GOODNIGHT SWEETHEART

Annie Groves lives in the North-West of England and has done so all of her life. She is also the author of *Ellie Pride, Connie's Courage* and *Hettie of Hope Street*, a series of novels for which she drew upon her own family's history, picked up from listening to her grandmother's stories when she was a child. *Goodnight Sweetheart* is based on wartime recollections of Liverpool from members of her family who come from the city.

Visit www.AuthorTracker.co.uk for exclusive news on your favourite HarperCollins authors.

By the same author:

Ellie Pride
Connie's Courage
Hettie of Hope Street
Some Sunny Day

ANNIE GROVES

Goodnight Sweetheart

HARPER

HarperCollins*Publishers*
77–85 Fulham Palace Road,
Hammersmith, London W6 8JB

www.harpercollins.co.uk

Published by HarperCollins*Publishers* 2006
1

Copyright © Annie Groves 2006

Annie Groves asserts the moral right to
be identified as the author of this work

A catalogue record for this book
is available from the British Library

ISBN 978 0 00 787937 3

Set in Sabon by Palimpsest Book Production Limited
Polmont, Stirlingshire

Printed and bound in Great Britain by
Clays Ltd, St Ives plc

Mixed Sources
Product group from well-managed
forests and other controlled sources
www.fsc.org Cert no. SW-COC-001806
© 1996 Forest Stewardship Council
FSC

FSC is a non-profit international organisation established to promote the
responsible management of the world's forests. Products carrying the FSC
label are independently certified to assure consumers that they come
from forests that are managed to meet the social, economic and
ecological needs of present and future generations.

Find out more about HarperCollins and the environment at
www.harpercollins.co.uk/green

I would like to thank the following:

All those at HarperCollins who helped to make publication of this book possible

Teresa Chris, my agent

Yvonne Holland

My fellow members of the RNA

Tony, who, as always, contributed to this book with driving and research help

And perhaps, most especially, to all those who endured the reality of World War Two.

For Maxine – confidence-builder extraordinaire

PART ONE

July 1939

ONE

'No! Don't.'

'Aw, what's up with yer?'

'It's not right, that's what,' Molly announced, keeping her arms folded tightly over her chest to prevent Johnny from making a fresh attempt to touch her breasts. It was a warm July evening and they had decided to walk home from the cinema on Lime Street to Edge Hill, the small tight-knit community of streets clustered together in a part of the Liverpool that didn't belong to the dock-side but wasn't part of the new garden suburbs like Wavertree either. A few yards ahead of them, she could see June, Molly's elder sister, locked in the arms of her fiancé, Frank.

'Aw, come on, Molly, just one kiss,' Johnny persisted cajolingly. 'Look at your June. She knows how to treat a chap.'

Molly didn't really want to look at June because June was with Frank, and just thinking about her sister's boyfriend always made Molly's heart ache painfully and her skin flush. But Frank was June's. And the only smiles he ever gave to Molly were kind and older-brotherly. Agreeing to go out with Johnny was the best way Molly could think of to stop herself from thinking about Frank. Frank belonged to June, and that was that.

'Come on, Molly, give us a kiss,' Johnny coaxed. 'There's nowt wrong in it. Look at your June and Frank.'

Molly tensed. There it was again – that pain she had no right to have. She had been struggling all evening to evade Johnny's amorous advances, and the eagerness she could hear in his voice now, as he pressed closer to her, made her feel wretchedly miserable and uncomfortable. What was wrong with her? Johnny was a good-looking lad, tall with thick dark hair. But his bold gaze and knowing smile intimidated Molly. Instinctively she knew that Frank would not make a girl feel uncomfortable when she was with him; neither would he start pressing her for intimacies she wasn't ready to give. Unhappiness clogged her throat and tears burned at the back of her eyes.

June and Frank were oblivious to Molly's plight. Not that June would have had much sympathy with her, Molly knew. It was June who had insisted on her going out with Johnny in the first place – he was a friend of Frank's and an evening out all together meant June could see Frank and keep an eye on her younger sister at the same time. Like every girl in the country who was walking out with a lad who had just received his call-up papers for the now obligatory six months' military training, June was anxious to spend time with Frank whilst she still could.

'June and Frank are engaged,' was all Molly could think of to say to Johnny to justify her own refusal, her voice slightly breathless as she wriggled away from his embrace.

'Well, me and you are as good as – leastways we would be if I had me way,' Johnny told her.

She stared at him with a mixture of dismay and shock. 'You can't say that,' she objected. 'We aren't even walking out proper. And besides . . .' She looked towards her sister and Frank.

'Besides what?' Johnny too turned to look at the other couple, then said sharply, 'You spend that much time looking at your June's Frank, you'll have me thinking you'd rather it were him you were with than me.'

'Don't be silly. Frank's engaged to our June.' Her heart was pounding now and her face was starting to burn. Her hands felt hot and sticky.

'Aye, and you could be engaged to me, if you was to play your cards right,' Johnny told her meaningfully, moving closer. 'Especially now that I've had me papers, and me and Frank have to report for training on Monday.'

To Molly's relief the other two had stopped spooning and her sister was turning round to face them.

'What's up with you, our Molly?' June demanded

when Molly and Johnny had caught up with them. 'You've got a face on you like a wet bank holiday.'

'Aye, that's what I'd like to know, an' all,' Johnny joined in, 'seein' as how I've just been telling her I want us to be engaged.'

'What? You're engaged!' June shrieked excitedly.

As usual June had got carried away and heard only the words she wanted to. Molly groaned inwardly. Now she would really have a job saying no to Johnny.

'Here, Frank, did you hear that? Our Molly and Johnny have just got themselves engaged. Course, me and Molly know that it's our duty to do everything we can to keep you soldiers happy.' She giggled, but her face started to crumple as she added, 'I was just saying to Frank that him and me should perhaps think about getting married sooner rather than later now that it looks certain there's going to be a war.'

'Now don't go getting yourself upset, June. We don't know that for sure yet,' Frank protested.

'Course we do. Haven't you seen them leaflets the Government has sent out to everyone?' she asked him scornfully, before turning to Molly and demanding, 'Here, Molly, give us it. You did put it in your handbag like I told you to, didn't you? We'll have to have it with us when we go to work on Monday, so as we can tell old Harding that we're going to need time off to go down to Lewis's and buy that blackout material it says we have to have.'

Molly nodded and obediently opened her bag to remove the notice. She could hardly bear to touch it, let alone read it again. When it had dropped onto the doormat of the little terraced home they shared with their father, she had been innocent of the realities of war. The leaflet's warnings about air raids, gas masks, lighting restrictions and evacuation alarmed her no end. She couldn't believe that the familiar streets of her beloved home town might one day be poisoned by gas or blasted by bombs. She could only hope that the Government were being overly cautious and that the war – if it even happened – would be short and not affect the city . . .

'See?' June had triumphantly finished reading the leaflet aloud to the men, jolting Molly back to the present.

'Well, we still don't know for sure,' Frank insisted, 'but if there is going to be a war, mind, Hitler won't be able to keep them tanks of his rolling against the British Army. Proper professional soldiers we've got,' he told them proudly.

'Oooh, Frank, don't say any more. You're making me feel right upset,' June protested tearfully, her earlier glee at being in the know having evaporated, whilst Molly shivered at her sister's side despite the warmth of the evening.

Everyone had been talking about war for so long without anything happening that it was hard to believe that anything *was* going to happen, despite the fact that the Government had already put in hand so many preparations. But its threat still hung over them like the dark rumbling shadow of distant thunderclouds. It was on everyone's minds and everyone's lips – a tension and anxious expectation that no one could ignore.

'Well, we'd better get ourselves home and tell our dad that you're an engaged woman now, Molly,' June insisted, rallying herself.

'That she is,' Johnny grinned, taking hold of Molly and hugging her so tightly that it hurt as he pressed a hot hard kiss on her mouth.

Molly's eyes stung with tears. She didn't think she really wanted to be engaged to Johnny, but of course it was too late to say so now. He was fun and so handsome, and she knew she should be happy instead of miserable. It made her feel guilty to think that she didn't want to be engaged to Johnny when he was going off to war. Besides, she could see how pleased June was. All her life Molly had done what her older sister had told her to do.

There were two years between them, and Molly could hardly remember the mother who had died when she was seven years old, other than as an invalid.

She could remember, though, lying in bed at night and listening to her mother cough. She could remember too the low anxious voices of Elsie from next door and the other women from the street when they came round to visit the invalid and do what they could to help. In the last weeks of their mother's life, Elsie had come round every day, bringing home-made soup for their mother and some of her elderberry wine for their father. But in the end her mother's illness had proved too much.

Their father had been devoted to their mother, and Molly knew how much he loved both his daughters. She and June were lucky to have such a good parent, and she was lucky, too, to have June as her sister. June had always been there for her, through good and bad, and Molly loved her deeply, even though she knew that other people sometimes found her sister a bit too know-it-all and bossy.

The four of them crossed the road, Johnny making a grab for Molly's hand as they did so, and then turned into the street that would eventually take them into Chestnut Close, the cul-de-sac of redbrick terraced and small semidetached houses, where the two girls and Frank lived.

'Dad will be wondering where we are,' Molly urged the others on, fearing that Johnny's sudden lagging behind meant that he was going to attempt to kiss her again.

'Don't be daft. He'll be down at the allotments,' June corrected her.

Their father, like many men in that community, rented a small allotment. It backed onto the railway line, and there he grew carrots, potatoes, turnips and peas as well as lettuce and tomatoes for salads.

In the summer months the men virtually camped

9

out there to take advantage of the long days, often sleeping in the small wooden huts they had put up, boiling up billycans of tea on Primus stoves and eating sandwiches packed up by their long-suffering wives. And now, of course, the Government was encouraging them to do so. Every spare bit of land was to be turned over to the pro-duction of food.

The house their father rented was not one of the larger semis, like Frank's widowed mother's, but a small terrace, down at the bottom of the cul-de-sac. The bedroom Molly and June had always shared was a bit cramped now that they were both grown up. June often complained that they needed more space, that the house was a bit old-fashioned and shabby, and their furniture had seen better days, but number 78 Chestnut Close was home and Molly wouldn't have swapped it for a castle.

'There's your mam spying on us, Frank,' June commented sourly as they walked past Frank's home. Molly stole a glance at the pristine house; the net curtains definitely seemed to be twitching.

Molly felt a little bit sorry for Frank at times, what with his mother forever trying to tell him how to run his life, vehemently taking against his choice of wife-to-be, and June equally determined to return Frank's mother's hostility towards her, but he was an easy-going, big-hearted young man, a right softie, always ready to do others a good turn.

They had all grown up together, although Molly,

at seventeen, was younger than the other three. They had shared so much together over the years – including the loss of a parent each. Both Frank's mother and Johnny's were widows, but whilst Frank's mother had been left with a bit of money and a pension, and only one son to bring up, her Bert having been killed in the Great War, Johnny's mother had been left with three children and no money, her husband having been killed when he had stepped out in front of a tram after drinking too much.

'If yer dad's down his allotment then why don't me and Frank come in for a bit?' Johnny suggested with a cheeky wink, much to Molly's dismay. She didn't want to have to endure any further intimacies with him. His kisses and wandering hands made her nervous.

To her relief, Frank shook his head.

'We can't do that, Johnny,' he protested. 'It wouldn't be right. We don't want to be giving our girls a bad name, do we?'

'Oh, and what do you think you'd be doing that would give us a bad name, eh, Frank Brookes?' June giggled teasingly. 'Chance'd be a fine thing, especially with your mam always waiting up for you,' she added grumpily. Brightening up, she continued, 'Look, seeing as how our Molly and Johnny have just got themselves engaged, why don't we go to Blackpool tomorrow and celebrate? I fancy going dancin' and having a bit of a good time.'

'It's Sunday tomorrow,' Frank reminded her, 'and there won't be enough time to get there and back after church.'

'Well, we ought to do something,' June protested, none too pleased at being denied her dancing.

'I don't mind if we don't,' Molly assured her. When the other three turned to look at her she coloured up and said quickly, 'I mean . . . what with everyone talking about the war, perhaps we shouldn't celebrate . . .'

They had reached number 78 now, where the girls lived, and were standing by the privet hedge that bordered the small front garden.

'Oh, Frank . . .' June's bottom lip trembled, her high spirits suddenly evaporating. Her emotions had always been able to change like quicksilver, although Molly wondered if they wouldn't all become as volatile if war did break out. 'I wish you didn't have to go, not so soon. I'll be glad when you've finished with this military training, and you're back home proper, like. I just hope we don't have this war. But if we do, you're not going off to fight without us being married first,' she warned him fiercely.

'I think we should have a word with the vicar tomorrow after church, and tell him that we want to be married as soon as we can, instead of waiting until next June. And I'll have a word with Mr Barker, the rent collector, and ask him to let me know if anything comes empty.'

'What's to stop you moving in with Frank's mam? She's got plenty of spare room,' Johnny asked June.

June tossed her head belligerently. 'I want me own house, thank you very much, and that's why . . . oh, Frank . . .' There were tears in her eyes and Frank put his arm round her and tried to comfort her.

Tactfully, Molly looked away, but at the same time she moved as far from Johnny as she could, not wanting him to get any ideas. To her relief she saw their father coming up the road, his familiar limping gait caused by the loss of a leg in the Great War.

'Dad . . .' Ignoring Johnny, she hurried towards her father, slipping her arm through his when she eventually caught up with him.

Albert Dearden was fond of saying that it was just as well his two daughters took after their mother and not him, reminiscing about how his wife had been a real beauty, and how, with her lovely naturally curly dark brown hair and her smiling blue eyes, Rosie had won his heart the moment he had laid eyes on her.

'Here, Dad,' June told him excitedly. 'You'll never guess what. Our Molly's only gone and got herself engaged to Johnny.'

'Well now. What's all this then, lass? You're only seventeen, you know.'

'There's a war on, Mr Dearden, and me being called up for the militia and like as not being sent off to fight—' Johnny began boastfully.

But Molly's father shook his head and stopped him, saying grimly, 'There's no war been announced yet, lad, and let me tell you, when we were called up to fight, the first thing we thought of was our country, not about getting hitched and leaving some poor lass worrying herself sick about us.'

'Aw, Dad, have a heart,' June complained.

'Perhaps we should wait,' Molly started to say, relieved a way out was being offered to her – for the time being, at least.

But her father was smiling lovingly at her, and he shook his head again and said warmly, 'Nay, lass, I'll not stand in the way of young love. But mind now, Johnny, my Molly is a respectable girl and there's to be no messin' about and getting her into any kind of trouble, and no marriage neither until she's eighteen.'

Molly smiled wanly, in stark contrast to Johnny's beaming grin. A year seemed a long way off but it would come round eventually and then she'd have no choice but to marry Johnny. The reality of being engaged to Johnny was so very different from the chaste daydreams of Frank she had blushed over in the privacy of her own thoughts. Frank, with his gentle understanding smile and brotherly kindness, made her feel so comfortable and so safe. She didn't feel either comfortable or safe with Johnny.

*   *   *

'What's up with you?' June demanded forthrightly later that evening as she and Molly prepared for bed. 'Anyone would think you'd lost a shilling and found a farthing.'

Molly put down her hairbrush and turned to look at her elder sister. 'The thing is, June, I'm not rightly sure I want to be engaged,' she said miserably, too tongue-tied to be able to explain just how confused and worried Johnny's constant urgings to allow him more intimacy were making her feel. Even with sisters as close as they were, it was unthinkable that she should tell June how little she enjoyed Johnny's kisses and how alarmed and uneasy they made her feel. June was so lucky to have Frank. Molly could see there was a world of difference in the way Frank treated June and the way Johnny kept on trying to pressure her.

'Don't be daft. Of course you do. And besides, you can't change your mind now. That would be a shocking thing to do with him about to go off and fight. Anyone can see that he's mad for you, and hundreds of girls would kill to be engaged to someone as good-looking as Johnny. He looks like a matinée idol, he does. But you be careful and play your cards right, our Molly, and make sure you don't go giving him nothing he shouldn't be having until after you've got his ring on your finger,' June warned her darkly. 'Frank's mam looks down on us enough, without you getting me a bad reputation by getting yourself in the family way before you've got a husband.'

Molly gave her elder sister an indignant look. As usual, June's thoughts were foremost with herself.

'Of course, that's not to say that now that you are engaged you can't let him have a few little liberties, like – especially if he does have to go off to war. A girl doesn't want to send her sweetheart off to fight without giving him a bit of a taste of what he's fighting for, does she?' June giggled. 'Wait till we tell them at the factory on Monday that you're engaged.'

The two sisters both worked as machinists at a small garment factory within walking distance of their home. Mr Harding, the factory owner, employed nearly twenty girls. June had got a job there when she left school, having seen it advertised in the Liverpool paper, and she had approached Mr Harding on Molly's behalf a couple of months before Molly was due to leave school, to ask that her sister be considered for any likely vacancy. It was piece work and unless you were very quick and didn't make any mistakes the pay wasn't good, but it was no worse than the girls would have earned anywhere else, and as June often said, at least the small factory was clean, and warm in winter as Mr Harding was well aware that cold fingers didn't work as nimbly and made mistakes – expensive mistakes for him if his customers rejected the work as not good enough. The other girls were a jolly bunch and, whilst they were all older than Molly, their company meant that there was always someone for her to have a laugh with.

The factory's main business came from a distributor who provided them with both pattern and fabric and who supplied clothes to the big Lewis's store in the centre of the city. Sometimes the girls were allowed to buy leftover pieces of cloth to make things for themselves. Two or three times a year, a very important dark-suited gentleman from Lewis's came up to the long sewing machine-filled room where the girls worked, to inspect their sewing. Molly was happy working there, even if June sometimes grumbled and complained.

Molly started to brush her hair again. Both girls had thick, naturally curly hair. June's was a mid-brown, but Molly's was much darker and richer, with a warm chestnut hue.

Pensively, Molly stared into the mirror, her cornflower-blue eyes clouding. Her mouth trembled and she blinked away tears.

'Now what's up?' June demanded, pinching her younger sister's arm almost crossly.

'Nothing,' Molly fibbed.

'I should jolly well think there isn't. You don't know how lucky you are, our Molly. There's a lot of girls in Liverpool would give their right arms to be in your shoes and engaged to a handsome lad like Johnny. And besides . . .'

Molly could see that June was looking very determined, and her heart sank. She had been hoping that June would understand her feelings

17

but now she could tell that she wasn't going to get very much sympathy from her.

'Besides what?' she pressed her anxiously.

'Well, the way I see it, Molly, is that this engagement of yours is a good thing for everyone. Frank has already hinted to me as how his mam will be on her own after we get married and that he feels it's his duty to have her come and live with us. Well, there's no way I'm going to have that, but Frank can be that stubborn when he really wants something, and his mam has brought him up to think she's got a right to tell him what to do with his life! Anyway, like I've said to him, with you marrying Johnny that'd leave our dad on his own, and that'd mean that we would have to have both of them to live with us and we can't do that.'

'But why would Dad have to live with you? He's got Uncle Joe at number 63,' Molly objected. 'And, anyway, he's always saying as how, once he's got us off his hands, Auntie Violet has said as how he's welcome to go and live with them in Cheshire.' Their father's elder sister was married to a farmer who lived near Nantwich.

'Well, yes, but there's no call for you to go saying any of that to Frank,' June warned her sharply. 'So far as he's concerned, you marrying Johnny means that our dad will need to come and live with us, because he'll be on his own just like Frank's mam. And since we won't have room for both of them we can't have either of them,' she announced triumphantly.

'You mean you want me to marry Johnny so that you won't have to have Frank's mam to live with you?' Molly protested.

'Oh, don't go looking at me like that. Just think how lucky you are to be engaged,' June told her firmly. 'And if war does break out, you'll know you'll be sending your Johnny off to war knowing he's got someone of his own here at home waiting for him. That means a lot to a lad, our Molly, and don't you forget that.'

TWO

'Oh Gawd, I've gone and laddered my stocking. Here, Molly, you put the roast in, will you – I've turned on the gas ready – whilst I go and change them, otherwise we'll be late for church.'

The girls' father worked on the railway sidings at Edge Hill station – 'the gridiron', as it was called locally – as a track maintenance man employed by the railway company. The work was back-breakingly hard and often dirty, but he never complained. Like many of the generation who had lived through the depression, he simply considered himself lucky to be in work.

Although he didn't earn much, with June and Molly's wages, they had enough coming in to be able to afford a joint of meat on a Sunday, to be eaten with the potatoes and vegetables Albert grew on his allotment.

Molly slid the roasting tin into the gas oven and then dashed upstairs to get her hat and gloves.

'Come on, you two,' Albert bawled up the stairs, 'otherwise we're gonna be late.'

Chestnut Close was a Protestant street, with all its inhabitants attending the parish church of St Michael and all the Angels.

The custom was that everyone filed into church in silence, merely exchanging nods of acknowledgement, and then got together for a good gossip after the service. So although the Deardens could see Frank and his mother walking down the street up ahead of them, June made no attempt to catch up with her fiancé.

'Look at her!' she muttered to Molly. 'Hanging on to Frank's arm for dear life, acting like he belongs to her. Well, if she thinks that Frank's going to be taking her to church every Sunday once he's married to me, then she's got another think coming. Of course, she thinks that I'm not good enough for him. That's why she's been sucking up to that friend of hers who lives on Carlton Avenue, in Wavertree – you know, them as has the laundry on the Scotland Road? Boasting all up and down the cul-de-sac she was at one time about how her Frank and their Angela would be perfect for one another.' June sniffed disparagingly. 'Maybe she would have been, an' all, if she hadn't got buck teeth and no bust.'

To Molly's relief, she couldn't see any sign of Johnny, although she spotted his mother and two sisters.

'There's your ma-in-law-to-be,' June told her,

nudging her in the ribs. 'You're going to have to watch those sisters of his: always on the cadge, so I've heard. Don't you go letting them boss you around, Molly.'

Despite herself, Molly smiled a little at the prospect of swapping a bossy sister for an equally overbearing sister-in-law.

As they walked to their pew, it struck Molly that the church seemed much fuller than usual, and when they stood up to sing 'Onward, Christian soldiers', it was obvious that Sally Walker in the pew in front of them, next to her soldier husband, Ronnie, in his uniform, was crying quietly. They'd only been married a year and their first baby was due in September.

Once the service was over, small groups of people started to congregate outside the church.

'You and Dad wait here. I'm going to find Frank so as we can have a word with the vicar,' June announced determinedly.

'His mam won't be happy about you wanting to bring the wedding forward,' Molly pointed out. 'She wasn't too keen on the pair of you getting engaged.'

'Well, she's going to have to lump it, isn't she, because me and Frank are going to be wed no matter what she thinks,' June responded, tossing her head before turning to disappear into the crowd. June usually got what she wanted, Molly thought, but wondered if perhaps she'd met her match in Doris Brookes.

All around her, Molly could see anxious faces, as families clung together, the men looking serious and grim-faced, many of the women crying and those with grown-up sons clinging desperately to their boys. It was easy to pick out Frank's tall, broad-shouldered frame as he stood with his arm around his mother.

Molly could see that several of the younger men had already gone over to talk to Sally Walker's husband, Ronnie, who was in the regular army and could tell them what life in the Forces was like.

'What's going to happen to us – that's what I'd like to know.' One of their neighbours started to sob noisily.

'Well, I reckon the first thing as is going to happen is that we're going to have to get used to wearing them ruddy gas masks,' her husband responded. 'Else we'll be having that Alf Davies, the ARP chap from number 14, giving us all a good ticking-off.'

'At least the kiddies will be safe,' another neighbour chimed in, 'seeing as how they're going to be evacuated.'

'Aye, and our brave lads will soon sort out that Hitler.'

'Will it soon be over, Dad?' Molly asked her father fearfully when he came to join her.

'I hope so, lass, but there's no telling,' Albert answered solemnly, whilst he and a couple of other men who had survived the Great War exchanged concerned looks.

'Seems we're going to be needing that ruddy air-raid shelter putting up at the bottom of the cul-de-sac, so we may as well make a start on it this afternoon,' their next-door neighbour, John Fowler, commented to Molly's father, adding grimly, 'They'll be calling all the young 'uns up, like as not now.'

Molly bit her lip. The Fowlers had a son working for the railways like John Fowler and her father, and a nephew in the merchant navy. Elsie Fowler's normally happy face looked pinched and strained. Molly reached out and took hold of her hand, squeezing it sympathetically.

Elsie had been a good neighbour to them, taking both girls under her wing, and giving them a bit of mothering after their mother had died. She'd plait their hair, sew them pretty things when she could get the material, and never once forgot to bake them birthday cakes, taking over all those little motherly duties that their father couldn't do. She'd been a godsend to Albert, who was desperately aware that, though he was doing all he could for his young daughters, they missed a mother's love and attention. Molly loved Elsie and was grateful to her, but she knew that June, with her more bossy nature, sometimes resented Elsie, claiming that her good intentions were 'interference'.

It was a good half-hour before June came back. Her eyes looked suspiciously puffy but she was still managing to smile.

'The vicar has said as how we can have the banns read right off so that we can be married just as soon as Frank gets some leave,' she told them, adding, 'There was that long a queue waiting to see him you wouldn't believe it. Seems like everyone is having the same idea as me and Frank.'

'What did his mam say?' Molly asked her anxiously.

A militant gleam sparkled in June's eyes. 'Just as you might expect. She was all for us waiting to see what happens, but Frank told her as how we didn't want to wait. When we go to Lewis's tomorrow to get that blackout material we can have a look at some wedding dress patterns as well. Frank has just had a word with Ronnie Walker, and he reckons it will be Christmas before Frank gets any leave, but there's no harm in being prepared.'

Slipping her arm through Molly's, she fell into step beside her as they headed for home.

By the time they had got back to number 78 and had had their dinner, it was well into the afternoon. Their father announced that he was off to join the other men from the terraced houses at the bottom of the cul-de-sac. Because their gardens weren't large enough for individual Anderson shelters, they had been told they would have to erect a shared one on the piece of unused land at the end of the cul-de-sac. The corrugated iron for it had already been delivered, but the men had to dig out trenches for it themselves and install it.

'I suppose we'd better measure up for those blackout curtains we've got to put up,' Molly suggested when she and June had finished the washing-up.

'Come on then,' June agreed reluctantly.

'I don't see as how we need to do this when we aren't even at war yet,' she grumbled ten minutes later as she made Molly climb up the ladders to measure the windows, whilst she wrote down the measurements.

'But if we don't, when the ARP warden comes round to check, we'll be fined,' Molly reminded her, her forehead pleating into a worried little frown. June hated being told what to do by anyone and wasn't afraid of saying so, but Molly was much more timid and keen to do her duty.

Half an hour later, when they had almost finished, June complained, 'I'm fair parched, Molly. Get down off them ladders, and go and make us a cuppa, will you?'

Molly had just filled the kettle when there was a knock at the back door, and Frank came in.

'June, it's your Frank,' she called from the kitchen.

'About time too,' June announced wrathfully. 'I was expecting you'd have bin here before now, Frank, seeing as it's going to be our last evening together.'

'I would have been,' he agreed placidly, giving Molly a gentle smile, 'but Fred Nuttall from next door asked me to give him a lift putting up his Anderson shelter.'

'Oh, I see, and of course he comes before me, does he?'

'Don't be daft. He's invited me mam to share the shelter with them, so I felt obliged to give him a hand. Don't let's fall out, June, not tonight, seein' as how me and Johnny have to report for our training tomorrow.'

Tactfully, Molly squeezed past them and closed the kitchen door.

Five minutes later the door opened and Frank told her quietly, 'Me and June are just going for a bit of a walk, Molly.'

Molly had never seen her lively sister looking so upset. She was clinging to Frank's arm as they left the house together and he was holding her tenderly as though she was something precious and frail.

What must it be like to love someone like that, Molly wondered. Part of her was glad that she did not know because she didn't think she could have coped with the pain of watching them go off to war. The thought of Johnny going away didn't fill her with dread at all. In fact, secretly she was looking forward to not having to evade his advances, or worry about the fact that she didn't really want him to kiss her or touch her. The truth was that she felt much safer and more comfortable with her girlish and innocent little daydreams about Frank's kind smiles and gentlemanly ways than she did with the reality of Johnny's urgent demands. But didn't that make her a terrible person, she worried guiltily. She ought to feel very different from how she did, she knew that. Perhaps if she just didn't think about how she really felt, somehow she would change.

June and Frank had been gone almost an hour when there was another knock at the door – the front door this time. Molly went to open it, her eyes widening with surprise when she saw Johnny standing there.

'Thought I'd come and say goodbye to you proper, like, Molly,' he told her boldly, winking at her, and then walking into the small hall without so much as a by-your-leave, pushing the door closed behind him. 'Come here and give us a kiss,' he grinned, making a grab for Molly as she backed away from him into the front parlour.

'Johnny,' Molly began in protest, but he ignored her as he took her hand, led her to the settee and sat her down, all the while kissing the side of her neck.

Frantically she tried to push him away but he grabbed hold of her other hand.

'We're engaged now, remember,' he told her, 'so how about showing me how much you love me before I go? I've gorra ring for you, look, Molly,' he added cajolingly. 'Bought it off a chap in the pub.'

Delving into his pocket, he produced a gold ring set with a small red stone, which he pushed onto her finger.

The slightly sour smell of his beery breath was making Molly feel sick. She didn't want to be engaged to him because she was afraid of the unwelcome intimacies being engaged would bring. His open hunger for her was too much, too soon, and it repelled rather than pleased her. But she didn't know how to tell him how she felt, and could only submit mutely to his kiss, longing for it to be over.

When June first started walking out with Frank, Molly, who had already begun to have a secret girlish crush on him, had envied her elder sister, but now she acknowledged miserably that sighing over a tender kiss on the cinema screen was far nicer than actually having to endure being kissed. Did other girls feel like her, or was there something wrong with her, she wondered unhappily as she finally managed to wriggle away from him far enough to warn him breathlessly, 'Our dad will be back soon, Johnny, and you know what he said.' She only hoped that it was true. She felt horribly guilty about not wanting him to kiss her, but she was too conscious of the fact that he could be going off to war to be able to tell him that she didn't want to be engaged to him.

'How many of us did you say had to fit in here?' Molly heard June demanding in disbelief as, along with the other women, they crowded into the Anderson shelter the men had spent the afternoon installing.

'The lorra us from number 56 down,' one of the men answered her, whilst the women exchanged concerned looks.

When the corrugated iron shelter had been sunk into the ground, the top had been covered with the earth that had been dug out.

'It will seem more like home once you get some curtains hung in it,' Brian, their neighbour from number 80, called out to his wife with a grin, whilst he winked at the other men.

'Curtains? But there aren't any windows...' Mavis Leadbetter began, and then shook her head when the men burst out laughing. 'Go on with you, you're nothing but overgrown lads, the lot of you. No one would think there's going to be a war on.'

'Come on, love,' her husband chivvied her. 'It's either laugh or cry.'

'Aye, well, there'll be a lorra crying done before we're out of this,' someone else chipped in.

'We've gotta sort the inside of this out yet,' Brian Leadbetter changed the subject firmly, 'but at least we've made a start...'

'Well, let's hope that none of us gets caught short whilst we're down here,' Nellie Sinclair, who lived on the opposite side of the cul-de-sac, said pithily.

'Don't worry about that, Nellie,' Molly and June's Uncle Joe grinned. 'I reckon the ARP lot won't miss a couple of those buckets they've told us we need to have in case of a bomb dropping.

Brian's a fair joiner and it won't tek him long to fit a nice polished seat on top of one of them for you.'

'Go on with yer, you've gorra lorra cheek, you have. And we'll have less of that mucky talk, if yer don't mind.' Nellie might be pretending to be shocked but Molly could see that she was laughing.

Uncle Joe was their father's cousin, not his brother, but the girls had grown up calling him Uncle Joe and his wife Auntie Averil. Following their father's example, Joe had moved into Chestnut Close shortly after he and Averil had married. He was a tall, well-built man, always ready with a smile and a joke, and much more outgoing than their own father, and so he had soon become a popular figure, not just in the close but also beyond it. He had a fine singing voice, and that, plus the fact that he could play the accordion, made him welcome at every local social event. Joe enjoyed a drink and a laugh, and he was a good father and husband as well as a kind-hearted uncle. He might tease June for being bossy, and make Molly blush with his saucy jokes, but Molly was always glad to see him. June might say disapprovingly that he had a bit of a reputation for being quick with a quip and even quicker with a silver-tongued compliment, but their father always defended him and said that there was no real harm in him.

As different as chalk and cheese was how people described the two men. Where the girls' father was quiet and self-effacing, Joe was boisterous and ready to put himself forward. Where Albert Dearden liked nothing better than to spend his spare time working on his allotment, Joe preferred to go down to the pub for a beer.

'What about your mam, Frank?' Albert asked a few minutes later as they all made their way home. 'I could go round and give a bit of a hand getting her shelter sorted out.'

'Thanks, Mr Dearden, but it's all sorted. She's to share with next door, and me and Fred Nuttall got it in this afternoon.'

'Well, don't you go worrying about her whilst you're away, Frank. I'll keep an eye on her.'

'I'd be obliged if you would, Mr Dearden. It's going to be hard for her, being on her own . . .'

'What about me? It's going to be hard for me as well, worrying about you,' June put in crossly. 'You don't want to be spoiling your mam too much, Frank.'

'Leave him alone, lass. Of course he's worried about her. If she needs a hand putting up them blackout curtains, Frank, you tell her that she's only got to say,' her father responded sharply.

'Never mind that. You remember to find out when you can have some leave, Frank, so that I can tell the vicar.'

'Ronnie Walker was saying that on account of me being a qualified electrician they might put me into the Royal Engineers.'

'Aye, and if'n you'd thought of it in time and

got yourself a job with the electric company you'd have been in a reserved occupation,' June reminded him tartly.

Unlike their father, and most of the other men in the cul-de-sac, Frank had been lucky enough to get a proper trade apprenticeship – thanks to his skill and his mother's determination. And that was yet another reason why Mrs Brookes felt that June wasn't good enough for her Frank, Molly suspected.

'Now that's enough of that, June,' Frank rebuked her gently, adding too quietly to be overheard, 'I want to do me bit, and I wouldn't want anyone thinking any different. Especially not folk like your dad.'

A couple of the women with young children were gathering them up and Molly went to help them.

'No way am I letting mine be evacuated,' Pearl Lawson was saying vehemently.

The Government had sent out notices earlier in the year advising people of their plans to evacuate city children out of danger in the event of war, sending them to live in the country along with their teachers, who would make sure that they continued to have their lessons. Pregnant women and mothers with babies were also included in the evacuation plans, but the mothers of Chestnut Close, like many mothers up and down the country, were divided in their feelings about the planned evacuation. Some accepted that it was a necessary decision if their children were to be kept safe but others were openly hostile to it.

'Aye, well, there's no way I'm going to let mine stay here and be bombed,' another said equally determinedly. 'And besides, I don't want mine missing out on their schooling and I've heard as how the Government will be closing down some of the schools here in Liverpool out of fear that they might be bombed. Why shouldn't our kiddies have as good as posh kiddies get and be sent into the country where it's safe?'

Pearl Lawson's next-door neighbour, Daisy Cartwright, chipped in, 'It's different for them. They'll be going with their schools and not sent off to some strangers like ours.'

It had been in the papers that some of the public schools based in cities were moving out wholesale to safer country locations where their pupils would board.

'Ta, Molly,' Daisy thanked her as Molly picked up the small toddler who had been making a determined effort to escape. 'Is it true that you and Johnny Everton are engaged, only I heard it from his mam that you are?'

'Yes,' Molly confirmed, blushing slightly.

'Well, you're a bit on the young side, if you don't mind me saying, and you're gonna have to watch him. He's gorra bit of an eye for the girls, from what I've heard,' Daisy told her. 'Marriage isn't allus all that it's made out to be, and once

34

you've gorra couple of kiddies to think about it's too late to change your mind.'

Pearl, sensing Molly's embarrassment, tactfully changed the subject. 'Have you measured up for them blackout curtains yet?'

'Yes, me and June are going to Lewis's to buy the material tomorrow,' Molly told her.

'I've told my George he's gorra make frames for the windows so that we can pin the stuff to them. Catch me mekkin' curtains when I've enough to do as it is! And wot's all this about not buying in food? Chance'd be a fine thing on what George brings home! Don't know what we'd do if it weren't for the allotment.'

Leaving the women to chivvy their children out of the shelter, Molly went to rejoin her own family.

'Has Johnny been round to see you, Molly?' Frank asked her in a kind voice.

'Yes. He called round earlier whilst you and June were out, but he couldn't stay.'

'Aye, well, I hope you didn't go and say anything daft to him,' June challenged her, adding for Frank's benefit, 'Daft thing's bin saying that she isn't sure she wants to be engaged, if you please!'

Molly could hear the impatience in June's voice.

'Well, if she isn't sure . . .'

Molly could feel herself starting to blush guiltily as her heart gave a funny little beat. She liked Frank so much. He was always kind to her, listening to her as though he really cared about what she was saying and treating her like a grown-up, while June was impatient with her. But then that was Frank all over, being kind to folk.

'Don't you go encouraging her to be daft, Frank,' June warned sharply. 'Of course she wants to wed Johnny – just like I want to wed you,' she added more softly, before demanding, 'Don't you, Molly?'

Obediently Molly nodded her head. What else could she do?

THREE

'Well, I'll tell you something for nothing, young Molly, you're not gonna be the only one sporting a new engagement ring this weekend,' Irene Laidlaw announced on Monday morning when the other machinists had all finished examining Molly's ring, 'seeing as how so many young men have received their papers. Of course, it's different for me,' she added loftily, 'since my Alan was one of the first to volunteer . . .'

'Probably because he wanted to get away from her,' one of the other girls muttered, causing a ripple of giggles to spread across their small enclosed work space, with its sewing machines and air smelling of new cloth.

Although she had no official senior status, it was accepted by the other girls that Irene was their leader. She had been working there the longest and, although opinionated, was a kind soul and the first to befriend a girl new to the factory and help her settle in.

All the girls worked in pinafore coveralls to prevent bits of thread and cotton from clinging to their clothes. And at least Hardings, unlike some of the factories, had windows big enough to let in proper daylight so that the girls weren't straining their eyes as they bent over their machines.

'I'll be glad when we've finished this bloomin' bloomers order, and start workin' on sommat a bit more glamorous,' one of the girls complained with a noisy sigh.

'Aye, I can't see your Bert getting excited about you tekkin' home a few pairs of these to surprise him wiv, Janet,' the girl working next to her grinned cheekily. 'I'm sick to me back teeth of 'em meself.' She too sighed as she surveyed the mound of bloomers waiting to be made up.

The girls were three-quarters of the way through a big order for 'quality undergarments', which in reality meant enormous pairs of bloomers as favoured by older women, and equally utilitarian brassieres. The kind of corsets favoured by most middle-aged women were supplied and made by specialist mail-order firms so that customers could be measured for them in the privacy of their own homes, and were so expensive that it was rare for the women Molly and June knew to own more than a best corset and a spare.

'Pity it's not some of them fancy French knickers we're mekkin' up,' Janet said longingly.

'Well, there's nothing to stop you getting a pattern from Lewis's and making yourself some,

Janet,' June pointed out briskly. She already had her eye on a nice piece of selvedge material. She reckoned she could get three pairs of drawers out of it if she got Molly, with her clever fingers and good eyes, to cut them for her. If she was very lucky she might be able to come by enough fabric to get Molly to make her a matching brassiere as well. There was a strict list that allowed each girl one piece of spare or unused fabric from any one contract, and the only way to get more was to ask one of the other girls to do a swap or to sell off her piece. Perhaps she'd ask Molly to let her have hers, June decided.

''Ere, guess what?' another of the girls demanded breathlessly, as she came hurrying into the room. 'I was just happening to be standing outside the office and what should I hear—'

'Come off it, Ruby. Admit it, you was listening on purpose,' May teased her.

'Do you want to know what I heard, May Dunning, or do you want to wait until old man Harding tells you?' Ruby demanded.

'Go on then, tell us,' May gave in.

'Well, old man Harding was talking to his missus, and saying as how they gorra take on more machinists, because of the Government wanting him to make a lorra stuff, like, for the army.'

'What, you mean uniforms?' May demanded excitedly. 'Cor, that will be a change from stitching bloomers. Just imagine the chaps as'll be wearing them: all fit and handsome, like . . .' May was notorious for having an eye for the men and often regaled them with saucy tales on a Monday morning of the latest man she'd met over the weekend.

'They might be fit and handsome when they first put on their uniforms, but they won't be for very long. Soon they'll start coming home dead, just like my Thomas . . .' The high-pitched emotional voice that joined the conversation belonged to Hannah Carter, the oldest and normally the quietest of the machinists, a small spare woman who had been widowed at the end of the First World War. Everyone turned to look at her with varying degrees of consternation or accusation.

''Ere, Hannah, there's no call for you to be saying stuff like that, and upsetting people,' Sheila Williams protested, her already florid complexion turning even pinker.

'Yes, there is. You don't know what it's going to be like, but I do. You don't know how it feels to send your husband off to war and never see him again.' Hannah had started to cry in earnest now.

Molly went over to try to comfort her.

'Watch out. Boss is on his way,' one of the girls called out, and immediately they all hurried to their machines so that by the time the door opened to admit a grey-haired middle-aged man and the thin-faced woman accompanying him, the room was filled with the sound of treadle machines busily stitching.

Robert Harding rang a small hand bell as a signal to the women to stop work, and then announced importantly, 'From today we're going to be making some changes at Hardings, on account of us being called on by the Government to make uniforms for our brave soldiers.'

'What kind of changes?' Irene demanded sturdily.

'Well, for one thing we're going to be taking on more machinists, and for another, Miss Jenner here is going to be in charge of all you machinists, to make sure that the uniforms are made to the proper standard.'

Molly gave a small shiver as she looked at the thin, hard-eyed woman standing at Robert Harding's side, surveying them all with unsmiling grimness. There was something about her that sent a chill right through Molly.

'All right, back to work, everyone.'

The sharp command was given almost before the door had closed behind Robert Harding, and although the girls obediently bent over their work, Molly was anxiously aware that some of them, June included, were not likely to take very well to Miss Jenner's arrival. It sent another shiver of apprehension all the way down Molly's spine to know that the supervisor was patrolling the narrow aisles between the rows of machines, standing behind each of them in turn to observe their work. Up to now Molly had liked her job. She was a good machinist, quick and deft, but

41

with the cold censorious weight of Miss Jenner's gaze on her back she was all fingers and thumbs.

'So when are we gonna be starting working on these uniforms, then, Miss Jenner?' May asked boldly, causing a collective sigh of relief to spread through the room at this breaking of the silent tension.

Their relief had come too soon though. Miss Jenner strode towards May and said coldly, 'In future you will speak only when you are spoken to. And let me remind you that you are all here to work, not to engage in time-wasting chatter. I have already told Mr Harding that I think he would do well to put in place a system of fines for workers who shirk their duties – in any kind of way.'

Molly could see the tide of angry red staining the back of May's neck.

Without the normal banter between the girls to speed them through the day, time seemed to drag, and Molly could scarcely conceal her relief when the dinner bell rang, signalling the end of the morning's work.

Immediately June stood up and called, 'Come on, our Molly. We'll have to put a bit of speed on if we're to get down to Lewis's and back . . .'

'You there, girl. Who gave you permission to stop work?' Miss Jenner demanded icily.

'The dinner bell's been rung and that means that it's dinner time. And me and me sister have got to get down to Lewis's and get our blackout material, just like the Government has told us to do,' June defended herself, raising her eyebrows as though defying Miss Jenner to claim a higher authority than that of the British Government.

'Very well then. But see that you are back here before the work bell rings otherwise you'll be docked half a day's pay.'

'You gorra be careful with that Jenner, June. It looks to me like she's going to give us a lorra grief,' May warned ten minutes later as they all streamed out of the room, heading for the small 'canteen' where they were allowed to eat their dinner and make themselves a hot drink.

'So what? Let her try, if she wants,' June shrugged. 'I don't care. Come on, Molly,' she instructed. 'We've got to get down to Lewis's.

'It'll be quicker if we walk instead of waiting for the bus,' June announced once they were outside the factory, but in the end, even though they ran almost the whole way down to Ranelagh Street, it still took fifteen precious minutes.

'Oh Gawd, look at the queue,' June complained when they hurried into Lewis's haberdashery department. The shop was filled with customers milling around amongst the rainbow-coloured bolts of cloth and shelves of pins, needles and buttons.

Lewis's was Molly's favourite store and she could remember the thrill of coming here as a little girl, holding tightly on to Elsie's plump hand for fear that she might be lost in the crowd of shoppers. Now that she was older, though, one of her favourite treats was to wander round the well-stocked haberdashery department. Unlike June, Molly loved sewing and was a dab hand at making things. She also had a good eye for the right bit of trimming to smarten up an old blouse, or last year's hat.

'Look, you go and get the blackout stuff,' June told her, 'and I'll go and look for a pattern for me wedding dress whilst you're queuing. Here's the measurements for the windows.'

'June, we're not going to get served in time to get back. Wouldn't it be better if we came back tonight?' Molly begged her.

'What, after we've gone and run all the way here? Don't be so soft. You go and get in that queue.'

Half an hour later, when Molly was only three from the front of the queue, June came hurrying up to her, pulling a face and complaining, 'I was hoping you'd have been served by now . . .'

'Did you find a pattern?' Molly asked her.

'Yes, but I wanted you to come and have a look at it with me and there won't be time now. Here, come on, it's our turn next,' she warned, digging Molly in the ribs.

'By, but this stuff is heavy,' June complained, stopping to push her hair off her hot face.

'We should have left it until tonight and then gone straight home on the bus,' Molly told her.

'Oh, give over saying that, will you, our Molly?'

It was just gone one o'clock when they finally trudged wearily into the factory yard, but when Molly would have made straight for the workroom, June shook her head at her.

'What are you doing?' Molly asked worriedly when she saw her sister heading determinedly for Mr Harding's office.

'Wait and see. And here, take hold of this lot for a mo, will yer?' June thrust her own parcel on top of Molly's, before knocking firmly on the office door.

'I'm sorry to disturb you, Mr Harding,' Molly heard June announcing when the factory owner opened the door, 'only I thought as how we should explain ourselves on account of us being late back from our dinner break.'

'You're late?' Molly saw him frown as he looked at his watch.

'Yes,' June confirmed, 'and I'm right sorry about it, only I felt it was our duty to go down to Lewis's just as soon as we could to get our blackout material, what with us getting notices about it from the Government, and all.'

'Well, yes, quite right. We must all be aware of our duty from now on,' Mr Harding agreed immediately.

'Of course we'll make up the time by working late,' June continued.

'No, that won't be necessary . . . June, isn't it?'

'Yes, Mr Harding. And this is me sister, Molly.'

'Very good, very good . . . Back to your machines now, both of you.'

'What did you do that for?' Molly asked curiously as they hurried away. It wasn't like June to admit to doing something wrong.

'By, you've got a lot of learning to do, our Molly,' June told her, shaking her head. 'Wait and see.'

The unfamiliar silence when they walked into the workroom almost caused Molly to miss a step and cannon into her sister.

All the girls were seated at their machines but none of them was working. Instead, they were all staring straight ahead whilst Miss Jenner stood in front of the machines watching them.

'And what time do you call this?' She pounced immediately on Molly and June.

'I'm sorry we're a bit late only there was a bigger queue at Lewis's than we were expecting,' June apologised.

'You are five minutes late, and since no work has been done by anyone whilst we have waited for you to return, that means that thirty lots of five minutes have been lost – the cost of that amount of time will be deducted from your wages, just as soon as I have spoken with Mr Harding.'

'Well, I've already seen him and he has said as how it was our duty to go and get our blackout material,' June told her, 'and if you don't believe me you can go and ask him yourself.'

Molly watched as an ugly red flush of anger spread up over Miss Jenner's thin neck, and then held her breath, fearing that her sister had gone too far. But the new supervisor didn't say anything, leaving June to give the other girls a triumphant wink behind Miss Jenner's back before sitting down at her machine.

'By, June Dearden, you've gorra lorra cheek,' Sheila Williams commented admiringly when the afternoon whistle had gone and they were all getting ready to leave.

'Aye, and you'll have made yourself an enemy as well,' Irene warned her darkly. 'She's not the sort who's gonna forget what you've done – she's gonna have it in for you an' for your Molly from now on, mark my words.'

'I'm not walking all the way home lugging this stuff,' Molly told June as they left the factory carrying the fabric. 'It's too hot.'

'All right then, we'll get the bus, but you're going to be doing the paying, mind,' June warned her. 'I wonder how long it will be before we get word from Frank and Johnny.'

The boys had been gone only a day but it had already affected the girls – though in very different ways. Underneath her bright exterior, Molly could tell that June was missing Frank keenly, while she herself felt as if a weight had been lifted from her shoulders with Johnny's absence – albeit with some guilt attached.

'I've told Frank as how he's got to write to me as soon as he can. I was thinking this afternoon that one of them uniforms we're going to be making could be for Frank. It gave me a rare old turn, an' all,' June admitted.

'Hannah's very upset that we're going to be making uniforms,' Molly commented sympathetically.

'Aye, well, she's got to snap out of that, otherwise she's going to find herself out of a job and she can't afford that. All she's got is that bit of a pension.'

'It must be awful for her, though, June. I was talking to her for a bit this morning and she was saying as how she'd been married only a few weeks when her husband was killed.'

'Maybe so, but that was nearly twenty years ago,' June responded bracingly. 'Things are different now.'

Their bus arrived and they both climbed on board, Molly paying both fares before slumping thankfully into an empty seat.

'What you got there, girls?' the conductor ribbed them jovially.

'Blackout material, that's what,' June answered.

'Want me to come round and give you a hand putting it up?' he offered, winking at Molly.

'Give over with yer cheek,' June told him firmly, but she was still smiling at him, Molly noticed with amusement.

The bus set them down on the corner of the

cul-de-sac and they walked up it together in their normal manner, Molly pausing frequently to admire the flowers growing in the small, neatly tended front gardens whilst June hurried her along, her attention concentrated on reaching home.

As they drew level with Frank's mother's house, Molly stopped walking and suggested warmly, 'Why don't you give Frank's mam a knock, our June, and see if she wants a hand with making up her blackout curtains? Those big windows of hers will take a lot of covering and we could easily run the curtains up for her on our Singer.'

'Why should I put meself out to do her any favours?' June demanded belligerently.

'You'd be doing it for Frank,' Molly said gently.

'You're a right softie, you are – just like Frank. But, aye, go on then, we might as well give her a knock,' June agreed.

Unlike their own, Frank's mother's gate did not squeak when it was opened, but Molly did not think that the Edwardian tiled pathway looked any cleaner than their own, nor the front step better donkey-stoned. Their mother had been as house-proud as the next woman, and June and Molly, encouraged by Elsie Fowler, had grown up maintaining those standards.

It was true that their front door did not have the coloured leaded lights adorning number 46's, nor did they have the advantage of a big bay window overlooking their small front garden, but their father kept their privet hedge every bit as neatly clipped.

'Come on, she mustn't be in, and I'm not wasting any more time standing here knocking again,' June announced, turning round.

Molly had started to follow her when she heard the door opening and stopped.

Mrs Brookes – a former ward sister at the hospital before her marriage, whose discipline and rigidity still remained – was a tall, well-built woman, firmly corseted, with a sharp-eyed gaze that rested disapprovingly on everything and everyone apart from her beloved son. It was certainly fixed less than welcomingly on them now, Molly recognised.

'Oh, it's you, is it?' she declared grimly.

She hadn't invited them in and quite plainly wasn't going to do so. Molly quickly realised that June was leaving it to her to speak.

'We were just passing on our way home and we wondered if you wanted any help with your blackout curtains, only me and June are going to be sewing ours tonight and . . .'

Was that a small softening Molly could see in the grimly reserved features?

'Yes, and whilst we were in Lewis's I had a good look at their wedding dress patterns,' June chipped in determinedly.

Immediately Frank's mother's hackles rose and her mouth pursed with displeasure.

'I'm already sorted out with me blackout curtains. My friend on Carlton Avenue and her daughter have invited me round there so that we can make them together. In fact, Angela is going to come round for me tonight in her car. Such a lovely girl. A schoolteacher, she is, and the whole family so refined.' She stepped back into the house and started to close the door, pausing to add coldly, 'Oh, and I wouldn't be making too many plans for any wedding, if I were you. From what I've heard, my Frank isn't likely to get any leave for quite some time and when he does, the last thing he's gonna want is to be rushed into a wedding.'

'Well, that's not what Frank has said to me,' June insisted angrily. 'And since it's him and me that is going to be gettin' married, it's our business what we do, and no one else's.

'Gawd, she's got her nose so stuck up in the air it's a mercy she doesn't fall over her own feet,' June complained to Molly as she slammed Frank's mother's gate forcefully behind them. 'So much for your idea, eh, Miss Clever Clogs?'

'Well, at least Frank will be pleased that you offered,' Molly told her, trying desperately to salvage something from the situation. Privately she half suspected that June quite enjoyed her set-tos with Frank's mother and even deliberately encouraged them, but her loyalty to her sister prevented her from saying as much.

'It works both ways,' June replied. 'So how about you going round and asking Johnny's mam if she wants a hand with her curtains?'

'She's got Johnny's sisters to help her,' Molly protested, but she knew her face was burning guiltily.

'What, them pair of useless articles?' June sniffed disparagingly. 'A lot of good them two will be, from what I know of them.'

'All right then,' Molly gave in reluctantly. 'I'll go round and see her as soon as we've had our tea.'

Half an hour later Molly was standing in her apron, slicing what was left of the Sunday roast for their cold meat salad tea, to be served with hot new potatoes from the allotment, while listening to the wireless, when she heard the sound of her father's heavy work boots on the back step. Leaving what she was doing, she went to fill the kettle.

'Kettle's on, Dad.'

His walk back from Edge Hill railway yard had brought a sheen of perspiration to Albert's sun-reddened forehead. As always, Molly was filled with a rush of love for him when she saw him. Left with two young daughters to rear alone, he could have opted to hand her and June over to their mother's family and got on with his own life, but instead he had done everything he could to provide them with a loving happy home. It must have been so hard for him. He had had to work long gruelling hours at the gridiron to ensure there was food on the table, but he had never once missed reading them a bedtime story, nor listening to them recite their times tables, nor checking their spelling homework. Tears pricked Molly's eyes. She could scarcely remember her mother but she knew from the way he still talked about her that her father had loved her and still missed her.

'I'll get washed up, love,' he called, disappearing into the small back scullery. Repairing railway lines and working on rolling stock was dirty and often heavy work, but Albert took pride in his appearance and was fastidious in scrubbing up the minute he got home. 'Costs nowt to be clean' was one of his favourite phrases. Medium height and slightly stooped, he faithfully clung to the small domestic details of family life originally put in place by the girls' mother. A bath once a week, their hair washed on Sunday night ready for school on Monday, a kitchen that was kept spick and span with the pans, like the family's shoes, polished so brightly that you could see your face in them. Albert had instilled in his daughters his own respect for cleanliness and neatness. There was another side to him, though, a side that had him cultivating flowers in the tiny back garden.

'Your mam allus loved them,' he had once told Molly when she had admired the scent of some roses, his arthritis-damaged fingers gently touching the velvety soft petals.

And he was not the kind of man to go off to the pub of a Saturday night, leaving his young motherless daughters to the care of a neighbour like some men in his position would have done. Instead, in winter the small family had gathered around the wireless after Saturday night's supper, whilst in the summer the girls had gone down to the allotment with their father.

'You'll never guess what's happened at the factory today, Dad,' June announced once they were all sitting down and eating.

'Aye, well, you don't want to go getting on the wrong side of that Miss Jenner,' Albert warned his elder daughter after she'd finished telling him with relish how she had outwitted the new supervisor. He knew June could be a firebrand at times.

Molly could see the worry in her father's eyes and vowed silently to do what she could to keep June from baiting Miss Jenner. No one else would take on a machinist who had lost her job for cheeking a superior.

Once the meal was over and everything cleared away, and their father had set off for his allotment, Molly ran upstairs to comb her hair. She knew she couldn't put off the visit any longer.

Johnny's mother and sisters lived three streets away from Chestnut Close, down a narrow backstreet. Its double row of small terraced houses were of poor quality. Unlike the houses on the close, those of Moreton Street did not have gardens or indoor bathrooms, but had to make do with small dank back yards and outside privies.

Two tow-headed little boys, playing in the dusty street, stopped their game to watch Molly until a young very pregnant woman, with untidy hair and wearing a grubby apron, called out to them to get themselves inside.

Moreton Street had a slightly rank smell, and Molly tried not to wrinkle her nose at it. On the cul-de-sac they had the benefit of more modern housing, the allotments, with their smell of fresh earth and air, and even the scent of roses from some front gardens. Not that some of the residents of Moreton Street didn't make an effort. Several of the houses had freshly donkey-stoned steps and clean windows with neat curtains hanging in them, but unfortunately Johnny's mother's house wasn't one of them.

Molly climbed the steps and knocked on the shabby door.

She could hear sounds of people talking inside the house, but it seemed an age before the door was finally opened to reveal the elder of Johnny's younger sisters, Deirdre, her hair in curling rags, and a grubby brassiere strap visible as she clutched at the front of her dressing gown.

''Ere, Mam, it's our Johnny's fiancée,' she called back to the darkness of the cluttered hallway.

Molly's tender heart couldn't help but pity Johnny's mother, with her nervous air, her hands disfigured and reddened from her cleaning job at the hospital. It must have been so hard to bring up three children alone with only one wage coming in. It was no doubt because their mother had had to work such long hours cleaning that Johnny's sisters were the way they were. The fact that their mother was out at work all day and most evenings meant that they had had far more freedom than most girls in the area, whose parents kept a much stricter eye on them.

'Well, I never . . . we wasn't expectin' you, otherwise—'

'Give over fussing, Mam,' Deirdre objected. 'If she's gonna marry our Johnny she's gorra get used to us the way we are, instead of expectin' us to put on a lorra fancy airs.'

'Deirdre, you pig, if you've bin using my rouge, I'll skin yer alive.' Heels clattered on the stairs, barely covered by a threadbare runner, as Johnny's other sister, Jennifer, came downstairs, her hair carefully curled to emulate the style favoured by the film star Jean Harlow, her flimsy short skirt all but showing off her knees.

''Ere, Mam, me hem's coming down. Have you gorra safety pin, so I can pin it? Only me other one needs a wash, and I ain't got nuttin' else to wear, like.'

'Perhaps it might be better to sew it,' Molly couldn't help suggesting.

'Give over,' Jennifer laughed, giving a dismissive shrug. 'I ain't gor any time for that. I've gorra meet me new fella in ten minutes and I don't want no other girl pinchin' him from us 'cos I'm late. Gizz us a woodie, will yer, Deirdre?' she demanded. 'I'm gasping for a fag.'

'You're gonna have to cut that out if we're going

to have a war,' her mother warned her. 'Fags'll be on the ration as well, you mark my words.'

'Then I'm just gonna have to find a fella to get them for me, aren't I?' Jennifer told her, blowing out a cloud of smoke that made Molly's eyes smart, before asking, 'So what's brought you round here then, Molly?'

'I was just wondering if your mam needed any help with her blackout curtains.'

'Blackout curtains – just listen to 'er,' Jennifer laughed. 'We ain't gonna be wasting our time messin' around with nuttin' like that; brown paper and sticky tape is all we're gonna be doin'. Bloody hell, Deirdre, have youse been pinching my scent again?' she demanded, sniffing the air as Deirdre attempted to walk past her.

'So wot if I have, an' all?' Deirdre responded sulkily. 'You took me last pair of nylons, didn't yer?'

'Hurry up and get yerself ready if yer coming down the dance hall wi' me 'cos I ain't gonna be waitin' for yer. Yer want ter come with us, Molly? . . . Catch me tying meself to one fella like you have with our Johnny . . . Why don't yer come wi' us on Saturday?' Jennifer asked.

'It's kind of you to ask, but me and June are going looking for some material for her wedding dress.'

'Well, if it's fabric you're wantin', there's a shop off Bold Street as sells all the best-quality stuff right cheap, on account of it having fallen off a lorry, if yer takes me meaning,' Jennifer added with a knowing wink.

Molly didn't make any response. It was impossible to grow up in Liverpool and not know about the brisk black market that existed, with so many goods passing through the docks, but Molly didn't want to get involved.

She could see through into the back room where the tea things were still on the table. The smell of cheap scent and stale chip fat was making her long to escape, but politeness kept her where she was.

'They're good girls really, my Deirdre and Jennifer,' Johnny's mother told Molly almost apologetically when both her daughters had gone to finish getting ready to go out, 'but they're young and they gorra 'ave a bit of fun, like. Mind you, I'm right glad our Johnny's going to wed you, Molly. You're gonna be good for him. Not like some as I could name as would only cause him a lorra trouble.' Her mouth tightened slightly.

It was a relief to be back in her own home, Molly admitted half an hour later, as she and June worked companionably together. 'At least we've got plenty of light to work in, what with this double daylight saving,' Molly commented, as they sat on the back step, tacking together the curtains they had cut out, and listening to Max Miller on the wireless.

'Here, was that the front door I just heard, our Molly?'

Molly put down her sewing and went to see.

Visitors didn't call on weekdays, and neighbours and friends always came round to the back, so she hesitated for a moment when she saw the shadow of a man through the frosted glass of the inner front door.

'ARP,' he called out. 'Come to mek sure you've got your government notice.'

'You'd better come in,' Molly told Alf Davies. He looked very official, with his clipboard and stern expression, but he accepted quickly enough when she offered him a cup of tea, and smiled approvingly when he saw that they were already busy making their blackout curtains.

'Not that I know why we have to do all this stuff, mind,' June challenged him. 'Not when there isn't even a war on yet.'

'Rules is rules,' he answered her importantly, puffing out his cheeks and then blowing on the cup of tea Molly had just given him. 'Gas masks are going to be given out this Saturday at Melby Road Junior School, so mek sure that you go and collect yours. You'll be given a demonstration of how to use it properly, like. Any children living here?'

Both girls shook their heads.

'Now what about an Anderson shelter?'

'We're sharing with the rest of the end of the cul-de-sac,' June informed him.

'Is it true that all the children will be evacuated even if their mothers don't want them to be?' Molly couldn't stop herself from asking him. The words of the government leaflet still haunted her, and she couldn't imagine how terrifying it would be for a small child to be sent off to a strange place to live with a strange family.

'I can't answer them sort of questions, but I can tell you that we are looking for volunteers to help wi' what's got to be done, if you twose wanted to help out.'

'Volunteer? We've got enough to do, sewing uniforms for soldiers – aye, and paid next to nuttin' for doing it, an' all,' June informed him sharply.

But for once Molly overrode her sister and asked quietly, 'Where would we go, if we wanted to volunteer?'

'You can just come round and have a word with me – you know where I am – number 14. The missus will take a message if I'm not there.' He stood up. 'Thanks for the tea, and remember, when the time comes for them curtains to go up, I'll be coming round to check that they ain't lettin' out no light, so make sure youse do a good job.'

'What's got into you?' June demanded when Molly had shown Alf Davies out. 'What did you want to go telling him you wanted to volunteer for?'

'Because if there is going to be a war, I want to do my bit,' Molly answered firmly. She'd been thinking for weeks about how helpless she would feel if – *when*, she now acknowledged grimly – war broke out, and so jumped at the chance to be able to do something for the war effort.

'Well, you're already sewing these blummin' curtains,' June grumbled. 'You're daft if you volunteer to do any more.'

She repeated her comment later when their father came back in, but he merely smiled and looked tenderly at Molly.

'You tek after your mam, right enough, Molly lass,' he told her gently. 'A right kind heart she had, an' all.'

'Now what am I supposed to do with it?'

Molly giggled helplessly as June struggled to put on her gas mask. 'Oh, give over larking about, do,' she protested. 'I'm laughing that much it hurts.'

'Well, let's see you put yours on then,' June challenged her.

They had arrived at the school an hour ago to join the tail end of the queue waiting to receive their gas masks, and now, despite the tension gripping everyone, several other people had joined in Molly's mirth as she watched her elder sister struggle.

'You gorra do it like this, love,' an elderly woman informed June, deftly demonstrating just how the mask should go on, after she had stopped laughing.

'We gor another of them leaflets come dis mornin',' a woman standing close to Molly announced. 'Full of a lorra stuff about food and rationing, it were, sayin' as how we gorra have ration books and that, like.'

61

Immediately the laughter stopped and the women looked worriedly at one another.

'Rationin'? What's that when it's at home?' a young girl with sharp features and a thin anxious face demanded.

'It's wot we had during the last war,' the older woman who had shown June how to put on her mask answered her grimly. 'The Government tells yer what food yer can buy and what yer can't.'

'That's all we need,' June told Molly glumly. 'Nothing to eat!'

'It won't be so bad. At least we'll have Dad's allotment – and if it helps our lads . . .' Molly tried to comfort her, as she packed her gas mask back in its box and shyly returned the approving smile of a pretty WVS volunteer she had been talking to earlier. June might not like it, but Molly was determined to join up for some voluntary work.

'Who's that you were just smiling at?' June demanded as they left the building, the summer breeze catching the cotton skirts of their dresses.

'I don't know her name. She was the one who gave me my mask. I was telling her about wanting to do some voluntary work. She's told me how to go about it. We could both do it,' she added hopefully.

'Huh, you won't catch me volunteering for anything,' June told her crossly. 'All them folk telling me what to do! We get enough of that at work. Daft, that's what you are. As if we don't have enough to do, and there'll be even more if this blummin' rationing comes in . . . What time did you say as we would meet the others?'

'Six o'clock,' Molly told her.

They had arranged to go to the cinema with some of the other girls from the factory, but despite this promised treat June was still looking glum, and Molly thought she knew why.

'Frank's bound to write soon,' she tried to comfort her.

'He better had, an' all, if he knows what's good for him. How the blinkin' heck am I supposed to organise a wedding when I don't know when he's going to get leave?' June sounded angry but Molly knew her sister well enough to realise that the anger masked her real feelings. Impulsively she reached out for June's hand and squeezed it.

Back outside on the street, Molly looked round for their father, who had gone to collect his gas mask with some of the other men from the allotments.

'It's our mam's birthday next week,' she reminded June.

Every year, on her birthday, among other days, the two girls and their father visited Rosie's grave to lay flowers on it.

'Aye, I know.'

'What was she like, June?' Molly asked her sister softly. 'I can't remember her properly at all.' She'd asked the question many a time over the years but never tired of hearing her sister describe their mother.

June paused for a moment as though she was thinking hard and then said slowly, 'Well, you look the image of her, and she was a bit of a softie too, like you, but by, she could give you a fair clout when she got angry. Allus laughing, she was, an' singing too, like – you've got her voice, our Molly. Fair gives me a turn sometimes to hear you singing 'cos you sound just like her. Right pretty she was, an' all, excepting for them last months.' Tears filled June's eyes and Molly was once again reminded of how much harder it must have been for June to see their mother fade before her very eyes. Molly had been too young to appreciate the extent of their mother's illness but June, two years older, had not been spared the reality of what was happening. 'Dead thin she went, just bones in the end. She'd been poorly all winter, coughing and the like. We thought as how she would get better when it came warmer weather . . .'

Molly gave a small shiver and moved closer to her sister. She might not always agree with June's way of going about things, and resent her control over her sometimes, but she was still her sister, the sister who'd been a substitute mother to her for so many years, and Molly loved her dearly.

'What about this?' Molly suggested, directing June's attention to the bolt of white satin fabric she had found wedged between some brightly patterned cottons.

'But I'd got me heart set on lace.'

'Haven't we all, duck, so mek sure you let on to us if you find any,' a woman with brassily bleached hair and bright red lipstick, standing close enough to overhear, chipped in. 'My Harry says as how he don't care nuttin' wot me wedding dress is made of just so long as he don't 'ave to waste a lorra time gettin' it off us,' she confided saucily.

'Common as muck,' Molly heard June muttering contemptuously, turning her back as the other woman reached past them both and picked up a bolt of bright blue fabric, calling over her shoulder, ''Ere, Marge, worra 'bout dis den for youse bridesmaids' dresses?'

'Who did you say told you this was a good place to get fabric?' June demanded, pursing her lips.

'May mentioned it and so did Johnny's sisters,' Molly admitted.

'Huh, I might have guessed.'

'The satin is lovely and heavy, June,' Molly tried to distract her. 'It would make up a treat and look really elegant. We could always trim it up with some lace . . .'

'I don't know . . . I'd got me heart set on lace, Molly . . .'

''Ere, Vera, you gorra come and luk at dis satin!' another female voice exclaimed. Immediately Molly snatched up the bolt of satin, hugging it tightly, and resolutely ignoring the look on Vera's friend's face.

''Aving that, are youse, lass, 'cos if you ain't . . .' the shopkeeper, who was keeping an eye on the proceedings, demanded.

'Looks like we'll have to now,' June grumbled. 'How much did the pattern say we needed?'

'Fifteen yards,' Molly told her, 'and that includes the train.'

Once the fabric had been parcelled up, Molly and June headed for Lewis's where they had arranged to meet the others for a cup of tea before going on to the cinema.

'It comes to something when you can't even buy what you want for your wedding dress,' June complained once they had explained to the other girls what was in her parcel, and ordered their tea.

'You gorra be grateful you got sommat,' Irene told June forthrightly, above the sound of Sonny Durband, the resident pianist in Lewis's restaurant.

'What I don't understand is why the Government's doing all of this, like, when Mr Chamberlain 'as promised that we ain't gonna be goin' to war,' Sheila protested.

'Are you daft or what?' Irene challenged her pithily. 'Of course there's going to be a blummin' war. Why the 'eck do youse think we're mekkin' all them bloody uniforms? Mind, if I had me way I wouldner be workin' at Hardings. I'd be down one of them munitions factories, like – Napiers, p'haps. Paying women two pounds fifteen shillings a week, they are, so I've heard,' she informed the others in awe-struck tones, 'and they get to have a bit o' fun and a laugh. Not like us – not now we've got that bloomin' Jenner woman spyin' on us all the time. You two will have to watch it,' she told June and Molly. 'Hates your guts, she does.' Then she added, 'Come on, you lot, it's time we was goin', otherwise we're gonna be late.'

'Not much of a film, that, and all them Pathé newsreels got on me wick. As if we don't have enough of that on the wireless, and with all them leaflets we keep on getting sent,' Ruby grumbled later, when they left the cinema.

'I thought it was interesting,' Molly protested. 'Especially that bit about the new National Blood Bank, and how the Government's making sure that the hospitals have plenty of beds and bandages, and building new operating theatres.'

'Listen to Florence Nightingale here. Next thing, she'll be wanting to give some of her own blood,' June grimaced.

Molly flushed but held her ground. 'Well, I would, an' all, if it was going to save someone else's life,' she retaliated stoutly, ignoring the derisory look her sister was giving her. Molly felt so passionately about 'doing her bit' and she was disappointed that June didn't share her own urgent desire to do what she could to help with the country's preparations for war.

FOUR

'Is that Pete Ridley outside with his milk float and horse?'

'Yes, Dad,' Molly confirmed, protesting when her father opened the back door. 'Where are you going? He'll leave the milk on the doorstep like always.'

''Tain't the milk I'm after, it's the horse muck,' he told her forthrightly. 'Right good for the allotment it'll be. And that reminds me, there's a few of the lads as will be coming round tonight to talk about the allotments. We're going to be forming a committee, seeing as how we're going to be part of the war effort and "digging for victory",' he told Molly proudly before disappearing through the door to speak to the milkman.

'Wait up, Molly,' June puffed. 'You're walking too fast.'

'I don't want us to be late,' Molly answered her worriedly as she waited for June to catch up with her. 'I'm sure that Miss Jenner is going to be looking for any excuse to make trouble for us.'

'So what? With old man Harding looking to take on extra workers, he's not gonna want to lose good machinists like us. He'll have the Government to answer to if he doesn't get them uniforms made on time.'

Since the other girls had also arrived a few minutes early, Molly suspected that they all shared her wariness of Miss Jenner. A handful of girls she didn't recognise were huddled together just inside the workroom, looking uncertain and anxious. One of them didn't look much more than fourteen, her thin arms and legs poking out of her worn dress.

Molly smiled at them as she tucked her hair up and pinned it back, before putting on her overall. Earlier in the year she and June had treated themselves to a new hairdo apiece at Lewis's, where Molly's hair had been cut into the style favoured by the actress Vivien Leigh for her role in the much-anticipated *Gone with the Wind*.

Molly had just seated herself at the machine when the work bell rang shrilly.

Immediately the door opened and Miss Jenner came in, her lips pursed as she silently inspected the rows of expectant machinists.

'From now on we shall be having a roll call every morning five minutes before you start work. Anyone not here for that roll call will lose a day's pay.'

An outraged mutter of protest filled the room but Miss Jenner ignored it, walking over to the new girls.

'Hardings has an important role to play in the war effort and you will find that I run this machine room with the same discipline and dedication with which an army commander controls his men. Since I understand that none of you has any previous experience as machinists, you will each sit beside a machinist and watch her work. Then this afternoon you will be given your own machine and you will start to work properly. Every garment made in this factory will be inspected by me, and if it fails to meet the high standards our fighting men deserve, then the machinist will be fined for the cost of the time and the material lost.'

A gasp of indignation filled the silence.

'Well, I'm gonna tell her straight I'm not puttin' up wi' it. Not for one minute I'm not,' Sheila fumed later, after the dinner bell had rung and the girls were all clustered together talking, after enduring a morning of silence.

'I'm tekkin' meself down to the Metal Box as was, first thing tomorrow morning. Crying out for workers there, they are, so I've heard,' said another girl.

The new girls all looked so exhausted and worried that Molly couldn't help but feel sorry for them.

'I'm right worried that they won't keep me on,' Jean Hughes, the girl who sat next to Molly, con-

70

fided whilst they ate their dinner, Molly having surreptitiously given half of her sandwiches to Evie, the stick-thin new girl, when she saw that Evie hadn't brought anything to eat.

Molly knew that Jean lived down on Daffodil Street, one of the 'flower' streets close to the docks, and, after listening to Irene, was worried that she wouldn't be able to keep a job that she had confided to Molly was a bit of a step up for her.

'You'll do fine,' Molly assured her kindly. 'It's just that we haven't got used to Miss Jenner yet.'

'I'm sick of this ruddy war already,' Ruby complained, 'and it hasn't even started yet. Our mam's acting like she's got ants in her pants ever since we got them blinking leaflets. She's had us at it all weekend up in the attic, clearing stuff out. 'Ave yer done yours yet?' she asked June.

'No. We could have done it tonight, only this one,' June emphasised scornfully, nodding her head in Molly's direction, 'has taken it into her head to go and sign up for the blinkin' WVS tonight.'

'Oh, me mam's in that,' one of the new girls chirped up, causing June to frown at her.

'Well, I'm thinking of joining,' Sheila put in quietly. 'They've bin asking for help round our way with this evacuation of all the kiddies coming up. Me sister's going mad about it. Seven months gone, she is, with her second, and her husband away in the merchant navy. She wants ter stay here in Liverpool, like, but our mam's told her as how she should do as the Government wants.'

71

Throughout every city thought to be at risk from enemy attack, parents had been issued with government instructions, telling them that they were to be ready for the mass evacuation of their children at the end of August. Children were to be taken to their local schools ready to be marched class by class and school by school to designated railway stations, from where they would be evacuated to the country along with their teachers. Parents had been told what clothes and other equipment each child was to have, and local industries and town halls had stepped forward with promises to give each child food and drink for the journey. Volunteers were needed to assist with this process and to help take charge of the children when they arrived at their schools ready for the evacuation.

Those people who would be housing the evacuees were going to be paid by the Government for doing so, and already there was a great deal of resentment being felt amongst the poor of Liverpool about the fact that other people were being paid to look after their children whilst they were denied any such help. The WVS, most of them mothers themselves, had been recruited to help the Government with this evacuation.

June was still in a huff with Molly about volunteering when they got home, but the discovery that the postman had brought letters from both Frank and Johnny evaporated the tension. June, pink-cheeked with excitement and relief, pounced on her envelope. 'At last. It seems ever such a long time since Frank left, and I've missed him that much.'

Late afternoon sunshine poured in through the back door, turning June's hair dark gold as she sat down on the step to read her letter.

Having put the kettle on to boil, so delaying the moment as long as she could, Molly went to join her, opening her own letter with a heavy heart.

Johnny's handwriting looked almost childlike. He wasn't allowed to tell her where he was, or what he was doing, he had written, before going on to complain that he hated the food. Her letter was much thinner than June's. There was no mention in it of when he might get leave, nor any hint that he might be missing her – but that made her feel more relieved than disappointed, Molly admitted to herself.

'What's the return address on yours?' June demanded.

Molly showed her.

'They aren't in the same camp then: Frank's is different. Does Johnny say when he's likely to get some leave?'

'No, does Frank?'

'He says they haven't been told anything much and that he'll let me know as soon as he's got some news.'

The kettle had started to boil. Molly got up and went to make the tea.

'Would you believe it?' June complained. 'Frank's put in his letter that he's worried about his mam being on her own. What about me?'

'He knows that you've got me and Dad,' Molly reminded her.

'Yoo-hoo . . .'

Elsie Fowler edged her way through the convenient gap in the hedge that divided their small back gardens.

'Seein' as how I haven't seen much of either of youse just lately, I thought as how I'd call round, like, with these,' she told them, handing Molly a bunch of sweetpeas. 'For yer mam for tomorrow,' she explained gently.

Emotionally, Molly hugged her and thanked her. She had to remind herself that Elsie must miss her old friend too.

'How are the boys?'

'They're fine, and you'll never guess what? Remember our Eddie, our nephew what used to come and stay wi' us when he were a kiddie, before his dad passed away and his mam took him back wi' her to Morecambe to her family? Well, his mam died last winter, and he called round here last night to ask if he can lodge wi' us. Took us right by surprise, he did. Not that we wasn't glad to see him. He's in the merchant navy now, I think I told you, and with both his mam and dad gone, it makes sense for him to be here in Liverpool wi' us.'

'Of course I remember him,' Molly smiled. 'He

used to protect me when the others tried to put worms down my back. I'm sorry to hear he's lost his mam, Elsie.'

'Aye, well, it's a mercy, if you ask me. She never got over losing our Jack, and she'd bin poorly for a good while, from what I heard. Not that she bothered to keep in touch wi' us much once she went back to her own folk. Eddie now, well, I've allus had a soft spot for him. The spittin' image of me own dad, he is,' she added with a fond smile. 'I told him he could bring his kitbag round here as soon as he liked, just as long as he doesn't mind sleeping in our boxroom. Have you heard from Frank and Johnny yet?'

'We got letters today,' Molly told her, 'but we don't know yet when they'll get any leave.'

'I dare say they won't be able to send word right away, but from what Sally Walker was saying, they should get some as soon as their training's finished, so you'd best hurry and get that wedding dress made, young June.'

'Well, we won't be doing that tonight,' June informed her, giving Molly a black look. 'Our Molly's off to join the WVS.'

'Good for you, love! There's two or three from the cul-de-sac joined up to it already, and I was thinking of doing the same meself, only with John and Jim working shifts on the gridiron an' all, it's a bit difficult.'

Molly looked quickly at her sister, hoping that Elsie's endorsement might make June change her mind, but she could see from her set expression that she was not going to allow herself to be coaxed into that.

'I won't be there very long, June,' Molly told her. 'We can have a look at the pattern when I get back, if you like.'

'There's no need for you to go putting yourself out on my account. Anyway, I've changed me mind and I'm going to spend the evening writing back to me fiancé,' she added pointedly, going back into the house.

'Perhaps she's right, and I shouldn't join the WVS.' Molly looked at Elsie unhappily.

Elsie snorted. 'Tek no notice of your June. If you want my opinion she's just feeling a bit put out, like, because you're doing sommat wi'out her having told you to do it. She'll come round. You wait and see.'

Molly reminded herself of Elsie's comforting words later that evening in the church hall whilst her head buzzed with all the information she had just been given.

According to Mrs Wesley, who was in charge of their local WVS group, the basic training members of the WVS would have to undergo, and the list of duties they could expect to be called upon to provide, included co-operating with ARP wardens and local authority services; organising and undergoing lectures for women in first aid; anti-gas and fire-fighting skills; manning of incident enquiry posts; co-operating in invasion defence schemes; staffing ARP canteens; feeding civil defence workers after raids; being trained to drive emergency vehicles; assisting in staffing NFS and police canteens; making and sewing sandbags; and all aspects of evacuation, including escorting, sickbay duties, running communal feeding centres, hotels and social centres. They were to provide staff for mobile office units and train as volunteers for emergency work, and a whole list of other duties so long that Molly was afraid she wouldn't be able to remember them all. Following the example of the girl standing next to her, she had put her name down for as many of the training programmes as she thought she would be able to do.

'Molly!'

She turned round, smiling as she saw a girl hurrying towards her in her uniform.

'So you came then? I'm so glad. I'm Anne – we met at the gas mask collection, remember?'

Molly nodded. 'I'm never going to be able to remember all that we're supposed to learn to do.'

'Yes, you will. I'll help you,' Anne told her stoutly. 'I'm going to go and put my name down for the driving lessons – why don't you do the same?'

'Oh, I couldn't,' Molly protested. She hadn't even been in a car, never mind thought of learning to drive.

'Yes, you can,' Anne overruled her. 'Besides, it's

our duty to do as much as we can.' She added more seriously, 'It's like Mrs Wesley just said: we've all got to remember that our help could make the difference between life and death.'

Molly looked at her uncertainly, uncomfortably aware of how June was likely to react to the news that she was planning to learn to drive.

'I won't take no for an answer,' Anne warned her. 'It would be marvellous if both of us could drive, and much more fun than unravelling old jumpers and making sandbags.' Anne pulled a face, and suddenly Molly found herself relaxing and laughing whilst her new friend dragged her over to sign up for driving lessons.

'I'm dreading this evacuation business we've got to help out with,' she admitted to Anne later.

'It will be a bit like jumping into one of the docks at the deep end,' Anne agreed, 'but it's got to be done. We can't have all those little ones at risk of being bombed, can we?'

The meeting had gone on longer than Molly had expected, and she hurried past the scout hut and across the main road after saying goodbye to Anne, who had explained that she lived in Wavertree. The garden suburb was considered 'posher' than Edge Hill, and it was obvious to Molly that Anne came from a better-off family than her own, and that she had had more experience of life. Anne's father, Anne had told her, had an office job at the town hall, and her mother did not go out to work. Her family home was semidetached, and she had mentioned that she was a member of Wavertree's tennis club. Molly knew that June would have said she was too pushy, but although she felt slightly awed by Anne, Molly couldn't help but like her open friendly manner.

Thinking of her sister made Molly wish all over again that June had agreed to come with her. It would help keep her mind off worrying about her Frank. She knew June was a kind person, deep down, but she came across as abrasive to many, especially those who didn't know her well. Maybe she would be able to persuade her to change her mind when she told her all she had learned, she decided hopefully.

The men were still working their allotments as she cut down the footpath alongside them, the scent of freshly watered earth mingling with that of their Woodbine cigarettes. Molly looked to see if she could see her father, but didn't stop walking. She was mentally rehearsing what she was going to say to June to persuade her to change her mind about the WVS.

When she got in there was no sign of her sister downstairs; even the radio had been turned off, and the table had been laid for breakfast, a task the girls always did last thing before they went to bed.

'June?' she called uncertainly from the bottom of the stairs, and then when there was no reply she hurried up, her initial surprise at finding her sister already in bed giving way to anxiety.

'Are you all right?' she asked.

'What's it to you?' June demanded truculently. 'Hours, you've been gone, and me here on me own. And me monthlies are giving me a right pain in me belly.'

'Oh, June, I'm sorry,' Molly sympathised. Of the two of them, June had always been the one who had suffered more each month. 'Would you like a hot-water bottle?'

June shook her head, thawing slightly. 'I'm feeling a bit better now. I'll come down and 'ave a cuppa, I think. It sounds like Dad's just come in – you'd better go down otherwise he'll want to know what's up.'

Her father was standing in the kitchen, holding a large cardboard box, which he placed almost tenderly on the kitchen floor.

'What's in there?' Molly asked curiously.

'Tek the lid off and have a look.'

Molly exclaimed in astonishment, as the moment she lifted the lid the kitchen was filled with the sound of cheeping.

'Day-old chicks, a gross of them, and our Joe's got another gross as well, and there's a gross for Pete – seeing as how he's promised to let us have his horse muck for the allotments. They're from your aunt's farm.'

'What are?' June asked, coming into the kitchen, her eyes widening as she saw the answer to her question.

'We've clubbed together at the allotments to buy

them. With a hundred and forty-four of them we should get a fair few fresh eggs. Only thing is, we need to keep them warm and properly fed for the next few days. I've got some mash, to start 'em off, like.'

'But where will you keep them?' Molly asked him.

'We're going to build a coop for them – I've got a bit of wood put by down at the railway yard.' He winked meaningfully at them and then added, 'Pete is going to pick it up for us, and once the chicks have grown they can scratch around down the allotments.' He picked the lid up and placed it over the boxful of chicks, immediately silencing them. 'And that's not all,' he told the girls enthusiastically. 'We've put in to have a pig as well.'

'A pig?'

'Aye, it's a scheme the Government is doing – them as keeps a pig gets ter keep a fair bit of the meat from it, so mek sure you don't go throwing away any scraps. Oh, and by the way, your Aunt Violet has sent a message to say they've got plenty of work down at the farm, if you fancy leaving that factory after all.'

June shuddered. 'Not likely – remember that time Dad took us there on the train, Molly, and them blinkin' cows? No, ta! You can keep the country. I'm staying here, even with that Miss Jenner at my throat.'

It was only later, when she was finally in bed

and almost asleep, that Molly realised that she hadn't talked to June about joining the WVS. Oh well, there was always tomorrow, she decided as she closed her eyes.

FIVE

The bright morning sun blazed down from a cloud-
lessly blue sky. It was far too hot to wear winter
clothes but, nevertheless, the three of them had
put on their darkest things and their father was
even wearing a collar and tie. People looked curiously at them when they got on the bus but they
ignored their sideways looks. They had made this
journey five times a year since Rosie's death: on
Mothering Sunday, on the anniversaries of her
birth, her marriage and her death, and at
Christmas. Now their coming here had gathered
its own small rituals: the flowers they brought –
daffodils on Mothering Sunday, the roses that bore
her name and which she had carried in her wedding bouquet on her birthday and the anniversary
of her marriage, violets in February, when she had
died, and at Christmas a home-made wreath of
holly and ivy to lay on the cold stone – their visit
to their own church before they left; their silence
like the silence of the cemetery where their wife

and mother was buried close to her parents and to her parents-in-law.

This morning, though, the cemetery wasn't silent. Instead, a group of men were moving and extending its boundary, whilst others were excavating the hard-packed earth.

Molly looked questioningly at her father. 'Are they going to turn it into allotments, do you think, Dad?'

'I don't think so, love. More like they're getting ready for a different kind of crop,' he told her heavily. 'Just in case, like . . .'

All the colour left her face as she realised what he meant. She looked from him to the bare stretch of land and then at the cemetery, visually measuring the grave-covered earth to the land that lay beyond it – land she now realised was being set aside for new graves.

A mixture of shock, fear and pain filled her insides. It was something she had not allowed herself to think of – the human cost of war. Tales of the Great War seemed from a different age.

'Surely there won't be so many,' she whispered.

Her father's mouth twisted. 'This is nowt to them as died last time.' His haunted expression aged his face. He had never told his daughters of the horrors he had witnessed in the trenches of France: of how he'd had to drink filthy, muddy water just to stay alive; of how he'd had to strip a dead soldier of his ammunition while he was still warm; of how he'd seen his best friend blown to pieces right beside him. 'A load of cardboard coffins we had shipped in on one of t'trains this week. There was talk as how the ice rink is going to be used as a morgue, if'n Hitler drops his bombs on us. Lorra rubbish. If'n he does it won't be whole bodies as they'll be buryin'.'

Molly shivered, her eyes widening in fear. 'Don't talk like that, Dad,' she begged him.

When he looked at her Molly realised that he had momentarily forgotten her and that he had been back in the past and his dreadful experiences of the last war. He squeezed her hand and kissed the top of her head, just like he had done when she was a child and had fallen over and scraped her knee.

'Don't you worry, love. With lads like Frank and Johnny to look out for us, we'll be just fine,' he assured her, although in his heart he felt mounting anxiety.

Sombrely the three of them made their way along the familiar footpath until they came to Rosie's grave. For once, even June was silent. The grave was marked with just a simple headstone, but at least she was with those she had loved and who had loved her, and as a child Molly had taken comfort from that knowledge.

One by one they kneeled down and offered up their flowers and their prayers. Molly could see that their father was trying not to cry.

Afterwards, though, when they made their way home, it was the sight of that empty land waiting to receive the bodies of those who were still alive that occupied Molly's thoughts and tore at her heart. For the first time she knew properly what it was to be afraid of war and death. So many graves; so many people who were going to die. She looked at her father and her sister, anguish inside her. It wasn't just the men abroad. What if one of them . . . ?

She could taste dust in the August heat when they got off the bus and walked up the cul-de-sac.

'I thought we'd make a start on turning out the attic tonight,' she heard June telling her once they were back home, briskly back to business.

Numbly Molly looked at her.

'What's up with you?' June asked her.

'All those graves, June, so many of them . . .' Molly's voice shook.

Immediately June's expression softened. 'Aye . . . I thought like that meself when I knew that my Frank would be joining up, but we've got to keep our chins up, Molly. Don't you worry about Johnny – he's a tough one.'

The two sisters looked at one another, both fighting against tears. Molly felt guilty that she was not thinking of Johnny but of every man fighting.

The door opened to admit their father, who had been upstairs to remove his collar. His shoulders were bowed, his expression drawn and sad.

Giving Molly a warning look, June said briskly, 'I expect you'll be off down the allotment, won't you, Dad, after you've checked on them blummin' chickens of yours. All over the kitchen, they are.'

June was so strong, Molly thought admiringly, as she watched their father respond visibly to her goading.

The chickens had escaped from their box and greeted their owners' return home with excited cheeps as they hopped and jumped all over the place. Their antics broke the sombre mood, and Molly couldn't help but laugh at them as she gave them their feed.

'Come on,' June instructed Molly, once their father had gone out. 'We'd better go up and make a start on that ruddy attic. Otherwise we'll be having that fusspot Alf Davies round.'

Molly nodded her head, determinedly putting her earlier despair firmly behind her.

'I could do with getting meself some new stockings before tonight, seeing as how Irene's set us all up to go dancing at the Grafton,' June commented. She and Molly clambered into the loft space and stood looking at the dusty boxes, illuminated by the bare bulb. 'Gawd, look at all this stuff! Just how long is it since we last came up here? We'll never get it all sorted out.'

But Molly wasn't listening. Instead, she was on her knees, examining the contents of a box she had found behind the pile of cardboard boxes stacked one on top of the other, labelled 'Christmas Decorations'.

'June, come and look at this,' she begged her

sister. 'This box has got all my exercise books from Neville Road Junior School, right back to me first year, in Miss Brown's class, and here's yours next to it.'

Molly could feel tears prickling her eyes as she saw the careful way their father had written their names on the boxes.

'Well, they can't stay up here. Everything that might catch fire has got to be got rid of – that's what the Government has said – and any glass taped up or removed in case we get hit by a bomb. Mind you, Jerry would have to be daft to be bombing us instead of aiming for the docks,' June added prosaically.

Reluctantly abandoning her school books, Molly started to help her sister go through the other boxes.

An hour later, Molly sat back on her heels and pushed her hair off her hot forehead with a dusty hand.

'We're nearly done,' June told her. 'There's just this box here that some fool has wedged right at the back.' Panting, she tugged it free, and then started to open it. 'Gawd knows what's in it . . . Oh . . .'

As June's voice changed and she suddenly went still, Molly stopped what she was doing and crawled over to her side, demanding, 'June, what is it?' And then her own eyes widened as she saw the crumpled, slightly yellowing lace that June was holding close to her cheek.

'It's Mam's wedding dress,' June said to her in a small choked voice.

The two sisters looked at one another. There were tears in June's eyes and Molly's own gaze was blurred with the same emotion.

'Let's take it downstairs so that we can look at it properly,' she suggested quietly.

As carefully and reverently as if they were carrying the body of their mother herself, between them they took the dress down to the bedroom they shared and then slowly unpacked it.

'Look how tiny her waist was,' Molly whispered, as she smoothed the lace gently with her fingertips. The dress smelled of mothballs and dust, but also of their mother – the scent of lily of the valley, which she always used to wear.

'Mam must have put it away up there when she and Dad moved here.' June's voice was husky, and Molly was startled at how much finding the dress had affected her normally so assured and controlled sister. It was at times like these that she realised June had a soft centre underneath her hard shell.

'It's too small for you to wear but maybe we could use some of the lace to trim your wedding dress,' Molly suggested.

June smiled with shining eyes. 'Oh, Molly, could we? I'd feel like I'd got Mum with me.'

'Does this lipstick look all right with this frock?' June demanded later that evening, as she scrutinised her appearance in the bedroom mirror. Molly, who had been applying pale pink lipstick to her own mouth, stopped what she was doing and put her head on one side to study her sister.

'It looks fine,' she assured her. 'What time are we supposed to meet up with the others?'

'Seven o'clock, outside the dance hall. Have you seen my shoes?'

'They're over there, by your bed,' Molly told her, watching as June slipped her feet into her silver dancing shoes and fastened the strap round her ankle.

The two sisters were wearing dresses cut from the same pattern, bought in Lewis's in the spring and carefully sewn by Molly. But whereas her own dress had a white cotton background printed with flowers in varying shades of pink and red, June had opted for a cotton with blue and yellow flowers, and whilst Molly's dress had a neat sweetheart neckline and puff sleeves, June's was a more daring halter-neck style. Both dresses showed off the sisters' neat waistlines and pretty ankles, though.

It was gone six o'clock before they were finally ready to leave, June complaining that she wasn't going to hurry anywhere because she didn't want her face to go all shiny, despite the powder she'd applied.

'At last,' Irene greeted them impatiently when they reached the dance hall ten minutes late. 'We was just beginning to think you weren't coming.'

'It was our Molly's fault,' June fibbed unrepentantly, as they all hurried inside in a flurry of brightly coloured cottons and excited giggles.

'It feels like I haven't bin dancing in ever such a long time,' June sighed, as they queued up to buy their tickets, even though the factory girls got together to go dancing every month or so.

'Here, look over there at them lads in their uniforms,' Ruby giggled happily, nudging Molly.

'Give over staring at them, will you, Ruby?' Irene chastised her. 'Otherwise they'll be thinking that we're sommat as we're not.'

'What do you mean?' Ruby demanded, oblivious to the looks the others were exchanging.

Several groups of young men, clustered round the dance floor, looked eagerly at the girls as they walked past, but Irene led them firmly to a table where they could sit down and then said sternly, 'Just remember that some of us here have husbands and fiancés, and we don't want to be embarrassed by the behaviour of those of you who haven't.'

'Well, if we're just going ter sit here all night, what have we come for?' May objected, eyeing up one of the young men.

'I didn't say as we wouldn't dance, only that I don't want to see none of you behaving like that lot over there,' Irene told them, nodding in the direction of another group of young women standing by the entrance, boldly eyeing up the men coming in and exchanging banter with them.

91

To her discomfort, Molly realised that two of the girls were Johnny's sisters, and when she told June as discreetly as she could, June looked past her to where they were standing and then warned her quickly, 'Well, don't say anything to the others. We don't want to be shown up. You'd best act as though you haven't seen them.'

The young soldiers the Hardings girls had seen on the way in had come to stand close to them and were quite plainly watching them.

Molly turned away whilst Irene raised an eyebrow as she lit a Woodbine and then told June drily, 'They're just a bunch of kids. My Alan would make mincemeat of them.'

'And my Frank,' June agreed, taking one of the cigarettes Irene was offering her.

Molly looked disapprovingly at her sister but kept quiet. She wanted them to have a good time – they all needed to release some tension after such an emotional day.

'June, Molly, I thought it was you two,' a male voice announced, and Molly's frown changed to a wide smile of delight as she recognised Eddie. 'Auntie Elsie said she thought you were coming down here tonight.'

'Are you on your own?' June asked him after they had introduced him to the others.

'I came down with our Jim, but I've met up with a gang of other lads off the ship. If you girls fancy dancing with us, I can vouch for them.'

'Oh, yeah? As if we'd believe that,' Irene teased

him, but Molly could see that she wasn't averse to the suggestion.

'Well, just you remember before you go introducing us to anyone that we're respectable girls and dancing is *all* we shall be doing,' June told him sternly.

'Auntie Elsie would have me hide if I was to say anything else. She thinks of you and Molly as part of the family,' Eddie assured her, before he disappeared into the crowd of young people now filling the dance hall.

Within five minutes he was back, along with half a dozen other young men, all slightly bashful but very eager to be introduced to the girls.

'How about you and me being the first up on the floor, Molly?' Eddie asked her with a big grin.

Molly laughed back at him. It had been Eddie, years ago, when they had all been children, who had been her partner at the dancing lessons they had had at the church hall in preparation for the annual Christmas party.

'Just so long as you don't tread on my toes,' she agreed.

'Well, I can't pull the ribbons out of your hair any more, can I?' Eddie laughed as he led her onto the floor, adding, 'But I promise I won't let anyone put any worms down your back.'

'Oh, do you remember that too?' Molly asked him eagerly, and then blushed slightly, as she realised that the music had started but she'd been too engrossed in their reminiscences to notice. As though he sensed her self-consciousness, Eddie gave her hand a small squeeze.

'I remember what a game little kid you were, Molly – aye, and a pretty little thing as well.'

As he swung her into his arms, there was a look in his eyes that made Molly's heart skip a beat. And when the band slowed into a new number and the lights dimmed, Molly didn't object when Eddie slipped his arm round her waist and drew her closer.

He smelled of Pears soap, the skin on his hands rough against her own softer flesh, just as the muscles of his thighs felt so much harder than hers as he pulled her into his body.

However, when the dance ended and they returned to their table, June gave them both a baleful look and demanded sharply, 'Why aren't you wearing your engagement ring, Molly?'

Molly's face burned. She had forgotten all about her ring, which she didn't like wearing because of the greenish mark it left on her finger. But June's tone of voice made it sound as though she had deliberately chosen not to wear it.

'It's all right, June,' Eddie said promptly and easily. 'I've already heard from Aunt Elsie that you and Molly are both spoken for now.'

Molly gave him a grateful look for rescuing her from her elder sister's disapproval and her own forgetfulness.

'I didn't mean to forget about my ring,' she told him quickly when he insisted on her getting up for another dance.

'You don't need to tell me that, Molly,' Eddie reassured her. 'I know you well enough to know you're not the kind of girl who'd cheat on a lad. I just wish I'd had the gumption to come courtin' you before Johnny did.'

Molly's face burned even hotter. He was just teasing her, that was all, she told herself. She had always got on well with Eddie, with his ready smile and twinkling blue eyes. He was fun and he made her laugh, and that was why she felt so much happier and more comfortable being held in his arms than she had ever felt being held in Johnny's. Eddie, she knew instinctively, was not the kind to press a girl for something she was not ready to give.

Johnny! She almost missed a step, causing Eddie to look down at her.

'I was just thinking about Johnny,' she told him honestly when he asked her if she was all right. 'It's horrible knowing there's going to be a war, but not knowing when it's going to happen. It feels a bit like waking up in the morning used to feel when it was Mr Roberts's arithmetic lesson that day, only worse. You sort of forget about it for a while but then when you remember . . .' She gave a small shiver.

'Aye, I know what you mean,' Eddie agreed soberly. 'The Government is going to be using the merchant navy to carry supplies and we've all been warned that Jerry submarines are going to be after us, trying to stop us.'

'Oh, Eddie . . .'

'I shouldn't have told you that,' he said gruffly. 'Not a word to me auntie about it, Molly, promise? 'Cos she'll worry herself sick about it, and she's got enough to worry about with Uncle John and our Jim working on the gridiron.'

'I promise,' she assured him solemnly, suddenly feeling very grown up and mature, not a girl any more but a confidante and an equal in this war that would soon be engulfing them all.

The Molly she had been last Christmas could not have imagined that the Molly she was now would be learning to drive, and going to first-aid classes, making notes on what to do if she was called upon to help out in an emergency. Being in the WVS wasn't just a matter of making cups of tea and knitting socks for soldiers, Molly acknowledged proudly. It was proper war work for women, and she was proud to be one of those women.

'When do you go back to your ship?' she asked Eddie.

'Tomorrow,' he told her, and then added determinedly, as he swung her round into another dance, 'So tonight I am going to mek sure I enjoy meself.'

'It's a good band, but I'm gettin' hot so shall we sit this one out?'

They had been dancing together non-stop for nearly an hour, so Molly nodded her head, fanning herself with her hand as Eddie led her back to the table.

All around them, Molly could see young men in uniform, holding their girls as tightly as they could, so determined to enjoy every minute they had together that the sight of them brought a lump to Molly's throat. Some couples were even embracing, something that would never have happened normally in such a public place without the management intervening, but tonight, instead of reacting disapprovingly to such intimacy, onlookers were viewing them with sympathy and understanding.

'Our Jim seems well taken with that Jean, who works with you,' Eddie commented to Molly, looking over at his cousin slow-dancing with Molly's work pal.

'Jean Hughes? She's really nice,' Molly told him.

'Where's she from?' Eddie asked. 'I've not seen her around before.'

'Her family's from down near the docks.' When Eddie started to frown, Molly told him quickly, 'The flower streets, Eddie, and she's a very respectable sort. I like her.'

'A Welshie, is she?' Eddie nodded his head approvingly.

June came up to join them, flushed and out of breath from dancing.

'The last time I came dancing here it was with my Frank.'

'Aye, and you'll be dancing with him at your own weddin' soon,' Eddie replied, trying to keep her spirits high.

'Yes, I will, an' all,' June agreed. 'I can't wait for my first dance as Mrs Frank Brookes.'

It was gone eleven when they finally left the Grafton, Molly laughing, her face flushed with the pleasure of dancing and the warmth of the camaraderie and laughter they had all shared, even if at times she had felt as though the frantic giddiness with which they were throwing themselves into the fun of the evening masked an awareness of what lay ahead that none of them wanted to acknowledge. It was almost as though they felt they had to enjoy themselves whilst they still could, Molly admitted to herself uneasily.

Eddie insisted on walking them home – Jim having mysteriously disappeared, along with Jean.

'Well, I suppose it will be all right walking home with you at this time of night – no one's going to gossip about it if they do see us with you,' June acknowledged, 'seeing as you and Jim are the nearest thing me and Molly have got to brothers.'

'Come on then, sis,' Eddie teased her, offering each girl an arm and then pretending to strut along the street like a comic turn, making Molly giggle and protest.

'Oh, give over, do, Eddie. You'll give me a stitch.'

'Fancy stopping at the chippy?' Eddie asked them, nodding in the direction of Harry Scott's chip shop up ahead of them.

'Go on then,' June agreed.

The three of them waited their turn in the queue whilst Hilda, Harry's wife, removed a new batch of chips from the fryer, testing one between her forefinger and thumb before expertly shaking them free of fat. The chips were the best in Liverpool and people flocked from the opposite side of the city to get their fish supper.

'Three penn'orths of mix, please,' Eddie ordered when it was their turn.

Nodding her head, Hilda placed three portions of chips on separate pages of the *Liverpool Echo*, then took the huge pan of mushy peas off the gas stove, and scooped half a ladleful out onto each pile of chips.

'Salt and vinegar?' she asked.

All three of them nodded.

Quickly wrapping their chips in another sheet of newspaper, she handed them over.

Now intent on eating their chips and peas, they slowed their conversation to match their pace as they headed for Chestnut Close.

The cul-de-sac was in darkness, and their chips long finished by the time they finally reached number 78. Knowing that Eddie was going to be rejoining his ship in the morning, Molly wanted to say something to tell him that she was conscious of the danger he would be facing once war came – that though she may be safe at home at the moment, she knew that things would change for ever for them all once hostilities were declared. But at the same time she was reluctant to spoil the happiness of the evening by reminding them all of what lay ahead.

Whilst she hesitated, not sure what to do, Eddie turned to June and hugged her, kissing her on the cheek. And then, having released June, he turned back to Molly. She had been in his arms for a good part of the evening whilst they danced, so she had no qualms about being held tightly by him now. But when he bent his head to kiss her, it was not with the same brotherly peck on the cheek he had given June, but a lingering kiss on her mouth that took her by surprise.

She looked up at him, her eyes wide with surprise and confusion. In his she could see a mixture of emotions. With the shock of an icy cold finger pressed against her spine, she recognised that what she was seeing in his eyes were the feelings of a man about to face the reality of war and death. With a mix of compassion, tenderness and a wholly female response to his need, she kissed him back, shyly and inexpertly, as though somehow her kissing him was a kind of magic talisman that would protect him.

'I'm off early in the morning,' Eddie told them both gruffly as he released Molly. 'Keep an eye on me auntie for me, won't yer?'

Both girls nodded. Molly hoped it wouldn't be too long before he was back home again, safe – and in her arms.

'I really enjoyed it tonight,' Molly told June

sleepily when they were both in bed. 'Did you?'

'I'd have enjoyed it a sight more if my Frank had been there,' June responded, immediately making Molly guiltily aware of the fact that she had not given Johnny much thought at all, apart from when she had spotted his sisters. As for the kiss she had given Eddie . . . Her face burned afresh, not just because she had given it, but also because she had enjoyed giving it.

SIX

Proudly Molly smoothed down the grey-green tweed skirt of her WVS uniform suit. Under the jacket she was wearing the red jumper that was part of her uniform, like the felt hat that she had pulled firmly over her curls. For winter there was a dark green coat to wear over the suit.

When Mrs Wesley had handed Molly the voucher to enable her to buy the uniform, she had praised her for passing her first-aid test, and had told her warmly to wear her uniform with pride. Although the suit was more functional than glamorous, Molly had managed discreetly to alter the fit of the skirt so that it looked more shapely. She had collected it earlier in the week and she was very conscious of wearing it, and also that she was about to play her part in a very important event. Today was the day when the children of the cul-de-sac and the surrounding area were to be evacuated from Liverpool to the safety of the Welsh countryside.

As she walked past the allotments she stopped to speak to Bert Johnson, who, despite the fact that he was coming up for eighty, still worked on his allotment. Rover, his mongrel dog, was lying faithfully at his side, and Molly stooped to pat the dog's head.

'Tell yer dad that he wants to get a rooster for them chickens of his,' he told Molly.

Her father often went round to check up on Bert, who lived several doors down from them on the opposite side of the road. Although he was older than their father, he too had served in the Great War and the two men got on well together. He had survived the war without any injury, but Bert had lost both his wife and his two young children in the influenza outbreak that had followed, and now lived alone apart from his loyal dog.

Promising him that she would pass on his message, Molly hurried down the road. She and the other WVS involved had been told to be at their designated schools well before the children to be evacuated were due to arrive. Molly's job was to tick off their names on a list she was going to be given and then later to help escort the children to Lime Street station to board the trains that would take them to their designated evacuation areas.

To her relief, the first person she saw when she reached the school was Anne, who beamed at her.

'I've been looking out for you. We're going to be working together. What luck!'

Two hours later, armed with her list, Molly was

busily asking children's names as they arrived at the school, whilst at the same time trying to reassure desperately worried mothers that they were doing the right thing. Already the school seemed to be full of children carrying suitcases tied with string, the older children with pillowcases containing the rest of their belongings slung over their shoulders. Many were also holding on to younger siblings, the gas masks they had been issued with hanging round their necks.

The boys, as boys will, were scuffling lightheartedly with one another, whilst the girls looked on disapprovingly. Molly knew that behind the teasing and jostling lurked real fear at what lay ahead.

'If you can, then do try to persuade the mothers to say their goodbyes to the kiddies here instead of going with them to Lime Street,' Molly's superior had told her, but it wasn't as easy as that. Molly found it heartbreaking to see the brown labels tied onto the children's clothes and belongings, their names often written in shaky handwriting, bearing silent witness to the mothers' anguish at the thought of the coming parting. The children were clinging resolutely to their gas masks, as they had been told to do.

'You'll look after them, won't you?' more than one mother had begged Molly with tears in her eyes, although there were some desperately sad little ones lined up, who seemed to have no one to care for them at all. Although she knew that she was not supposed to do so, Molly discreetly gave just that little bit more attention to these children, some of whom were very shabbily dressed and didn't seem to have with them the new clothes and personal items the Government had instructed that each child was to have.

'A toothbrush each, if you please, and how am I supposed to give my three that, when they all share the same one at 'ome?' Molly heard one mother demanding indignantly of one of the other WVS girls.

By and large, though, the children she was dealing with were well fed and properly clothed. It tore at Molly's sensitive heart, though, to see their wan little faces and anxious expressions when they thought that none of the grown-ups was watching them. How would she have felt if this had been her and June? She would have been crying and looking every bit as upset as the little girl she had just tried to comfort. But it was all being done for the children's own good – to keep them safe if the cities were bombed.

Molly tried to remind herself that she was here to do a job and that she must not let herself give in to her emotions. It wasn't easy, though, especially when one poor mother handed over her little girl wearing a heavy metal calliper on a badly twisted leg, and begged Molly, 'She has to have her leg rubbed every night with warm olive oil. I've written it down on her label, look. You'll mek sure that whoever she goes to knows that, won't you, miss?'

'I'll do my best,' Molly promised her gently.

Every child had been given a block of Cadbury's Dairy Milk and a bottle of Edmondson's lemonade for the journey, but some of the children hadn't been able to wait and had already consumed the whole lot.

She had lost count already of the number of times a small hand had tugged urgently on her skirt and a small voice had piped up shrilly, 'Please, miss, I want the lav,' or, 'Please, miss, me bruvver's peed his pants,' or, 'Please, miss, our kid's bin sick.' It made Molly think again of her mother – all the tiny, thankless tasks she'd done for her and June, and how they had fallen to her father after her death.

She had been thinking of her mother such a lot since they had found her wedding dress. How would she have felt if she were alive? She would have been worrying about the war like they all were. Would she have been proud of Molly for joining the WVS; might she have even joined with her and persuaded June to do the same? Molly sensed that their mother's presence in their lives would have had a softening effect on June's sometimes determined nature. She would certainly have shared in June's pride that Frank was doing his duty. Their mother would have liked Frank – Molly knew that instinctively. But what would she have thought of Johnny? Would she have understood how confused Molly felt, or would she have taken June's side and told Molly that she was being silly? Molly liked to think that she would have understood.

The day seemed to be passing in an unending toing and froing, but eventually the supervisors came round to collect the lists and to announce that they would shortly be leaving for Lime Street.

'There seem to be a lot of gaps on my list,' Molly apologised.

'I'm afraid that rather a lot of the mothers have changed their minds at the last minute,' the supervisor told her, as the children were marshalled into a crocodile, ready, along with their teachers and helpers like Molly, to walk to Lime Street station to wait there for the train that would take them to North Wales.

Molly was just about to leave the school when she caught sight of Sally Walker. She looked pale and unwell, one hand pressed into her lower back as though to ease away an ache.

Hurrying over to her, she exclaimed, 'Sally, aren't you coming?'

Women who were pregnant, or who had babies and very young children, had been offered the opportunity to be evacuated. The more well-to-do could afford to rent houses for themselves, but for most people evacuation meant having to live under someone else's roof, and very few women were keen to do that, especially when it meant moving away from their own homes and their families.

Sally shook her head. 'No. I want to stay here just in case my Ronnie gets leave unexpected, like.

107

Besides, I don't fancy having to live alongside strangers, and having to ask every time I wanted to mek meself a brew and all that. I like 'aving me own home and me own things around me.' Her eyes were swollen and she had obviously been crying. 'I came down with me neighbour. She's sending her kiddies off. Bloody awful it is, an' all, poor little mites.'

'It's the best thing for them, Sally,' Molly tried to comfort her.

'What would you know?' Sally demanded sharply. 'You haven't got any kiddies.' She winced as she spoke and Molly asked her worriedly if she was all right.

'Stop goin' on, will yer, Molly, and leave us alone,' Sally snapped.

The walk down to Lime Street seemed to take for ever, and some of the younger children had already started to flag. In an attempt to cheer them up and spur them on, their teacher started to sing loudly 'Sing As We Go', urging the children to join in. One little girl, too exhausted to walk any further, suddenly dropped down on her bottom, sobbing. Molly bent down and picked her up. She was wet through and crying, and Molly comforted her as best she could, wondering how she would be feeling if she did have children.

Had it really only been a week ago that she had been dancing and laughing at Grafton Dance Hall? Now, watching Liverpool's children wrenched away from their homes and their mothers, she couldn't believe she would ever laugh again.

'Miss, will they have pictures where we're going?' one little boy asked her. 'Only I ain't going if'n I can't see Flash Gordon of a Saturday no more.'

'I'm sure there will be a cinema,' Molly reassured him, treating his concern seriously. 'And there'll be lots of places for you to play as well, nice green fields, and fresh air.'

'Fields?' one sharp-faced boy asked her warily. 'What's them, then?'

These were city children – some of them slum children, Molly reminded herself as she struggled to find the right words to calm their fears.

'Fields are where farmers grow things for us to eat,' she told them. 'I dare say that those of you who get billeted with farmers will be able to collect your own eggs from the farmer's wife's hens. My auntie has a farm and she used to let me do that when I was your age.'

'Will there be ponies for us to ride?' one little girl asked eagerly.

'Maybe . . .' Molly answered her cautiously, adding firmly, 'I expect you'll all make lots of new friends at your new schools.'

Although some of the children accepted her words happily, she could see that others were not so easily convinced or appeased, and she could hardly blame them.

Once they reached Lime Street station, the

combined noise of so many people packed into one place was such that Molly was tempted to put her hands over her ears. She had never seen so many children. They were everywhere – crying, sobbing, shouting, throwing tantrums, or else completely silent, as if they had been struck dumb by the trauma they were enduring, whilst mothers wept, and harassed officials did their best to make some sort of order out of the chaos. The trains that were to take the children away stood silently beside the platforms, their doors firmly closed. No one would be allowed to board until they were queuing up in the right order, their names ticked off the appropriate list. So much careful planning had gone into this operation to protect the country's young, but right now all Molly could think of was its emotional cost to the families involved.

A small boy tugged on her sleeve, and demanded, 'Did all these kids get a bar o' chocolate, miss?'

'I expect so,' she murmured. She knew that from now on the smell of Dairy Milk was always going to remind her of this heart-rending scene.

Behind the barriers, mothers were standing ten deep, calling out their children's names, and as Molly watched, one young woman reached over and grabbed her child, refusing to give her back.

'This is so awful,' Molly whispered to Anne, who had just materialised at her side.

'It's for their own good, Molly. We must remember that, and think of how much safer they are going to be instead of thinking of this.'

Mutely, Molly nodded. She was still holding the little girl she had picked up in the street. The child had stopped crying now and, instead, had fallen asleep. She couldn't be more than five, Molly guessed.

'She's wet herself,' she told Anne unhappily. 'I was wondering if I could take her somewhere to change her. I hate to think of her sitting on the train and being uncomfortable.'

Anne sighed. 'There's some done worse than that to themselves,' she told Molly forthrightly. 'I know the Government meant well, giving them that chocolate, but I can't help thinking it might not have been a good idea.'

Molly grimaced as the loudspeakers suddenly boomed out teachers' names and classes.

'Here we go,' Anne told her as the children surged forward towards the waiting LNWR train.

'I just keep thinking about those children and their poor mothers,' Molly said back home, pushing her dinner around her plate without eating it.

She had told June all about her day when she had got home. June, despite her cynicism at Molly volunteering, had actually been interested and touched by the children's plight.

'Like I'm allus saying, you're a right softie, our Molly.'

'Sally Walker was there at the school. She's refused to be evacuated in case her Ronnie comes home on leave,' Molly told her.

'I wish my Frank blinkin' well would. Every letter I get says the same thing – he doesn't know yet!'

'Now that I've tacked your wedding dress, I need you to try it on before I start machining it,' Molly reminded her. 'We don't want Frank coming home and it not being ready,' she added, trying to cheer June up a little bit, as well as shake off the feelings of misery the evacuation of the children had left her with.

'If he *does* come home,' June stressed sombrely.

'Oh, June, you mustn't say that,' Molly protested. 'Of course he will. You know what Ronnie Walker said. He said that the trainees were bound to be given leave before they go on active duty.'

'I know what he said all right, but Ronnie Walker isn't the blinkin' Prime Minister, is he?'

Molly could see how upset and unhappy her sister looked and wished she could offer her some proper reassurance.

'Let's have the wireless on, eh, Dad?' June suggested to her father, who had just come into the room. 'A bit of Tommy Trinder will give us a laugh.'

Molly looked in the mirror and straightened her hat, pressing her lips together to set the lipstick she had just carefully applied. She was wearing her navy-blue 'going to church' suit, bought from Lewis's sale in the spring. Her hat was last year's but she had retrimmed it to match her suit, and her polka-dot blouse she had made herself.

June was also wearing a navy-blue suit in a similar style – they had bought them together, agreeing that they were a sensible buy – but her blouse had a floral pattern and a different collar, and she had bought herself a new hat.

On Sundays they used the front door, and their father beamed proudly as he walked up the cul-de-sac with a daughter on either arm.

'How's them chicks of yours?' one of their neighbours, Gordon Sinclair, called out to him, crossing the road with his wife to walk along with them, shaking his head and telling Albert, 'It would have saved youse a lorra messin' if'n you'd got point-of-lay pullets.'

'Chicks is best,' the girls' father insisted, the two men arguing good-naturedly as the small group made its way to the church.

'By, but it's quiet without the kiddies,' Gordon's wife, Nellie, commented, adding, 'You was at the school helping, wasn't you, Molly? I heard as how Sally Walker didn't go. Mind you, I don't blame her, what with her due any week now. Oh Gawd,' Nellie continued without pausing to take a breath, 'there's Alf Davies. Up and down the cul-de-sac all the time, he is, sticking his nose into other people's business.'

The Sinclairs were Scottish Liverpudlians and had family connections down in the tenements by the docks. It was no secret that Gordon was the person to ask if you wanted to get hold of something, no questions asked. Some inhabitants of the cul-de-sac looked down on the Sinclairs and considered them to be rough, but for all her outspokenness Molly knew that Nellie Sinclair had a kind heart, and she knew too that, despite conceiving several children, Nellie had miscarried them all and lamented the fact that they had no family. Every child in the street knew that if you went round to number 39, like as not Nellie's face would crease into a smile and she would reach into the special jar she kept in her kitchen and give you a bit of Spanish or a humbug.

'Oh dear, I thought we was going to be late,' Elsie puffed as she and John caught up with them.

'Your Eddie gorn back to his ship then, 'as he, Elsie?' Nellie asked, whilst Molly and June shared eloquent glances. Not for nothing was Nellie known as the cul-de-sac's most enthusiastic gossip.

'Last week,' Elsie confirmed, 'and our Jim won't be coming to church this mornin' either. He's doing a Sunday shift on the gridiron.'

'I was just sayin' to my Gordon last night that I don't envy them who's got fellas working on the railways when this war does come. Bound to try to bomb the railways, that Hitler is,' Nellie announced tactlessly.

'Why don't we try and catch up with Frank's mam?' Molly suggested hurriedly to June. 'Then you could ask her how she's going on.'

'What's to stop her asking how I'm going on?'

June challenged Molly, before adding miserably, 'Oh, our Molly, I'm missing him that much. I never thought it'd be like this.'

Molly squeezed her hand sympathetically.

They had reached the church now and instead of going straight inside as usual, people were gathering outside to talk in angry and anxious voices.

'It seems so quiet without the children,' Molly murmured, echoing Nellie's earlier sentiments. She loved hearing the little ones sing every Sunday.

Almost as soon as she had finished speaking she saw Pearl Lawson hurrying towards the church, defiantly holding the hands of her two children, the expression on her face both mutinous and challenging as she came over to Molly, whilst her husband, George, hung back slightly.

'I heard as you was down at the school yesterday 'elping with the evacuation,' she announced to Molly. 'Sally Walker told me. No way was I letting my two go, not once I'd heard as how they would be mixing with that lot from down the docks,' she sniffed disparagingly. 'My kiddies have been brought up to mind their manners. They know how to behave proper, like. 'Ere, Georgie, get that finger out of yer nose,' she commanded the younger of her two sons crossly, before turning back to Molly and continuing, 'It's not right, sending decent respectable kiddies off wi' the likes of them – Gawd knows what they might pick up. You should be ashamed of yourself, helping to send them away. Mine is staying right here wi' me.

'Ere, Sally, are you all right?' she demanded as Sally Walker walked slowly towards them, one hand pressed into the small of her back.

'Just a bit of backache, that's all.'

'How long now before you're due?' Pearl asked her sympathetically, deliberately keeping her back turned towards Molly to emphasise her disapproval of Molly's role in the evacuation.

'Another two weeks.'

She looked pale and tired, and Molly's heart went out to her. It must be so hard for her with her husband so far away, and no family of her own to speak of.

The vicar gave a longer than normal sermon, and when his sonorous voice began to read 'Suffer the little children to come unto me', audible sobs could be heard from the mothers amongst the congregation.

'Fancy choosing to read that out,' Nellie Sinclair complained to Molly once they were all outside again, adding forthrightly, 'Daft bugger. He should have known it would set all the mams off crying. Did I tell you I saw old Bert this morning? Getting himself in a real state, he is, on account of Alf Davies telling him that he'll have to have that dog of his put down, dogs not being allowed in air-raid shelters in case they goes wild and bites folks. Thinks the world of it, he does, and who can blame him, since it's all he's got? Here . . .' She broke off in mid-breath to frown at the sound of a bicycle

116

bell being rung loudly and continuously as a young lad pedalled frantically towards the church, skidding to a halt.

'It's war,' he yelled breathlessly. 'It's just bin on the news.'

Immediately Alf grabbed hold of him to question him, whilst the rest of the congregation turned to one another in uncertainty and fear.

Several of the women were crying, including Elsie, Molly saw, whilst the men looked anxious and uncertain what to do. Out of the corner of her eye Molly noticed that Frank's mother was standing on her own, her face white and set. This was a time for families to be together and automatically Molly started to go over to her.

She had just reached her side, when Sally Walker suddenly collapsed.

'Oh my Gawd, it's the shock, it's gorn and killed her,' someone said dramatically, whilst one of the other women snorted derisively and said, 'Don't talk so daft.'

'Let me have a look at her,' Frank's mother said sharply, and Molly discovered that she was somehow holding Frank's mother's handbag and gloves, as the older woman crouched down beside Sally, who was now groaning and moaning and clutching her belly.

The men had stepped back, allowing the women to take over, and were standing together looking slightly embarrassed.

'Looks like she's gorn into labour,' Pearl

announced knowledgeably. 'We'd better get 'er to the hospital.'

'Her labour's too far advanced for that,' Frank's mother responded, standing up. 'We'll have to get the men to carry her to my house.'

'Well, she did say as how she'd bin having pains,' Pearl added, 'but the little 'un isn't due for another two weeks.'

Molly saw Frank's mother's mouth compress. She certainly looked every inch the fearsome hospital ward sister she was known to have been as she instructed some of the men to carry Sally to her house.

'I'll need some help . . .' Doris Brookes announced.

'You've been havin' some first-aid lessons, haven't you, Molly?' Elsie offered.

Apprehensively Molly started to shake her head. It was true that all the new WVS were being taught first-aiding skills and that she now had her basic first-aiding certificate. She could clean and dress minor wounds, splint broken limbs, and she knew what to do in the case of gas poisoning or minor burns, along with shock and lack of consciousness, but childbirth was not something that had been included in the course.

But before she could say so, Frank's mother was commanding her sharply, 'Very well, you'd better come with me then.'

Molly looked imploringly at June but her sister shook her head, her mouth set. Even for Sally,

118

June wasn't prepared to come to Molly's assistance and willingly spend time with her future mother-in-law.

Reluctantly Molly followed the small procession being marshalled by Frank's mother, who was walking alongside Sally whilst the men carried her.

'You'd best take her up to my Frank's room but don't put her on the bed until I've covered it with a rubber sheet,' she warned them. 'And you – Molly, isn't it? – you'd better come up as well.'

Obediently Molly followed the men upstairs, into a spick-and-span room with a good-sized bed and gleaming furniture.

'All right, you can put her down now,' Doris instructed the men, quickly stripping off the jacket of her suit and then rolling up the sleeves of her blouse.

Sally was lying on the bed with her eyes closed, moaning and whimpering. The men were just straightening up when the sound of an air-raid siren filled the room.

For a few seconds all of them were too shocked to move, and then one of the men said urgently, ''Ere, isn't that that air-raid siren Alf's been blethering on about? The one he said as meant we had ter get into them ruddy Anderson shelters?'

The men looked at one another and then at Doris.

'Best get her downstairs again,' one of them said uneasily.

Sally suddenly screamed loudly.

119

'You lot best go,' Doris told the men calmly, her attention focused on Sally as she bent over her.

The siren was still wailing and Molly longed to clap her hands over her ears to blot out the terrifying sound. The men looked at her but she shook her head.

In the silence that followed the men's departure, Molly could hear the sound of them running down the street. Terror and panic engulfed her. What if one of the bombs landed right here on Frank's mother's house? Cold sweat ran in beads down her face whilst she shivered in fear.

'Still here, are you?' Doris demanded as she turned round and saw Molly cowering. 'Hmm, different kettle of fish it would be if that sister of yours was here.' She sniffed disparagingly.

'You've got no call to say that about June,' Molly defended her sister.

'Mmm, well, since you are here you might as well make yourself useful,' Doris told Molly grimly. 'Not that you're likely to be much use. Wait here a minute.'

She was gone only a few seconds, returning with a white starched overall. 'Go downstairs, and give your hands a good scrubbing with carbolic soap right up to your armpits, then put this on and come back.'

Molly marvelled that Frank's mother could remain so calm in the face of the danger they might be in, and then winced as Sally suddenly screamed loudly again.

'Hurry up,' Doris chivvied her. 'I need to examine her and I can't do that until I've scrubbed up meself.'

Molly did as she had been told as quickly as she could, leaving her jacket and blouse downstairs and hurrying back to the bedroom dressed in the voluminous overall she had been given.

'Scrubbed yourself properly, have you, like I told you?' Frank's mother demanded.

Molly nodded her head. Her hands were red and stinging slightly from the carbolic.

'Good, 'cos we don't want no dirty germs getting everywhere. You stay here whilst I go and get scrubbed up.'

Sally, who Doris had by now undressed, was moaning and panting, pushing the sheet down off the white dome of her belly.

When Doris came back she was wearing an overall like the one she had given Molly, her hair forced back off her face by the starched cap she was wearing, her arms glowing pinkly from their scrubbing.

Sally's screams were getting louder, interspersed with sobs and pleas to God to spare her any more pain, but unlike Molly, Doris was unmoved by Sally's travail. All the while the siren continued and Molly could hear people running and shouting in the street below.

'She'll forget all about this once her baby's been born,' Doris told Molly confidently as she lifted the sheet and proceeded to examine her patient.

'By the looks of you, you've been in labour a good while,' she announced disapprovingly to Sally when she had finished.

'I was havin' a lot of twinges all day yesterday,' Sally panted. 'And then me waters broke just before I left for church.'

'Well, you are very foolish for not saying so,' Doris rebuked her sharply.

'Oh. Oh . . . oh Gawd, it hurts,' Sally yelled, grabbing hold of Molly's hand and holding on so tightly that it felt as though her nails were cutting into her flesh.

Somewhere outside Molly heard a sound she guessed must be the all clear, but between them, Sally and Doris were keeping her too busy to pay any attention to it – Sally with her groans and protests, and Doris with her sharp instructions.

'Eee. But I'm never gonna let that bugger near me again,' Sally moaned, gasping for breath. 'It's fair killing me, this is.'

'Push,' Doris commanded her, ignoring her complaints.

And then, so quickly that Molly could hardly believe it had happened, Sally's baby slithered into the world and gave his first mewling cry.

As soon as she had cut the birth cord, Doris handed the baby to Molly and told her crisply, 'Wash him and then give him to Sally,' before turning back to Sally and cleaning her up.

The baby was so tiny and yet so vigorous, so full of life. Tears blurred Molly's sight as she washed him carefully in the warm water Doris had told her to bring up earlier. He was bawling, his eyes screwed up and his little legs drawn up towards his distended belly, but then as she washed him he stopped crying and seemed to be trying to focus on her.

A feeling like none she had ever experienced before gripped her. Her emotions were so intense that she wanted to both laugh and cry at the same time.

'Give him to me, Molly,' Sally demanded huskily.

Molly looked at Doris, who nodded her head. Very gently she carried the baby over to his mother.

An expression of intense joy flooded Sally's face as she took hold of him and instinctively put him to her breast.

'You're lucky you're the kind that can give birth as easy as shelling peas,' Doris told Sally unemotionally, 'otherwise you might not be smiling right now.'

'I was frightened I'd be sent away, and I wanted to be here in case my Ronnie gets some leave,' Sally protested.

Someone was knocking on the door. Nodding to Molly, Doris told her, 'Take these things down to the back kitchen for me, will you, whilst I go and answer the door.'

The caller turned out to be Doris's neighbour, come to see how Sally was and to explain that they'd heard that the air-raid siren had simply been a test.

'Over an hour we was in that Anderson shelter,' she complained after she had admired the baby, and accepted the offer of a cup of tea.

After that the visitors came thick and fast, and Molly was kept busy making tea and washing up until, at five o'clock, Frank's mother told her that she could go.

'You're not a nurse but at least you've got a bit of gumption about you, not like that sister of yours,' she told Molly grudgingly. 'What my lad sees in her I'll never know.'

'Frank loves our June and she loves him,' Molly defended her sister heatedly. 'She's missing him so much,' she added.

Was that a small softening she could see in Doris Brookes's eyes? Molly hoped so.

'When will Sally be able to go home, only I thought when she does I could go round and give her a bit of a hand?' she asked quietly, changing the subject.

'She'll be back in her own bed tomorrow night,' Doris answered her.

Why should she be feeling so tired, Molly wondered wearily as she walked home. It was Sally who had had the baby, not her.

'You're back, are you?' June greeted her as she walked into the kitchen. 'What took you so long? Elsie was round here hours back, saying as how Sally had had a little boy.'

'People kept coming round to see them and I was making them cups of tea,' Molly told her tiredly.

'I don't know why you wanted to go putting yourself forward like that anyway, offering to help. What do you know about nursing? You've changed since you got involved with that WVS lot,' she accused Molly sharply. 'Become a bloody do-gooder and helping others rather than your own.'

Molly suddenly realised that June felt threatened by her voluntary work, scared she wouldn't be there for her, especially now she was so lonely with Frank being away. It made her heart go out to her sister.

'I didn't offer; it was someone else who said—'

'Mebbe not, but you didn't refuse, did you? A lot of use you must have bin.'

'I didn't do anything really, only fetch and carry. Oh, June, the baby is so gorgeous.' Molly burst into tears. 'I wish you could have seen him.'

'Aye, well, I shall have to wait until Sally goes back to her own place. I'm not going knocking on Frank's mam's door and begging to be let in.'

'Why don't you, June?' Molly suggested impulsively, adding before June could say anything, 'She must be feeling lonely without Frank, and worried about him too, just like you are. I know she always seems a bit standoffish, but I'm sure if you let her see how much Frank means to you and sort of, well, talked to her a bit about the wedding and things, make her feel involved—'

'What?' June put her hands on her hips and glowered. 'Me go round there making up to her?

125

Don't make me laugh. I'm not going round there to be shown up and told how she wants Frank to marry someone else.'

Molly sighed. She wanted to urge her sister to adopt a less antagonistic attitude towards Frank's mother, but she could see she was in no mood for such talk.

'I don't notice you going round to Johnny's mam's, making up to her,' June accused.

'That's different,' Molly protested. 'Me and Johnny have only just got engaged, and his mam's not living on her own.'

'It seems to me that you aren't that bothered about poor Johnny. You hardly ever talk about him,' June sniffed disparagingly.

'I write to him every day,' Molly defended herself. It was true, after all, even if Johnny's letters back to her didn't arrive with the fatness and frequency of Frank's to June. She wondered, though, if her regular letter-writing was more down to guilt than anything else. She certainly didn't look forward to receiving Johnny's letters, not like June did her Frank's.

And not like she would have done if it had been Eddie who was writing to her.

'And you don't wear Johnny's ring,' June pointed out critically.

'It made my finger go green and you said that that was because it wasn't proper gold,' Molly reminded her, trying to subdue her guilty feelings over how much time she now spent thinking about

Eddie. Eddie's warm but gentle kiss had not left her feeling worried and wary like Johnny's fiercer kiss had done. Eddie was familiar and his return to her life welcome, whereas she felt she hardly knew Johnny at all.

'Well, that's as maybe, but from the way you were kissing Eddie Saturday night, no one would ever have guessed you were engaged to someone else.'

Molly could feel her face starting to burn, betraying her guilt.

'It was you who wanted me and Johnny to be engaged, not me. I don't want to be engaged to him – I never have,' she burst out, angry tears filling her eyes. Her heart was thudding and she felt sick, but relieved as well, now that she had finally said how she felt.

She could see how much her outburst had shocked her sister, who was simply standing staring at her.

'Well, you can't break your engagement to him now, Molly,' June said finally. 'Not with 'im definitely about to go to war. A shocking thing that would be!' she pronounced fiercely. 'It would bring shame down on all of us, me and our dad included.'

Molly tried to blink away her tears. A hard lump of misery lay like a heavy weight inside her chest. She knew that what June had said was right, but she still wished desperately that she was not engaged to Johnny.

Because of Eddie?

Something about his gentleness reminded her of Frank. Eddie made her laugh and she felt safe with him. He didn't possess Johnny's brash self-confidence, and he didn't share Johnny's desire to take things further than she wanted to go. From listening to the conversation of the other machinists, Molly was well aware that not all girls felt as she did. Some of them, like May, actually not only welcomed the advances of men like Johnny, but also actively encouraged them. But May was nearly twenty-two and Molly was only seventeen.

She wasn't too young, though, to know that the kiss Eddie had given her had been more than that of a childhood friend, and she wasn't too young either to know that she had liked being kissed by him. They had been children together, she and June playing hopscotch in the street, whilst Eddie and the other boys played football, all of them sitting down together on Elsie's back steps to eat meat paste sandwiches and drink their milk. It had always been Eddie who had taken Molly's side and defended her from the others, and Eddie, too, who had comforted her when she had accidentally allowed Jim's best marble to roll down the street grid. Luckily he and Jim had been able to rescue it. Eddie who had carried her safely piggyback, in the mock fights the close's children had staged, telling her to 'hang on' whilst she had screamed and giggled with nervous excitement. In the winter, when it was too cold to play outside, they had

128

done jigsaws together on Elsie's parlour table, and then later, when they were more grown up, had scared themselves silly with ghost stories. But then Jim and Eddie had left school and moved into the grown-up world of work, Jim joining his father at the gridiron and Eddie getting work on a fishing boat out of Morecambe Bay so that his visits became infrequent and then fell off altogether.

Molly couldn't say honestly that she had missed him. She had been busy growing up herself, anxious to follow in June's footsteps, and leave school and get a job. But now that he'd been back she discovered how much she enjoyed his company, and how their relationship was all the sweeter for the years they had been apart and the growing up they had both done.

But now June's accusation forced Molly to confront a truth she hadn't wanted to recognise. It had been bad enough being engaged to Johnny before, but now when the first person she thought of when she woke up in the morning was Eddie, just as he was the last person she thought of when she went to bed at night; when every time she did think about him her heart lifted and bounced so hard against her chest wall that it made her feel dizzy, her engagement to Johnny was an unbearable burden.

'Where's our dad?' Molly asked June. She felt unable to look at her sister, but somehow she had managed to stem her tears.

'Gone down the allotment to have one of them

committee meetings. Uncle Joe came round for him half an hour back.' June's voice was terse. 'Seemingly Uncle Joe has been asked to take charge, and make sure that them as has allotments looks after them proper, like. I heard him telling Dad that he wants to set up some sort of plan so that they can grow enough stuff for everyone in the close. Mind you, it will take a bit more than him telling a few jokes to get some of that lot from the allotments to listen to him. Even Dad admits that some of them are that cussed they won't listen to anyone.'

'It's different now. We're all in this war together,' Molly reminded her stoutly.

'Oh, I see, and that's why you've been making eyes at Eddie, is it, and letting him think you was some fast, flirty type like May?'

'I haven't . . .' There was panic as well as misery in Molly's denial. Was that what Eddie thought of her? That she was a flirt? Or even worse, *fast*?

'Yoo-hoo, it's only me – can I come in?'

Instantly both girls tensed and looked at one another, June giving Molly a small warning look, as she called out, 'Yes, of course you can, Elsie,' and pushed the half-open door fully open to smile at their neighbour.

'I've brought yer some of me pressed tongue for your teas. I know your dad likes it. And I've brought some of that strawberry jam we made the other week as well. We might as well enjoy it before we gets bombed to bits. I were that worried when that siren went off, what with our Jim down at the gridiron.'

'Would you like a brew, Elsie?' Molly asked her, desperate to avoid any more gloomy talk, for a few minutes at least. Besides, she acknowledged guiltily, Elsie might have some news about Eddie.

'Yes, ta, love,' she confirmed, sitting down with a relieved sigh.

'So tell us all about the baby then, Molly. Came quick, didn't he?'

'Sally told Frank's mother that she'd been having pains all day yesterday but hadn't wanted to say anything,' Molly answered her obligingly.

'Aye, well, I reckon the shock of hearing that we're at war can't have done her any good in her condition. We're gonna see some hard times from now on, you just see if we don't. When I think about my lads . . .'

The evening air was warm but Molly still shivered, tears blurring her eyes, as she had a sudden mental image of Eddie.

What was happening to her? She had known Eddie all her life. He had fixed her doll for her when Jim had pulled off one of its arms. He had always been there, as an accepted part of her life – how could she suddenly be feeling all breathless and giddy just because she was thinking about him?

'I went right cold all over when I 'eard.'

'I were that shocked, I could hardly breathe, and then when that air-raid warning went off . . .'

The girls might be trying to outdo one another as they described their feelings on hearing the previous day's announcement but none of them was exaggerating the strength of the emotions they had felt. All of them had waited anxiously for every wireless news bulletin, and most of the girls had stopped to buy a paper on their way in to work.

'Our boys'll be needin' these uniforms now,' Irene announced sturdily, 'so we'd best not waste any time gettin' them made.'

'Me cousin Lizzie wot works at the hospital were tellin' us last night as how she's seen empty cardboard coffins stacked up fifty deep and that they've bin told that Hitler will be blitzing Liverpool, on account of the docks,' Ruby informed them ghoulishly, her voice trembling.

Molly's hands were shaking as she put her gas mask over the back of her chair. The morning paper was full of the dangers Liverpool's merchant fleet would be facing from Germany's U-boats, along with reminders about blackout regulations, and the importance of attending regular air-raid warning drills.

'I thought we'd really had it when that bloomin' siren went off yesterday,' Jean admitted. 'Scared me to death, it did. Ran as fast as we could for the nearest shelter. I didn't sleep a wink last night for fear of us being bombed.'

There were heartfelt murmurs of agreement from the other girls, several of whom were yawning tiredly.

'Watch out, here comes our own bloody little Hitler,' Irene warned them all just before the door opened and Miss Jenner came in.

'What's up wi you, Hannah?' Ruby asked after the dinner bell had rung and the girls were crowded together in their blacked-out canteen, eating their dinner.

Molly looked over to where Hannah Carter was sitting staring into space, her fingers plucking fretfully at her clothes.

'It's all them bodies,' Hannah told her in a high-pitched voice. 'They keeps saying as how we're to blame for making them those uniforms.'

Some of the younger girls nudged each other and started to giggle, whilst Irene frowned and said firmly, 'Don't talk so daft, Hannah. There's no bodies here.'

'Yes, there are. They're everywhere, wi' their arms and legs cut off, just like my hubby . . . Sent him back wi'out his legs, they did . . .' She had started to rock herself to and fro, as though trying to comfort herself. 'There's no sense in mekkin' uniforms for dead men, and that's what they'll all be soon enough; all of them dead. You just wait and see. Them uniforms as we're making for them will be the death of them, just like last time. Sent me his uniform back they did . . . but he weren't in it . . .'

One of the new girls started to sob noisily, protesting, 'Me bruvver's in the territorials and bin called up . . .'

'Gorn orf 'er head, she has, and no mistake,' Irene pronounced grimly, as the bell summoned them back to work. 'Tek no notice of her,' she consoled the distraught girl.

Hannah's machine was directly in front of Molly's, and for the rest of the afternoon Molly could hear Hannah talking agitatedly to herself whilst she worked. And then suddenly she got up from her machine and went to where all the finished uniforms were folded, waiting to be inspected.

It was Molly who saw the scissors she was carrying first. Getting up from her own machine, she called out anxiously, 'Hannah, no . . .'

But it was too late: Hannah was cutting frenziedly into the uniforms, slicing and tearing at them.

As quickly as she could, Molly hurried over to her and gently took the scissors from her whilst Hannah screamed and cried out before collapsing on the floor, shuddering violently.

'What's going on in here?'

Still in shock, the other girls turned away from Hannah to look at Miss Jenner.

The supervisor stared at Molly in furious disbelief, and then strode towards her, grabbing hold of her arm with one hand and wrenching the scissors from her with the other.

'What have you done?' she demanded savagely. 'Answer me.' She threw down the scissors and slapped Molly so hard across her face that her

134

head jerked back and she bit her own tongue.

'Here, don't you go hitting my sister,' June protested fiercely, but she was too shocked to say anything more.

'You're sacked, both of you,' the supervisor told them. 'You're nothing but troublemakers, the pair of you . . . and the cost of these uniforms will be deducted from your wages. I'm going to go and get Mr Harding now and show him what you've done. You'll have the police to answer to for destroying government property,' she told them threateningly.

'We haven't done anything,' June told her angrily. 'It was Hannah who did it. Gone mad, she has, as you would see for yourself if you had any sense,' she added contemptuously, pointing to where Hannah was sitting rocking whilst she stared blankly at the scene in front of her. But instead of making Miss Jenner rethink her accusation, June's words only incensed her.

'Silence! Wait here, both of you, whilst I go and inform Mr Harding about what you've done.'

'Right, that's it,' June announced as soon as the supervisor had gone. 'I'm not staying here to be called a liar again by her. Come on, our Molly, we're going.'

'We can't just leave,' Molly protested shakily, but June was ignoring her, gathering up their things, and then, taking hold of her arm, practically dragged her to the door.

''Ere, June, hang on a mo,' Irene protested.

'Wait till old Harding gets here. We can tell him what's happened.'

'What, and have that nasty piece of work threatening us every time we do sommat as she doesn't like?' June demanded sharply. 'There's plenty of other jobs going, and better paid ones too.'

They were out in the street before Molly could say anything, June leading her towards the bus stop.

'There's Frank's mam watching us,' June pronounced as they walked past number 46. 'I bet she'll be wondering what we're doing home this time o' day. Well, she can wonder, for all I care.'

'You don't think Mr Harding *will* send the police round here after us, do you?' Molly asked her worriedly.

'Don't talk so daft. What for? We haven't done anything wrong. It was Hannah who went mad and cut up them uniforms. Is yer face still hurting?' June asked her sympathetically. 'It's a mercy she didn't knock yer teeth out, she hit yer that hard.'

'You should have seen her face when you answered her back like that.' Molly shook her head, marvelling at her sister's bravery, unable to stop herself from laughing as she remembered the look of disbelief on the supervisor's face as she turned round to see June bearing down on her.

'Aye, well, she's lucky I didn't give her a swipe like the one she gave you,' June replied, and then started to laugh herself.

'Here, wot's got into you two?' Pearl demanded sharply as she came out of her house to find the two of them rocking with laughter, their arms round one another. 'There's a war on, yer know . . .'

'Aye, and we're both out of a job, an' all,' June informed her, still laughing.

'I reckon Pearl thought we had lost our wits,' Molly told June as they let themselves into number 78.

'Aye, probably caught it from Hannah, we have,' June agreed, adding, 'Let's have the wireless on, Molly, in case there's any news.'

There was and it instantly banished their laughter. A Glasgow-based liner, the *Athenia*, had been sunk by a German U-boat and one hundred and twelve lives had been lost.

Molly and June listened to the broadcast in white-faced silence, holding one another tight.

'Oh, those poor, poor people,' Molly whispered. She could not help thinking about Eddie and wondering where he was and if he was safe. If the Germans would attack an innocent passenger ship, then what chance did a merchant navy vessel have?

The newscaster was announcing the appointment of Winston Churchill as First Lord of the Admiralty, before continuing to warn people of the importance of adhering to the strict blackout regulations that had been enforced, but Molly had stopped paying attention. All she could think

about was the dreadful news about the *Athenia* –
and Eddie.

'I've got a WVS meeting tonight,' Molly told
June once they had finished their evening meal and
were washing up.

'We'll have to start looking for new jobs
tomorrow, remember,' June warned her. 'I fancy
working in munitions meself. The pay's good and
they lay on buses and entertainment.'

'Perhaps we should have waited to see Mr
Harding,' Molly suggested. She was still fearful
about the repercussions of their walking out.

'What, and have that Jenner woman making
out that we were lying? No, thanks.'

It felt different wearing her WVS uniform now
that they were at war, Molly realised as she hesitated in front of the dressing table she shared with
June and then, on impulse, slid Johnny's ring onto
her finger in a futile attempt to ease her guilt at
thinking of Eddie all afternoon.

She'd arranged to meet Anne under the Picton
Clock so that they could go to the meeting together.
As she hurried towards it, she saw that Anne was
already there.

'Isn't it dreadful news about the *Athenia*?' Anne
greeted her sombrely.

'Those poor people,' Molly agreed.

'What's that you're wearing?' Anne demanded,
catching sight of Molly's ring.

Molly blushed and told her about Johnny.

'You're engaged? You never said. When . . . ?'

'I don't wear me ring because it's a bit loose,' Molly told her, and then added in a low voice, 'I'd just as soon not be engaged to Johnny, really, but . . . when he was called up for the army . . .' She was desperate to confide in someone and be listened to sympathetically.

'He's one of our fighting men? Then you can't possibly break your engagement to him, Molly. It isn't the done thing. Not when a man has got to fight for his country, and all he has to keep him going is the thought of his sweetheart waiting at home for him, and being true and loyal,' Anne told her reproachfully.

Molly looked pleadingly at her friend. 'But, Anne, I don't love him, and . . . and the truth is that . . . that there's someone else.' Molly could see from Anne's shocked face that every word she said was only making things worse, but she longed so much for her friend to understand her plight and sympathise with her that she just could not stop the words from tumbling out, even though Anne's disapproval was growing by the minute.

'I'm surprised at you, Molly,' Anne told her sternly. 'Yes, and shocked as well. I thought you were a decent sort of girl who knew the difference between right and wrong.' She shook her head. 'Please don't tell me any more. I'm going to pretend that we haven't had this conversation. If you're the girl I thought you were, Molly, you will forget all about this other chap and put him out

139

of your thoughts and your life. I'll say no more on the subject, except that it's up to us to do everything we can to support our boys, not go falling in love with someone else behind their backs.'

Molly was quiet for the rest of the evening. Now even Anne disapproved of her. It was very easy for others to talk about what she should do, Molly decided miserably, especially when they weren't the ones who were in love with Eddie.

It was still light when Molly got home just over an hour later, but that didn't seem to be stopping Alf Davies from marching purposefully down the cul-de-sac.

'Blackout in half an hour,' he told her, checking to see that she was carrying her gas mask. 'Just bin down the allotments to see that old fool Bert.'

'He won't really have to have Rover put down, will he?' Molly asked anxiously.

'Rules is rules and no dogs are allowed in air-raid shelters. I've told him that. And what if he were to get bombed and his bloomin' dog left to roam all over everywhere, causing a nuisance?'

'But Rover is all he's got,' Molly protested.

Ignoring her comment, Alf looked at his watch. 'Time I was on me way. I want to check the whole of the cul-de-sac at blackout time, and then I've got them streets behind to do, an' all.'

By rights she ought to go home. She was only a few doors away now and, as Alf had just pointed out to her, it was almost blackout time, but ever since they had heard the news about the *Athenia*, all Molly had been able to think about was Eddie, and she was guiltily aware that she should not be thinking about him – leastways not in the way that she was.

The Saturday night they had danced and laughed together might as well have been a lifetime ago, so many terrible things had happened since then. She and June had lost their jobs, and whilst it was all very well for June to talk nonchalantly about them getting other work, Molly liked the girls they had already worked with and the friendly familiarity of Hardings. June enjoyed confrontations but she didn't, and it made her feel sick and shaky to remember what had happened. And what if Miss Jenner or Mr Harding did report them to the police? The country was at war and everyone was being exhorted to do their bit, with severe punishments threatened for those who did not abide by all the new rules the Government had brought in.

And if all that wasn't bad enough, she kept imagining Eddie on his ship and those awful German U-boats. She felt so worried and upset that even the thought of old Bert and his dog was enough to fill her eyes with tears.

She glanced disinterestedly at a man turning into the cul-de-sac. He was walking with that slight roll of seagoing men, and . . .

Her eyes widened and she stiffened in disbelief. It was Eddie.

SEVEN

'Molly!'

'Eddie!' She didn't know whether to laugh or cry, and discovered that she was doing both as he started to run towards her.

'I can't believe it's you,' she told him. 'How can you be here? I thought—'

'We had orders from the Admiralty, telling us to turn back,' he answered excitedly.

'I can't believe it,' Molly repeated. 'I was just thinking about you and . . .'

'Was you?'

His voice had deepened and suddenly he was standing much closer to her whilst the dusk wrapped its own protective and concealing blackout around them.

'By, Molly, but I like to think of you thinkin' of me.'

'I meant just as a friend and neighbour,' Molly told him hastily, flushing guiltily as she did so, agitatedly twisting Johnny's ring with her fingers.

'I didn't kiss yer when I said goodbye like you was just a friend and neighbour to me, Molly,' Eddie told her thickly. 'I kissed yer like you was my girl. And I want yer to be my girl, Molly.'

'But I'm engaged to Johnny,' Molly told him miserably.

'But you don't love him, do you?' Eddie probed.

Molly shook her head, and then murmured a small apprehensive protest as Eddie drew her deeper into the shadows and into his arms.

'Aw, come on, Molly love, don't cry,' he begged her.

'I can't help it,' Molly told him. 'Everything's so awful. Our June says that I can't not be engaged to Johnny on account of him going off to fight, me and her have lost our jobs, and the *Athenia*'s been sunk and it could have been you, and poor Bert will have to have Rover put down, and even Anne, me friend at WVS, has taken the huff with me.'

As she sobbed out all of this, Eddie held her closer, stroking her hair and murmuring comforting words into her ear.

'Oh, Eddie, why did this have to happen to us after I'd got engaged to Johnny?'

'I don't know, lass. Mebbe it teks sommat like a war to make us see what's bin under our noses.'

'What are we going to do?'

'Well, I reckon that Johnny is bound to get some leave before he's sent into action. When he does,' he squeezed her hand gently, 'I reckon that would be the time to tell him what's happened.'

'Tell him about you and me, you mean? Do you think I should?'

Eddie nodded.

'But what would people say?' she asked. 'I'd feel so . . .'

And then he kissed her, and Molly recognised that nothing else and no one else mattered more right now than her love for Eddie.

Being kissed by Eddie was every bit as wonderful the second time as it had been the first, she discovered dizzily. So wonderful, in fact, that she didn't want him to stop – not ever.

But he did, his voice unfamiliarly gruff and husky as he told her, 'You've got to be my girl after kissing me like that, Molly, even if we are going to have to keep it to ourselves until you've told Johnny.'

Suddenly Molly knew she had no choice. It was Eddie she wanted, not Johnny.

'How long will you be home for?' she asked him.

'I don't know yet. But like as not it won't be for very long.'

Molly's heart sank at the words but she berated herself hurriedly. This time together was an unexpected blessing and she would cherish every second of it.

It was almost dark now, and Eddie bent his head and kissed her again, a quick, hard, very grown-up kiss that left her tingling from head to foot as they looked at one another through the darkness.

'Come on, before I do sommat as I shouldn't,' Eddie told her gruffly, releasing her and turning her firmly in the direction of their homes.

'It seems really funny, not seeing any light anywhere,' Molly commented, smothering a soft laugh as Eddie accidentally stepped off the pavement and into the gutter because they couldn't see where they were going. Her laughter turned to a protest of her own as she bumped into a privet hedge.

'If them in charge don't watch out, this blackout's going to be causing a fair few accidents,' Eddie prophesied as they reached number 78.

'What are you doin' tomorrow?' he asked.

'June was talking about us going to look for new jobs.' She had already told him about the earlier incident at Hardings.

'I'll pop round in the morning then, just to come and show me face, like. Leastways, that's what I'll tell your June. Go on,' he gave her a small tender push, 'you get yourself inside. I'll stay here and watch to mek sure you're all right. And, Molly.' She turned to look up at him. 'Don't wear Johnny's ring any more.'

She looked helplessly at him, desperately tempted to run back to him for one more kiss. She didn't tell him that the ring had been off her finger and in her pocket before they'd even finished kissing.

* * *

145

'Watch that light you're letting out. You'll have Alf Davies down on us,' June commented critically when Molly opened the back door. 'You're late. I thought you said you would be back before dark,' she added.

'I got a bit delayed,' Molly told her, bending down and pretending to brush some fluff off her skirt so that she could hide her telltale guilty flush from her sister.

'What's to do with you this morning? You're like a cat on hot bricks,' June complained as Molly glanced towards the back door for the umpteenth time.

'As soon as I've finished writing this letter to my Frank I thought we'd go down into town and get it posted and then go and 'ave a word at Napiers – see if they're still taking folk on.'

Molly's heart sank as she listened to her sister. What excuse could she give for not wanting to go out that wouldn't betray her? Eddie had said he would come round this morning. But it was half-past ten already and Molly was beginning to wonder if, in the cold light of day, he was having second thoughts about what he had said to her last night or – her heart thudded into her chest wall at the thought – could he now be thinking of her as a girl who was not only 'fast' but who was also guilty of betraying another man?

Desperate to find something to do that wouldn't further alert June's suspicions, she picked up the old blue cardigan she had brought downstairs earlier.

'What are you going to do with that?' June asked her.

'I thought I'd unpick it and use the wool to knit something for Sally's baby,' Molly explained.

'Aye, well, when you go and see her why don't you ask her if you can borrow that frock her bridesmaid wore last year? I can't see how we're able to afford to buy you a new one, not now we haven't got jobs, and even if we could I don't know where we'd get any fabric.'

'Yes, I'll do that,' Molly agreed, too relieved at having successfully distracted her sister to protest that she didn't particularly want to wear the bright pink, shiny, mock-taffeta frock Sally's bridesmaid had worn. She'd look like the Sugar Plum Fairy. She could remember how, at the time, Sally had complained bitterly that she hated it, but that Ronnie's sister had insisted that it was what she was going to wear.

'Yoo-hoo . . .'

The cardigan slipped from Molly's fingers as she turned towards the back door, tense with hope, uncertainty and self-consciousness that Eddie would be with his aunt.

'You'll never guess what,' Elsie beamed as she bustled into the kitchen. 'Our Eddie's home.'

'Aw, Auntie Elsie,' Eddie protested with a grin as he followed her into the kitchen, and then looked at Molly.

Oblivious to anything and anyone else, she looked back at him, whilst her heart threw itself at her ribcage with much the same force as she wanted to throw herself into his arms.

'Oh . . . not that I wasn't sorry to 'ear your bad news about your jobs, of course. A right shame, that is,' she could hear Elsie saying. 'I couldn't believe it when our Eddie walked in last night. Already in bed, we was, on account of me spending all day mekkin' piccalilli and bottlin' soft fruit. Our Jim managed to get me a whole box of Kilner jars, and I thought sooner than waste 'em and leave 'em empty, I might as well fill 'em wi' sommat, especially since . . .'

'. . . there's a war on,' Eddie chanted in time with his aunt, and then laughed.

'I've already told you, Auntie, you want ter be careful wi' them jars, wi' our Jim bringing them home for yer.' He winked. 'Checked 'em for cracks, did you, in case they got broke when they fell off that goods wagon?'

'That's enough of that, our Eddie,' Elsie began, and then laughed herself when she saw that he was teasing her.

Teasing her and making them all laugh, and somehow at the same time managing to close the distance so that he was standing right up next to Molly and was able to give her hand a reassuring little squeeze under the oilcloth cover on the table.

She dared not look up at him because if she did she knew she would give herself away.

'Aye, well, you don't need to go feeling sorry for us, Elsie. Me and Molly'll soon have new jobs – better jobs, an' all, than working at Hardings,' June prophesied. 'I've heard as how they're taking on at Napiers to make armaments—'

'You're never thinkin' of going working there?' Elsie protested immediately, while Eddie also frowned.

'Why not?' June demanded as she licked the envelope she had just put her letter into and sealed it. 'It's good pay and—'

'It's too dangerous,' Eddie said tersely. 'And besides, mekkin' shells and that is men's work.'

'Huh, and how are men going to do it when they're all being called up?' June challenged, tossing her head.

'Aye, well, I have heard as how they're tekkin' women on down there,' Elsie agreed. 'But I wouldn't want any daughter of mine working there. I've heard as 'ow only last week one poor lad had his arm blown off, and there's tales of lads gettin' all sorts of skin rashes and the like . . .'

'Any news yet, June, as to when your Frank is likely to get leave?' Eddie broke in diplomatically, and Molly sent him a look of grateful relief.

'No. He's not in the merchant navy with leave every other week,' June sniffed crossly.

'Aye, well, I wouldn't be here neither if we hadn't been sent orders to turn back,' Eddie answered, knowing June of old and that her concern for Frank was making her tetchy.

'So you're home now until the war's over, are you?' June demanded jealously.

'Of course he isn't, June,' Elsie objected, 'but he's not allowed to say what's happening, are you, Eddie, on account of loose talk costing lives?'

Eddie shrugged. 'I doubt that June would go blabbin' to anyone, Auntie, not with her Frank in the army. Sent him over to France now, have they then, June?' he probed.

'He's still in Clacton, doing his training,' June informed him loftily.

'Lucky Frank. In the merchant navy we does our training on the ship, and if a U-boat gets yer in its sights before you're ready, it's just too bad,' Eddie drawled meaningfully.

Molly could see that an angry red flush was spreading across June's face. It was obvious to her that her sister did not like the fact that Eddie was refusing to let her have the last word.

'The Admiralty gave instructions for us to turn back on account of them deciding that merchant navy vessels are to travel in convoy and be protected by warships from now on,' Eddie continued in a milder tone. 'How do you fancy goin' to the pictures tonight, Molly?' he added casually.

'She can't,' June answered sharply before Molly could speak. 'None of the picture houses or the dance halls are opening, on account of the blackout. And, besides, she's an engaged woman.'

'Aye, and we know whose idea that was,' Eddie began angrily.

Molly looked at him imploringly and shook her head.

'And what exactly do you mean by that?' June started to demand, only to frown as someone began banging on the front door.

'Who the hell is that?' June protested, adding, 'You go and see, will yer, our Molly?'

Molly could make out the outline of a man through the frosted glass. Uncertainly she opened the door, her mouth opening in a startled 'Oh' of surprise when she saw Mr Harding standing outside.

'Oh, Molly . . . may I come in?'

'Who is it?' June called out.

'It's . . . it's Mr Harding, from the factory,' Molly called back shakily.

She could hear sounds of movement from the kitchen and then June demanded sharply, 'Give over having me on and messing about, our Molly,' followed by silence as her sister came to stand beside her, and she realised that Molly had been speaking the truth.

'I've come to have a word with you both,' Mr Harding announced. 'Is there somewhere . . . ?'

'You'd best come into the front room,' June told him, giving Molly a loaded look as she opened the door.

The front room smelled of polish, and the worn leather sofa creaked slightly when Mr Harding sat down on it.

'I've come to talk to you about yesterday,' Mr

151

Harding began, having already refused June's offer of a cup of tea.

'It weren't us as were to blame,' June told him swiftly. 'We didn't touch them uniforms.'

'No. I know that, June. The other girls have explained everything. I've had a word with Hannah's doctor and he feels that the shock of hearing we are at war has affected Hannah's brain and that was why she did what she did. But I'm not here to talk about poor Hannah. I'd like you both to come back to work. Hardings can't afford to lose girls as skilled as you two.' He smiled warmly at them both. 'And, of course, there'll be no question of any wages being lost, not even for today.'

'I'm not going back to work under that Jenner woman,' June announced flatly.

'Miss Jenner is no longer with us. She has handed in her notice to join the ATS,' Mr Harding informed them, adding, 'I won't keep you any longer. And I hope to see you both back at your machines tomorrow morning.'

'Who was that then?' Elsie asked curiously whilst Molly looked delightedly at June, then explained, 'It was Mr Harding from the factory. He's offered us our jobs back and said as how he knows what really happened. And he said that Miss Jenner has left to join the ATS.' Molly beamed.

'Well, that's all right then. All's well that ends well, eh?' Elsie said mundanely.

'It might be for him, but I dunno as I want to go back to Hardings,' June announced. 'Four pounds a week I've heard they're getting down at Napiers. That's nearly twice as much as we get at the factory.'

'Oh, June, you don't mean that, do you?' Molly protested. She liked working at Hardings and she liked the girls they worked with.

'If June wants to work at Napiers, then that's up to her, but there's nothing to stop you going back to Hardings if you want to, Molly,' Eddie said firmly.

'And what gives you the right to start telling our Molly what she can and can't do, Eddie Granger?' June demanded.

'I'm not telling her to do anything – you're the one doing that, June,' Eddie retorted. 'I'm just saying that Molly doesn't have to leave Hardings if she doesn't want to just because you do.'

'Eddie's right, June,' Elsie chipped in. She smiled at Molly. 'You do what you want, love,' she said, adding, to Molly's relief, 'I'd better get back. I promised Sally Walker I'd get her a bit of shoppin' in. She's finding it hard being on her own with baby, and no family around her to help whilst her Ronnie is away.'

'That Eddie's got some cheek,' June said scathingly after their neighbours had left. 'It seems to me he's got a sight too much to say for himself where you're concerned, our Molly. I hope you haven't forgotten where your duty lies. I wouldn't want a sister of mine being talked about by every gossip in Edge Hill and Wavertree as the sort that forgets where her loyalties lie. Why don't you write to your Johnny and tell him how much you're missing him?'

'I haven't had a reply yet to the last two letters I wrote,' Molly told her quietly.

'Well, you can't expect a fighting man to have the time to be writing every five minutes.'

'Why not? Frank writes to you every day, and besides, they aren't fighting yet, are they?' Molly pointed out sturdily. 'They're both still training.'

'You've got a sharp tongue on you today,' June told her. 'Let's get changed and go down to Lewis's. We can have a cup of tea there, I'll post me letter, and then we can go and see if they're taking on at Napiers.'

Molly shook her head, ignoring the guilty twinge she felt at June's astonished look.

'No, I don't want to. I'm going to go back to Hardings,' she told her sister.

'Well, if you don't mind turning down four pounds a week, that's up to you,' June announced, but Molly could see that she had surprised her.

Half an hour later, when June came downstairs all dressed to go out, with her hat on, Molly had to fight to suppress her own qualms about going against her. All her life she had gone along with what June had told her to do, and it felt strange to be defying her now. She felt bad, but somehow strangely lighter at the same time.

'If you change your mind, you know where to find me,' June told her firmly.

After she had gone the house felt oddly quiet. She and June had always done everything together. Perhaps she should get changed and go after her. After all, working at Napiers was surely a small price to pay to be with her sister.

She headed for the stairs and then stopped as she heard a soft tap on the back door.

'I saw your June walk past,' Eddie announced when Molly let him in. 'You shouldn't let her tell you what to do all the time, Molly.'

'She means well,' Molly defended her sister. 'She's just looking after me, that's all.'

'Aye, well, from now on I'm going to be the one doing that,' Eddie told her softly, reaching for her hand.

Her heart felt as though it was jumping around all over the place. She could hardly breathe for the excitement fizzing inside her like Edmondson's best lemonade. She looked at her hand, so small against Eddie's.

'We shouldn't be doing this,' she whispered. 'Not whilst I'm . . . people will talk, Eddie,' she told him anxiously, 'what with me supposed to be engaged to Johnny.'

'I've got to go back to me ship tonight.' He was playing with her fingers, and Molly could sense his desire. 'I wish I could make you mine, Molly, so that if I don't come back, you'll never forget me,' he began gruffly.

'No, you mustn't say that,' she protested, tears stinging her eyes, as she went into his arms. When they wrapped around her, she closed her eyes, lifting her face towards his for his kiss.

'You're right, we shouldn't be doing this,' he told her thickly.

But he still kissed her, and she still kissed him back, even though she knew she shouldn't.

'I'm going now,' he whispered hoarsely as he released her and stepped back from her, 'because if I don't . . . Will you come and see me off tonight? We're sailing from Brunswick Dock.'

Molly nodded. She didn't want to let him go but part of her was glad that he was going. She didn't trust herself to refuse him if he stayed.

There had been a girl two streets back from Chestnut Close, who had got herself in trouble last summer. The shame of it had forced her parents to up sticks and leave the area. It made Molly shudder just to think about it. She wanted her and Eddie to be together for ever, and in every way a man and woman could be together – but not just yet . . .

'A WVS meeting again tonight?' June grumbled. 'And what am I supposed to do with both you and our dad out? Sit on me own and twiddle me thumbs?'

'You could go round and see Sally,' Molly suggested lamely.

'What, and risk bumping into Frank's mam? No, thanks. From what I've heard she's round there every day, telling Sally how to go on.'

Molly was too guiltily aware of the lie she had told June to press her to change her mind.

The atmosphere between them had been very strained since June had returned from posting her letter to Frank to tell Molly that she was definitely not going back to Hardings but was taking a job with Napiers instead.

'But we've always worked together,' Molly had protested.

'Well, it's not me that is changing that,' June had told her. 'There's a job for you at Napiers, if you want one.'

But the truth was that Molly didn't. She wanted to go back to Hardings and the friends she had made there. It wasn't so much the danger of working at the munitions factory that put her off as the gossip she had heard about some of the girls who worked there.

'They're a real rough lot,' Irene had pronounced when they had talked about the good wages Napiers paid. 'Thieving and all sorts goes on.'

Her guardian angel must really be looking out for her, Molly decided with fervent gratitude as she risked giving a final guilty glance over her shoulder and hurried out of the cul-de-sac. Molly didn't have to lie to June about why she was going out supposedly to a WVS meeting out of uniform, because June had announced immediately after the tea things had been cleared that she too was going out for the evening, to see an old school friend she had bumped into earlier in Lewis's.

'She's working in a baker's now and said as how she would do her best to sort me out with a wedding cake.'

Although food wasn't as yet rationed, certain things were very hard, sometimes even impossible, to get, and everyone was being exhorted to remember the war, and reminded of the penalties for not doing so. Molly could well understand June's desire to take full advantage of the opportunity that had arisen.

With any luck she should be back home before June. Eddie, who had nipped in to say a public goodbye to both her and June during the afternoon, had said that his ship was due to sail at half-past seven.

Now, just thinking about him made her quicken her pace, whilst her heart raced in a mixture of excitement, guilt and concern.

Brunswick Dock was a fair walk, so Molly decided to take the bus as far as she could to save time and shoe leather.

The dock was busy, and Molly hesitated, not sure where to go.

'Your fella sailing on the *Aronsay*?' another girl called out cheerfully to her, falling into step alongside her when Molly nodded.

The closer they got to the side of the large ship

looming up out of the docks, the thicker the press of people was. Eddie had told Molly he would meet her at the stern end of the vessel, and to her relief the other girl informed her that she too was heading in that direction.

'New to this, are yer?' she asked in a kindly way, adding when once again Molly nodded, 'Well, mek sure you tell him what ter bring yer back – nylons, I've told mine to get us, and a lipstick as well. Allus get a bit o' sommat special when he's over to New York.'

Molly's eyes rounded. 'I thought they weren't supposed to say where they are sailing to?'

Her new friend smirked. 'My Jimmie wouldn't dare as not tell me. Oh, there he is,' she announced. 'Will yer be OK?'

'Oh, yes . . .' Molly began to assure her politely, relief bringing a wide smile to her face as she heard Eddie's familiar voice calling her name.

'I should have remembered how busy it gets down here and not asked you to come,' he said ruefully, holding her hand as he led her through the crowd into the shadows of the great hull.

'I didn't realise you were going to New York,' Molly told him worriedly. 'It's such a long way, and there'll be U-boats and—'

'Nah, the *Aronsay*'s a good ship – and fast. I'll be there and back before you've had time to miss me, and I promise I'll bring you sommat pretty.' He had in mind his Auntie Elsie's comment that June was thinking poor Molly could wear Sally

Walker's sister-in-law's cast-off bridesmaid's dress, and he was hoping he would have time in New York to get her some pretty fabric.

There was a long, loud blast on the ship's whistle. Eddie took Molly in his arms and kissed her fiercely. Oblivious to everyone and everything but him, Molly kissed him back equally eagerly.

'I've got to go, otherwise I'll be swimmin' over Liverpool bar to catch up with the ship,' Eddie joked. But he still kissed her a second time, whilst all around them men started to hurry on board.

'I love you, Molly Dearden,' he whispered to her, as he finally released her.

She wasn't going to cry, Molly promised herself sturdily. She didn't want him to remember her with tears in her eyes. So instead she smiled as she waved, and watched him disappear, her heart soaring and breaking at the same time.

She was just about to start making her way back through the crowd when she saw Johnny's sisters, standing a few yards away, staring at her. Her heart thumped guiltily. Had they seen her with Eddie? She knew that she couldn't ignore them, and was just about to make her way towards them when they turned round and disappeared into the crowd.

Although she was relieved not to have to speak to them, Molly still felt sick with worry and guilt. What if they *had* seen her with Eddie, and they told Johnny?

She shouldn't have come down to the dock to

say goodbye to Eddie, and she most certainly should not have kissed him, she knew that. She was engaged to Johnny, and it didn't matter that she had never wanted that engagement. If Johnny's sisters had seen her kissing Eddie they would tell everyone, and there was nothing she could say to explain or defend herself. She wished desperately for the umpteenth time that she had never let herself be talked into her engagement to Johnny.

All the way home on the bus, her head was filled with dreadful images of everyone's disapproval. And it wouldn't just affect her, it would affect her sister and her father as well. Once one member of a family did something that made them a social outcast, that reflected on everyone else in their family. Yet she couldn't regret having gone to see Eddie off, and nor could she bring herself to deny her feelings for him.

These were such dark and dangerous times. If the unthinkable should happen, and his ship should be attacked by one of Hitler's U-boats and sunk, at least she would have the memory of having held him and parted lovingly from him.

Molly looked wanly at her breakfast. She had barely slept and this morning her head was aching.

'Come on, drink up your tea, else we're going to be late for work, and I don't want old Harding moaning at us,' June urged her.

Molly frowned in confusion. 'What about Napiers?'

'What about them?' June shrugged. 'I didn't say as I would take their job, I just said as I'd think about it. As it happens, I have thought about it and I've decided I might as well stay where I am. Now get a move on, will yer?' she demanded, pulling a face when Molly jumped up, her corn-flower-blue eyes shining with delight as she flung her arms around her sister, exclaiming with heart-felt delight, 'Oh, June, I'm that glad you've changed your mind.'

'Oh, give over being so soft, will yer?' June complained, but Molly could see that she was smiling.

It was such a relief to know that she and June would still be working together, Molly thought as they set off for work, linking arms to walk speedily down the cul-de-sac.

'I really would have missed you if you'd gone to Napiers,' Molly told June, squeezing her arm affectionately.

'Aye, well, it seems to me that someone has got to look out for you, and make sure as you don't go getting yourself into trouble.'

Molly was relieved to see their bus lumbering towards them, sparing her from betraying her guilt. It was tearing her apart.

'So then Mr Harding says, "Well, Irene, it seems to me that you should be in charge of the girls from now on,"' Irene told them, mimicking the factory owner's way of speaking, as she filled June and Molly in on what had happened since they left.

'But poor Hannah, what will happen to her?' Molly asked worriedly.

'Gorn mental, she has,' Ruby opined, 'and no mistake.'

'Her sister come in yesterday and said as how Hannah will be moving in wi' her so as she can look out for her,' Irene answered Molly, before saying crisply, 'Now come on, all of you, we've got work to do. There's a war on, you know.'

Within a few minutes the room was filled with the busy whirr of sewing machines – and the chatter of the girls as they returned to the familiar exchanging of comments whilst they sewed, calling out questions and answers to one another without lifting either their eyes or their hands from their work. They were working hard for their men and for their country, but it didn't mean they couldn't have some fun doing it.

EIGHT

'I heard last night as how all the cinemas and dance halls are opening up again on account of there not having been any bombs,' Ruby told the other girls one October evening as they hurried to put on their hats and coats ready to go home.

'Well, that's something to be pleased about,' Irene said approvingly. 'Right fed up of havin' to stay in, I'm gettin', especially with the blummin' blackout.'

'Well, I heard as how some poor chap was run over the other night on the Scotland Road. Walked right in front of a bus, he did, and never even seed it on account of it being blacked out.'

The newspapers were full of stories of accidents in the blackout, and men had been urged to walk with their shirt tails hanging out at night so that drivers could see them. All over the country people were complaining about the rules being forced on them to protect them from Jerry's bombs, of which, as yet, there had been no sign.

Molly combed her hair and put on the coat she wore for work. She had bought it the January before last, having queued up outside Lewis's at the start of their sale. She'd saved up for it out of her wages. Secretly she still preferred it to her going-to-church coat. It was brown tweed, darted at the back and nipped in at the waist, with a soft flare that emphasised her neat figure. It fastened with proper horn buttons. Some of the other machinists didn't care how they looked, coming and going to work, but their father had brought June and Molly up to take a pride in their appearance. She pulled on her hat, dark brown and trimmed with feathers, automatically adjusting it to the right angle before reaching into her pocket for the brown gloves she had knitted to match her coat.

It had been raining all day and the streets gleamed greasily under the leaden sky as the two sisters huddled beneath a shared umbrella.

'Look, there's our dad,' Molly said, as they got off the bus and turned into the cul-de-sac.

'He must have had to work over his shift,' June commented. 'He said last night that he would be finishing at two today and that he would go straight to his allotment.

'Here, Dad, wait up,' June called out as the girls hurried to catch up with him.

'I hope you haven't got more eggs,' June teased him.

His chickens had become a bit of a standing

joke in the cul-de-sac, which he took in good part, claiming that at least they would be more tender to eat than the two pigs the allotment holders had applied to keep.

'You're late finishing work,' said June.

'Aye, we had to get some extra wagons emptied and ready for Napiers.' He rubbed a dirty hand across his eyes. 'Some of the lads were saying that they'd heard that there's bin U-boats up at Scapa Flow and that they've sunk the *Royal Oak*. Gawd help our merchant men if blummin' Jerry can sail right into Scapa and let loose his torpedoes. John from next door isn't saying much but you can tell that he's worrying about that nephew of his, and who can blame him? Seems like there's news of another ship sunk every day.'

All the time her father had been speaking, Molly's heart had been thumping relentlessly in her chest.

It was nearly a full month since Eddie had sailed and Elsie had let slip when she had called round last night that she had been expecting him home before now.

'Didn't you say you had a WVS meeting tonight?' June asked Molly as they all hurried inside, shaking wet coats and shivering in the cold dampness of the kitchen.

When Molly nodded, June told her, 'Put the kettle on, Molly, whilst I go and see if there's any letters come.'

The kettle was almost boiling, and June hadn't

come back into the kitchen. So Molly left her father still tuning in the wireless and went to the door, calling out to June that she was making the tea.

'I thought that would bring you,' she called over her shoulder a few minutes later when she heard June come into the kitchen. When there was no response she turned round and almost dropped the teapot.

June was holding a letter in her hand and tears were rolling silently down her cheeks.

'June, what is it?' Molly demanded, putting down the teapot.

'It's Frank,' June told her, causing Molly's heart to lurch, before a huge smile replaced June's tears. 'He's written to say that he's bin told he will be home for Christmas and that I'm to get everything sorted out for the wedding.'

'Oh, Junie . . .' Molly hugged her.

'I'm so happy, but fancy him not writing to let me know before now. How am I supposed to get everything sorted out?' June demanded, reverting to her normal manner. But Molly could see how truly happy she was.

'Well, at least your dress is nearly finished.'

'Aye, but I'll still have to see the vicar, and our dad will have to have a suit, and then there's the wedding breakfast.'

'What about Frank's mam?' Molly began.

'Frank says that he's written to her and told her. I think I'm going to have to sit down,' she added faintly. 'I've come over all of a shake. Oh, and he

167

said as how your Johnny will be coming home as well and that he's asked him to be his best man.'

Molly's smile faltered.

'Looks like there's a letter here for you from Johnny, an' all,' June told her, handing her an envelope. Molly hadn't seen Johnny's sisters since the night she had seen Eddie off on his ship, and there had been no hint in the two letters she had received from Johnny since then of them saying anything to him.

She was dreading having to tell Johnny that she wanted to end their engagement, but at the same time she was longing to be able to do so. She couldn't help wishing, though, that Frank had not asked him to be his best man, especially with her being June's bridesmaid. It was going to be very awkward.

'Oh, Molly, I was beginning to think Frank'd never get leave.'

June's face was glowing with happiness, and Molly had to force herself to put her own feelings to one side, for her sister's sake.

'Molly, we've heard today that my brother is to have leave from the RAF over Christmas,' Anne announced excitedly as the two girls met up at their now regular meeting point of the Picton Clock. There was an air-raid shelter reasonably close to the clock so they had agreed it made sense to meet there 'just in case'.

'Frank and Johnny are to get leave as well,'

Molly told her more circumspectly. Although Anne seemed to have forgotten her own heated words, Molly was very mindful of Anne's disapproval of her desire to end her engagement, as well as troubled by her own deceit. But what else could she do? She could not confide in Anne, knowing how she felt. And, anyway, it was only right that she told Johnny first that she wanted to end their engagement.

Once she had, she would then have to tell Anne, but if she then chose to turn her back on Molly, then Molly would just have to accept it. The love she and Eddie had for one another was too precious and dear for her to give up – much as she would hate to lose Anne's friendship.

'And Frank has written to tell our June to go ahead with their wedding plans.'

Arm in arm, the two girls headed for the school building where the WVS held its meetings.

'It's dreadful news about the *Royal Oak*, isn't it?' Anne said quietly, once they were inside. 'So many lives lost, and at Scapa Flow, where they thought it was impossible for any U-boats to get. I'm so glad my brother isn't in the navy.'

Molly started to tremble, choking back the anxious words she knew would betray her. It hurt so much, not being able to say how she felt about Eddie and to share her fear for him, but it had upset her to have Anne criticise her so sharply. It was obvious from her manner since then that she assumed that Molly was sticking by her engagement, as she had urged her to do. Anne didn't realise how it felt to be in love, otherwise she would have been more understanding, Molly comforted herself.

The news of the torpedoing of the *Royal Oak* had thrown everyone into a sombre mood that wasn't lightened when Mrs Wesley, the head of their group, announced that she had received a number of complaints from her fellow WVS members in the area to which the Edge Hill and Wavertree children had been evacuated.

'It seems some of those who were kind enough to take in the children are reporting a very serious lack of good manners indeed. And I'm afraid we have also had reports of a boy of seven who has, on several occasions, lost control of himself and wet his bed. Naturally he has been punished, and severely, but of course such shameful behaviour reflects on us all.'

Molly bit on her bottom lip as she listened to her. A small rebellious voice inside her was telling her that a young boy, separated from his mother and his home, and handed over to strangers, might be so upset and afraid that certain accidents might happen. She felt more pity and compassion for the child than the righteous anger their superior obviously thought they should feel.

'There are also reports of children stealing, and refusing to do as they are told,' Mrs Wesley continued sternly. 'It is a shameful thing indeed when good people take these children in out of the kindness of their hearts and that kindness is abused.'

'But surely the Government is *paying* them to house the evacuees,' a young blonde-haired woman spoke up firmly, much to Molly's admiration.

'Well, yes, that is true, but it does not excuse such behaviour. I have been in touch with the mother of the boy concerned and informed her that he will be returned to her. Now, how are we doing with our knitting for our soldiers programme . . . ?'

Molly had discovered in the weeks since she had joined the WVS that their leader was considered by some of the younger members to be a little too set in her ways and old-fashioned. Molly shared those views, and could see in Anne's eyes that she did too, as did the smart blonde girl who had spoken up.

'Poor little chap,' Anne whispered to Molly. 'I can't see that beating him would do any good. It will only frighten him all the more.'

'Now, I want volunteers who are willing to learn to drive. The Government has informed us that it wishes us to ensure that as many of our members as possible are able to drive, and Mrs Noakes's husband has kindly offered to teach those who want to learn.'

Anne was nudging Molly. 'Come on! Remember we signed up to do it when we first started?'

The thought of being in charge of a motor car still terrified Molly, but she thought it would be useful to learn, and might prove a welcome distraction from the turmoil of her emotions.

At the end of the evening, when the volunteers were asked to line up, Molly was pleased to see that the smart blonde woman was also volunteering, along with several of the other younger members of the group.

'Oh, Molly, thank you. He's growing so fast, he's out of nearly everything I had already,' Sally Walker said as Molly handed her the little matinée jacket and romper suit she had knitted up from her own old cardigan. 'I've got the frock from our Dawn for you. It's upstairs in the spare room. Come on, I'll take you up.

'I had a telegram this morning from Ronnie,' Sally continued. 'He's bin given a week's leave and he's on his way home. I can't wait to see him, and neither can this little lad, can you?' She smiled tearfully. 'He hasn't met his dad yet, have you?'

The pink dress was laid out carefully on the bed in the immaculately tidy room. It was obvious that Sally had done her best to display it nicely but Molly's heart still sank when she saw it. The bright pink colour was even more brash than she had remembered, the fabric shiny and stiff.

'It's very kind of you to lend it to me,' Molly began, trying not to reveal what she was really thinking, but Sally was no fool.

'I'm right sorry it isn't better, Molly love, especially after what you've done for me. That Dawn never had no taste, and I did everything I could to get her to choose sommat else, but she weren't having none of it. And I reckon it will be too big for you, an' all.'

'I can make a new sash for it,' Molly assured her. What did it matter what she wore, after all? It was June's day, not hers. And who knew, perhaps one look at her in it would be enough to make Johnny break off their engagement. She cheered herself momentarily with that thought.

'So your June's set the date then?' Sally asked as they went back downstairs, Molly carrying the dress and Sally the baby.

'Yes, the Saturday before Christmas.'

'What about the wedding breakfast? Where is she having that?'

'She says she's not having much of a do on account of the war and everything. The vicar has said she can use the church hall, and Elsie from next door has said she'll help us with everything,' said Molly.

'Aye, I reckon the whole cul-de-sac will lend a hand, Molly. Frank's mam was round here this morning. I reckon she's a bit put out that they aren't having sommat a bit posher. Frank's the apple of her eye and no mistake.'

Molly didn't say anything. She liked Sally, but she didn't want to fuel any gossip about Frank's mother's disapproval of the fact that Frank was marrying June.

* * *

'There!' Molly announced, through a mouthful of pins, as she finished pinning the hem of June's wedding dress, and sat back on her heels to ease her aching back and survey her handiwork. 'You can take it off now. I've only got to hem it.'

It was gone six o'clock and she had been working on the dress since they had cleared away the remains of their Sunday dinner.

As soon as June had stepped out of the dress Molly put it on a hanger and wrapped it carefully in its protective sheet.

'Elsie said she'd come round this evening so we can sort out what we're going to 'ave for the buffet,' said June. 'I've had a word with me friend up at the baker's, and she's promised to let us have some baps.'

'Oh, I nearly forgot,' Molly broke in, 'I was telling Anne about the wedding and she said to tell you that there's a butcher up on Edge Road who makes his own potted meat, and she reckons she can get you some, if you want.'

It was getting harder by the day to buy food, unless you were prepared to pay black-market prices, or knew someone who knew someone. June was understandably concerned at what the situation would be, come the wedding.

'Dad's had a word with Auntie Violet and she's promised us a nice piece of ham and some of her home-made sausages. If you want, you can tell that Anne she's invited, seeing as how she's helpin' with the food,' said June.

'I thought we'd go down to the hall the week before and give it a good clean out – scrub the floor, and that, and the vicar says we can have the Christmas decorations up if we want to make it look a bit festive,' June told Molly, adding, 'Oh, and guess what I've heard. I saw that Sandra, and she told me that Daisy Cartwright has had to bring her two kiddies back from Wales on account of her Davie wettin' the bed.'

Molly stiffened. Was their neighbour's little boy the child the WVS supervisor had been talking about so unkindly?

'Yoo-hoo.'

Molly hurried downstairs to welcome their neighbour and then came to a full stop when she saw Eddie standing behind his aunt. She blinked once to make sure she wasn't seeing things, and then a second time to blink away her happy tears.

The temptation to run to him almost over-whelmed her. She heard June come downstairs and into the kitchen, but she couldn't stop looking at Eddie, greedily absorbing the reality of him. She could hear June and Elsie talking, but she was oblivious to what they were saying, oblivious to everything and everyone but Eddie.

'I've brought you a bit of summat back wi' me, like I promised,' she heard him telling her as he offered her a big flat parcel.

'What's going on here? You buying our Molly presents, Eddie?' June asked sharply, but Molly wasn't listening to her.

Very carefully she opened the brown-paper-wrapped package. Inside it was sky-blue silk taffeta of the most beautiful shade she had ever seen.

'It was me Auntie Elsie as put the idea into me head,' Eddie told her gruffly. 'She said as how you were having to wear Sally's sister-in-law's bridesmaid's dress, and that you didn't much like the colour. I thought this would match your eyes.'

'Oh, *Eddie*.' Right there in front of his Auntie Elsie and her sister she whispered his name in such a way that she knew she must have given herself away.

'I would have bin back wi' it before now, only we came up against Jerry's torpedoes in the Atlantic. Did for another ship, they did, right in front of us. Poor sods on board never had a chance.' Eddie shook his head, his eyes clouding over at the memory.

White-faced, Molly looked at him, everything she was feeling revealed in her expression.

'How about me and you going to the pictures tomorrow night?' Eddie asked her thickly.

'Yes,' Molly agreed quickly, at exactly the same time as June said a firm, 'No.'

'Don't think I don't know what's going on,' June warned Molly after Elsie and Eddie had gone, and they were alone together in their bedroom, getting ready for bed in the angry silence they had shared since Elsie had almost dragged her nephew out of

176

number 78's kitchen. 'I'm not daft, you know, and I wasn't born yesterday. I've got two eyes in me head, our Molly, and I could see how you was looking at Eddie, so don't you go thinking I couldn't.' June gave up any pretence of brushing her hair, throwing her hairbrush down on the bed and starting to pace the linoleum-covered floor.

'Have you no shame? Looking at him like you wanted . . . and you engaged to someone else as well. I don't know what's got into you. And him bringing you that silk and saying it were the same colour as your eyes. Cheek of it, when he knows you're engaged. As for you going to the cinema with him, you're going nowhere with him, my girl.'

Molly had heard enough. She stood up to confront her sister. 'Who says I'm not? You can't tell me what to do, June. I love Eddie and he loves me, and just as soon as Johnny comes home I'm going to tell him that I don't want to be engaged to him any more.'

For a moment there was silence and then June exhaled and said angrily, 'You can't do that.'

'Yes, I can, and you can't stop me,' Molly retorted, repeating emotionally, 'Me and Eddie love each other. You heard what he said about that other ship being torpedoed. That could have been him.' Tears filled her eyes. 'Who knows how long we might have together and I'm not going to give up a second of it.'

'But what about Johnny?'

'I never wanted to be engaged to Johnny in the

first place. It was always you who wanted it. This is my life and I'm going to live it my way!'

'Well!' June exclaimed, her mouth tightening as she turned her back on Molly and sat down on her bed.

She hated falling out with her sister, Molly admitted wretchedly, half an hour later, in the darkness of the bedroom she shared with June, her pillow already damp with her silent tears. But she was not going to give Eddie up. She was not! And she *was* going to the pictures with him tomorrow night, no matter what June said to try to stop her.

NINE

Only June didn't say anything at all – not when they got up, not over breakfast, not one single word.

When their father asked what was going on, June told him bitterly, 'You'd better ask *her* that question, Dad. Seeing as she's the one who's to blame.'

'I don't want to be engaged to Johnny any more, Dad,' Molly admitted.

'Well, I did say I thought you was too young.'

'She hasn't told you everything, Dad. She's only got it into her head that she's in love with Eddie from next door.'

Molly bowed her head.

'Eddie's a decent lad,' her father pronounced, 'but it's bound to cause trouble if you go breaking your engagement with Johnny to tek up wi' him, lass.'

'That's exactly what I told her,' June announced triumphantly.

'It's all right for you,' Molly stormed back, losing her temper. 'You're the one who made me get engaged to Johnny, even when I didn't want to, just to suit your own ends, and it's yourself you're thinking about now, not me.'

June's face burned a dull shade of angry red. 'I suppose you've gone and told Eddie that, an' all, have you? That it were me as wanted you to get engaged?'

'What if I have? It's the truth.'

'Lassies, lassies,' their father protested unhappily, but neither of them paid any attention. Hostility and anger had suddenly replaced sisterly love and loyalty.

'I'm going to work,' June announced, standing up and ignoring Molly.

'I'm sorry, Dad,' Molly muttered before going to get her own coat and trailing after her sister.

''Ere, Molly, there's someone outside asking ter see yer,' Ruby announced, bursting into the room excitedly ten minutes after the dinner bell had rung. 'Said his name were Eddie.'

Immediately Molly's face went bright pink whilst June glared furiously at her.

Ignoring her sister, Molly ran to the door and down the stairs.

Eddie was standing outside, watching the door anxiously. The moment he saw her he put out the cigarette he had been smoking and hurried over to her.

'I've just come to tell you that I've had word that we're sailing today.'

'Oh, Eddie . . .' Her elation was instantly replaced by a dull dread.

'I didn't want ter go wi'out saying goodbye proper, like,' he told her, 'although I've told me Auntie Elsie to tell you that I'd gone.'

Molly looked at him with helpless yearning, longing to beg him to stay with her, but knowing that she couldn't. She was acutely conscious of the fact that the factory windows overlooked the small yard, and that no doubt if she were to turn round and look up, she would see the curious faces of her workmates looking down at her.

'Might be gone a bit longer this time,' he warned her, 'but wi' a bit o' luck I'll be home by Christmas.'

'*Christmas!*' Molly protested. 'That's weeks away!'

'I want you to wear this for me.' He reached into his pocket and brought out a fine chain supporting a small locket in the shape of a heart.

'Oh, Eddie . . .' Suddenly it didn't matter any more who could see them. This moment and Eddie were far too important.

'There's nothing I'd like more than to give yer a proper ring, Molly, but that'll have to wait until . . .' They looked at onc another, each knowing what the other was thinking.

Molly gave a small nod and told him quickly, 'I'll tell him as soon as he comes home.'

She could hardly bear it that he was leaving again so quickly, and on a sudden impulse she reached up on her toes and placed her lips against his, unable to let him go without physically showing him how much she loved him.

'Aw, Molly . . .' He hugged her so tightly she could hardly breathe, but that didn't matter, not with the big solid warmth of him all around her, holding her.

'I wish I could come down to the dock with you and see you off properly,' she whispered.

'Aye, well, best you don't, not this time . . . 'cos if you did I might be tempted not to go.'

He kissed her quickly and then released her, leaving her to watch him walk away. When he got to the end of the road he turned round and waved.

The busy bustle when she walked back into the room, all the girls apparently engaged in what they were doing and carefully avoiding looking at her, told its own story, Molly realised guiltily as she picked up the cup of tea she had been drinking before Eddie had arrived and took a quick defensive sip, even though it had gone cold and tasted of tannin.

'Well, I know what ter think when I see a girl who's already engaged – and to one of our brave soldier lads – mekking up ter another fella as bold as brass without any shame in her,' Irene announced condemningly to the room at large as she banged down her own cup and left the room, quickly followed by several other girls, including, Molly saw, her own sister.

In the silence that followed Irene's condemnation, Ruby came over to Molly and said sympathetically, 'Don't tek no notice of her, Molly. He looked a right 'andsome lad ter me.'

Hot tears filled Molly's eyes.

Jean, who was still walking out with Eddie's cousin Jim, looked uncertainly at her and then looked away as though not sure whether to sympathise with her or condemn her.

It was a relief when the bell rang, summoning them back to work. Molly was glad of the excuse her sewing gave her to keep her head bent over her machine.

'Seein' as how they've opened the Grafton Dance Hall up again, why don't we go there this Saturday? I'm getting fed up of staying in every night,' one of the girls called out above the noise of the machines.

'Ooh, yes,' Ruby agreed eagerly.

'Well, it's up to them as wants to go to mek up their own minds,' Irene chipped in. 'Not as most of us needs to guess who will want to go and who won't. There's some of us as has too much respect for them as we're promised to and who won't be here to want to go dancin' whilst they're fightin', and then there's some of us as doesn't,' she announced with a meaningful look at Molly. 'And, of course, there's them of us who wouldn't want to be seen in public wi' a girl who's bin seen kissing one lad whilst she's engaged to another.'

There was no point in her trying to defend herself or to point out that less than two months ago Irene had been perfectly happy to go dancing without her fiancé. Molly knew that she had been tried and judged by her peers, and found guilty. Irene was making it very plain what she thought of her, and Molly was acutely aware of the cold looks she was receiving from several of the other girls, as they followed Irene's lead. In a small enclosed society like theirs, where a young woman's reputation reflected on her family and her friends, people were often quick to judge and then exclude those who broke the rules.

'See what you've done? I hope you're happy now,' June hissed at Molly as they got off the bus and crossed the road, heading for home. 'And to think I didn't take that job at Napiers on account of me not wanting to leave you. I wish I had taken it now. It'll be all over the cul-de-sac what you've done,' said June angrily. 'And what my Frank's goin' to say about it I don't know! Proper shocked, he's going to be. And as for his mam—'

'If you don't want me to be your bridesmaid any more then I won't be,' Molly cut across her angry outburst.

'Oh, yes, and a fine lot of gossip that would cause, an' all. It's bad enough as it is, wi' out making it any worse.'

As they turned into the cul-de-sac, a small group of women who lived there were chatting together, but they broke off their conversation to turn and look at the sisters.

Molly forced herself to smile at them, flushing hotly when none of them smiled back, and one of the women even went so far as to grab hold of her son's hand and turn her back very deliberately on them.

'Looks like they've heard already,' June seethed.

They had almost drawn level with Frank's mother's house when unexpectedly the door opened and Doris Brookes came out to say sharply, 'If you've got a minute, please, June.'

Giving Molly a bitter 'I told you so' look, June reluctantly followed her future mother-in-law into the house, leaving Molly standing alone outside.

While deliberating whether or not to wait for her sister, Molly saw Sally Walker coming towards her wheeling her pram. When she saw Molly she checked and looked as though she was about to cross the road to avoid her, but then she changed her mind and came up to her.

'Well, Molly,' she announced forcefully, 'if what I've just been hearing from Pearl about you is true, I'm very disappointed in you. I never thought of you as the sort of girl who would do sommat like that. I'm grateful for you helping me when I was having me baby, but I can't forgive you this.'

Without giving Molly the opportunity to say anything, she wheeled the pram past her.

It seemed that the whole world was against Molly as she hurried into the kitchen of number 78, relieved to escape the censorious scrutiny of her neighbours. What she had done *was* wrong, she knew that, but when she had allowed June to convince her to remain engaged to Johnny she had had no idea what falling in love would be like or how it would make her feel.

Tears filled her eyes and ran down her face to drip onto the draining board as she reached for the kettle.

'Yoo-hoo . . .'

Molly shrank visibly as the kitchen door opened and Elsie came in, but she saw immediately from Eddie's auntie's face that she at least was sympathetically inclined towards her.

'Eh, Molly love,' she clucked, putting her arms round her and giving her a cuddle. 'What's to do?'

'Everyone's so angry with me because of me and Eddie, and me still being engaged to Johnny,' Molly wept.

'There, lass, don't tek on so. Of course there's them as disapproves – there's bound to be. But for meself, there's no one I'd sooner see married to our Eddie. I can see in yer eyes that you love him. Aye, and he loves you, an' all. And as for young Johnny . . .' she added, her voice taking on an unfamiliar note of disapproval.

'What?' Molly asked her uncertainly.

'It's not my place to say, and it's perhaps only a bit o' gossip anyways,' Elsie announced, mad-

186

deningly refusing to be drawn or to say any more, even though Molly pleaded with her to do so.

'No. Least said, soonest mended, lass. So did our Eddie get ter see yer then?'

Molly nodded her head, happiness illuminating her expression as she remembered the sweetness of their goodbye.

'Where's your June?'

'Frank's mam asked her to go in.'

'Aye, it'll be about the weddin', most like. I have heard as how Doris is worried that she's going to be shown up in front of them posh friends of hers.' Elsie gave an inelegant snort. 'Well, I might not be able to boast that I've bin a ward sister, but everyone who knows me knows that me cookin' is the best in the cul-de-sac, so she needn't worry that them friends of hers will be turnin' up their noses at it.'

Molly had to laugh, and she was still laughing a few seconds later when June came in, scowling darkly, taking her temper out on Molly as she declared, 'I wouldn't be laughin', if I was you, Molly, because you haven't got nowt to laugh about. I've just seen Sally Walker, and she was telling me about how shocked she was to hear what you'd bin up to. She says as how all the mothers in the cul-de-sac have taken right against you on account of it.'

'Oh, leave 'er alone, do, June,' Elsie defended Molly firmly. 'Poor lass can't help how she feels.'

'You wouldn't say that if it were your son she

were engaged to,' June retorted. 'Showing us up like that, and getting talked about behind our backs.'

'What did Frank's mam want then?' Elsie asked June determinedly, whilst Molly held her breath, dreading hearing June say that her future mother-in-law had called her into her house to complain about Molly's behaviour.

'Oh, nowt much,' June shrugged disinterestedly. 'She only wanted to ask about the wedding and to have a bit of a go at me, an' all, complaining that she hadn't been consulted about anything.'

'Aye, well, it's natural that she should want to know what's goin' on,' Elsie agreed cheerfully. 'So would I, an' all, if it were my lad as was marryin'. Luckily for me I'll be living right next door when our Eddie weds Molly here,' she added with a chuckle that brought an angry frown to June's face.

'Don't you go encouraging her, Elsie,' she stormed. 'And I'll thank you to remember that our Molly is engaged to Johnny.'

'Aye, well, she might be now,' Elsie answered her back, 'but she won't be for much longer, if what I've heard about him is true.'

'And what does that mean?' June demanded suspiciously.

Elsie shook her head. 'Like I've already told Molly, I ain't saying no more. I'm no gossip,' she sniffed virtuously. 'Unlike some folks about here.'

Once that comment would have been enough

to unite Molly and June in a shared grin of mutual understanding, but on this occasion June didn't even bother to look at her, Molly acknowledged miserably, as Elsie left.

TEN

Tenderly Molly touched the shimmering blue folds of the fabric Eddie had given her. June had flatly refused to allow her to use it to make herself a new bridesmaid's dress, claiming that Molly's relationship with Eddie had caused her enough trouble already.

June's dress, finished now, had been carefully folded away. With less than a month to go to the wedding, June was becoming increasingly on edge and anxious, and – or so it seemed to Molly – increasingly hostile about Molly's feelings for Eddie.

Molly had grown accustomed now to being ignored in the street by the other women from the cul-de-sac, but their coldness towards her still hurt.

With daylight saving time over, and the clocks put back, a grey darkness seemed to have settled over everything, exacerbated by the blackout. Most people who had to be out after dark now carried a torch with them, making sure to point its beam downwards.

'Instead of t'hospital being filled with folk wot have been bombed, it's filled with them as has fallen off of t'pavements,' Bert had complained pithily earlier in the week.

It made Molly smile to see the way in which Bert was steadfastly refusing to pay any attention to Alf's warnings and threats, claiming that since there hadn't been any air-raid sirens, there was no need to go into the shelters, which in turn meant that his dog was not going to panic and bite anyone out of fear.

'Poor old Bert.' The girls' father had shaken his head dubiously. 'It's all very well him arguing wi' Alf now, but once rationing comes in there'll be plenty of folk ready to complain about 'im feeding his dog whilst their kiddies are going wi'out.'

'But Bert feeds Rover on scraps, doesn't he?' Molly had protested.

'Aye, he does, but folks won't take account of that, Molly, if'n they gets their dander up. That's the nature of 'em, you see.'

The last of the sweet juicy tomatoes had long since been plucked from the vines in the allotments' greenhouses, and the cold dampness of the November air sent a mist swirling over the brown earth and a warning of colder weather to come.

Eddie was back at sea, his ship barely having had time to unload on its return before it was off again across the Atlantic, and Molly listened anxiously to every news bulletin, her stomach tightening with sick fear every time she heard the words 'the Atlantic'.

Everyone knew that Hitler had his U-boats patrolling the icy grey wastes of that ocean, hoping to destroy the merchant ships ploughing steadily to and fro across it, bringing into Britain much-needed supplies.

Although the girls at work had thawed slightly towards her, Molly was still conscious of their disapproval. The women in the cul-de-sac, though, whom she had always thought of as friends as well as neighbours, especially Sally Walker, were making it very clear that they did not intend to forgive her. She had been 'sent to Coventry', their backs turning to her whenever they saw her in the street.

No one, it seemed, sympathised with her apart from Elsie. Molly hadn't dared confide her misery to Anne, knowing that she too would disapprove.

Only her driving lessons were bringing a small ray of light and laughter to her days, since it had turned out, to her own astonishment, that she had what Mr Noakes had approvingly described as 'a natural aptitude' for driving. Seated beside him in his Wolseley, she had followed his brisk instruction to her to watch what he did, and then she had listened carefully whilst he explained to her about the gears.

'See this here,' he had commanded, motioning to Molly to get out of the now stationary car and stand beside the open driver's door whilst he demonstrated the use of the pedals to her. 'This first one is what we call the accelerator, this one next to it is the brake and this last one is called the clutch. ABC, that's what you've got to remember, ABC. And what you have to do once you've got the engine turned on is get the car in gear and you do that with the clutch.'

That lesson had been followed by a nerve-racking interlude during which Mr Noakes had lectured Molly on the importance of good clutch control. Despite that, she had still had the car kangaroo jumping all over the road the first time she had tried to put this lesson into practice. Now, though, she knew to the second when the clutch had bitten and she could change gear as smoothly as anything.

Even Mrs Wesley had given Molly a frosty smile on being told of her new accomplishment.

'Driving!' June had exclaimed when Molly had told her what she was doing. 'Getting ideas above your station, you are, my girl,' she had added, insisting, 'Tell her, Dad.'

But to Molly's relief their father had said, 'I reckon now that they've brought in conscription, it's a good thing if women do learn to drive, 'cos if Hitler does drop his blummin' bombs, they're going to be needin' someone as can drive ambulances and the like.'

'I don't know if I'll ever be that good, Dad,' Molly had protested.

'So what will you be driving then?' June had demanded.

'The WVS are going to have sommat as they call mobile kitchens,' Molly had explained. 'That Lord Woolton has designed them.'

'And what's them when they're at home?' June had derided her.

'It's a van with a bit of a kitchen at the back so as we can drive them into bombed places and make sure that folk can have a cuppa and a bite to eat,' Molly had explained patiently.

The driving was in small part helping take her mind off Johnny. But now, with less than a month to go before Frank and Johnny came home on leave, before being sent into action, Molly was becoming increasingly apprehensive. Over and over again inside her head she had rehearsed the words she would have to say to Johnny. Nothing could change her mind about her feelings for Eddie, she knew that, but she also knew that she was scared of telling Johnny their relationship was over.

What would she do if he refused to accept that their engagement was at an end – if he lashed out at her with his fists, or threatened her, she worried, as she hurried back from her Saturday afternoon driving lesson.

The cul-de-sac rang with the sounds of the activities of its children, most of whom had now been brought back home by their mothers when the threatened bombs had failed to appear. Over the last few weeks, the sound of children playing, quarrelling and laughing had increased in the Edge

Hill streets once more. Smoke curled upwards from chimneys to hang on the still autumn air. A handful of little girls, skirts tucked into their knickers, were skipping, one at either end of the rope, whilst the others jumped in and out of it in time to the words they were singing.

'Wallflowers, wallflowers, growing up so high, we're all little children, we all have to die.'

Molly paused to watch, shuddering inwardly as she listened to the familiar schoolyard songs she and June had once sung, aware now as she had not been then of the dark warning of the words.

'Excepting little Betty, and she's the youngest child, half a shame – half a shame – turn your face to the wall again.'

A few boys were pretending to fight, firing imaginary guns, one of them almost running into Molly. She laughed as she recognised Pearl's younger boy, glad to be released from the darkness of her own thoughts of war and death, reaching out to steady him.

But instead of returning her smile, he pulled away from her and said fiercely, 'Me mam says we're to have nowt to do with you on account of what you've done.'

White-faced, Molly watched him dart away, oblivious to his mother's approach until Pearl had drawn level with her.

'I'll thank you not to go interfering wi' my kiddies, if you don't mind,' she began sharply. 'I don't want you goin' tittle-tattlin' about them to them

WVS friends of yours, like you done with poor Daisy's little lad. Shamed her, you did, and no mistake, letting it out that they'd had to be brung home on account of wettin' their beds when they was evacuated. Not that either o' mine would go wettin' their beds, mind . . .'

Molly stared at her and then demanded, 'What do you mean? I haven't said anything about Daisy's children to anyone.'

Pearl started to frown. 'Well, that's not wot we 'eard. First Daisy goes rushin' off to bring her kiddies back wi'out saying anything, and then Beryl from number 71 starts tellin' everyone who'll listen that they had to come back on account of wettin' their beds. Of course, it didn't tek long for us to put two and two together and guess that it had to be you wot had bin talkin' about it, wot with you being in the WVS an' all. Ashamed of yourself, you want to be,' Pearl denounced her roundly.

'Pearl, it wasn't me,' Molly insisted. 'We *were* told that one of the children had had an . . . an accident and was being sent home, but Mrs Wesley didn't mention any names. And even if she had,' Molly lifted her chin and said firmly, 'we have to swear an oath to keep confidential things confidential.'

'Are you saying that it wasn't you who let it out about Daisy's lad?'

'It certainly wasn't,' Molly assured her.

'Well, I don't know now what to say.' Pearl was suddenly frowning as she said slowly, ''Ere, I've just remembered, doesn't Beryl's cousin's lad walk out wi' the maid wot works for that Mrs Wesley?'

Molly shook her head. 'I don't know. I don't know her.'

''Ere, Molly, if it was her that told on Daisy, then I'm right sorry we've bin thinking it were you,' Pearl told her gruffly.

Molly felt there was no point telling Pearl that she had assumed the crime she was being punished for was that of falling in love with Eddie.

'I'm goin' to have a word wi' Beryl and get to the bottom of this. If'n it weren't you then—'

'It wasn't,' Molly interrupted her quietly. 'And I'd just as soon forget the whole thing, Pearl. I don't want any more upset, not with our June's wedding getting so close, an' all.'

'You're a good lass, Molly,' Pearl told her, looking uncomfortable. 'I never thought as it would be you, but Daisy were that upset. All ready for the weddin', are yer now? Only if there's owt as any of us can do . . . My hubby has a contact as he can get a bit of beer and the like from, if your June wants me to have a word wi' him.'

'I'll tell her.' Molly accepted this olive branch, although privately she was not sure that the vicar would welcome 'contraband' alcohol being served in the church hall.

'You're looking mighty pleased with yourself,' June commented when Molly walked into the kitchen.

'I've just seen Pearl,' Molly told her. 'You'll

never guess what, June. They've been thinking that it was me that let it slip that Daisy had been told to bring her little lad back from North Wales on account of him wettin' the bed. That's why they've all been so off with me.'

'Don't talk daft.'

'It's true,' Molly insisted. 'Pearl has just told me. Oh, and she said that her George can get some beer and that for the wedding, if you want him to.'

'Oh, aye, and I can just imagine what would happen if we let George and that lot bring it in. The vicar would have sommat to say about that – aye, and Frank's mam as well.'

Molly had detected a slight softening in the hostilities between June and Doris Brookes in the run-up to the wedding, and Frank's mother had even offered June the loan of her best lace table-cloth. Toasting her toes in front of the back-room fire, Molly allowed herself to smile properly for the first time in weeks. She was pleased to have the reason for Pearl and the others' recent frostiness towards her out in the open, and even more pleased that it wasn't anything to do with her relationship with Eddie.

'I can't believe that by this time next week Frank will be home,' June smiled happily, whilst Molly shifted her heavy shopping basket onto her other arm. Both girls were well wrapped up in their winter coats against the raw November weather, their hands and ears protected by the brightly coloured gloves and scarves Molly had knitted from leftover scraps of wool.

'We were lucky to get that suet,' June commented. 'The Co-op didn't have any at all, and they were out of sugar an' all.'

'I saw Pearl this morning and she said her George had got a load of tinned stuff from some warehouse that had had a fire. Nothing wrong with it, but all the labels had come off. She said she'd let us have a couple of dozen tins.'

'Dad said that one of his chickens was missing. He reckons someone has taken it for the pot.'

The two sisters looked ruefully at one another.

'Gawd knows what it's going to be like when rationing does come in,' June grimaced.

'At least we've got everything sorted out for the wedding,' Molly offered comfortingly, but stopped speaking when she saw Johnny's sisters walking purposefully towards her.

'We was just on our way round your house,' Jennifer announced meaningfully.

'Our mam wants ter have a word with yer about our Johnny. She said to tell yer as it were important.'

June's mouth tightened. Although she had ceased to criticise her, Molly knew she had not been forgiven.

'I'll come round later,' she offered as she tried to hide both her reluctance and her apprehension.

'It'd be best if you was to come now.'

'We'll both come,' June announced firmly.

Molly could see June's nose wrinkling in distaste at the acrid sour smell of bad drains permeating the street where Johnny's family lived. Stalwartly she managed not to follow her sister's example, for fear of offending Johnny's sisters.

'Going down the dance hall tonight, are yer?' Deirdre asked them both.

'Me and Molly have got far too much to do for that, what with my Frank and her Johnny coming home soon,' June told them, giving Molly a warning look.

'I can't see our Johnny coming when he finds out what's happened,' Jennifer muttered half under her breath, causing her sister to give her a sharp nudge.

'I knew sommat like this would happen,' June whispered angrily to Molly, but in a low voice so that the other girls couldn't hear. 'I told you it would get back to Johnny's family about you and Eddie.'

Molly could feel her face burning, as she and June stood behind Johnny's sisters and waited for them to open the door.

'It's us, Mam,' Deirdre shouted, 'and we've brought Molly back wi' us like you told us.'

The two girls then disappeared into the dark recesses of the house, leaving June and Molly standing in the hallway.

It seemed to take for ever for Johnny's mother finally to appear, looking even more pale and worn than when Molly had last seen her. Wiping her hands on her apron, she pushed open the warped door to the front room, ushering them both inside.

'I'm right sorry to have to do this, but I couldn't think of what else to do. We only heard about what's bin going on yesterday, and a real old shock it's given me, I can tell you. What our Johnny's going to say when he's told I don't know, and he will have to be told, that's for sure. The whole street's talking about it already.'

Molly couldn't bring herself to look at June. She knew all too well what her sister would be thinking.

'Eeh, Molly, I just don't know what ter say to yer, lass. I know yer a decent, well-brought-up lass and I'm hopin' that yer will do wot's right . . . aye, and I'm hopin' that our Johnny will do wot's right an' all, because if'n he doesn't—'

'Have yer told her yet, Mam?' Jennifer interrupted her mother, putting her head round the door. 'Only they've come back . . .'

There was a commotion in the hallway and then a man strode into the room, almost dragging a young and very pregnant girl with him.

'She's no daughter o' mine no more,' he announced belligerently. 'She can stay here with you from now on, seein' as it's your Johnny that's got her like this, 'cos she ain't staying under my roof.'

The girl had started to cry, whilst Johnny's mother looked on helplessly.

'Stop that racket, will yer?' the man demanded, cuffing the side of the girl's head angrily. 'You should have had more sense than ter let 'im get into yer knickers in the first place. If I'd bin at home ter see what was goin' on instead of in bleedin' prison, I'd 'ave soon sorted 'im out. He'd have had a kick up his backside that would have sent him into the middle of next year, and no mistake. No one messes wi' my daughter and leaves her in the family way and unwed, and just as soon as he gets off that train next week, he's going into church to make a respectable woman of my lass.'

'Are you trying to say that Johnny is the father of your daughter's child?' June demanded fiercely, squaring her shoulders and taking charge.

'And 'oo might you be?'

'Johnny is engaged to my sister,' June announced.

'Oh ho, he is, is he? And is she in the family way, an' all, then?'

'Certainly not,' said June.

'Aye, well, in that case my Doreen is gonna be the one he weds, because there's no way she's gonna be making me the grandfather of a bastard. Shut up your noise, yer silly cow,' he commanded the sobbing girl.

'Oh, Molly, I'm that sorry,' Johnny's mother was saying pitifully.

'Not 'alf as sorry as that bleedin' son of yours is gonna be. I'm warning yer that he'd better do the right thing by my Doreen 'cos if he doesn't

202

he's gonna know about it, even if it gets me back in bleedin' prison.'

'Of course Johnny must do the right thing by your daughter,' Molly agreed, unable to believe what was happening.

'Eeh, lass, but that's right generous of you, ter be so understandin',' Johnny's mother smiled in relief. 'I know how you must be feelin'.'

'Aye, and so do I,' June agreed meaningfully as she looked at Molly.

'Well!' June announced half an hour later after they had left Johnny's mother's house. 'Aren't you the lucky one, an' all?'

'I wouldn't have been very lucky if I had loved Johnny, though, would I?' Molly couldn't resist pointing out sturdily. 'That girl was nearly eight months pregnant, according to what Johnny's sisters were saying, and that means—'

'I know what it means, thank you very much,' June stopped her hastily, before adding, 'I can tell you, I'm going to have a thing or two to say to my Frank when he gets home.'

'It isn't Frank's fault,' Molly objected, easing the ache out of her arm from carrying her shopping basket.

'Mebbe not, but he must have known what Johnny were up to wi' that other lass, and he never said anything to me about it when I told him to bring a friend along with him to make up a foursome with you.'

203

Molly hid a small smile. It was typical of her sister that now that the truth about Johnny's reprehensible behaviour had come out, she was blaming someone else for introducing him to Molly. But right now the unexpected turn of events was making Molly feel so light-hearted and filled with relief that all she could think about was her eagerness for Eddie to come home so that she could tell him that she was free of her engagement. If there were such things as guardian angels, hers had most certainly been looking down on her and had heard her prayers, Molly decided gratefully.

ELEVEN

'Your sister looks so happy, Molly,' Anne whispered as the two girls sat together watching Frank whirling June round in his arms to the sound of the lively music coming from Brian Leadbetter's accordion.

'It was a lovely wedding,' Anne added warmly, 'and your dress is so pretty. The colour matches your eyes perfectly.'

Molly smiled, gently smoothing the blue fabric. She had been so determined to make up the fabric that had been Eddie's gift to her into a new bridesmaid's dress that she had sat up virtually all night in order to get it finished. Her fingers had ached painfully most of the next day but it had been worth it. She just wished Eddie could see her in it.

Deprived of his intended best man on account of Johnny's furiously angry future father-in-law practically dragging Johnny from the train the moment it drew into Lime Street station, Frank had asked Ronnie Walker – who, as luck would have it, had also been granted Christmas leave – to take his place.

Because of that, Molly had cheerfully given up her official 'right' to claim Ronnie as a dance partner, insisting instead that he and Sally enjoyed some fun.

The news in November that butter rationing was to be introduced a week before the wedding had thrown June into a panic, but the neighbours had rallied round and provided enough food for the wedding breakfast.

Watching her new brother-in-law looking so proudly at June now as they danced together brought tears to Molly's eyes. She was desperately disappointed that Eddie couldn't be here, but he had told her that he hoped to be home for Christmas. Happily she hugged to her the memory of the precious few hours they had managed to snatch together earlier in the month when his ship had docked.

They had gone to the cinema, cuddling up on the back row, exchanging whispered confidences in between kisses and declarations of their love, Molly virtuously saying 'no' when Eddie had whispered in her ear that since her father and June were both out, they could go back to number 78.

Eddie had burst out laughing when she had given him a graphic description of the scene at Johnny's mother's house, with Doreen's irate father, but he had stopped laughing when Molly had confided in him that Doreen's father had been a recent inmate of one of His Majesty's prisons, shaking his head and saying that Johnny had better make sure he didn't get on the wrong side of his future father-in-law.

'It could be Christmas before we're back,' he had told Molly, adding warningly, 'but when I do get back, I'll be asking you to set a date, Molly, and I won't want to be waitin' long for us to get married. Not with this war on.'

Immediately Molly had pressed her finger against his lips, pleading with him not to remind her of the dangers he faced.

She couldn't wait for him to get back. John and Elsie had both made it clear to her how much they were looking forward to welcoming her into their family. A small secret smile curved her lips as she remembered the passionate kiss she and Eddie had exchanged when they had said goodbye. The intimacies she had been so reluctant to share with Johnny were intimacies she couldn't wait to share with Eddie once they were married.

'Oh look, do!' Anne exclaimed delightedly. 'Isn't that your dad dancing with Frank's mam?'

Molly laughed. Frank's mother had unbent enough to give her approval of June's frock, and everyone had seen the gusto with which her posh friends had tucked into the food.

'Folks like that don't know how to cook proper,' had been Elsie's comfortable comment. 'All they know is posh shop-bought food. That cousin of

Doris Brookes's said as how my tongue was the best he 'ad ever tasted,' she had boasted to Molly earlier.

'Dad doesn't look very comfortable,' Molly giggled.

Her father was a couple of inches shorter than Frank's mother and a good deal thinner.

'It's like watching a Mersey tug taking on a big liner,' Anne's brother, Richard, observed, laughing.

'I heard the best man talking to your brother-in-law, Molly. He was saying that he's heard that more of our troops are to be moved out to France.'

'Ronnie's in the regular army,' Molly explained, looking over to where Ronnie and Frank were now deep in conversation. 'And his unit's already over there. They've given him leave to come home for Christmas and to see the baby.'

'Excuse me, girls,' Anne's brother smiled as he stood up and looked meaningfully towards Frank and Ronnie, 'I think I'll go over and join them.'

'Rick's heard that he'll be going out to Nantes any time,' Anne explained quietly once he had gone. 'The Royal Engineers are based there and some of the RAF ground crew like Richard.

'It's still so hard to believe we really are at war,' she continued. 'I know there've been enemy planes up at Scapa Flow and down on the Thames Estuary, but somehow it is hard to believe it's all real, despite our practising our drills and doing all the things we've been told to do.'

'It is real, though. Rationing has started,' Molly

reminded her. 'And we've lost ships,' she added in a lower voice.

Anne reached out and squeezed her hand in silent acknowledgement of Molly's anxiety. Molly had told her about the ending of her engagement and, to her relief, when she had learned the reason why, Anne's hostility towards Molly's love for Eddie had thawed immediately and completely.

'Come on, Molly, it's your turn to dance with Frank,' June laughed, puffing slightly as she and Frank came to a halt in front of them.

'Thanks for everything you've done for June, Molly,' said Frank.

Molly shook her head, matching her steps to his as they started to dance. 'We've all done our bit, Frank.'

She liked Frank. He was a big, easy-going young man with a kind heart, whom she suspected her sister would bully unmercifully, much as she guessed his mother already did.

The newly married couple were to have two nights in a hotel in Blackpool, before returning home for Christmas. Since there was no room for them at number 78, they were to share Frank's old room at his mother's whilst he was on leave – not that June was too happy about the prospect of that.

'I'd have sooner rented a place of our own,' she had told Molly, 'but Frank says that there's no point, with him going away.'

* * *

Molly smiled with sleepy satisfaction as she snuggled deeper into her bed. In the end all the wedding guests had gone to Lime Street station to wave Frank and June off on their honeymoon, laughing and joking as they did so, before returning to the village hall to clear everything away. The perfect day could only have been made more perfect by Eddie's presence. But it wouldn't be long now before he was home, Molly reminded herself happily.

PART TWO

Christmas 1939

Part Two

Christmas 1939

ONE

'And then last night, when we were at the Tower Ballroom, they gave out that they were going to play a special dance number for all the newlyweds, seeing as how they'd heard there was so many couples honeymooning in Blackpool. The dance floor was that packed you could hardly move, and, of course, wi' them great size eleven feet of his, Frank were standing on me toes . . .'

'Oh, size eleven, is it?' Uncle Joe broke into June's monologue with a knowing wink.

'Give over, do,' she gave back, before calling out, 'Molly, where's that tea? I'm dying for a proper brew – that hotel tea was awful.'

The newlyweds had arrived back in the cul-de-sac just over half an hour earlier, and June had talked non-stop ever since, whilst Frank had looked on indulgently. He was obviously still as besotted with his new bride as he was when they left for Blackpool.

'I'm on me way with it,' Molly assured June

when she came into the kitchen. Her cheeks were flushed from bustling around in the heat from the oven, buttering the scones she had made earlier in the day, in between laying out their late mother's best tea service, bought at Preston Pot Fair, the year before Molly's own birth.

'What's all this for?' June asked, pushing the door to so that they couldn't be heard by the others.

'You, of course,' Molly told her, pausing to wipe her hands on her apron as she did a quick count of the scones, wondering if there were enough to go round with so many neighbours having called in to see the newly married couple.

'Ah, you daft bugger.' June shook her head, but Molly could see the pink tinge of pleasure warming her skin.

'I wanted to do something a bit special, like, to welcome you and Frank home, June,' she said softly. 'I've missed you. I know that we've had a few words these last few months, specially about Johnny, and me joining the WVS, but . . .'

As Molly's voice trailed away, June put her arms around her and gave her a fierce hug.

'We're sisters, you and me, our Molly, and nothing can ever change that, specially not a few cross words. When our mam died it was just you and me and our dad, and I had to tek charge a bit, like, me being the eldest, an' all. I felt it were me duty to look out for you just like Mam would have done. I know you thought it was being a bit hard on you, like, with Johnny and that, but I was just trying to do me best for you,' June told her earnestly.

For a moment Molly was too overwhelmed to say or do anything other than look at her pink-cheeked sister, suddenly seeing her through more mature eyes. They were equals now and even June was acknowledging that fact.

'Oh, give over looking at us like that, do,' June protested, as tears welled in Molly's eyes, and she hugged June tightly.

'Where's that tea? I'm dying for a brew to wet me whistle.'

Both sisters burst out laughing as they heard Uncle Joe's complaint outside the door.

'Here, give me the teapot; you bring the tray,' June ordered, adding wryly, 'I'll tell you something, Molly, I'm not looking forward to having to sleep over at Frank's mam's tonight. I'm not saying that I'm not right glad that I married Frank, because I am, but having to live with his mother until we can find somewhere of us own to rent is something I could do without. It doesn't seem right somehow, me not being here at number 78. With you and Dad. Even though me and Frank are married now, this house is still me home.'

'I miss you too, June. But you won't have to stay with Frank's mam for long,' Molly consoled her.

'I hope not. You should have seen her face when I told her that me and Frank would be having our

Christmas dinner here. Mind you, she soon changed her tune when she heard that our Auntie Violet was sending a nice big turkey up from Nantwich for our Christmas dinner.'

'It came yesterday, with one for Elsie as well,' Molly informed her. 'Me and Elsie spent all morning taking out the giblets and making a bit of stuffing for it.'

'Well, mind you don't start cooking it until I'm here. I don't want you burning it and showing me up in front of Frank's mam,' June warned her, reverting to her normal bossy elder-sister role. Molly smiled. Her sister might be married now with more responsibilities, but she would always give Molly her twopenn'orth, and Molly wouldn't have it any other way.

It was late afternoon before all the well-wishers had left, Frank having been dispatched to bring his mother round to join in the merrymaking, only to return with the information that she was suffering from a headache and had gone to lie down.

'Headache, my foot,' June protested angrily to Molly as the two sisters carefully washed their mother's tea set whilst Frank and their father sat talking about the war in the parlour. 'If you ask me, she was just pretending to be poorly.'

'Oh, no, June, surely she wouldn't do that,' Molly replied. The steam from the hot washing-up water had turned her cheeks pink and a few stray curls clung damply to her forehead, whilst the pinny she was wearing emphasised the slenderness of her waist.

'You don't know her like I do, Molly,' June retorted. 'I've already told Frank that I'll not stand for his mam trying to tell me what to do like she does him. He's a married man now, and he's got a wife to think about, and the sooner his mother knows that the better.

'Me and my Frank had best be on our way,' June told her when the tea set had been carefully put away in the china cupboard in the front room. 'I'll come over early tomorrow to give you a hand with everything. Eeh, Molly . . .'

To Molly's surprise, she saw that June's eyes had filled with tears.

'It doesn't seem right somehow, me not being here on Christmas Eve. Do you remember when you was little how we allus used to hang up our stockings together?'

Molly nodded her head, remembering those childhood Christmases and their innocent happiness. They never had much money but there was always a turkey on the table and stockings hung above the fireplace, which would be full come Christmas morning. The festive season had never lost its magic for Molly. She still felt like a child every year, creeping downstairs as dawn gave way to the early morning light.

'I knew, of course, that there was no Santa, but of course I had to pretend I still believed in him because of you. I knew it was what our mam would have wanted me to do.'

'One year you took my sugar mouse and put your dates in my stocking instead,' Molly remembered with a chuckle.

'I never.' June tried to look innocent but the corners of her mouth were twitching.

'Yes, you did,' Molly laughed back, and then they were crying and laughing and holding on to each other as tightly as they could, reminiscing about the Christmases they had shared as young girls.

'You're sure then about Eddie, are you?' June demanded as they recovered themselves.

Molly nodded so vigorously that her curls bounced, her blue eyes shining with love and conviction. 'I know he's the one for me, June.'

'How long will it be before he's back?'

'He said that he hoped he'd be home for Christmas, but obviously that's not going to happen now. Maybe it will be before the new year,' Molly told her.

It was almost midnight. June and Frank had left to go to Frank's mother's, and Molly looked tiredly round the spick-and-span kitchen, checking to make sure she had left nothing undone.

'Come on, lass,' said her father. 'It's time you was in bed, otherwise Santa might not come.'

Molly smiled lovingly at him as she took off her apron. 'I want everything to be right for our

June tomorrow, Dad, what with Frank's mam going to be here.'

'Eeh, but you're just like your mam, Molly, allus worrying about others. Aye, and you look like 'er an' all,' he added gruffly. 'A right bonny girl was my Rosie. Thought that the minute I set eyes on her, I did. It was in Ma Wheeler's pie shop that I first saw her, standing waiting to be served. I knew straight away that she were the one for me. Come over from Ireland, she had, to stay with her auntie, after she lost her mam and dad. I'd not long bin living in Liverpool meself then. Come here looking for work, I had, aye, and bin lucky to be took on by the railways. I was living in digs then down on Daffodil Street and it turned out that your mam was living just round the corner. I asked her if I could call on her and she told me that I could. Walking out for two years, we was, before I were earning enough for us to get married. We were that proud when we paid our first week's rent on number 78. I can still see your mam's face now when we came to look round and she saw that it had its own bathroom. I told meself then that I'd find the money to pay the rent even if I had to work round the clock to get it. Never a day goes by wi'out me thinking about her, and even more so at this time of year. She loved Christmas.'

'You must have loved her so much,' Molly whispered. She had heard how her mother and father had met dozens of times, but she never grew tired of the story. She had grown up without her mother, and over the years had learned to accept her absence, but now, loving Eddie as she did, she recognised how very hard her mother's death must have been for her father.

'Aye, I did. And you think on about that, lass,' her father told her. 'I knew the moment I met your mam that she were the one, and I reckon that you tek after me that way, Molly. So you mek sure you listen to what's here inside yer in future,' he urged her, touching his own chest, 'and not what other folk tell yer to do. Our June – now, she's different. She's got more of a practical head on her shoulders, just like me sister.'

'Oh, Dad,' Molly choked, 'I'm sorry I've caused everyone so much trouble, but I do truly love Eddie.'

'Aye, lass, I can see that. I've bin worrying about you these last weeks, I admit. I could see as sommat were wrong, and I'm right glad that everything's bin sorted out now.'

It was the longest speech she could ever remember her father making to her. She ran over to him and hugged him fiercely. She knew how lucky she and June were to have their father. Never once in the whole of their lives had he said an unkind or sharp word to them, never mind taken his belt to them.

'All I want is for the two of you to be happy like me and your mam was,' he told her. 'Best thing that ever happened to me, meeting your mam were, and I shall want to hear that this young man of yours thinks the same about you an' all.'

Molly was so tired she could barely climb the stairs after she had bade her father good night and Happy Christmas. She paused as she opened her bedroom door, her eyes widening in disbelief as she saw the small stocking hanging from the mantelpiece, her tiredness suddenly vanishing, her eyes sparkling with happiness.

'Oh, June,' Molly whispered to herself as she ran over to the fireplace and removed the sock, just as eagerly as if she were still a child. She could feel the nuts stored in its toe and something round and hard, which she suspected would be an apple. There was a pencil too – a reminder of childhood Christmases of the past when Molly would laugh with glee when presented with another coloured pencil for her collection.

She sat down on the bed, both laughing and weeping. It was so typical of June – always so touchy on the outside and so loving on the inside.

June had sworn that just because she was married that didn't mean that anything was going to change. She had said that she and Frank would find somewhere to rent close by, and that with Frank in the army she would probably end up spending more time in her old home than her new one, but Molly knew that June was making those assurances for herself as much as for her, and that they both knew that their old set-up as older and younger sister, bound together by the loss of their mother in a relationship in which June took charge and gave the orders, and Molly obeyed them, had already gone. She had outgrown her childhood need to have June 'look out' for her, Molly knew, but if anything she loved her sister more now that they had to look out for each other.

She undressed quickly after washing in the chilly bathroom, burrowing into her small bed, and luxuriating in the warmth of the hot-water bottle she had put there earlier, squeezing her eyes tightly closed so that she could think about Eddie.

Eddie. She couldn't wait for him to come home. She touched the golden heart he had given her, a small secret half girl's, half woman's smile curving her mouth as she dreamed of being with him and of the future they would share.

Excitement and longing bubbled up inside her, but it was different from what she had known as a child on Christmas Eve. She wondered what next Christmas would bring. Hopefully peace and married life for her and Eddie.

Restless, she tossed and turned, thinking of the presents she had made and wrapped so lovingly and which were now carefully tucked beneath her bed: a warm muffler and a pair of fingerless gloves for her father to wear through the winter when he worked on the allotment; a pretty tray cloth she had embroidered for June, ready for when she got her own home; some handkerchiefs for Elsie next door; and, best of all, the two pairs of thick warm socks she had knitted for Eddie from the oiled wool she had unpicked from an old fisherman's sweater she had bought from a second-hand market stall.

'Oh, Eddie,' she whispered lovingly. She couldn't wait for the time to come when they would spend Christmas together as man and wife.

'Listen up at the fellas putting the world to rights,' Sally Walker laughed, cocking her head in the direction of the parlour that Christmas morning.

'Aye, well, they'll have to talk up a bit to hear themselves over Frank's mam's snoring,' June grinned. 'How many glasses of Elsie's sloe gin did you give her, Molly?'

The three girls were in the kitchen washing up the dishes from their Christmas dinner, whilst Frank's mother slept off the effects of her after-dinner drink, whilst supposedly keeping an eye on Sally and Ronnie's baby, Tommy. When Sally had told Molly that they would be on their own for Christmas because there wasn't any room for them with their families in Manchester, Molly had invited them to come round and join in their own festivities.

'I dunno how I kept me face straight when Frank's mam started telling them bawdy jokes,' Sally giggled.

'Huh, don't be fooled by her,' June complained. 'Got a face like thunder most of the time. Done nothing but boss me about, she has, and I'm fair sick of it. The sooner the war is over, and him and me get a place of our own, the better.'

'Well, she has got a bit of a reputation for having a sharp tongue,' Sally agreed, 'but I haven't forgotten how good she were to me when I were having baby. I don't mind bettin' that you'll see a change in her once you and Frank have a little 'un, June.'

'Aye, well, when we do she'd better not start trying to interfere, 'cos I won't stand for it,' June said crossly.

The combination of the hot kitchen, a glass of sloe gin and the conviviality they had all shared around the dinner table had brought a pretty flush to all three young female faces and the kind of mood that led to shared confidences.

'I dunno if it's on account of this war and living for the moment or what, but my Ronnie has been that keen on having his you-know-whats whilst he's bin home that you'd think we was newly married,' Sally informed Molly and June frankly, with a small giggle. 'I've told him that I don't want to be left with another kiddie on the way, not while he's away.'

'No, me neither,' June agreed. 'Not that my Frank isn't very mindful of what he's doing,' she added, blushing self-consciously.

'Oh ho, "mindful", is it?' Sally ribbed her, grinning. 'Well, you wait until he comes back from the pub late on a Friday night, wanting his nuptials – he won't be so "mindful" then, you mark my words. I remember when we was first married my Ronnie used to give me this look, and quick as you like he'd have me upstairs, and out of me knickers that fast . . .'

'Oh, he never,' June protested, before confiding, 'Me and my Frank was in bed every night before ten when we was on our honeymoon and some afternoons as well. One tea time the landlady came up and knocked on the door when we was . . . you know, and he called out to her that we was checking that the blackout worked!'

'I can't see you gettin' away with that at his mother's, June,' Sally laughed. 'You'll have to come up with sommat else. Whilst your Frank's coming up with sommat of his own.'

'Oooh, cheek! I don't want none of that kind of talk in front of our Molly, Sally,' June protested, suddenly remembering her younger sister was in the same room. 'It's not fitting, her not being married yet.'

From their position as married women, Sally and June exchanged smugly knowing looks, whilst Molly blushed furiously. Whilst she no longer envied her sister her happiness with Frank, she couldn't help enviously imagining sharing the married intimacies June and Sally were describing with Eddie.

'Well, from what I've seen, it won't be long before Molly's gettin' wed herself,' Sally relented, giving Molly an arch look. 'We've all seen how keen Eddie is on her. And her on him!

'You're miles better off wi'out that Johnny, Molly,' Sally continued. 'A real wild 'un he is, from what my Ronnie has said. Aye, and that lass he's got in the family way isn't the only one he's bin messin' with, by all accounts. He were even givin' me the eye at one stage! Mind you, there's no denying that he's a handsome-lookin' lad wi' a bit of a way about him. I've heard as his dad were just the same. A real good looker, wi' enough blarney in him to get into a nun's knickers. That sort's all right for a bit o' fun but when it comes to settling down a girl needs a good steady chap she can depend on. 'Ere, June, have you put those mince pies in the oven?'

'Oh Gawd, I'd forgotten,' June groaned, grabbing for the tray of pies they'd made with precious butter and flour rations. 'We've got half of Chestnut Close coming round 'ere tonight, so we'd better crack on and get the supper sorted out ready.'

Molly had never known a Christmas Day pass so quickly. Whilst Sally took baby Tommy upstairs for a feed, she and June worked side by side preparing a cold buffet.

'I just hope that John from next door remembers that he said he'd bring along some beer, because Dad and Uncle Joe haven't held back this afternoon.'

'He will do,' Molly reassured June. 'And Elsie has promised to bring a couple of jellies.'

'We was lucky that Aunt Violet sent us that turkey,' June admitted. 'Mind you, when I saw it last night I was worried that it were going to be too big for the oven. I didn't eat hardly any breakfast so as to save my appetite. It felt that funny this morning, waking up at Frank's mam's and not here. There was no stockings put up there, for one thing, and Frank's mam had bin to church before I was even up. Frank got up early to go wi' her so I didn't get no nice cuppa in bed like we always have. Mind you, I did tell Frank that I would be wanting me and him to go to church wi' you and our dad, so he ended up having to go twice. There's no going downstairs in a dressing gown there like we do here neither. She doesn't approve of that, and she wouldn't let Frank bring me up a cuppa neither 'cos drinking tea in bed is something else she doesn't hold with.' June sighed before adding, 'That sounds like Sally coming back downstairs. I'll stay here and finish off, if you want to go up and get tidy.'

As she brushed her hair at her dressing table, Molly touched her heart necklace through the tartan fabric of her best winter dress. All the worry and upset of the last few weeks had caused her to lose weight so that the tartan dress was now a little bit loose on the waist. Molly had cinched in the spare fabric with a little black belt. So much had changed since last Christmas, and so much more was going to change. This time next year she, like June, would be sharing Christmas with

227

her husband. The only shadow darkening her life now was that of the war. Molly shivered inwardly, praying that it would soon be over and their lives could return to normal. Neither Sally nor June had said a word about their fears for their soldier husbands, but Molly had seen the looks they'd exchanged during the King's speech, and she had seen too the way that June had clutched tightly at Frank's hand as if frightened that if she loosened her grip, he would vanish into thin air.

An hour later Molly had no time to think or worry about anything other than how to stop her sides aching from laughing at Uncle Joe's jokes, covering her ears when the men started singing 'Roll Out the Barrel'.

Uncle Joe had just struck up another tune when someone banged on the front door.

'If it's that Hitler, tell 'im to go and salute himself,' one wag yelled out, cheered on by the other men, whilst Molly struggled through the press of people filling the small house and opened the door.

Alf Davies was standing on the step, wearing his ARP uniform.

'Oh, it's you, Mr Davies. Happy Christmas,' Molly said uncomfortably.

'Aye, just checkin' up to mek sure that everyone's observing the blackout,' he told her brusquely.

''Oo is it, lass?' Molly's father asked.

'It's Mr Davies, Dad—' Molly started to tell him before Alf interrupted, 'Come round to check up on the blackout. I could see a light coming from here.'

''Ere, Molly, shut that door, will yer?' Ronnie called out, coming into the hall with Frank.

Frank immediately sized up the situation and said quietly, 'You wouldn't begrudge two fighting men a bit of fun before they go off to war, would you, Alf?'

'Rules are rules,' the ARP man insisted, 'and if there's any light showing then it's a three-pound fine.'

Molly looked towards her father, who had just entered the hallway, and gave him an anguished look. Three pounds was almost half his weekly pay.

Several men had crowded into the hallway now, and Molly could hear their angry mutter.

'Here, Alf, get this down yer,' Ronnie Walker invited, thrusting a small glass of sloe gin into the other man's hand. 'It's a cold night and a thankless job you've got on, I reckon. But don't you go blaming Albert or his lasses if'n there's a bit o' light showing – not that I'm saying there was, mind. I reckon it were likely me as done it when I looked out of the window to see if it were snowing. None of us here wants to give Jerry owt but the bloody nose he deserves.'

'Aye, well, happen there's no harm done,' Alf said reluctantly.

'Course there ain't. Pity you 'ave to be on duty, otherwise you and your missus could have joined

us and 'ad a bit of fun, couldn't they, Albert?'
Ronnie appealed to Molly's father.

'Aye, they could.'

'I'd best be on me way, but mind now – no
breaking the blackout,' Alf warned them sternly.

'And Happy Christmas to you, Ebenezer,' Uncle
Joe called out after Alf, amidst chuckles all round.

TWO

''Ere, Molly, are you and your June goin' to the New Year's Eve dance down at the Grafton?' Ruby asked Molly, over the noise of the bell ringing to announce the end of their day's work. It was three days after Christmas, and Molly and the other girls had been back at work a day already, although June had decided to take some time off without pay so that she could spend as much time as possible with Frank, who did not have to report for duty until early January.

'Yes,' Molly confirmed. 'Are you?'

'Of course I am. You wouldn't catch me staying at 'ome on a New Year's Eve, war or no war,' Ruby told her scornfully.

When she stepped out into the street, Molly instinctively looked down towards where the docks lay hidden from her view by the buildings of the city, bracing herself against the icy cold wind as she wondered where Eddie's ship was and when he would be home. He was supposed to be back

231

before New Year's Eve but she dared not hope he would be, because she knew she would hardly be able to bear her disappointment if he wasn't. It seemed such a long time since she had last seen Eddie. So much had happened in those few short weeks.

It was Thursday night and *ITMA*, the comedy show, would be on the wireless, to cheer her up, she reminded herself. No doubt Frank and June would be coming round to listen to it as well, since June was flatly refusing to spend any more time than she had to underneath her mother-in-law's roof. Although, naturally, June had not said so, Molly had guessed that it was the privacy of an empty house that brought them to number 78 as much as June's open resentment of her mother-in-law, and for that reason she had taken to rattling the handle of the back door to announce her own return home, when she thought they might be there.

The Government's original determination to impose a total blackout had now given way to its reluctant acknowledgement that doing so was causing too many accidents, and Molly was glad of the light from her small torch as she made her way down the cul-de-sac in the cold darkness of the wintry evening.

The wireless was on when she walked into the kitchen, and June and Frank were already sitting together listening to it as she predicted.

'Me and Frank are going to the pictures tonight,

Molly. You can come with us, if you want,' June informed her.

Molly shook her head. 'Ta, but no thanks. It's *ITMA* – my favourite – and besides, I've got me frock to sort out for New Year's Eve,' she told June cheerfully.

'I thought you said you was goin' to wear your bridesmaid's dress again,' June reminded her.

'I am, but the hem needs a stitch in it where I caught me heel in it at the wedding. Besides, I don't want to be playing gooseberry with you and Frank.'

'I'll have you know that me and Frank are an old married couple now, so less of your cheek.'

Molly laughed. 'Oh, yes, and I suppose it was because the two of you were taking a nap while you were here that you had the bedroom curtains closed all afternoon yesterday, was it?'

'How do you know . . .' June began, and then stopped, blushing hotly when Molly laughed even more.

Molly and her father had laughed at *ITMA*, with Tommy Handley, and listened to the news, and Molly had just finished making their bedtime cocoa when they heard the knock on the back door.

'That'll be our June, forgetting her key and come to tell us about the pictures, so as she can have a bit more time away from Frank's mam,' Molly called out to her father, who was on his way upstairs.

Opening the door, she announced warningly, 'You can make your own cocoa if you want some, because me and Dad are just having ours.'

'Well, that's a fine way to greet a sailor home from the sea,' a familiar male voice answered her ruefully.

'Eddie!' Molly gasped, torn between shock and delight, and then gathered herself together to demand excitedly, her face going pink with happiness, 'Oh, is it really you? When did you get back? How—'

'Wait up a bit,' Eddie laughed, as she stepped back so that he could follow her into the kitchen. 'We docked an hour ago, and I came round as soon as I could.'

She almost flew into his open arms, exhaling a shaky little sigh as they closed tightly round her, burying her face against his shoulder. She could feel the warmth of his lips pressing against her head, and also the slight tremble of his body.

'Molly, you don't know how much I've bin wanting to hold you like this.'

'You've missed me then?' she couldn't resist asking.

'Missed you? There hasn't been a minute when I haven't thought about you. You're my girl now, Molly,' he told her, 'and I'm never going to let you go.'

Molly could have stayed in his arms for ever but reluctantly released him when Eddie said he had to go next door and see Elsie and John.

234

'I'll be back to see you tomorrow, mind. Maybe we can go to the pictures?'

After they had kissed goodbye, Molly ran up the stairs to her bedroom as fast as her feet would take her. It overlooked the close, so Molly was able to lift just enough of the blackout curtain to call out and wave to Eddie, and blow him a swift kiss as he stood below her. Dropping the curtain, she leaned against the wall, her heart pounding. She felt as though she was going to burst, she was that excited and happy. Hugging herself, she danced giddily round the bedroom. Eddie was home and now everything was going to be all right. No, from now on and for the rest of her life, everything was going to be wonderful. She stood still and closed her eyes, reliving the sensation of his lips on hers. Oh, Eddie!

Quickly Molly checked her appearance in her bedroom mirror, patting her hair and pressing her lips together to set her lipstick. The last thing she felt like doing now that Eddie was home was going to work. But there was a war on, and the uniforms they were making at Hardings were going to be needed by all those young men who were being called up – many of whom would be married with young families. Things must be serious if the Government was having to call up more men, but you wouldn't know it, not from listening to the news or reading the *Liverpool Echo*.

Her father was working an early shift and had left at six. Molly had gone downstairs to make sure he had some breakfast before leaving, and then returned to bed.

She shivered as she opened the door and stepped out into the cold air, quickly locking the door behind her and then hurrying into the street, where she came to an abrupt halt, her face breaking into a delighted smile as she saw Eddie standing outside the gate, rubbing his hands together and stamping his feet to keep warm.

'Eddie, what are you doing here?' she asked, trying to sound casual and grown up, not realising that the glow of happiness in her eyes gave her away, or how much it meant to the man watching her to see it there. He had thought about her, longed for her, all the way across the Atlantic and back.

'Waiting for you, that's what,' he answered her. 'I thought I'd walk you to work, like. I saw your dad going off to the gridiron earlier, so I didn't knock in case anyone thought we was up to a bit of hanky-panky.'

He had taken off his cap and he was holding it in his hands as shyly as a schoolboy, his blond hair almost flattened straight with Brylcreem. He looked so handsome that Molly felt as though the sudden loving swelling of her heart would suffocate her.

'You didn't have to get up out of your warm bed to walk me to work, you daft thing,' she chided him, but her expression was giving her away and revealing how thrilled she was to see him.

'I know I didn't have to – I've done it because I wanted to. Because I wanted to be with you, Molly,' he told her. 'That's what I want more than anything else. For you and me to be together, for always . . .'

Molly had never imagined that walking to work could be so wonderful. When they finally reached the factory she could barely bring herself to leave Eddie.

'Will you still be here New Year's Eve?' she asked him. 'Only there's a dance down at the Grafton, and there's a few of us going.' The expression on her face gave away her longing to go to the dance with him.

Seeing it, Eddie crossed his fingers behind his back and told her nonchalantly, 'I don't reckon we'll be sailing for a good few days.' The truth was that he already knew they were on a quick turnaround but right there and then he decided that even if he had to jump ship and get another passage, he would do so, just to see the happiness in Molly's eyes when he held her in his arms and danced the New Year in with her, the first of many, many New Year's Eves they would spend together.

THREE

'And Richard says that they'll both be on leave until the sixth of January, so I've suggested that we all go to the New Year's Eve dance at the Grafton tomorrow night.'

Molly nodded, listening to Anne's whispered conversation about her brother on Saturday morning, at the same time as they were supposed to be listening to a lecture from Mrs Wesley whilst they all rolled bandages, ready for some first-aid practice.

'So what's he like then, this Philip?' Molly whispered back, referring to the friend Richard had brought home for Christmas, who had obviously had a profound effect on Anne.

'Oh, he's really nice, Molly,' Anne enthused, blushing, her face alight with excitement. 'He's got really lovely manners and he'd brought us all Christmas presents. Mine was ever such a lovely boxed set of lace-edged handkerchiefs, embroidered with an "A". I'm glad that things have worked out for you, Molly. With Eddie, I mean. I know that at first I said that I thought you were wrong to get involved with him when you were already engaged, and I still don't hold with an engaged girl seeing another man behind her fiancé's back, but things happen so quickly in wartime, and it looks like everything's worked out for the best after all. You're my friend, Molly, and I'm glad to see you looking so happy, truly I am.'

Anne put her arms around Molly and gave her a quick hug, which Molly returned.

'Did you have a good Christmas?' Anne asked.

'Well, I managed to cook the turkey that our Aunt Violet in Nantwich had sent,' Molly chuckled. 'It was a bit touch and go, though. It was that big I thought it wasn't going to go in the oven and our June was having forty fits on account of her Frank's mam having her Christmas dinner with us. In the end it all worked out, even though it was a bit of a tight squeeze with so many of us. And then in the evening we had some of the neighbours in for a bit of a knees-up.'

'Watch it,' Anne muttered. 'Mrs Wesley is looking this way.'

When the meeting was over Anne had to dash off because she had promised her brother and his friend that she would go ice-skating with them. Her excitement at seeing Philip was palpable, and Molly wondered if he could be the cause of her friend's complete understanding and acceptance of her own love for Eddie.

'Ice-skating?' Molly laughed. 'The last time I went, I was still at school. Elsie knitted me this red skating dress, and I fell over so often that by the time we left it was soaking wet through. I ended up having to walk home with it dripping everywhere, and June and the others yelling at me to keep away from them because I looked as though I'd wet me drawers.

'See you tomorrow night at the Grafton,' she added as they hugged one another and Anne darted off to join her brother and the dark-haired young man who was standing with him.

Molly could see the appeal of Philip, even from across the street. He was tall and broad-shouldered with ink-dark hair. His face lit up when he saw Anne.

Molly waved goodbye to them, then hurried eagerly towards Eddie, whom she could see waiting for her on the corner.

Tucking her arm through his, she squeezed it lovingly.

There wasn't a prettier girl in the whole world than his Molly, with her sense of fun, her dark curls, and those eyes of hers that could steal a man's heart away with just a smile, Eddie reckoned – no, nor a happier man than himself. His chest swelled with pride as he looked at her. She was a real gem, a sweetheart, inside and out.

'Brr, I've never known it so cold,' Molly shivered, moving closer to Eddie as they hurried past the Picton Clock, heads bowed against the steel-cold wind that was stinging colour into the pale Celtic skin Molly had inherited from her mother and trying to tear her firmly secured hat from her head.

The main street was busy with people shopping, and in the bus queue several young couples were standing close together, making an excuse of the cold, and the fact that all too soon they would have to part as the young men went to fight, to share a physical intimacy that would normally have been frowned upon.

Molly could feel the warmth of Eddie's body pressed up against her side and she moved closer to him, blushing when he stopped walking to look down at her.

'Don't you go getting any ideas,' she laughed. 'I'm just cold, that's all . . .' But her laughter died as she saw the way he was looking at her – so hungrily and . . . and . . . so dangerously that her heart seemed to turn right over inside her chest.

Everyone was saying it was the coldest winter they could remember, and despite the pleasure of being able to walk arm in arm with Eddie, Molly was relieved when they finally reached number 78.

'Dad must be out,' she told Eddie, unlocking the back door. 'He's probably down at the shelter with the others from the allotments. They meet up there sometimes for a brew and a natter.'

'So we've got the house to ourselves, have we?' Eddie asked her, drawing her towards him.

'Oh, Eddie . . .' Molly protested, but it was a

very half-hearted protest, and when he started to kiss her she didn't even try to resist.

When he finally stopped they were both breathing heavily, and Molly's cheeks were flushed a deep shade of pink.

'I've got to go and get changed out of my uniform, remember,' she told him, pulling herself free of his arms and laughing as he refused to let go of her hand.

'You look beautiful to me whatever you wear,' he told her thickly.

'Wait here,' she said, showing him into the back parlour and then hurrying upstairs. In her bedroom she took off her uniform and her blouse, rushed into the cold bathroom in her slip and stockings, to wash quickly and clean her teeth, before scurrying back over the cold linoleum to her bedroom.

She was just about to put on her sweater when the bedroom door opened and Eddie came in.

Her eyes widening with shock, Molly let the sweater drop onto the bed, pressing her hand flat to the creamy skin of her chest as though to suppress the fierce uneven thudding of her heart.

'Molly.'

She trembled at the urgency in Eddie's voice, shaking her head in denial, but it was too late. He was holding her and kissing her, pressing frantic little kisses all over her face and then her throat, whilst he whispered to her how much he loved her.

'Eddie, we mustn't,' she warned him breathlessly, but he didn't seem to hear her as his hands stroked her bare arms, their male touch making her quiver with sweet pleasure. He kissed her mouth, sliding the straps of her slip and brassiere off her shoulders. She felt him shudder as he pressed his hot forehead against the coolness of her cheek, his hand trembling as he touched her breast.

'I want you so much . . .'

'We mustn't . . .' But her head still fell back against his arm when he kissed the side of her neck, his hand a hot exciting pressure against her slip-covered breast.

'Sweet Molly! Let me love you . . . let me show you . . .'

Molly shuddered, her belly turning somersaults in response to the desire in his voice.

'I've been thinking about this for so long . . . wantin' you for so long . . . I love you, Molly.' His voice cracked with emotion.

'And I love you too. But we mustn't, Eddie,' she told him frantically.

Eddie ignored her words, kissing her fiercely instead. Helplessly, Molly let him, her own body gripped by the same hunger as his. How could it be wrong for them to be together when they loved one another?

But it was wrong, she reminded herself.

'No, we mustn't,' she repeated, pulling away from him. 'There's bin enough talk already shaming me dad and our June, and if anything were to happen . . .'

The fear in her voice checked Eddie and made him frown. 'I'm sorry,' he whispered. 'I didn't mean to upset yer, Molly. I just got carried away, what wi' wantin' yer so badly an' all.'

'You must go downstairs, before me dad gets back.' She was trembling slightly, her normal exuberance dimmed, and there was a shamed, unhappy, confused look in her eyes that made him ache with guilt.

'If anyone knew about this, they'd say that it was my fault and they'd be right,' she told him miserably.

'Don't talk so daft. How could it be your fault? It's me as is to blame.' He could see that she was close to tears. 'Eeh, lass, I never meant to upset yer – that's the last thing I want to do,' he told her.

Molly took a deep breath and shook her head. 'I'm not upset, Eddie, not really, and I . . . and I . . . I feel the same way you do,' she admitted bravely, 'but I've caused me family enough upset. I'm not blaming you, but—'

'Well, you should be,' Eddie stopped her, 'because it's me wot is to blame. I should be protecting yer, Molly, not . . .' He stopped speaking to swallow against the emotion gripping his chest when she looked up at him, her eyes filled with such a look of love and trust that he had to ball his hands into fists to stop himself from reaching out for her.

'I'll go downstairs and wait for yer there,' he told her thickly.

Her hands were trembling so much she could hardly pull on her sweater. If she hadn't sent Eddie away, right now they could have been . . . A wave of hot sweetness stole away her breath. Oh, but what she was thinking was so very wrong. Everyone knew that and everyone knew too what happened to the girls who broke the rules and let lads have their way with them outside of marriage. Shamed, they were, and their families too. But whilst her conscience might know that, her body still ached longingly for Eddie. All those lonely nights when she had lain here in her bed, thinking about his kisses, and now when she had had the opportunity to have more than just kisses she had gone and sent him away.

'Is me lipstick all right?'

Dutifully Molly scrutinised June's mouth as best she could in the dim lighting of the Grafton Dance Hall.

'It's fine,' she assured her sister, raising her voice to make herself heard above the band.

A whole gang of them had met up at the Grafton: Molly, June and Frank, Sally and Ronnie, plus some of the girls from work and their dates, as well as Jim Fowler and Jean.

Molly had even persuaded Anne to join them, along with Richard and Philip.

They had taken over two large tables, with a

good view of the dance floor and the band, and the mood of the evening, which had started out as one of energetic enthusiasm, had suddenly become more sombre now that it was almost midnight.

Couples were swaying together on the dance floor as the band started to play slower, smoochier numbers. A girl at the table next to Molly's party had started to cry as she clung to the hand of the young man with her.

'There's that many girls scriking, you'd think that every lad in Liverpool had bin called up,' June whispered witheringly to Molly. 'When your hubby really is fightin' for his country, you owes it to him to act with a bit of self-control, instead of cryin' all over him.'

Everyone knew that the Government was exhorting women to send their men off to war with a brave heart and a warm smile instead of with tears.

'It's almost midnight – come and dance with me,' Eddie begged Molly.

The girl singer with the band was singing George Gershwin's 'The Man I Love', and the lights had been turned down low. All around her couples were dancing together, lost in their own worlds. Molly could see June dancing with Frank whilst Anne was wrapped tightly in Philip's arms.

At almost midnight, the band stopped playing. Eddie took hold of Molly's hand and practically dragged her back to their table. As midnight struck and everyone roared and cheered, Eddie reached into his pocket and brought out a small box.

'I've bin carrying this around wi' me ever since I bought it for yer in New York, Molly.' He shook his head as his emotions overwhelmed him, and then opened the small box. Molly gasped as she saw the ring nestling on the little velvet cushion, the stone in the centre glittering. 'Will yer marry me and be me wife, Molly?' Eddie asked her.

'Oh, Eddie . . .' Her eyes shining with happy tears, Molly nodded. 'Yes, oh, yes, of course I will.'

She examined the ring. 'It's beautiful. What is the stone?'

'It's a diamond solitaire, of course,' he told her proudly, as he slipped the ring onto her finger.

A diamond solitaire. No one Molly knew had a real diamond ring with a proper stone in it and not small chips of diamanté. She was so over-whelmed that she couldn't speak. Tears trickled down her cheeks, causing June, who had just returned to the table, to rush over.

Still speechless, Molly simply extended her left hand. Within seconds, or so it seemed to her, the whole table was cheering and whooping, the men congratulating Eddie and demanding to kiss her whilst the girls all crowded round her to admire her ring.

'So when will you be gettin' married then?' June asked.

'I don't know. We haven't talked about it yet. I didn't even know that Eddie . . .' Molly shook her head, setting her dark curls dancing. With her cheeks flushed and her eyes shining just as brightly as the diamond ring on her finger, her lips slightly parted in a tremulous smile, she looked radiant.

Molly could hardly believe what had happened. She knew that Eddie loved her, as she did him, but the unexpectedness of his romantic gesture had made her feel so wonderfully special.

'I'll remember tonight for the rest of my life,' she whispered to him later, locked in his arms whilst they shared the last dance of the evening. 'It's been so wonderful. *You* are so wonderful, Eddie.'

'You wait until we get married – then I'll show you what wonderful is all about,' he whispered, buoyed up on the inhibition-dissolving effect of love and the beer he'd drunk during the evening.

'Sauce!' Molly checked him automatically, but the gaze she gave him was liquid with love and delight as she nestled closer to him, a happy smile curving her lips. Tonight she was the happiest girl in the whole of Liverpool and she didn't care who knew it.

FOUR

'Blimey O'Reilly, it's cold,' June protested, huddling deeper into her coat, against the biting wind with its thick flurries of snow. 'I hope this isn't a sign of what 1940 is going to be like.' They had had freezing temperatures all week and the pavements were treacherous, with frozen snow lying beneath fresh falls.

Molly glanced down towards the docks. It was the second week of January and Eddie's ship wasn't due to dock for another week. She couldn't help worrying about him even more now, exposed to the danger from Hitler's submarines, and the worst winter weather anyone could remember.

June was walking alongside her, her arm through Frank's, whilst Sally and Ronnie were up ahead, Ronnie carrying Tommy whilst Sally clung to his arm.

They had just got off the bus outside Lime Street station, where they had come to see the men off to rejoin their units, as had the other wives and families crowding into the station.

Ronnie had told them he had heard they were being posted to France to join the British Expeditionary Force that was helping to fight off a German invasion of that country.

A group of WVS volunteers just inside the station were dispensing cups of tea from a huge urn, as well as taking charge of lost children and answering anxious questions.

Molly studied them discreetly. Her own group had already been warned that in the event of battle-weary and injured men being returned to England, they would be called upon to take their turn at the station, giving what assistance they could.

Now, for the first time, as she saw the swirling mass of people filling the station and felt the sombreness of the mood – could almost taste its heady combination of female fear and male tension – Molly was sharply aware of the stark reality of the country being at war. The jolliness and togetherness of Christmas, and the fun and excitement of New Year's Eve, had almost made her forget there was a war on, but just one look at the concerned faces all around her brought the fear and dread flooding back in an instant.

Everywhere, there were men in uniform, along with wives, parents and children. She could see the pride and the anxiety in June's eyes as her sister looked up at her own husband, and she had to blink away sudden tears herself.

'That's our lot over there,' Ronnie called out to Frank, gesturing to a group of men standing several yards away, surrounded by their families.

Ronnie and Frank forged a pathway through the crowd, Sally and June clinging to their arms, whilst Molly hurried along with them.

When they reached their watching comrades they were given a rousing cheer, and introductions were quickly performed that left Molly with a confusing mix of nicknames to pin to the unfamiliar faces. Typically, the men were soon exchanging jokes and banter.

'Look at 'em. Anyone'd think they was off to a football match and not a war,' June said witheringly to Molly.

'Mark my words, your Frank will be a sergeant before this is all over,' Ronnie predicted.

The train was already filling up with men.

'You'd better get on, Frank, else you'll not get a seat,' June warned.

'Don't you worry about your Frank, missus,' one of the other men grinned. 'He'll get a seat even if he has to chuck someone else out of it first.'

'Aye, and like as not it will be you, Benjy,' Frank quipped in response, turning back to hug Sally and then Molly. Molly could see the genuine affection in his eyes. She hugged him back and then released him, stepping back so that June could stand next to him.

Whilst the men were ribbing one another and

joking, the women were slowly growing quieter and more concerned.

'Here, why don't I take Tommy, Sally?' Molly offered. 'Then you can say goodbye to your Ronnie proper, like.'

'Ta, Molly.'

Feeling that it wasn't her place to watch other people's private goodbyes, Molly settled the baby in her arms and walked back into the crowd.

Three men were hurrying towards the train, the tallest of them wearing his cap pushed back off his face and his army greatcoat open, causing several women to admire his broad physique and handsome face, looks which he brazenly returned, whilst Molly stood staring at him in consternation, unable to move.

He was almost abreast of her before he saw her, his grin faltering before quickly returning as he winked and said easily, 'Hello, Molly. Come to see Frank off, have you?'

'He-llo, Johnny,' Molly managed to stammer. 'Yes. He's over there with Ronnie Walker.'

'Heard about your engagement,' Johnny told her, gesturing towards her glove-covered hand as she held the Walkers' baby.

'You didn't waste much time there, did you?'

Had he no shame, Molly wondered indignantly, her initial self-consciousness forgotten as she tossed her head and told him pithily, 'By, but you've got your cheek, Johnny Everton!'

Instead of being properly shamed, Johnny's grin

simply widened. Bending his head, he whispered close to Molly's ear, 'Bet he isn't as good a kisser as me.'

Molly blushed bright pink, but managed to retort firmly, 'I should have thought you'd be showing a bit more shame, seeing what you've done. That poor girl . . .'

Immediately Johnny's grin vanished. 'Her!' he grimaced bitterly. 'That kid she's claiming is mine could be anyone's, and the whole of their street knows it – aye, and that father of hers, an' all.

'Hello, gorgeous,' he called out to a passing blonde, his attention instantly diverted from Molly. 'Fancy catching a train with me?'

'Oh, Johnny,' Molly protested. Despite herself she grinned. He would never change and, actually, she decided, she wouldn't want him to. In an ever-changing world, Johnny Everton's cheek and charm were reassuring constants. Now that she wasn't engaged to him she no longer felt so over-whelmed by his sexuality, like a young girl appre-hensive in the face of something she didn't really understand. She did, after all, know how it felt to want someone now. She wasn't sorry that they had met accidentally like this. For one thing, it took away any awkwardness, were they to meet in the future, and for another it made her all the more sure that it was Eddie she loved. Eddie . . . A small secret smile played on her lips as she thought about him.

'Ah, don't get jealous, Molly – I still like yer the best!' Johnny teased.

'Don't even think about it, Johnny Everton,' Molly replied with a smile. 'My Eddie's worth ten of you.' She meant it. Narrowly avoiding being married to Johnny had been a lucky escape, and though she could still see why virtually every woman stopped in her tracks when she clapped eyes on him, she knew that what she had with Eddie was worth far more.

Giving her a mock salute, Johnny turned and headed for the train.

Funny how things worked out, Molly decided happily as she made her way back to June and the others. When she had been engaged to Johnny she had felt trapped and afraid – of him and of marriage. Now that she was engaged to Eddie she felt far more at ease with Johnny than she had ever done when they had been together. And as for being afraid of marriage – she laughed happily – she couldn't wait. A rush of pleasure filled her. She hugged the baby tightly. When Eddie came home she was going to tell him that she didn't want to wait, and that she wanted them to get married as quickly as they could. Maybe he could get work down at the gridiron, alongside her dad as well as his uncle and cousin. Her father had said only the other night that more men were needed because of all the munition trains. It would be hard, dirty work, she knew that, but surely it would be better and safer than being in the merchant navy. Perhaps she ought to have a word with Elsie to see what she thought.

Life and love were both so precious. She didn't want to waste a single minute of either.

'How do you fancy going to Lewis's and having a cuppa before we go home?' Sally suggested as the three girls struggled to stay together in the press of people leaving Lime Street, whilst they battled against the icy wind and driving snow.

'I suppose we might as well,' June agreed.

'I'll have to call at the butcher's on the way back and collect mine and dad's bacon ration,' Molly put in, 'otherwise our dad won't be able to have his bacon butties.'

'I'll come with yer then, and collect mine,' June told her. 'And then you can come with me to Frank's mam's and help me take me stuff back home. I told Frank there was no way I was going to stay on at his mam's with him gone, and that the first thing I'd be doing was moving back to number 78.'

'Ronnie told me that some of the wives have bin taking lodgings down south so as to be close to the barracks,' Sally informed them. 'Then if the men are on home duty they can get to see a bit more of them, rather than spend two days of it travelling there and back. I've bin thinking about doin' the same, if my Ronnie got a home posting.'

'I shouldn't bother, if I was you, Sally,' June told her. 'With any luck they'll be back soon. That

Hitler will be running off with his tail between his legs once he realises our lads aren't going to let him invade France.'

All three of them were shivering when they finally reached Lewis's. The store was already busy with Saturday shoppers seeking warmth. In the cosmetics department the shelves were already half empty.

'It's all right for you,' June proclaimed to Molly. 'Your Eddie will be able to bring you back stuff from America . . . Ooh, Molly . . . I feel ever so funny,' she added, suddenly turning white as a sheet. 'I think I need to sit down.'

Quickly Molly and Sally took hold of her, guiding her to a nearby chair.

'It's the shock of her Frank going,' Sally told Molly knowledgeably. 'Same thing happened to me the first time I saw my Ronnie in his uniform. Takes yer by the throat, it does . . . You feeling all right now, June?'

'I feel ever so sickly,' June admitted. 'Perhaps we better not have that cup of tea after all . . .'

Molly hummed happily along with the wireless as she sewed. Mr Harding had put the wireless in the factory because he had heard that listening to music helped to increase productivity, specially of women workers.

Eddie's ship was due to arrive back at Garston Dock tomorrow, and finally, after the frighteningly severe frost and heavy snow that had hit the country the previous week, the weather had started to turn a little bit milder.

It felt like a lifetime since she had waved goodbye to Eddie, and Molly was aching to see him. Sometimes, without her diamond ring to remind her, she suspected she might wonder if she had only dreamed those few precious happy days they had had together.

'Anyone fancy coming to the pictures wi' me tonight? They've got a new film on so I've heard,' Irene shouted above the sound of Vera Lynn singing.

'I'll come with you, if you like,' Molly shouted back, giving the girl next to her a nudge and telling her, 'Go on, Jean, you come as well. You deserve a bit of a treat.'

Jean's mother had taken sick just before Christmas and, as well as having to work, Jean had had to nurse her and to take charge of the house, and look after her father and two younger brothers. Elsie had told Molly that she had sent Jim round to Jean's with some of her quince jelly for the invalid and a bottle of her elderberry wine.

'Oh, if you're coming wi' us, Molly, I suppose it'll have to be the three-and-sixes, wi' you wearing that posh ring,' Irene joked, referring to the most expensive seats in the house.

Molly took her teasing in good part, saying chirpily, 'Oh, I don't mind slumming it, Irene, and sittin' in the one-and-threes . . . Oh, I've just remembered, I can't go. It's WVS.'

'Well, one thing's for sure,' June broke in morosely, 'none of us would have bin wanting to sit in the back row with our lads all away.'

'You wouldn't catch me sittin' there wi' my Algy, anyway,' one of the new girls Mr Harding had taken on to cope with the extra work announced cheekily. 'Not with the way them hands of 'is are all over the place like he were an octopus or sommat.'

Irene gave a disapproving sniff. 'Well, I say that it's up to a girl to make sure her lad behaves his-self as he should.'

'Aye, well, there's plenty o' lasses who are that feared they might never see their lads again that they haven't the heart to say no to them when there's a war on,' someone else joined in frankly.

Molly remembered how difficult she had found it to resist Eddie before he left to go back to sea. Before the war, she would have been appalled to hear of girls sleeping with their men before they were married, let alone consider it herself, but wartime had made everything feel different.

'Do you want to stop off at your Frank's mam's on our way home?' Molly asked June later, as they walked home together in the darkness of the winter evening. 'We didn't get a chance to last night, and you only had things for overnight.'

'If we must,' June replied miserably.

'Dad said this morning that he'd see if he could

get her a bit of extra coal,' Molly reminded her sister, 'seeing as how she's family now.'

'Huh, well, you wouldn't think so sometimes from the way she treats me.'

'I reckon she'd be better with you if you went round a bit more often,' Molly told her, trying to be as tactful as she could, as she added, 'She'll have seen you going round to Sally's and she only lives a couple of doors down.'

'And what if she has?' June sniffed. 'That's my business.'

'But with Frank away, she's on her own,' Molly mumbled.

'If you're trying to say that I should bend over backwards to please that old cow—' June began sharply.

'Course I'm not. Don't be so daft. But there's folk who live in the cul-de-sac who haven't spoken to their in-laws for years – we both know that; I wouldn't want my kiddies growing up not knowing who their dad's family were.'

'Well, I suppose you've got a point,' June admitted grudgingly, 'although it's a bit early for you to be thinking about kiddies, isn't it? You and Eddie aren't even married yet. Me and Frank have decided to wait until this war's over before we have any . . . So you're off to the WVS tonight then, are you?'

'Yes,' Molly confirmed. 'We're all going down to Mill Road Hospital so that we can learn what we'd have to do if there was an emergency.'

'Sally said as how she might call round tonight,' June told her.

They had almost reached number 46, but Molly knew better than to suggest a second time that June call in to see her mother-in-law.

Her sister had become increasingly short-tempered since Frank had left for France, and whilst Molly sympathised with her sometimes, she had to bite her tongue to stop herself from reminding June that she wasn't the only girl who was worrying about her man's safety.

Every day or so it seemed to Molly there was another report in the papers of merchant ships being attacked and sunk by Hitler's warships and submarines. There were rumours that the whole of the east coast had been mined by enemy ships so that nothing could put to sea from British ports without risking being blown up. Molly gave an involuntary shudder. Every night she prayed for the safety of all the brave men who were doing their bit for Britain.

Everyone was being exhorted not to waste valuable fuel that was needed for the war effort, but Molly admitted guiltily that it was wonderful to walk into the parlour and find a good fire burning, thanks to their father's 'perk' of being allowed to collect loose coals from the goods yard.

An hour later, after a hasty supper of corned beef hash, Molly was ready to go out again, her curls pinned back beneath her WVS cap.

'See you later,' she called, putting her head

round the door to the back parlour, where her father and sister were sitting beside the fire, listening to the wireless.

As usual Molly had arranged to meet Anne under the Picton Clock and on this occasion she got there first, although she didn't have to wait long to see Anne's familiar figure hurrying towards her.

'Sorry I'm late,' Anne apologised. 'Only Dad was kept late at work on account of some shocking news they've had. I'm not really supposed to say anything, but I know I can trust you, Molly.'

'What's happened?' Molly asked her as they set off for Mill Road Hospital where they were to meet up with the others.

'Well, you know that Dad is an accountant with the council?'

Molly nodded.

'This afternoon they were all called to a meeting and told that there's this chap, really important he is, a ship repairer, and seemingly he's done himself in. The Admiralty found out that he's stolen money from them by claiming wages for non-existent jobs and employees, and stealing materials to sell elsewhere. Dad said that he's stolen over twenty million pounds, enough money for the Admiralty to have built a new warship.'

'How dreadful!' Molly gasped.

'Yes, isn't it? It all came out when Mum was telling Dad about how pleased she was at getting some stuff from a friend of hers.' Anne pulled a face. 'You know, Molly, off the black market. Dad was really angry and said that Mum was being unpatriotic, and then he told us about this man.'

Anne looked so upset that Molly put her arm round her shoulders and gave her a small hug.

'I don't suppose he meant to upset you, Anne,' she consoled her.

Eddie had already told her that virtually all merchant seamen brought things back with them that they knew they could sell at home for more than they had paid for them. Like her father's pieces of coal, that was considered an unofficial perk of the job. 'Course, some of them go a bit too far and get themselves hauled over the coals for it,' Eddie had added, 'but there's that much stuff goes over the side at the docks when they're loading and unloading the ships that what we bring in is nothing.'

Selling on goods that had 'fallen off a lorry' was a way of life for dock workers, as everyone who lived in Liverpool knew. Molly didn't condone it but could understand the need when money was tight and there were children to feed and clothe.

Mill Road Hospital had been built at the end of the nineteenth century, and had originally been the West Union and Derby Poorhouse Infirmary. But unlike other poorhouse infirmaries its nurses had been trained by methods set down by Florence Nightingale herself. During the Great War the hospital had started taking in wounded soldiers, changing its status from an infirmary for the long-term ill, and becoming instead a hospital where acute cases were operated on.

The purpose of their visit was, Mrs Wesley explained when they were all gathered together, to familiarise themselves with the floor plan of the hospital and its wards, so that, should it be deemed necessary by the authorities, members of their group could help out at the hospital in an emergency in a variety of practical and non-medical ways.

'In the event of Liverpool being bombed it will be our role to facilitate the identification of the injured and to provide them with support as and where necessary whilst they wait to receive treatment,' Mrs Wesley explained. 'And if there are other tasks we are called upon to perform then I would exhort you all to do them efficiently and speedily.'

'If she means we're going to have to empty bedpans, the 'ospital can find someone else,' a woman standing next to Molly muttered behind her hand, whilst the girl beside her tittered.

'I also want volunteers for Lime Street station next week. We've got any number of troop trains leaving and, of course, we shall want to send our boys off with a hot cup of tea and a sandwich inside them.'

'Oh, that must have been what my fella was after the other night,' the girl who had made the comment about bedpans whispered to her friend, who immediately started to giggle and ended up having to cough to conceal her amusement.

'I'm so glad we're proper friends again, Molly,' Anne told her when they were all taken to the nurses' canteen for a welcome cup of tea. 'I thought at the time I was acting in your best interests, trying to persuade you to do what seemed right, but I didn't realise then what it's like to fall in love.' She blushed self-consciously. 'I expect you've guessed about me and Philip?'

'I had wondered,' Molly admitted, 'especially when I saw the way the two of you looked at each other.'

'It happened so quickly, Molly. On Christmas Day Richard was teasing us both with a piece of mistletoe so poor Philip had no option but to kiss me. I wasn't expecting . . . that is, I knew I liked Philip but . . .' Blushing and laughing, her eyes shining with happiness, Anne confessed shyly, 'Oh, Molly, I never imagined that kissing someone could feel like that. And on Boxing Day, when Philip and I went out for a long walk together and we were talking about it, Philip said that he had thought exactly the same. I thought of you then, and I felt so bad about how unkind to you I'd been. You're the dearest girl, Molly, and I want us to stay friends so much, especially now. Tell me that you forgive me.'

Molly's heart overflowed with emotion. 'Of course I forgive you,' she assured Anne, her words muffled as they hugged one another fiercely.

'We'll be able to support one another now, Molly,' Anne told her. 'It isn't going to be easy with both Eddie and Philip doing their bit, but at least you and me will have each other. It's like Philip was saying to my parents when he asked Dad's permission for us to be engaged, things are different in wartime.'

'You're engaged!'

Automatically Molly looked at Anne's left hand, but there was no ring on her finger.

'Only unofficially at the moment,' Anne sighed. 'Dad's a bit old-fashioned and he insisted that we have to wait until my twenty-first birthday in May, on account of us not knowing one another very long yet.' She pulled a face, and then said fiercely, 'I know that I won't change my mind and that I shall love Philip for ever.'

Mrs Wesley was signalling that their tea break was over. Exchanging mutually understanding looks, Molly and Anne rejoined the others.

An hour later, when they had tramped for what felt like miles down long disinfectant-smelling corridors, getting to know the layout of the hospital, Molly turned to whisper to Anne, 'I'm glad I'm not a nurse. Me feet are killing me.'

'Mine too,' Anne agreed.

Her and Anne's feet might have been aching, but their hearts were filled with happiness and love, Molly reflected joyfully as she hurried home to number 78, huddling deep in her coat to avoid the icy cold.

Perhaps Sally would still be there. She hadn't seen her for a few days. The bitter cold and the short dark days had meant that the women of the close had kept themselves very much to themselves during January, apart from exchanging gossip whilst they queued with their ration books, and grumbling about having to stand for so long in such a biting wind.

Because they were both at work, Molly and June had had to rely on Elsie for information on what was happening to everyone else, and it seemed that every family in the street now had a husband, a father, a son or a brother in uniform and ready to fight for his country. Every household now had an air-raid shelter box ready to snatch up in case of need, and, thanks to Alf Davies and the leaders of the local Cub and Scout troops and the Guide and Brownie packs, all the children in the area knew their gas mask and air-raid shelter drill. Some of the older boys had been formed into a messenger service to be used in case the telegraph lines went down. Molly had seen them practising racing one another up and down the streets on their bicycles as they challenged each other to see how fast they could deliver any message.

But despite all this activity, people's initial fears had subsided. The attacks people had feared had not happened and a new mood of confidence was beginning to take over, as people assured one another that Hitler would soon be sent packing with his tail between his legs by the BEF, and the celebratory flags would be out all over Britain by the summer. Even Molly's fears had begun slowly to subside, especially knowing Eddie was due home any day.

'There's no need for you to rush into getting married, Molly,' June told her once Molly was settled in front of the fire with a mug of hot cocoa. 'The war will be over by summer, and then you can have a proper do with a proper frock.'

'Well, I just hope our boys don't come home via Paris. Not after what I've been reading in the papers,' Sally said. 'I don't want my Ronnie having his head turned by one of those French mademoiselles, thank you very much.'

They all laughed.

'When's your Eddie back, Molly?' Sally asked her.

'Tomorrow.' Molly was unable to stop a huge grin from breaking out across her face.

'Are you going down to Garston Dock to wait for him?' June asked her.

Molly shook her head. As a precaution, just in case Jerry should attempt to bomb them, the convoys crossing the Atlantic were coming into Liverpool's docks under cover of darkness, often arriving in the early hours of the morning, and were quickly unloaded so that they could put back to sea. Eddie had said before he left that he wasn't sure what time they would dock and he didn't want Molly waiting around in the cold and dark for hours.

'He said not to, just in case they were delayed. I've told Mr Harding that I'm going to take a day off without pay when Eddie does get back, though. Eddie said that before he left they'd been told it would have to be a quick turnaround this time, without any proper shore leave: the country is depending on the merchant navy to bring in as many supplies as they can,' she added proudly.

Sometimes it seemed to Molly that June and Sally, both with husbands in the army, seemed to forget that other men were doing their bit for the war effort as well and that it was just as important, their bravery just as great. A man didn't always need a gun to do his duty.

When Sally announced that it was time for her to go home, Molly noticed that June had left her cocoa.

'Are you still feeling queer?' she asked her sister when they had closed the door behind Sally.

June shook her head. 'I've bin feeling a bit sickly like all day,' she admitted. 'It must have bin sommat I ate.'

Molly looked at her sister. She knew that June had said that she and Frank weren't planning on starting a family whilst there was a war on, but with June now saying that she felt sick, and knowing that her sister normally had a healthy appetite, Molly couldn't help but wonder. Not that she had any intentions of telling June what she was thinking. With the mood June had been in these last few days she would probably snap her head off if she did.

She tried to imagine how she would feel if she and Eddie were married and she was feeling sickly on account of them having started a baby. The feeling of longing that swept over her made her eyes ache with tears. Once she and Eddie were wed there'd be no waiting for the war to be over; she already knew that she couldn't wait to hold his baby in her arms. Elsie would be thrilled as well. She knew that. And Elsie wasn't just Eddie's auntie: she was as good as an adopted mother to Molly as well. She was so lucky to have so many people in her life to share her love with, Molly decided, and even more lucky to have her wonderful, wonderful Eddie. She couldn't imagine her life now without him. It just wouldn't be worth living.

FIVE

It was almost dinner time and there was still no sign of Eddie. Molly was beginning to wonder if she should go down to Garston Dock after all, to see if his ship was now putting in at a different time from when it had been expected. Both June and her father were at work and Molly had the house to herself. She had kept busy by giving the front parlour a good turn-out and then going round to Elsie's to see if she had heard any news, and now, even though she was pretending to listen to the wireless, she was hurrying into the front room every few minutes to look anxiously through the lace curtains.

She was wearing the blue sweater that Eddie said matched her eyes, and her best pink lipstick, carefully painted on with a little brush to make it go further. Her tummy was so full of nervous butterflies, she couldn't even manage a cup of tea, never mind anything to eat. She wasn't going to go to the window again, she wasn't . . .

She almost jumped out of her skin when she heard the knock on the door, ran to open it and only just managed not to fling herself into Eddie's arms in full view of the whole cul-de-sac when she saw him standing on the step.

'Where have you bin?' she demanded breathlessly as he followed her inside. 'I was expecting you ages back.'

'We got delayed. Jerry subs,' he said to her lightly, adding with a reassuring grin, 'Mind you, we wasn't in any real danger, 'cos they can't aim straight for toffee. And then when we did get back we was anchored up out over the Liverpool bar, waiting for a pilot boat to bring us in.'

Molly was laughing and crying at the same time. 'I've missed you that much,' she told him, too relieved to see him to realise that he was deliberately making light of the perils of his return voyage.

Barely giving him time to drop his kitbag, she hugged him tightly in the privacy of the dark enclosed hallway, eagerly lifting her face for his kiss. She hadn't realised until now, when she was in his arms and he was kissing her, just how much she had missed him and how afraid for him she had been.

'I feel like I've bin holding me breath ever since you left,' she told him dizzily. She loved him so much she could hardly bear it. She wanted to stay with him like this for ever, held tightly in his arms, his lips on hers, his body hard and warm against hers.

'How many days leave have you got?' she

271

asked, not really wanting to know when they would be parted again.

There was a small pause before he answered, 'We're not getting any proper shore leave this trip, lass.'

Molly could feel her stomach muscles tensing in protest. 'Oh, Eddie, what do you mean? Why not?' she protested, unable to keep the shocked disappointment from her voice.

'I'm sorry, lass. Rightfully speaking, I shouldn't be here at all,' he told her quietly, 'but the captain said we could have a couple of hours.'

'A couple of *hours*!' Molly's eyes brimmed with tears of sadness. 'But, Eddie, they can't turn the ship round in that time. They'll have to take off the cargo and re-equip the ship with fuel and food before it can set sail again.'

With her head resting against his shoulder, she couldn't see the anxious look that crossed his face, but she did see the movement of his Adam's apple as he swallowed.

Immediately she raised her head and looked at him. 'Eddie, what is it?' she demanded. 'And don't tell me there isn't something because I can see that there is.'

She could feel the stiff resistance in his body, and her heart lurched with an awareness of his pain.

'Tell me,' she insisted.

She felt him take a deep breath, and then the words came spilling out.

'We lost a ship out of the convoy on the way back. Jerry torpedo got it. It went down so fast, one minute it was there and then the next . . .' A violent shudder went through him. 'Sister ship to ours, she was. We'd bin out wi' the lads off her in New York, and now they're gone, not a one of them left . . .'

Deep juddering sobs overwhelmed him. Molly gathered him as close to her as she could. He was such a tall broad-shouldered man and she was so small, but she cradled him in her arms, whispering comforting words to him as she did so.

'I'm sorry, lass. I shouldn't have told you about that.' He shook his head, raising his sleeve to wipe away the tears on his face.

Wordlessly, Molly clung to him, so afraid for him that she could hardly breathe. What if Eddie had been on that ship that had gone down? What if he had been taken from her?

All of a sudden she was overwhelmed by feelings she didn't fully understand: desperation; urgency; fear; a compulsion to hold him and never ever let him go; and something else – a different feeling, and a very different need that was so unfamiliar to her she could hardly comprehend where it had come from.

'Eddie, there's no one else here. Let's go upstairs.' She was talking quickly, her eyes brilliant with emotion, as she took hold of his hand and tried to tug him towards the stairs.

But Eddie refused to move.

For a minute she did not think he had understood what she was saying because he stared at her, whilst a dark tide of colour burned up under his skin. And then shook his head.

'Eddie, I want us to be together,' Molly begged him. 'Like we were already married. Like you wanted to before you left last time,' she added.

'Oh, Molly, Molly . . .'

Suddenly Eddie was holding her tightly, his whole body shaking, fresh tears filling his eyes as he looked down at her.

'There's nothing I want more than . . . than for you and me to be together properly, and bless your sweet heart for offering yourself to me, Molly, but it wouldn't be right. Not now, when I don't even know . . .' He took a deep breath. 'If anything should happen to me, Molly, and one day I don't come back . . .'

Immediately Molly put her hand over his mouth to silence him. 'Don't say that,' she implored, frantically shaking her head. 'You mustn't.'

Very gently, Eddie removed her hand from his lips and kissed it, before holding it tightly within his own, as he continued gruffly, 'There's a war on, Molly, and some things need talking about. If anything were to happen and I weren't to come back, I wouldn't want to think I'd left yer in any kind of trouble. I love yer, Molly. I love yer so much it gives me a pain right here,' he thumped his heart, 'just thinking about yer, when we're not together. But I respect yer, as well, as a man should respect the woman he loves – aye, and I want others to respect yer as well.

'There's nothing I want more than to hold your sweet body next to mine, and for two pins . . . I'd . . . but I can't, Molly. It wouldn't be right. I want us to be properly wed before you give yourself to me.'

'I hate this war!' Molly whispered passionately as she wept in his arms. 'I want us to be together *now*, Eddie.' Now before it was too late, but superstitiously she couldn't bring herself to say those last words to him.

She felt his arms tightening round her and her heart thudded into her ribs as he groaned and then kissed her with fierce passion. Her belly quivered, her veins running molten with an urge far stronger than any rules of society when she felt his response to her. But then, just when she thought she had won and that he would take her upstairs, instead, he kissed her hard and then released her.

'I've got to go.'

'No,' Molly begged him. 'No! Not yet, Eddie . . . no.'

'I've got to. It's for the best. Let's set a date for the wedding, Molly,' he told her urgently.

Her face lit up. 'When?'

'We're gone just short of three weeks at a time, so why don't we say in nine weeks? I'll be due a bit of extra leave by then so we can have a bit of a honeymoon. I'll sort that out if you sort out having the banns read with the vicar.'

'Nine weeks. Oh, Eddie!'

'Is that too soon?'

'No . . . I wish it could be nine days,' Molly told him honestly, and then blushed when she saw the look in his eyes.

'Eeh, lass,' he whispered, kissing her fiercely and then saying huskily, 'Come wi' us whilst I go next door and tell me Auntie Elsie that I'm not staying ashore this time home, and that she'd better start trimming her wedding hat.'

'I'll come down to the dock with you,' Molly said as he opened the door, wanting to prolong their reunion for as long as she could.

'No, lass. It's best that you don't. Come on now, give us a smile to tek away with me – something to remember you by. I haven't forgotten that it's your eighteenth birthday coming up, and I promise I'll bring you sommat special back wi' me next time.'

She tried her best to be strong but when he kissed her, her tears ran down her face, dripping onto their intertwined mouths, so that their kiss was flavoured with the bitterness of her grief.

'Nine weeks!' Elsie exclaimed when they told her their news. 'Well, that isn't going to leave us much time to get everything sorted out.' Her face softened when she looked at them. 'Mind, I can see by the looks of you that you don't want to wait. And you've got a sensible head on your shoulders, Molly, for all that you're only seventeen.'

'She'll be eighteen in a few weeks,' Eddie reminded his aunt.

Molly smiled lovingly at him. She certainly felt more than grown up enough to be marrying Eddie.

'Well, I don't know why you're going round wi' such a glum face on you, our Molly,' June chided her over supper. 'At least you got to see your Eddie.'

'I know you're disappointed that Eddie's had to sail again so quickly, but our June's right, lass,' their father said gently. 'Now come on, cheer up, there's a good girl.'

She *was* being thoughtless and selfish, Molly acknowledged guiltily as she went over to her father and hugged him. She was upsetting her father and no doubt June would have given anything to have seen Frank, even for five minutes.

'Sorry, Dad. I was just a bit upset, that's all,' Molly admitted, forcing herself to smile as she tried to make light of her feelings.

'Molly, go round to Elsie's, will yer, and ask her if she's got any of them sour baking apples still stored away?' June appealed, trying to lighten the mood. 'I've got a right taste for them at the moment.'

To both Molly and June's astonishment, their father started to chuckle and shake his head.

'I remember that yer mam craved them when she was carrying you, our June. Couldn't get her enough of them, I couldn't. All hours of the night and day she were eating them.'

June's face lost its colour in a flash whilst Molly looked at her sister and said cautiously, 'June, that sickly feeling you've bin having, you don't think—'

'No, I don't,' June denied angrily, 'and I don't want to think it neither, thank you very much. I've already told you that me and my Frank don't want no kiddies until the war's over, and don't you go saying nowt to anyone about me fancyin' stuff, neither.'

'So you don't want me to go round to Elsie's to ask for an apple, then?' Molly teased her mock-innocently.

'Oh, give over with yer teasing, Molly,' June begged her, with a reluctant smile. 'This isn't a joke. The last thing I want is to be carrying, with Frank away and a war on.'

Molly could see that her sister was genuinely upset and worried. She went and sat down beside her.

'You're feeling a bit shocked now, June – it's only natural – but if there is to be a baby . . .'

'I've already told you there *isn't*.' June looked close to tears. 'There can't be. Me and Frank . . .' She shook her head, her bravado suddenly crumpling as she clung to Molly's hand and begged her, 'Oh, Molly, what if I am? What am I going to do? What will Frank say when he finds out? And that mother of his . . . I can just imagine what she's going to say, blaming me and saying as how we should have bin more careful. And besides, I don't know anything about babies.' June's face puckered and she wept, 'Oh, Molly, I wish our mam was here.'

Molly bit her lip as June's eyes filled with anxious tears. Her sister had always been so strong and so fiercely independent. Now suddenly she was vulnerable and afraid. It was up to her to help her, Molly told herself, just as June had helped *her* when they were younger.

Taking a deep breath, she squeezed June's hand reassuringly and said, 'Stop worrying. Your Frank will be over the moon and you'll have Sally to help you and tell you how to go on.' She added teasingly, 'And Frank's mam can even deliver it for you.'

'*What?* Have her delivering my kiddie and probably torturing me out of spite?' June objected vigorously, the militant sparkle returning to her eyes. 'Over my dead body.'

SIX

February might be the shortest month but to Molly it was dragging by as though it was anchored up in Garston Dock. They were still only just over halfway through it and life was getting harder by the day. Ration queues were getting longer, and the shop shelves were getting emptier of those things that weren't rationed.

June's pregnancy was making her tetchy, and, of course, nothing could be said about it publicly until she reached her fourth month and was safely over any chance of miscarriage, although one evening when Molly and June were at Sally's, Sally badgered June until she gave in and told her, before admitting herself, 'Same here. I reckon mine's due in September, what about you?'

'The same,' June responded. 'Our Molly here's already fussing about knitting for it.'

'I reckon no matter what the Government has to say about it, there's gonna be a lot of kiddies being born soon. Stands to reason, doesn't it? It's only nature, after all. Mind you, there's gonna be them as aren't wearin' a weddin' ring wish they weren't carryin'. Aye, and them as well 'oo won't be able to say rightly who the father is. You've only got to go down the Grafton on a Saturday night to know that.'

Sally had got a job at the Grafton as a hat check girl, and Elsie and Molly had volunteered to mind her baby whilst she was out at work, knowing how much she needed the extra money.

'All sorts goin' on down there now, there is,' Sally confided, as she eased her shoes off her aching feet. 'I saw them two sisters of Johnny Everton's there last week, showin' themselves up. Aye, and I've seen women I know is married wrapping themselves around some chap wot isn't their husband. Shockin', especially when they've got hubbies off fighting.'

'I suppose they feel lonely,' Molly offered, flushing slightly when June and Sally both turned to look at her with identical expressions of disapproval.

'Well then, they should find sommat useful to do, instead of goin' chasin' after men and mekkin' a show of themselves,' Sally said. 'I got ter admit I could have done wi'out this,' she added glumly, patting her still flat belly. 'I'm bound to lose me job, and they were paying me good money.'

'Maybe the war will be over before you have the baby, Sally,' Molly suggested hopefully.

'I don't know about that. I had a letter from

my Ronnie this morning. He said as how they were gettin' well dug in at this Nantes place he's bin moved to. They've had them building an airfield and they've got RAF an' all sorts there now. 'Ave you heard from your Frank lately, June?'

'Yes, but he didn't say much about where they were.'

'Is everything sorted out for the wedding, Molly?' Sally asked, desperate to lighten the mood.

'Just about. The vicar has said we can get married the third Saturday in March, to fit in with Eddie's ship docking.'

'He'll be back before then, though, won't he?'

'Yes.' Excitement shone in Molly's eyes. 'He should be back this week.' She could hardly wait. It seemed like for ever since she had last seen him. But she was luckier than June and Sally, she knew. At least Eddie's ship came back to Liverpool regularly, even though it had to suffer the dangers of crossing the Atlantic to do so. Mr Churchill was full of praise for the brave men of the merchant navy, and the warships that sailed with them to protect their convoys from enemy submarines. There was so much she wanted to tell him about the wedding, but most of all she wanted to be held tightly in his arms. Just thinking about him kissing her made her whole body tingle.

'What about your wedding dress?' Sally asked.

'She's altered my frock, and trimmed it up a bit different, so as it will fit her, haven't you, Molly?' June answered for her.

Molly nodded. She had taken the dress in, and shortened it. She loved the fact that, like June, she would be wearing some part of her mother's wedding dress. It made her feel closer than ever to her sister. Who knew – maybe she would have a niece and then perhaps a daughter to pass it down to in time?

'Me and June went to the baker's to see about a cake,' Molly told Sally, laughing as she added, 'Because of the sugar rationing they're renting out a dummy cake they've made out of cardboard and painted up to look like it's been iced all fancy.'

'Aye, well, that's no loss, is it?' Sally comforted her practically. 'Meself, I've never bin keen on fruitcake. Besides, I expect your Aunt Violet will be able to help out with some stuff from the farm.'

'Yes, she will,' Molly agreed.

'And even if she couldn't, there's allus George Lawson from number 79, who works down the docks. He can get his hands on anything, so 'e says,' June chipped in.

'Aye, and from what I've heard that includes any girl daft enough to be taken in by his soft-soaping,' Sally said forthrightly.

Molly was listening to them but at the same time she was thinking excitedly of Eddie's return and their wedding. She was counting the hours now until he got back, knowing that even with bad weather his ship should be putting in to port soon.

* * *

283

Molly looked impatiently at the clock. Eddie's ship was due to have docked in the early hours of the morning under cover of darkness, although she hadn't heard from him yet. This Saturday it was her turn to go down to Lime Street station with the WVS to man the tea urns and be on hand to offer whatever practical help she could to the new conscripts going off to their training barracks, and the families who came to see them off. Molly had hurried through her morning's chores, torn between impatience and excitement, humming happily under her breath, imagining Eddie's ship docking and Eddie wanting to see her just as impatiently as she was longing to see him.

Her chores now finished, she hurried upstairs to get washed and changed, and then quickly drank a cup of tea before grabbing her cap and cramming it down on her curls, ready to leave the house.

She had just stepped out through the front gate when she saw the telegraph boy cycling up the cul-de-sac.

Daisy Cartwright from across at number 77, who was obviously on her way to the shops and marshalling her two small exuberant sons in front of her, waved at Molly, and called out to her, 'Wonder where he's goin'. Makes me go cold all over, it does, whenever I see 'im.'

Molly was just about to agree with her, when the boy drew level with her and called out, 'You from number 78?'

Quickly she nodded, her heart pounding as she took the telegram from him. It was addressed to her. Everyone knew that the buff envelopes brought bad news of loved ones being injured or killed.

''Ere, Molly, let me go and get your dad.'

She looked blankly at Daisy, numbly aware of the shocked pity she could see in her eyes. She hadn't even seen or heard Daisy cross the road.

Whilst she stood gripping the telegram, Daisy put her arm round her shoulders and instructed her sons, 'Run round and knock on the back door of number 78 and tell whoever answers the door to come quickly.

'Come on, Molly lass, let's get you back inside before the whole of the cul-de-sac comes out nosying. Not that anyone'd mean any harm, but at times like this yer wants yer bit of privacy . . .'

'What's going on?' June asked sharply as they walked into the front room.

Daisy answered quickly, 'There's bin a telegram delivered, June, for your Molly.'

Molly was distantly aware of June taking the telegram from her and opening it, and then exclaiming crossly, 'Well, of all the daft things . . . Molly, it's all right. It's from your Eddie, to say that they've docked but that he won't get no shore leave this time because he's being transferred to another ship that's going out today.'

'*What?* Let me see,' Molly demanded. When

June passed the telegram to her, her hands were shaking so much she could hardly hold it.

At the bottom Eddie had written, 'See you in church.' And he had signed it with a kiss.

'Daft bugger,' Daisy said bluntly. 'Fancy sending her a telegram. Half scared her to death, he has. Men! I'd best be on me way otherwise the queue at Hodsons will be all the way up Edge Hill and back again.'

'Are you all right?' June asked Molly after Daisy had gone.

'When he gave me the telegram and I saw me name on it, I thought . . .' Tears of relief welled in Molly's eyes.

'Like Daisy said, your Eddie is a daft bugger,' June declared, putting her arm round her comfortingly. 'You'd better come back inside and have a cup of tea.'

'I can't. I'm going to be late for the WVS as it is, and they're relying on us down at the railway station. Some of the families have come from miles out to see their men off. You know yourself what it's like.'

'Well, get yourself a cuppa there and have a couple of extra sugars – it'll help you calm down.'

'I'm all right, June, honest.' Suddenly Molly started to laugh.

'What's so funny?' June demanded, puzzled.

'I was just picturing meself, standing there, thinking that Eddie was dead when he wasn't.'

'Well, I can't see owt much to laugh about in

that,' June grumbled. 'If it had been my Frank that'd given me a shock like that, I'd have boxed his ears good and proper the next time I saw him.'

'Have you told your Frank about the baby yet?' Molly asked her.

'No, he'd only start worrying, and since I'm not three months I don't see the point. Time enough to tell him once it's for sure. With any luck he'll be getting some home leave soon anyway.'

'It would be nice if he were here for the wedding. Eddie would like that, an' all. He and Frank really get on.

'June, do you ever wake up in the morning and can't believe how much has changed?' Molly asked her sister impulsively. 'Dad was telling me the other day as how he and our mam were walking out for two years before they got married, and yet this time last year you were only just walking out with Frank, and I was with Johnny and now . . .'

'Aye, well, it were different in Dad's time and war makes people act a bit quicker – you can't take time for granted. You've got the church booked, and the church hall so you're all sorted. Of course, Elsie will be giving us a hand.'

Molly smiled happily. So what if she had to have a pretend cardboard wedding cake? She didn't care. All she cared about was that in three weeks' time she and Eddie would be getting married.

SEVEN

'And you could have knocked me over with a feather when I got a letter from my Frank yesterday, saying as how he would be home before Easter. Molly, how do you think it will look if I put a bit of trimming on me straw hat for the wedding, so that it matches up with me blue frock, and then pin a few flowers to me jacket?' June demanded, breaking off from telling Sally about her good news, and then continuing without waiting for an answer, 'I could do with some of that Cyclax leg cream as well. I'm clean out of stockings and my legs need some colour.'

'You want to have a word with Pearl. She told me the other day that if I ever wanted any stockings to have a word with 'er as her George has a contact,' Sally said. 'It's a pity you didn't get a chance to have a word with your Eddie before he left, Molly. I reckon it would be easy enough for 'im to bring us both in a few pairs of stockings, what with him toing and froing across to America all the time. Did he say exactly when he'd be back when he wrote you that telegram?'

Molly shook her head, using her teeth to snap off the thread from the hem she was sewing. 'He's only bin gone just over a week, so I reckon he won't be back until a couple of days before the wedding.'

'It's a pity he's going to miss your birthday, tomorrow,' June commented.

'He can miss that, just so long as he doesn't miss our wedding,' Molly answered stoutly. Of course she would have loved it if Eddie could have been with her tomorrow to celebrate her eighteenth birthday, but what did a birthday matter compared with a marriage? 'I went round to see Elsie last night. Eddie had left a parcel with her to give me on me birthday if he wasn't back. She was asking me if he was going to wear his uniform or if she ought to sort him out a suit.'

The three young women were spending Sunday afternoon together, discussing the wedding, and listening to the wireless, June and Molly's father having gone down to the allotment, whilst Sally and Ronnie's little boy slept in his pram.

'Well, we're certainly going to celebrate your birthday, even if Eddie isn't going to be here to share in the fun,' Sally announced determinedly, 'and not just with Elsie's elderberry wine. You're only eighteen the once, and tomorrow night we'll mek sure you have a good time.'

Molly, June, Sally and some of the girls from

Hardings were all going to Lewis's after work for a bit of tea, before going on to the pictures. 'Not that goin' to the pictures wi' us can compare wi' going with Eddie,' Sally teased, laughing when Molly blushed and then laughed herself.

She was disappointed that Eddie wouldn't be home to share in her birthday celebrations but she was still looking forward to them, and to going out and having fun with her friends. After all, it wouldn't be long before he was home and then she would have their wedding to look forward to. Just thinking about becoming Eddie's wife made her feel giddy with happiness and excitement.

'So what's the present he left for you, then, Molly?' Sally asked.

'I haven't opened it yet.'

'Oh, go on, get it open. Eddie won't mind,' Sally urged her.

Molly shook her head, but the other two insisted that she satisfy their curiosity and in the end she gave in, going upstairs to collect the neatly wrapped square box.

'It doesn't look like stockings,' June commented, obviously disappointed.

Molly wasn't listening to her. Instead she was staring at the contents of the small box she had just opened, her lips parted in a shocked 'Oh' of delighted disbelief.

'What is it, then, Molly?' Sally demanded, peering over her shoulder.

'It's a watch,' Molly told Sally and June breathlessly, her face flushing with pleasure, as she continued to stare at the pretty dainty watch with its neat leather straps. 'Eddie's bought me a watch.'

'Let me have a look,' June demanded. 'Well, I never. That must have cost him a pretty penny, Molly,' she teased, breaking off to complain, 'Who's that knocking at the front door on a Sunday afternoon? You go, our Molly. Don't worry, we'll mind your watch.'

Laughing, Molly put down her birthday gift and went to see who was there.

A young man stood on the path. He was dressed in the everyday uniform of the merchant navy, a smear of oil on his cheek.

'Are you Molly Dearden?' he asked her.

'Yes.'

'I've come about your Eddie.'

'You're a friend of Eddie's?' Molly opened the door properly, smiling warmly at him.

But he stayed where he was, twisting his cap in his hands as he looked down at the ground and muttered, 'I've come wi' a bit of bad news for you.'

Even then she didn't have any kind of premonition or sense of warning, her first thought being that he had come to tell her that Eddie's ship was going to be delayed.

'It's Eddie's ship, see,' the young sailor told her desperately. 'Torpedoed, it was, three days out of Liverpool. Our ship was on our way back, see,

291

and so we was able to pick up them as had survived . . .'

Molly stared at him, unable to take in what he was trying to tell her. It couldn't possibly be true. She wasn't going to let it be true.

'Where's Eddie?' she demanded, repeating frantically when she saw his face, 'Where is he? Where . . . ?'

'He was a goner when we pulled him out of the water – anyone could see that – but he still grabbed hold of me arm and said how he wanted me to come and see you and . . . tell you how much he loves . . . loved you. Them were his last words: "Tell Molly that I love her."'

Molly opened her mouth to scream that it couldn't possibly be true; that he couldn't possibly be standing there and telling her that Eddie, her Eddie, who was to marry her in two weeks' time was dead. But no sound emerged. She felt as though a giant hand had seized hold of her, squeezing the breath from her throat and the life from her heart.

Eddie couldn't be dead. He mustn't be. Not Eddie.

'Molly, who is it?' June demanded, coming to the door to find out what was keeping her, her impatience changing to concern as she saw the way Molly was standing there like a statue, whilst a young man June didn't know stood on the front path, twisting his cap and stammering, 'I'm sorry, missus, it's her Eddie . . . Bought it, he has. His ship were shot out of the water by Jerry. Poor sods didn't have a chance . . .'

'Are you saying that Eddie is dead?' June asked shakily.

'Yes. I'm off of the *Aegeus* – we picked up the men from his ship, and his last words to me were to come here and tell his girl.'

Suddenly Molly came to life. 'But if he spoke to you he can't be dead. Tell him, June,' she pleaded, turning to her sister. 'Tell him that Eddie can't be dead.' Molly's voice had started to rise and the young sailor was looking increasingly uncomfortable, whilst June whispered to Sally in an urgent undertone to go round to Elsie's and tell her what had happened.

'He got it in the gut, missus,' he told June in a gruff voice. 'It teks longer ter die that way, but he knew as he got it. Said so himself . . . when the medic was pumping him full of morphine. I've got ter go and get back ter me ship. You'll be hearing official, like, of course . . .'

June had her hand on Molly's arm and she could feel her trembling.

'Thanks for your trouble,' she told the sailor, adding to Molly, 'Come on, let's get you inside.'

'I don't want to go inside. I want to go to Eddie,' Molly told her. 'He needs me, June. He needs me . . .'

EIGHT

Four days ago she had been eighteen, but she might as well have been eighty. That was how old she felt, how empty of any desire to go on living. There was no point to life for her any more without Eddie, and she wished passionately that instead of standing here in the bright sunlight of this cold March morning she was in that dreadful wooden coffin with Eddie. At least that way they would be together, she would be in his arms, lying heart to heart with him, even if their cold lifeless flesh couldn't register the joy of that shared intimacy.

She looked dry-eyed at the coffin up ahead of her, borne aloft on the shoulders of his shipmates. John Fowler, dressed in funereal black, walked immediately behind them. Elsie had been too distraught to attend the funeral of the young nephew she had brought up almost as though he were her own child. Molly too had been gently advised not to come, in case it was too much for her, but how could she let Eddie be locked away in that box and buried in the black coldness of the earth without her being there? Eddie, whose last words had been for her, whose last thoughts had been of her; Eddie who had loved her as no one else ever could.

The whole cul-de-sac had turned out to walk him to his grave, along with many of his shipmates and officers from the merchant navy.

'Why did he have to sail on that ship?' Molly had asked brokenly when June had led her into their front room, the raw agony of her loss permeating her numbness. 'Why did it have to be him, my Eddie? Why . . . ?'

It had been Frank's mother – reluctantly summoned by June when she had realised that the fits of shivering that gripped Molly, alternated with hot sweats, needed more experienced help than she could give her – who had finally answered her terrible question.

Doris Brookes had taken hold of Molly's hot and sweaty hand, clasping it in the firm coolness of her own as she told her calmly, 'When there is no reason or explanation, we have to accept that some things are God's will. Eddie has gone, Molly, but if he was here do you think he would want to see you like this? Do you think you are the only young woman to lose the man she loves?' The sympathy in her voice took June by surprise. She'd forgotten that Doris was not much older than she was herself when she lost her husband.

Her words had made Molly turn towards her, remembering that she had been widowed in the Great War.

'Eddie wouldn't want to see you upsetting yourself like this. He'd want to be able to be proud of you, just as you should be proud of him.'

'Proud of him? For dying?' Molly had challenged her bitterly. 'For leaving me here without him?'

Huge sobs racked her body. She had never dreamed she could feel like this, or that she would have to. Her pain was shot through blood red with anger. Anger because Eddie had had to change ships; anger against the Germans; anger against the authorities; anger against other people whose men were not dead; but, most of all, anger against Eddie himself for leaving her here alone without him.

She had tried to drag her hand free of Doris Brookes's but she had refused to release it, saying with firm authority, 'It will get better, Molly, I promise you, but you have to help it. You have to be strong and brave, and think about what Eddie would have wanted you to do.'

Molly had tried to take comfort from her words but she couldn't. How could it be God's will that Eddie had to die so young and so cruelly?

But he was dead, and now she was walking slowly behind his coffin, four days after her eighteenth birthday, her head bowed beneath the brim of her borrowed black hat to conceal her tears.

She ought to be wearing a bridal gown, not mourning clothes. Her father and her sister were on either side to support her, whilst Frank, newly returned on leave, walked up ahead of them in his uniform.

Inside the church, dust motes danced on beams of sunlight. But despite the sunshine outside the church, here inside it was bitterly cold. As cold as the grave. The thought tormented her and she had to force back an anguished sob. She had promised herself that today at least she would be brave for Eddie, not disgrace him.

June was standing next to her in the pew with their father on her other side. June, who was carrying a new life inside her, a child who would never see the man who would have been his uncle. Molly pressed her hand flat to her belly as a steel-sharp pain twisted it, taunting her for the emptiness of her own womb. She should have pressed Eddie harder that last time they were together. Then at least she might have had something of him to fill the emptiness inside her and take some of the pain from her loss. Eddie's child would have been a blessing, a ray of hope at this bleakest of times.

Tears filled her eyes and spilled down onto her cheeks. At her side June reached for her hand and squeezed it tightly, whilst on her other side, Molly could see out of the corner of her eye how her sister also reached for the comfort of her own husband's hand. An unfamiliar bitterness gripped her.

Eddie hadn't even been in the forces. He had been a merchant seaman, a soft target for Hitler's torpedoes. She had to bite the insides of her cheeks to stop herself from crying aloud.

'Why don't we go home now, Molly?'

She turned her head to look at Frank, staring at him as though his quiet compassionate words had been spoken in a language she didn't understand. His hand was on her arm, his eyes filled with sadness and pity for her. They were outside the church now, waiting for Eddie's body to be conveyed to its final resting place.

A huge wave of raw pain tore at her, savaging her, as she shook off Frank's hand and went to join the other mourners making their way to the graveside.

'Molly lass.' Her father was standing in front of her, blocking her way. 'Come on home now. You don't need to see this.' He knew from experience that seeing your loved one being put into the ground for ever was the worst thing imaginable, and he feared for his younger daughter.

Stubbornly Molly looked away from him. Couldn't he, of all people, understand?

'Molly . . .' her father urged.

'I can't leave, Dad, not yet. I've got to stay with him until . . . until it's over.' Tears she wasn't going to let herself cry burned the back of her eyes and her throat felt like there was something lodged within it. She should have been there with him to share his last moment and hear his last words, to send him from her with her love and the touch of her hand in his. His flesh was cold now and far beyond feeling her touch but she still felt a need to be with him at the very last.

'I'm taking June home,' she heard Frank saying quietly to her father.

Had she really once dreamed foolish girlish dreams of Frank? How distant and unreal all that seemed now when she was suffering the adult pain of loving and losing Eddie. Of course, Frank would be concerned for June, and all the more so now that he knew she was to have their child.

She would never have a child now, never love another man, never stand in church with Eddie at her side, whilst they exchanged their marriage vows.

A narrow grassy pathway led to the place where the grave was discreetly covered, but nothing could truly conceal the yawning pit of dark earth.

Her father tried to screen her from it by standing in front of her, but Molly pushed her way past him. The other mourners averted their faces when they saw.

Only the vicar looked directly at her, his watery blue eyes kind behind his spectacles.

There was a movement at the edge of Molly's line of vision and then the men were lifting the coffin. Suddenly, as they started to lower it, one of them let go of a rope just a bit too fast and the box lurched towards her as though inside it some life force was pleading to be set free. Molly reached forward towards it, crying out Eddie's name, struggling against the arms that held her back. Through her tears she saw the coffin being lowered into the earth.

'It's all right, Molly. Eddie is being laid to rest now.'

Laid to *rest*! He was twenty-one – he hadn't wanted to *rest*. He had wanted to live and to love.

The vicar was speaking, each word stabbing Molly's heart: ' "Earth to earth . . ." '

Her father leaned forward and picked up a handful of the rich black soil, letting it crumble through his rough and calloused hand onto the coffin.

Soon others were doing the same, but Molly couldn't. How could she throw the heavy black choking earth that would entomb him onto her beloved Eddie?

Eddie, please don't, please come back . . . The pleading words filled her head, but what was the use of speaking them? How could Eddie hear her when the sound of the earth being thrown down on top of him was drowning out her voice?

Most of the other mourners had left number 78 now. Only Elsie was still here, her homely face shadowed with abject sadness. Momentarily

Molly felt guilty – Elsie had loved Eddie too, as much as she loved her own son, and Molly hadn't tried to comfort her in any way since they'd heard the news. But at least Elsie had Jim and John left. Working down at the gridiron was back-breaking, low-paid work, but at least there they were safe, since Jerry had miraculously not dropped the bombs they had all been told to expect. God willing, Elsie would see the end of this war with both her husband and her son still alive, and probably a grandchild on the way as well if her Jim got wed, Molly reflected, gripped by her own pain.

Elsie watched Molly. She had loved Molly and June since they were born and she had helped Rosie out with both babies. But there had always been an extra special place in her heart for Molly. She couldn't have been happier, knowing that her much-loved nephew was going to marry the girl she had always loved as much as though she were her own daughter. Now she was grieving not just for Eddie but for Molly as well.

Thank God Frank was here now for June, Elsie thought, his arm wrapped comfortingly and protectively around her, but there was no saying what might happen to him once his leave was over and he went back to France. They were a lovely family, the Deardens, but they had not had much luck, what with Albert losing Rosie so young, and now Molly losing Eddie before they had even had time to wed.

Fresh tears filled Elsie's eyes and she welcomed the warmth of her John's sturdy arm to lean on. Poor, poor Molly. What a terrible thing to have happened.

Numbly Molly watched as Frank looked down at June, giving her a little hug and smiling gently before bending his head to whisper something to her that brought a smile to her sister's lips.

The emptiness inside Molly became a huge roaring burn of pain. Once that would have been her, with Eddie holding her. But she would never have that love again. Not now. Eddie would never look at her like that, nor hold her like that. She would never be able to put her hand on her still flat belly as June was now doing and look up at the man she loved, filled with love and happiness at the knowledge that between them they were bringing a new little life into the world to love and cherish. Never . . .

The sun was just coming up, lifting thin mist from the graveyard. Somewhere close at hand Molly could hear the early morning twitter of waking birds.

This was the day she should have been marrying Eddie, instead of visiting his grave.

In another week it would be Easter; the Church's celebration of the resurrection and the triumph of life over death. She was walking faster now, almost slipping on the wet grass in her haste.

The kind cloaking cloths of Eddie's burial had gone now, leaving the raw scar of the disturbed earth. There was no headstone as yet, just a small cross with Eddie's name written on it. Very carefully Molly kneeled down beside it. Her skirt would be muddied but what did that matter now? She put down the basket she was carrying and started to scratch at the earth with her bare fingers, and then dug more fiercely into it. Tears ran down her face to drip onto the soil as she tore at it, panting and sobbing. It was so newly dug that it fell back into the hole as soon as she had made it. She stopped to push her hair out of her eyes, leaving a smear of dirt on her forehead, and sat back on her heels, trying to catch her breath.

The sun was coming up, throwing long early morning shadows across the graveyard. One of them moved slowly towards her but she was oblivious to it as she went back to her self-imposed task.

'You should have brought a trowel with you instead of getting your hands all muddy like that. Here, give them to me and let's see if I can clean you up a bit.'

She turned obediently at the gentle familiarity of her father's voice, holding out her hands to him in the same way that a young child might have done.

Very slowly and carefully he wiped the soil from them with his handkerchief.

'How did you know I would be here?' she asked him.

'I heard you get up so I got up too.'

'I decided about the flowers the day we buried him. I bought the plants off Mr Thomson at the nursery.'

'Yes. He told me.'

'Heartsease,' she told him, giving the tiny purple and yellow violas their popular name. 'And there's rosemary for remembrance, and lavender for later in the summer.' Her father took out his trowel and within minutes he was tucking the small plants into the little pockets he had dug for them.

'You put them in nice and square, with plenty of room for their roots so as they can breathe, and then you mek sure that when you put the soil back it's holding them in good and firmly. Good sturdy plants, these are, as deserve a proper planting.'

They worked together for nearly an hour, Albert Dearden tenderly cherishing the plants Molly had bought, and equally tenderly cherishing his daughter, unable to find the words to tell her how much he grieved for her and for the fine young man who had died.

'I can remember as clear as though it were yesterday the day we buried my Rosie,' he told her quietly. 'A black day that was for me, Molly.'

'At least you and Mam were married, Dad. At least you'd been together,' Molly burst out.

Her father sighed, guessing what she was feeling. 'Aye, lass, and you've bin cruelly denied that, and that's hard to bear.'

'I don't know how I can bear it,' Molly told him. 'I don't want to bear it . . . Oh, Dad, Dad . . .'

He took her in his arms, comforting her as best he could.

NINE

March was dying into April, the days turning with agonising emptiness. Molly had grown accustomed to the uncertain sideways glances of the other girls at the factory, the guilty indrawn breaths whenever they forgot and talked in her earshot about their own loves and lives. But the truth was that she could feel barely anything through the numbness of her grief. It filled every hour of her life, her days and her nights, with its cold relentless ache that somehow had become so familiar that she was now afraid to be without it.

June's pregnancy had already begun to show, and she was spending more and more time with Sally. The two of them had more in common now than she and June did. *They* were both married, both carrying, both waiting impatiently for the war to end and their husbands to come home to them, in between talking excitedly about the long-awaited arrival of the film *Gone with the Wind*.

Sometimes Molly felt that she couldn't bear to be anywhere near them, their futures contrasted so sharply with her own, and yet she knew that they were doing their best to comfort her and she didn't want to hurt their feelings.

She was alone in the house, June and Sally having taken advantage of the sunny Saturday morning to go shopping. They had invited Molly to join them but she had refused. Her father was down at his allotment and when the doorbell rang she tensed, hesitating before reluctantly going to answer it.

The sight of Anne standing on the front doorstep brought a fresh shadow to cloud her thoughts, although she wasn't really surprised to see her friend, the fresh spring breeze tangling Anne's honey-blonde curls.

'I've just come from the church hall,' Anne informed Molly, determinedly stepping into the hallway without waiting for an invitation. 'Mrs Wesley keeps asking where you are.'

Molly made no reply, turning her face away.

'Molly, I know how you must feel,' Anne told her gently, closing the front door.

'No, you don't. How can you? Your Philip isn't dead. He's still alive.'

'Oh, Molly.' Dropping her handbag, Anne put her arms round Molly and hugged her tightly. 'I'm so very, very sorry. It must hurt dreadfully badly. I know how much you loved Eddie, and I can imagine how I would feel if I lost Philip.

I can't bring Eddie back for you, Molly, but please don't shut me out. I thought you and me were friends, but when I came round to see you earlier, June told me that you didn't want to see me.'

The tears Molly had been holding back overwhelmed her. She hadn't wanted to see Anne because she hadn't been able to bear the thought of Anne talking about Philip and their love, and their plans for their future together.

'You can't go on like this, Molly, shutting yourself away from everyone.'

'Why not?' Molly demanded, pushing her friend away and digging in her pocket for her handkerchief so that she could dry her tears.

'Because when you and me joined the WVS, Molly, we made a commitment to do our bit, just like your Eddie and my Philip, that's why not. I never took you for the kind of girl who would go and let others down, Molly, and that's what you will be doing if you stop coming to WVS. And what about your driving? You were so proud after Christmas when Mrs Wesley said that she was going to put you forward for special emergency vehicle driving training on account of you being so good.'

'That was before I lost Eddie.' Molly felt a small pang of guilt. It was true that she had been thrilled by Mrs Wesley's decision. 'Anyway, it's too late for that now.'

'No, it isn't. Mrs Wesley said to tell you that

there's an Air Raid Precautions ambulance driver course starting the week after next and that you're to report to the ARP headquarters on Monday night to enrol for it. She said to tell you as well that she's spoken to Mr Harding and he's agreed that you can have time off to go on it.'

'I don't want to.'

'Oh, Molly, how can you say that? It's such an honour. I wish I'd been chosen but my driving isn't good enough. Just think how proud your Eddie would have been.'

Fresh tears prickled Molly's eyes. She didn't want Eddie to be proud of her. She wanted him to be here with her.

'I'm not leaving this house until you promise me that you'll go. I'll come with you, if you like,' Anne offered coaxingly.

Molly felt too tired to argue with her any longer. What was the point? 'Very well, I'll go,' she gave in dully.

'Oh, Molly.' Anne smiled in relief, giving her another hug. 'Just wait until I write and tell Philip. He will—' Anne's face went pink and she bit her lip, suddenly aware of how much it must be hurting Molly to hear her talk about Philip when Eddie was dead.

'Why don't we go and see a matinée, Molly? It's only just gone dinner time, and the main film doesn't start until two.'

'I'd just as soon not do, thanks all the same, Anne.' The thought of having to sit through

309

newsreels that could include scenes of merchant shipping putting safely into England's ports was more than Molly could bear.

Under normal circumstances the thought of what lay ahead of her would have had her shaking in her shoes, feeling both proud and a little bit scared, Molly admitted as she stood with the other women who had been selected to train as voluntary emergency services drivers, in the yard of the ARP headquarters at the Police Training School in Mather Avenue. But Eddie's death had left her feeling as though nothing really mattered to her any more. The only reason she was even here was because of the fuss Mr Harding had made when he had insisted on telling everyone how proud he was that one of his employees had been selected for such important work.

'And you never said so much as a word to me,' June had complained when they had walked home together.

'It didn't seem that important,' Molly had defended herself, tempted to add that nothing could be important to her any more.

But then when they had got home, June had insisted on going round to Elsie's and telling her all about it, and then Elsie had burst into tears and told Molly how proud she was of her and how proud Eddie would have been, and after that Molly hadn't been able to bring herself to say she didn't want to do the training.

So now here she was, feeling slightly sick as a very stern-looking uniformed policeman strode up and down in front of them.

Several feet away, on the other side of the yard, a row of ambulances and lorries was drawn up facing them, a driver standing beside each one.

'We've been told that all of you have the makings of first-class drivers, but first-class drivers and first-class emergency drivers are two very different things,' the fierce-looking police officer announced warningly. 'Those of you that succeed in completing this course will be first-class emergency drivers, and your responsibility will be a heavy one. People's lives will depend on your driving skills, and on your knowledge of this city. If a bomb drops in the street ahead of you when you're on your way to hospital or driving one of the rescue detail lorries, then you need to know how best to divert to make sure you get there safely and speedily. Therefore part of your course will involve learning by heart the road map of the city of Liverpool. There's no place for slackers or time-wasters on this course. Anyone missing a lesson will be dismissed. Those of you who complete the course successfully will be given official recognition as trained emergency services drivers and your names will be placed on a rota of available drivers.'

Molly could feel a tremor of uncertainty and dismay running through her, and it was obvious the other women felt the same. But oddly, instead of leaving her daunted, for the first time since Eddie's death she felt a small prickle of interest and an unexpected surge of determination.

Two hours later, having driven one of the ambulances under the watchful eye of its regular driver, and won his approval of her neat three-point turns, as well as having collected the city map she had to learn and listened to a lecture detailing an imaginary emergency situation, she returned home feeling both exhausted and yet more alive than she had felt since she had received the news of Eddie's death.

'So how did it go then?' June asked her when she got home.

'There's so much to learn, June. We've got to know every street in Liverpool off by heart, for a start, and not just their names, but where they are, where they go and if they're wide enough to drive down or turn round in. It's like the inspector told us – us knowing the quickest way to the nearest hospital could mean the difference between life and death for those we've got in an ambulance.'

'So it's ambulances you're going to be driving then, is it?'

'Maybe, but we've got to practise on lorries as well because they'll be used for transporting men and equipment to bomb sites.'

'I'd have thought they'd be using men for dangerous work like that,' June protested.

'There aren't enough men who can drive,' Molly told her, 'and a lot of the older ones want to do their bit but they don't want to learn to drive. Mrs Wesley says that she'll be putting my name down to drive the WVS mobile canteen vans as well, when I'm not on duty for emergency services driving.'

June shook her head but didn't say anything. She didn't entirely approve of what Molly was doing but at least it seemed to be bringing her back to life again.

Since she was now taking the emergency services driving course, Molly couldn't think of any plausible reason for not attending her WVS meetings, so reluctantly on Wednesday evening she put on her uniform and set off for the church hall.

Mrs Wesley acknowledged her presence with a brief nod of her head, and to Molly's relief didn't say anything about either her absence or Eddie's death.

It seemed strange to be back amongst the others, as though nothing had happened. It was hard for her, though, to hear them talking about their menfolk, and as though she sensed what she was feeling, Anne deliberately drew her away from the others when they were having their tea break.

Molly saw the local ARP warden hurrying in and going up to Mrs Wesley, but she didn't think anything of it until their organiser clapped her hands and called for their attention.

'Ladies, I'd like volunteers, please, to go down to the docks immediately. A convoy on its way to New York has been torpedoed. Two ships were sunk and another so badly damaged that it has had to turn back with those men who survived. Our help is needed to provide the men who don't require hospitalising with blankets, hot drinks and whatever other assistance we can.'

'Come on, Molly, let's volunteer,' Anne urged her, already putting up her own hand, but Molly shrank back and shook her head.

'I can't.' Her face was white and she was trembling.

'Yes, you can,' Anne told her, grabbing hold of her wrist and lifting Molly's arm before Molly could stop her.

'You shouldn't have done that. I can't go down to the docks.' Molly felt sick with shock and anger. How could her friend have been so insensitive? But Anne was ignoring her protests, tugging her with her as Mrs Wesley gathered up all the volunteers. She couldn't make a scene and refuse to go now, Molly realised, as Mrs Wesley urged them all to hurry, and collect everything they might need.

Willing hands packed blankets into Mrs Wesley's car whilst the ARP man assured her that a mobile kitchen would be in place by the time they reached the docks.

The dock was already busy with volunteers when Molly and Anne got off the tram. A pilot boat was nursing the dark hulk of the slow-moving merchant ship into its berth. Molly's stomach churned sickly just looking at it, and then it churned even more when her eyes adjusted to the darkness and she saw the gaping hole in its side.

How many men who had set out from Liverpool in the convoy would not be coming home? How many on this ship were injured and dying like her Eddie?

A shudder tore through her. She couldn't bear being here. It was too much. She could see Eddie's face; she could hear him crying out to her as he died.

'I can't do this.'

'Molly, you've got to pull yourself together,' Anne warned her fiercely.

'That's easy for you to say. Your Philip isn't dead.' The pain was unbearable. She had to escape it. Dropping the blankets she had been holding, Molly turned to flee, but Anne was suddenly standing in front of her, blocking her escape route.

'Molly, you can't leave now. Mrs Wesley will see you.'

'I don't care. I can't bear this,' Molly wept.

Anne grabbed hold of her and gave her a small shake. 'Yes, you can and you will. I never thought you would turn out to be a coward, Molly Dearden, but a coward is what you will be if you leave here. What do you think your Eddie would say if he could see you now? He'd be ashamed of you, that's what – and I'll be ashamed of you as well. We've got a duty to help these poor men, Molly. I know it must be hurting you being here, but running away and feeling sorry for yourself

315

won't bring your Eddie back. He's gone and you've got to face up to that, and be proud that you loved him and he loved you.'

Molly had stopped struggling as she listened to her friend, and now she straightened up in Anne's hold, her eyes brimming with tears. Somehow Anne's words had reached past her pain, and her self-pity.

'The men are coming off the ship now,' Anne told her, releasing her.

Very slowly Molly turned round. Hunched, weary-looking figures moved slowly down the gangplanks, the white flashes of bandages showing up starkly against the darkness of their uniforms, the stretcher bearers coming off first. Through her tears, Molly watched as the injured were taken to the waiting ambulances.

'Come on,' Anne urged her, bending down to pick up the blankets they had dropped.

Mechanically, Molly followed her, joining the line of WVS volunteers as they waited to offer hot drinks and hand out blankets to those who needed them.

Any one of these men could have been her own dear Eddie, Molly reflected, as weary faces lightened with relief and gratitude.

'Ta, duck,' one sailor thanked Molly as she handed him a cup of tea. 'Blew out the galley, Hitler did. All we've had for the last three days is cold food. Mind you, at least we was alive, unlike so many poor buggers. Didn't stand a chance, they didn't. Bloody Hitler,' the man swore, his face darkening.

Molly was trembling so hard that tea slopped wildly from the next cup she picked up, but to her relief the sailor taking it from her did so in silence.

Dawn was just beginning to lighten the sky when Molly let herself into number 78. Before they had parted to go to their homes, Anne had hugged her fiercely and said emotionally, 'Molly, Eddie would have been so proud of you for tonight.'

Molly's course ended, and to her relief she was passed as an emergency vehicle driver. She still went to bed every night reciting the names of Liverpool's streets, which at least helped to stop her from crying for Eddie.

In May the tempo of everyone's life began to change as the dreadful news came that Germany's blitzkrieg had resulted in the fall of Norway and Holland and Luxembourg. June and Sally exchanged anxious looks as the three girls sat in front of the wireless one Friday evening listening to the news.

'Our lads will sort out Jerry, you just wait and see,' Sally pronounced loyally but with hesitation, causing a sharp thrill of anguish to pierce Molly's heart.

'Where are you going, Molly?' June asked her when she got up and went to the back door.

'I feel like a bit of fresh air, so I thought I'd go down to the allotment and walk back with Dad.'

She could almost feel the look she knew June and Sally would be exchanging behind her back – a mixture of pity and guilt.

It had been a warm day, and the scent of late spring hung softly on the evening air.

As she approached the allotments she could hear angry raised male voices, loudest amongst them Alf Davies's.

'. . . And I'm telling you that that bloody dog of yours has got to go.'

A group of men were gathered in one of the allotments, Molly's father amongst them.

'Take it easy, Alf,' Molly heard him saying as she approached them.

'You can't blame the dog for doing what comes natural, like. He didn't know that you'd trapped them rabbits for your own dinner, did he?' one of the men laughed.

Bert Johnson was standing next to her father, his dog at his feet, whilst Alf Davies stood in front of him, red-faced with fury, refusing to join in the other men's good-natured banter.

'If he'd obeyed the law then the bloody dog wouldn't have got me rabbits, would it? No dogs to be allowed exceptin' for working dogs – that's what the Government has said. Anyone who has a dog has ter have it put down . . . and if he doesn't do it then I'll tek a gun to the thing meself.'

'You touch my dog and it'll be you as is facing the wrong end of a gun.' Bert's voice was thin and tremulous, and Molly felt tears prick sharply at her eyes. Why she should feel so concerned for old Bert and his dog she didn't know. She only knew that somehow Bert's plight touched a raw nerve with her.

'Come on, Alf. Leave it be now,' Molly's father urged. 'It were only a couple of rabbits, after all.'

'That's not the point. The law's the law and the law says no dogs exceptin' for working dogs,' Alf insisted, plainly resenting the fact that the other men were siding with Bert against him.

Molly shivered, despite the cardigan she was wearing over her short-sleeved blouse, and wrapped her arms around herself. She had never really taken to Alf Davies, nor his wife, if she were honest, and she knew that the couple weren't popular in the cul-de-sac.

'Molly lass!' her father exclaimed, suddenly seeing her.

'I came out for a bit of fresh air,' she told him. 'It's bin on the news again about the Germans invading Holland . . .'

'And that won't be the end of it, neither,' one of the other men prophesied grimly. 'No matter what bloody Chamberlain says.'

Molly shivered again. She slipped her arm through her father's, turning to frown over her shoulder as she heard Alf continuing to berate old Bert.

'He can't really make Bert have his dog put down, can he, Dad?'

'He might think he can, but I reckon between

319

us we can find a way to keep the dog out of sight until he's calmed down a bit,' her father comforted her, patting her hand. She had become so thin and pale since Eddie's death, her once-ready laughter now silenced. He ached with sympathy for her, but he knew from his own experience that only time could soften the sharpness of her pain. She was so young that she was bound to feel it all the more keenly, but young enough, he hoped, to find happiness with someone else – although he knew he could not tell her that.

That night Molly couldn't sleep. The scented sweetness of the night permeated her bedroom as she lay awake listening to the soft wuffling sound of June's breathing.

She and Eddie would have been married for nearly two months by now. Eddie . . . Eddie . . . She rolled over and buried her face in her pillow, longing for the relief of tears. Somehow, these last few weeks, she had found it impossible to cry properly for Eddie, as though everything inside her had dried up into a barren emptiness.

It was Pete Ridley, the milkman, who brought the news, leaving his horse to make its own ambling way down the road with the milk cart, as he paused to tell everyone, shaking his head and saying as how it were a crying shame. Molly stood as whey-faced as blown milk, listening to him telling her father that old Bert had been found dead this morning, having shot his dog and then hanged himself.

'That dog were closer to him than many a man is to his missus – closer. Meant the world to him, it did. Of course, I blame that Alf Davies, allus threatening to have it put down. Well, now poor old Bert's gone and done the job for him. Aye, and finished himself off as well.'

Suddenly Molly realised that she was crying. Great choking sobs tore at her body, making her chest heave as she wept for old Bert, who had not been able to go on living without the dog he loved. But she had to live without Eddie, and she wept for him, and for all those men who would die, and all those women who would have to go on living without them.

Molly wasn't surprised to hear her father saying later that week that he had heard that Alf Davies and his wife had decided to move out of the cul-de-sac and rent somewhere else in another part of the city.

But the gossip about Alf Davies was soon forgotten in the excitement of Mr Chamberlain stepping down as Prime Minister and Winston Churchill taking his place.

'Now we'll show Jerry what's what,' John Fowler beamed, coming round to talk about the latest news with Albert.

Unlike Mr Chamberlain, the new Prime Minister did not minimise the danger of Hitler or the German blitzkrieg.

* * *

'Here, listen to what it says 'ere,' Jean called out sombrely, causing the other girls to leave their machines and cluster around her as she waved the latest copy of the *Picture Post* in the air. 'It says "The Darkest Day of the War, Arras and Amiens fall to the Germans." Where are they when they're at home?'

'France, yer dafthead,' Irene told her sharply. 'Go on, what else does it say? Oh, give it here and let me read it . . .'

Molly listened, aware of but somehow unmoved by what she was hearing, as though set apart from the anxiety of the other girls. After all, what did it matter now to her what happened? It couldn't bring Eddie back.

She was the only person who *wasn't* tensely waiting for every fresh news bulletin, though – she knew that. You could feel people's tension, and see it in their faces. Only she seemed to be immune to it, sealed off from it by her bitterness and grief.

'My father says that the Germans won't take France because the BEF is sure to hold them back,' Anne told her that evening as they left their weekly WVS meeting.

'I hope your father's right, Anne,' Molly answered. 'There's enough good men dead already.' She yawned loudly. She hadn't been able to sleep for the last few nights, and when she did she dreamed of old Bert and his dog, the animal howling mournfully until suddenly it wasn't the dog she could hear but Eddie, crying out to her in agony.

Her loss had begun to sharpen the softness of her smile and to strip the flesh of her girlhood from her bones. She had retreated to a place inside herself where she could shut out everyone else, a place where she could mourn Eddie and the loss of her own future. The girls at Hardings whispered when she excused herself at dinner, not knowing what they could do to help their friend.

'I hope that Dad is right as well,' Anne agreed. 'What with our Richard in France and Philip too . . .' She took hold of Molly's arm, her eyes dark with fear. 'Molly, I'm scared for them.' The two girls looked at one another, and then Anne shook her head and said firmly, 'Just listen to me! Our Richard would give me a right telling-off if he could hear me.' But nevertheless there were tears in her eyes and Molly could feel her trembling.

Seeing Anne so distressed pierced the protective wall Molly had built around herself. She reached out to Anne and hugged her reassuringly. 'Try not to worry,' she said. 'I know it isn't easy but, Anne, you have to believe that they will be safe, for their sakes. Try to tell yourself that they'll be home soon.'

'Oh, Molly, I do hope they will. I know it sounds silly but, do you know, I have to look at Philip's photograph now to remember what he looks like.'

Comforting Anne made her own pain lessen a

little, Molly recognised as she did her best to calm her friend's fears.

She had promised to call in at Sally's on her way home so that she could walk back with June, who was now spending most of her spare time there.

Sally and June were laughing together when Molly walked in.

'Oh, Molly, there you are. Me and Sally was just saying that we could do with you getting started with a bit of knitting for these two,' June laughed, patting her belly.

The sound of their laughter and the sight of their happiness brought a resurgence of Molly's pain. 'Is that all you can talk about, you two – babies, and how your Frank and Sally's Ronnie are going to push Jerry back to Germany single-handed?' she demanded bitterly.

June flushed and looked shocked. 'There's no call for you to act like that,' she protested.

'We just thought that doin' a bit of knittin' would give yer sommat to take yer mind off . . . everything . . . but if you feel like that then you do not have to bother,' Sally said huffily.

'Do you really expect a bit of knitting for someone else's baby is going to take me mind off losing Eddie?' Molly laughed mirthlessly.

June looked uncomfortably at Sally and then shook her head. 'Molly, we all know what you've bin through, but carrying on like this isn't going to bring him back—' She broke off as there came an urgent knock on the door. Looking worried, Sally got up to answer it.

'I thought you'd both want to know,' Frank's mother breathlessly announced as Sally invited her in. 'I've just come from Mill Road Hospital – I've got a friend there, one of the sisters. She's got *connections*, like, and she's just told me that she's heard that orders have gone out to our lads that they are to fall back. May God help them.' Doris Brookes's voice quavered slightly, and June, who had stood up when she had seen her mother-in-law, gave a small moan, and collapsed in a dead faint.

Immediately Doris reverted from anxious mother to professional nurse, instructing Molly to help her get June into a sitting position with her head between her knees, and commanding Sally to go and get a bowl.

'Like as not she'll be sick when she comes round,' Doris pronounced matter-of-factly.

'Will she be all right? Only she said as how she felt a bit faint, like, when she got here,' Sally informed them worriedly.

'She's not said anything about any bleeding or that, has she?' Doris asked, frowning.

Sally and Molly shook their heads.

'Well, that's all right then. No, I reckon it's just a bit of shock done it. Allus bin a bit highly strung, your June has, Molly. If you had a bit of cork we could burn, that'd bring her round,' Doris announced, as she took the bowl Sally had brought her, adding, 'Put yer radio on, will yer, Sally, just in case there's bin any more news. It's all right, lass,' she told Molly bracingly as she saw her expression. 'Like I said, your June has allus bin one for a bit o' drama, and I warned my Frank so when he first said as how he were walking out with her. I told him he'd be better off walking out wi' you! "You'll end up having to fetch and carry for her, our Frank," I told him, but he wouldn't listen.' Doris patted June's hand. 'She's coming round now . . .'

June moaned faintly, slowly lifting her head. 'Oh, what's going to become of me and the baby if anything should happen to Frank? I told 'im all along not to join up.' She gagged suddenly, giving Molly just enough warning to get the bowl in front of her before she was sick.

'Oh, I feel right badly,' June sobbed.

'Come on now, that's enough of that,' Doris told her briskly. 'Bawling your head off like that isn't going to help anyone. How do you think you're going to go on when you go into labour if you carry on like this after a bit of a faint?'

'A bit of a faint?' June objected angrily. 'It were you as made me faint, frightening me half to death like that, and me carrying.'

Doris gave an unsympathetic snort. 'There's women carrying who go through far worse than that, I can tell you. I did myself—'

'The news is coming on,' Sally interrupted her.

All four women fell silent. As if he too sensed

the tension around him, even baby Tommy stopped gurgling, but the newsreader made no mention of any retreat by the British Army.

'You want to be ashamed of yourself,' June rounded on her mother-in-law, her face bright red, 'coming round 'ere and frightening folk half to death like that. That friend of yours wants to get her facts right before she goes spreading any more gossip, otherwise someone will be reporting her to Mr Churchill, and he'll have her locked up.'

'Don't tek on so, June. You'll mek yourself poorly again,' Sally warned.

'I'm all right,' June told her, 'no thanks to some folk I could name.' She sniffed. 'I know you never wanted your Frank to marry me, but he has done and I'll thank you to remember that in future. Frank isn't going to be happy when he hears about this, not with me being in my condition.'

June was looking triumphant whilst Frank's mother's face was set with anger and contempt.

'I'll walk back with you if you like, Mrs Brookes,' Molly offered, hastily stepping in between them. June might claim that Frank would blame his mother for what had happened, but Molly suspected that Frank would not be happy if a permanent rift were to develop between his mother and his wife.

'Thank you, Molly, I'd appreciate that. At least one of you has manners.'

TEN

'It's true, I tell yer. I heard it from a lad I know down the docks. Navy's bin sent to Dunkirk to bring home what can be saved of 'em poor buggers, and that won't be many, not with Jerry and his bloody blitzkrieg after them. Gawd help those poor lads, that's all I can say – aye, and their families, an' all.'

'And Gawd help us,' Molly's father said sombrely. 'There'll be nowt to stop Hitler invading England now.'

Something in her father's voice made Molly quickly look up at him. What she saw broke through the protective barrier her grief had made her throw around herself. She went to him and he put his arm around her.

'Dad,' she whispered.

Her father was afraid for them, for what might happen to her and to June. She had seen that in his eyes. Her heart started to pound inside her chest as waves of panic and pain seared through her.

'Not a word about this to our June yet, lass,' her father warned her. 'There's no point in having her frettin' before she needs to.'

'No, not in her condition,' Molly agreed soberly.

'It ain't just a matter of that,' her father said. 'See, Molly, June isn't like you. For all that she's one for telling other folk what to do, she's not strong like you are. Think on, lass, because, God forbid, if her Frank were not to make it, then June would need you to help her through. If'n your Eddie *is* lookin' down from somewhere, watching yer, Molly, he will want ter be proud of you and I know that he can be. But our June . . .' He shook his head worriedly.

Molly's chin lifted. Her father was right. She *was* strong. Strong enough to bear the pain of losing Eddie and to do whatever she was called upon to do to help others. A new sense of pride and purpose began to fill her, driving out the bitterness that had gripped her since Eddie's death. 'Don't worry about me, Dad. I'm all right now and I'll do whatever I have to do for our June, if it comes to that.' Her face suddenly crumpled. 'But, oh, Dad, those poor boys . . .'

By the end of that week the whole country was waiting with heavy hearts and many prayers for news of the safe return of the retreating army.

White-faced, June and Sally clung to one another in the kitchen of number 78 as they all listened to the news.

On 28 May it was announced formally that Belgium had fallen to the Germans.

'I'll never see my Frank again,' June sobbed noisily.

'Our lads will be all right, June,' Sally insisted sturdily. 'You see if they aren't.'

Molly could see that June was struggling to contain her tears and to mirror Sally's brave optimism, and she went over to hug her, telling her fiercely, 'Sally's right, June. You've got to be strong for Frank's sake, and for the baby's as well.'

June gave a hiccuping sob as Molly held her tightly.

At that evening's WVS meeting, Molly and the others were told that they would be needed to meet the trains coming up from the coast, bringing home the men who had been saved.

'You must remember that these men will have seen dreadful things – comrades wounded and dying, civilians left behind to face the Germans. They will have suffered and endured things beyond our own grasp, and you may find yourselves having to witness and listen to things they would be too proud to tell their wives and loved ones,' Mrs Wesley told them, adding, 'I would caution you all to remember that it is your duty to your country to give our brave soldiers what comfort you can. A cup of tea, a gentle touch, a listening ear – all of these things are important.'

The girl standing next to Molly giggled and

whispered, 'Gawd, I wondered what she was going to tell us we had ter give 'em for a moment.'

'You will also be required to supply field post forms to those men who have not already filled them in, so that their families will be informed of their safety and whereabouts. There will be nurses and doctors on hand to help those men who need medical attention, and you will direct the injured to the first-aid station.'

'Have you heard from your brother yet?' Molly asked Anne after the meeting was over.

Anne shook her head, biting her lip. 'No, not yet. Oh, Molly, it is all so dreadful. I heard Mum crying last night. I can't stop thinking about our brave men.'

'No, neither can I,' Molly admitted. In her mind's eye she could see them, line after line of them, waiting patiently and bravely on Dunkirk's beaches for salvation – or death. She gave a deep shudder. It was too late now for her Eddie, but there were other men who needed her prayers and whatever help those who waited here at home could give them.

A new sense of purpose and determination had filled her these last few days. For Eddie's sake and in his memory she would do whatever was asked of her to help those men.

You could see it in other women's faces, Molly thought as she walked home from work with June, carefully slowing her pace to match June's in the heat of the late May afternoon: that look, that light in their eyes, or lack of it, that said they had received good news – or they had not. Her sister looked drawn and tired, the curve of her belly growing bigger every day whilst the rest of her body seemed to grow thinner.

'I'm on duty at Lime Street tonight,' Molly told her quietly as they walked into number 78. 'Anne ran across at dinner to tell me. They're expecting the first of the trains, bringing men as has been brought home from Dunkirk back up North to their units.'

'Frank's mam's gone up to the hospital to see if she can do anything to help out,' June told her. 'She said as how she couldn't bear just to stay at home waiting for news. Good for her, I say.'

Molly smiled – maybe the war would bring one good outcome.

'Oh, Molly, if anything's happened to my Frank . . .' June started to cry helplessly. Molly put down the shopping bag such as every woman carried with her in case she should hear of a shop getting in some extra supplies, and went over to her, putting her arms round her, and doing her best to comfort her.

An hour later, when she came downstairs, having changed into her WVS uniform, she found June waiting for her by the kitchen door.

'I'm coming with you,' she announced determinedly, 'just in case my Frank is on one of them trains.'

'June, you can't,' Molly protested. 'It isn't allowed. And besides, in your condition it might not be safe for you.'

'I'm only five months, and as for it not being allowed –' June tilted her chin stubbornly – 'if my Frank's on that train then I want to be there.'

Molly shook her head, and said as gently as she could, 'June, you'd have heard if Frank was back.'

'Mebbe, mebbe not . . .'

Molly looked at their father, who was sitting polishing his shoes.

'Come on, June lass, be sensible. Our Molly's got her duty to do, and like she says, there's no sense in you going to Lime Street and wearing yourself out standing around in this heat when like as not your Frank won't be on t'train. You'd be far better off staying here wi' me.'

'Dad's right, June,' Molly told her softly. 'I'll look out for Frank, I promise, and will send word if he's on the train. How about that?'

June grudgingly nodded her head and Molly set off, not knowing what horrors might await her at Lime Street.

The streets were hot and humid, and Molly wished she was wearing something a bit lighter than her uniform. The rough cloth was making her itch, and the heat inside the busy station made her long to be able to remove her jacket, but she must keep it on to identify herself as WVS.

She had to struggle through several groups of people before she saw her colleagues.

'Has June heard from our Frank yet, Molly?'

'Mrs Brookes!' Molly exclaimed as she saw Frank's mother. She was wearing a nurse's uniform and was standing with several other volunteers.

'No, she hasn't. She wanted to come with me tonight but me and our dad managed to dissuade her.'

'Best thing if she stays where she is, if you ask me.'

'Over here, Molly,' Mrs Wesley called out imperiously.

'Sorry, Mrs Brookes,' Molly excused herself, 'but I'd better go.'

'Right now, Molly, you can have these forms and some pencils, and when Anne and Mary have given the men a drink, you can find out whether or not they've already filled out a form. If not, then you can give them one. Then the men will be taken to the transport that will carry them back to their units, or to hospital if they need medical treatment.' She looked at her watch. 'Right then, ladies, is everyone ready?'

Molly gulped and nodded her head.

The first thing that Molly noticed when the train pulled in was the silence. It was thick and smothering, unnervingly so compared to the noise she could remember filling Lime Street when the men had left for the war.

The second was the smell: a sour wave of sweat mixed with the acrid smell of damp khaki and leather, and something else that her mind was already labelling as the smell of defeat and exhaustion.

'No, ta, luv.'

'Thanks, duck.'

'Filled one out already, I have.'

The flattened male voices all held the same tone as Molly followed Anne and Mary down the line. Grey-faced and unsmiling, the men marched towards the exit, something in the hunch of their shoulders tearing at Molly's heart in a different way from the pain she felt at Eddie's death. This pain was new, an adult pain, she realised, not for herself but for others, for all that these men had suffered.

'Have you filled in a field post form yet?' she asked repetitively, waiting patiently whilst exhausted men tried to focus on the form she was holding and then nodded their heads before moving on.

'Have you . . . ?'

'No, and I'm not going to neither.'

'Johnny!' Molly stared in disbelief at her ex-fiancé. His face looked thin and his cheeks sunken, his uniform hanging loosely on his tall frame. He badly needed a shave. He swayed slightly as she looked at him and she could smell the spirits on his breath. His right arm was in a sling.

'Are you all right?' she asked him as he grabbed hold of her arm to steady himself.

'I'm alive,' he told her shortly. 'Unlike those poor buggers we've left behind us.'

'Would you like a cup of tea?'

He gave her a rictus-like smile and started to shake his head before changing his mind and saying instead, 'Go on then.'

'Wait here,' Molly told him, before hurrying over to Anne to get Johnny a drink and a pork pie.

'Is there anywhere to sit down?' he asked her.

'There's a bench over there, behind you,' Molly told him.

She started to turn away, offering a form to the next in line but Johnny grabbed hold of her arm and demanded, 'Come wi' us for a minute, Molly.'

'I can't, I'm on duty.'

'Aye, and isn't it part of your duty to help us poor lads?' he pleaded with her.

Unwillingly, Molly let him pull her along with him to the empty bench.

''Ave you had any news from Frank yet?'

'Not yet,' Molly told him, 'but we're keeping our fingers crossed that he's all right, and Ronnie Walker too. We've been praying for all of you,' she told him quietly.

Johnny started to laugh bitterly. ''Ave you, an' all. Well, it'll tek more than prayers to help them as we've had to leave behind – some of 'em dead and left there to rot, and others . . .' A dark, brooding expression hardened his face. 'I've seen things that no man should see, Molly – no, and no woman hear about neither. Things as you wouldn't imagine even if you was in hell. Men blown up and lying there wi'out their arms and legs, their bellies ripped open and their guts spilled out, screaming to be put out of their misery. I put a bullet in the head of one of them, poor sod, and kept one for meself as well, just in case.'

Molly swallowed against the sour sickness threatening to overwhelm her. Inside her head she could see the most dreadful and unwanted images, but she fought them down and waited silently. Wasn't this what Mrs Wesley, obviously more informed than they had known, had warned them to expect?

'There was one lad with us, only seventeen – and he nearly made it, an' all, and then the bloody Luftwaffe came strafing us like we was vermin, shooting us down as we stood in line. Got it in the leg, he did. Shot off right to the hip. I used to go down the abattoir after school to earn a bit of pocket money – screamed just like them pigs did there, he did, only his screaming didn't stop. We took him to the first-aid station they'd got set up on the beach. I heard the nurse asking the doctor if she was to give him some morphine and he told her, "No, give him heroin instead."'

Molly looked at him.

'He wasn't going to be coming back, see. They knew that so they give him sommat as would stop him from knowing about it.'

'What . . . what happened to your arm?' Molly asked him jerkily when she was physically able to speak.

'Nothing much. Just a bit of Jerry shrapnel – first-aid lot have taken the worst of it out.'

'Molly, what are you doing?'

Molly stood up guiltily as she saw Mrs Wesley hurrying angrily towards her.

'Thanks for that, missus,' Johnny told her, giving her back the now empty cup and winking at her like the old Johnny as he too stood up and started to limp painfully, something Molly was sure he had not done when he had dragged her with him to the bench. 'Your lot are doing a hell of a good job for us lads,' he told Mrs Wesley with a soulful look.

Immediately Mrs Wesley's stern expression softened slightly.

'Come along, Molly, we need those forms,' she told her.

ELEVEN

'Molly . . . Dad . . . !'

June's scream brought both Molly and her father running to the front door where June was standing holding a telegram, tears pouring down her face.

'It's Frank.'

Molly fought the sickening lurch of her stomach.

'He's safe. He's *safe!* He's somewhere down south and he's all right. Oh, I'm so happy.' June was laughing and crying at the same time, whilst their neighbours, alerted by the noise and knowing that June was waiting to hear about her husband, were opening their own front doors to see what was going on.

'She's had news then?' Daisy called across.

'Frank's arrived in England, Daisy. June's just had a wire from him,' Molly called back.

'Oh, thank the Lord for that,' Elsie breathed, her head poking over the fence. 'I were that worried for her.'

Now that they knew the news was good, Daisy and Pearl both came across the road to hug June, whilst Elsie reached for Molly's hand and gave it a gentle pat, telling her quietly, 'You're a good kind lass, Molly. Our Eddie would be proud of you.'

'I knew all along your Frank would be back safe and sound,' Pearl pronounced. 'Has Sally Walker heard from her hubby yet?'

June shook her head. 'I don't know . . .'

'Frank's mam will be glad to hear the good news,' Elsie broke in. 'Will she get her own wire, June, or are you going to go up the cul-de-sac and tell her, like?'

'I'll go up later. I'm all of a shake, what with seeing the telegraph lad and thinking it were bad news.'

'I'll go up later and tell Frank's mam, if you like,' Molly offered.

June gave her a grateful look. Molly knew that her sister still hadn't forgiven her mother-in-law for her sharp words at Sally's.

'I'll call in on Sally as well and see if she's heard anything, unless you want me to hang on until you're feeling better so that you can walk up with me?'

'No, you go, Molly. This heat is really getting to me and me ankles are swelling up that big I can hardly walk.'

'Are you two going down the Grafton tonight?' Pearl asked. 'Only I've heard as how they're putting on a bit of a special night on account of Dunkirk, like.'

'Our Molly can go, if she likes, but I won't be going,' June answered for both of them.

'I'm on WVS duty down at Lime Street again tonight,' Molly told her. She hadn't said anything to anyone about seeing Johnny, although she didn't really know herself why she had not done so, unless it was because of the horror of the verbal picture he had drawn for her.

June did look a bit pale and sweaty as she announced that she felt that shaken that she was going to go in and make herself a cup of tea.

'I'll come with you,' Molly offered.

'You sit down and I'll put the kettle on,' Molly said to June, once they were back inside number 78.

'Look at that. Me hanky's wet through,' June hiccuped, still crying.

'Here, tek mine, it's clean,' Molly removed her own clean handkerchief from her sleeve and handed it to her sister.

'I don't know why I'm crying, I've got nowt to cry about now that I know my Frank's safe. Oh, Molly, if I'd lost him . . . Oh, Molly, what you've gone through, I can only imagine.'

'Well, you mustn't, and you've got baby to think about as well, so you'd better start pulling yourself together,' Molly told her firmly.

'I don't know what I'd have done without you and Sally these last few days,' June admitted shakily, 'and I've got ter tell yer, Molly, I've been feeling right ashamed of meself for not understanding how it must be for you, losing your Eddie. I felt for yer, of course, and I thought I understood, but I know now that I didn't,' she added with unusual humility.

Such an admission from her normally abrasive sister made Molly's hand shake slightly as she filled the kettle.

'I'm getting better, slowly but surely,' she told June determinedly. 'I'll never forget Eddie, of course – how could I? – but . . . I don't know, June, it's a bit like I've bin through the worst thing that could happen to me and for a while I thought that I just couldn't go on wi'out him but then hearing about our lads nearly getting killed by Jerry and then being saved has somehow made me feel that I want to do me bit to get this war won and Jerry sent back where he belongs. For Eddie – so he didn't die in vain. If one of us had to lose their lad it's better that it should be me.' She looked meaningfully at June's belly. 'There's going to be enough kiddies left without their dads wi'out yours being one of them.'

She waited for the tea to brew and then poured them each a cup, going to sit down on the back door step.

For a few minutes they sat in mutual silence, and then June said unsteadily, 'I hope that Sally's Ronnie is all right.'

'They've bin saying on the news that the navy

and all them little boats are going back time and time again to bring everyone home,' Molly reminded her, determinedly refusing to think of what Johnny had told her about the death and destruction he had witnessed.

It was no wonder that the church was so full today, Molly thought, as they waited to file out and shake the vicar's hand. Everyone wanted to give thanks for the miraculous rescue of so many men, against so many odds. Over three hundred thousand had been brought back safely.

Sally, white-faced and drawn, clung to Molly's arm. She had still not had any word about Ronnie, and now, where there had been closeness between her and June, there was awkwardness and tension.

It was Frank's mother June was talking to as they left the church, their differences temporarily forgotten in their relief at the safety of the man they both loved.

Once they were outside the church, Molly whispered to her father to keep an eye on Sally and then slipped quietly away, into the cool shadows of the graveyard.

She hadn't visited Eddie's grave for over a month and it shocked her to see the stark line of new graves stretching beyond his.

She hunkered down beside the grave, and touched the smooth cold surface of his headstone, dipping her head to kiss the sharp carving of his name. Tears clogged the back of her throat, but today there was no bitterness in them, only sorrow and her own sense of loss.

'So many of you lost, Eddie,' she whispered to him. 'But at least you'll not be alone.' She laid her hand flat over the body of the grave like a mother comforting a child. 'I'll never forget you, not ever.' As she talked to him she was busily removing weeds, smoothing the cover of his last resting place with gentle, loving hands.

She looked up at the church clock. It was time for her to go. They were having a chicken for dinner – sent up from the farm – and she'd have to get back to make sure it didn't spoil.

'Where've you bin?' June demanded as Molly caught up with them outside the church.

'I just went to have a bit of a chat with Eddie, tell him that your Frank's safe, and that,' Molly told her, adding when she saw the quick tears filling June's eyes, 'and I told him, an' all, that you'll be moaning your head off if we don't get back and get our dinner.'

'They was saying outside the church some of them boats have gone back over and over again to get the men,' June told Molly emotionally as they made their way home. 'Haven't they, Dad?'

'Aye, brave lads they are too, an' all. It fair lifts yer spirits and meks yer feel proud, when yer hear about how brave our lads are, standing waiting in line to be taken off the beaches. That takes courage, that does, and no mistake. Aye, and it takes courage to keep going back again and again across the Channel with Jerry doing his best to kill yer, too.' His chest lifted as he heaved a huge sigh and gave both girls a watery smile.

'Do you fancy coming back with us for a bit of dinner, Sally?' Molly asked, hanging back until Sally had caught up with them.

'No, ta. I won't, if you don't mind. My Ronnie is bound to be getting in touch to let me know he's safe,' Sally told her valiantly. 'So I'd best stay at home so as I don't miss any message.'

Silently, Molly nodded.

They all knew that the Germans were advancing on Dunkirk and that it was a desperate race for the navy to get as many men off the beach as they could before the Germans arrived. But everyone knew not all of them could be rescued. Some men would be left behind. Molly prayed that Ronnie wasn't one of the unlucky ones.

That fear lay heavily on Molly's heart as she joined Anne and the others at Mill Road Hospital on Monday night, where their WVS unit was on duty, helping the hard-pressed nursing staff.

'We still haven't heard anything from our Richard,' Anne confided to Molly gravely as they stood together beside the tea urn they had set up inside the hospital's foyer. 'Dad tries not to show it, but I know he's beginning to worry.'

'You said he was at the airfield at Nantes, though, not Dunkirk,' Molly reminded her, trying to cheer her up.

'Yes, I know, but the Germans are bound to want to take the airfield and what will happen then? Oh, Molly, it doesn't bear thinking about.'

'Mr Churchill will get them home,' Molly told her stoutly with more confidence than she was feeling. 'You just see if he doesn't. Look at how many we've got back from Dunkirk, and still coming too.'

'I was talking to one of the nurses earlier. She'd had a letter from her sister down south saying that her husband had got back safe and sound but that he had the most dreadful look in his eyes and he wouldn't talk to her, not even to say hello,' Anne told her unhappily.

'The men are bound to be shocked,' Molly responded quietly, 'and some will take it worse than others.' She was thinking of Johnny and what he had told her, and how some men needed to talk about what they had seen and heard while others preferred to keep it all locked up inside themselves.

One of the jobs of the WVS was to go round the wards, taking magazines and newspapers others had donated to the wounded soldiers. This always seemed to take Molly longer than the others because she found it so hard to leave the bedsides of those who were reluctant to let her go, so grateful were they to have someone to talk to, especially those whose families hadn't been able to visit them for one reason or another.

'I'm afraid there aren't any newspapers left,' Molly began to apologise as she reached the final bed on the ward. 'But I have got a *Picture Post*, and . . . oh, Johnny. It's you.'

'You know what they say about bad pennies,' Johnny joked, grinning.

His arm was strapped up and someone had shaved him so that he looked far better than he had done when she had seen him a week ago at Lime Street.

'How are you?' Molly asked him. 'Do your family know you're here? Do you want me—'

'Course I want you. Allus have done,' he told her cheekily, winking at her whilst Molly blushed and shook her head. 'Mam's bin in, but I've told her not to bring the girls, scriking and showin' me up. She told me about your Eddie, Molly. I'm sorry.'

Before she could stop him, Johnny had reached for her hand and was holding it. His skin was calloused but warm, alive, and very male. Her face started to burn. Quickly she pulled her hand free.

'I should have married you, Molly,' Johnny told her fiercely. 'Aye, and I would have done, an' all . . .'

Molly turned away.

'I'm sorry,' he apologised gruffly. 'I wasn't thinking. I didn't mean ter upset yer. I just meant that if that lying whore hadn't claimed I'd fathered her bastard, then you and me—'

Molly shook her head. 'You didn't want to marry me really, Johnny,' she told him. 'It was our June who pushed us together.'

'Your June and me own natural curiosity, if you know what I mean,' Johnny laughed, winking at her.

It was strange how his innuendos didn't worry her any more, Molly thought as she gave him a firm look and told him, 'That's enough of that, Johnny Everton. How's your arm?'

'Jerry's damaged the tendons, according to the doc. Seems like the war is over for me, Molly, and from now on I'm going to be back in civvies,' he told her.

By the end of the week it no longer shocked Molly to see men break down in tears in front of her, nor to hear them tell her about the terrible things they had witnessed, even though her heart ached for every single one of them – and for those who would not be getting on any train ever again.

She had also sat through the cinema newsreels showing the men being taken off Dunkirk's beaches so many times with June, whilst her sister looked to see if she could spot Frank, that she knew every word of them by heart.

Not that June was the only one going back to the cinema over and over again to see those newsreels. The girls at the factory talked of nothing else, and neither did the newspapers – and who could blame them, Molly admitted. Everyone you talked to was saying how proud they were to be British, and those rescued from Dunkirk were greeted as true heroes by their families and friends.

Two days before her birthday, June had had a letter from Frank to say that he had been told he would be given leave but that he didn't know when it would be. It was the best birthday present she could wish for, June had said, before biting her lip as she remembered too late the news Molly had received on the eve of her own.

'Tell Sally,' Frank had written, 'that her Ronnie is safe back but that he's in hospital with a broken leg.'

June had sent Molly running round to Sally with the news and the letter, but Sally had heard from Ronnie now herself. He was in an army hospital down south.

'I just wish that I could see him, that's all,' she told Molly emotionally. 'I daren't let myself believe it until I do.'

Sally wasn't the only one to feel like that, Molly knew. She had heard the same words so many times from families coming to the station looking for their loved ones when they got word that a troop train was going to be coming in.

'What about those that are still there in Dunkirk?' Molly said starkly to her sister and father on the following Friday night as they sat drinking their cocoa. She gave a small shiver. 'How must they be feeling?'

'Don't, Molly. I can't bear it,' June protested, putting down *Feeding and Care of Your Baby*, the book she had been reading by the famous Dr Truby King. The book had been Elsie's birthday present to her.

'Now then, our June, don't go getting yourself all upset,' their father warned.

Molly wrapped her hands tightly round her cocoa mug. 'When we were at the factory this morning I couldn't help noticing how them as had had good news were all talking together, laughing and chattering, whilst them as hadn't were holding back, not saying anything, but you could see in their faces what they were thinking and how afraid they were.'

They looked at one another in silence and then June said chokily, 'Them poor lads . . . aye, and their families, an' all.'

Phew, but it was hot! Molly lifted the heavy weight of her hair off the back of her neck to try to cool herself down. She had already taken off her WVS jacket, and she could feel the perspiration prickling on her scalp. She had walked all the way back from Lime Street station, thinking it would be quicker than waiting for a bus. The stream of men returning from Dunkirk had slowed to a trickle now.

Molly guessed that June would probably still be round at Sally's, helping her to get ready for the journey down south to see her Ronnie. June and Frank's mother, for once united, had insisted that she must take advantage of the Government's offer to provide a travel warrant for her to go and visit Ronnie, and that between them they would look after Tommy for her.

Molly walked up the narrow path that led to the back of the houses and into their small back garden, the movement of the gate wafting the scent of roses and honeysuckle towards her. She pushed open the back door and then came to an abrupt halt.

Frank was sitting at the kitchen table, holding his head in his hands.

'Frank?' she queried gently.

When he looked up at her, her heart ached for him. He had lost weight, his face almost gaunt, dark shadows under the blue eyes, which had lost their habitual sparkle and were bloodshot with exhaustion.

'Oh, it's you, Molly.' He spoke without any emotion, as though it was an effort for him to frame the words.

Putting down her jacket, Molly walked over to the table and calmly pulled out a chair opposite him.

'June's over at Sally's,' she told him lightly, knowing now, from her experience of talking to so many returning men, that a very gentle touch was needed on such bad emotional and mental bruises. 'I dare say she'll be back soon but I can run over and get her for you, if you like.'

'No, not yet. I still can't get me head round being here. All them hours, standing waitin' on that bloody beach, thinkin' that we might not be taken off.' His voice was hoarse and harsh, and Molly suspected that he wasn't even fully aware of who he was talking to.

'Why don't I make us both a cuppa?' Molly suggested.

'No . . . no, don't go,' Frank demanded, reaching across the table to put his hand on hers. 'I never thought as I would mek it, Molly. Strafing us, the bloody Luftwaffe were, picking us off like we was . . .' He shuddered violently. 'One of them got them lads as was standing behind me.' Tears filled his eyes and he tried to blink them away.

Molly got up and went to him, standing next to him and putting her arms around him in the motherly way she had held so many returning men as they had wept out the pain of what they had seen. 'It's all right, Frank,' she told him softly.

'There were a young lad . . .' he said jerkily.

There was a look in his eyes that made Molly's throat ache. He wasn't looking directly at her but focusing on something only he could see, his disjointed words delivered in a low monotone. Molly had seen this behaviour in other men still in shock from what they had endured.

'Only a bit of a kid, crying out for his mam, with his guts spilling out of his hands as he held his belly.' He knuckled his damp eyes, whilst Molly fought to control her own reaction. 'There were these lads right next to me, standing there joking

352

one minute and gone the next . . .' Abruptly, he seemed to come to himself and realise where he was and what he was saying. 'I shouldn't be upsettin' you wi' all of this.' His voice started to get stronger. 'You've had enough to bear, what wi' losing your Eddie.'

'Listening and caring are the least that those of us at home can do, Frank,' Molly told him, as she released him and went back to her chair. 'We want to do our bit, an' all, you know.'

'Aye, I know that, and you do so much more than that, Molly,' he agreed. 'T'uniform suits you, Molly – meks you look proper grown up.'

'I am grown up,' she told him half indignantly.

He was smiling now, looking much more like the Frank she remembered.

'You should have seen our lads, Molly,' he told her warmly, reaching across the table to take hold of one of her hands. 'They were that brave and strong. I were proud to be wi' them.'

'And we are proud of you, Frank – all of us, the whole country.'

'You're a good lass, Molly.' He looked at her and said quietly, 'I'm not going to say anything to June about what I was just telling you – about the other men, I mean.'

'I won't say a word,' Molly assured him. He was still holding her hand and he gave it a small squeeze. It was funny to think that, a year ago, just the thought of being on her own with Frank would have sent her giddy with excitement.

Inwardly she shook her head over the foolishness of the girl she had once been.

She returned the pressure of Frank's fingers and looked into his eyes, relieved to see that some of the old light was coming back into them.

'You're a good 'un, Molly,' Frank told her emotionally. 'I never thought I'd be able to tell anyone about that young lad, but somehow it were easy to tell you.'

Silently they looked at one another. Molly felt her heart miss a beat and then thud unevenly. There would always be a soft spot in her heart for Frank, but he was her brother-in-law now and nothing more, she told herself firmly. This was neither the time nor the man for 'what could have beens', she acknowledged as she gently removed her hand from Frank's.

'Why don't you walk down to Sally's, and let June know that you're back?' she suggested. 'And don't worry, what you've said to me is just between the two of us and it always will be.'

'Thanks, Molly,' Frank said gratefully. 'There's no sense in upsettin' June, not in her condition, and with me going back just as soon as Mr Churchill has got us all re-equipped.'

'The armaments factories are going to be going on seven-days-a-week working,' Molly told him. 'Mr Churchill says that the whole country is going to be working on the war effort. I'll go down to the allotment and find our dad.' She hesitated, and then said a little bit guiltily, 'Happen it'll be best not to say anything about me seein' you before our June had a chance to.' She hated being deceitful but she knew how she would feel herself in June's shoes.

Frank nodded and got up from the table.

Frank, in common with others who had been at Dunkirk, had been granted a fortnight's leave. He was still at home and they were still celebrating his safe return when Sally arrived back from visiting Ronnie in hospital in the south of England, where he was recovering well from his injuries. But she brought shocking news.

'Apparently they aren't supposed to say anything about it, though of course it was all over the hospital,' she told them when she came round to collect Tommy.

'What was? What's happened?' June demanded.

'There was a ship as was taking our lads off at this St-Nazaire place, wot's bin bombed by Jerry, and according to wot we was hearin' at the hospital, thousands of men on board have drowned. It was bringing back the RAF men from Nantes, and the Royal Engineers and all that lot. Its captain had been told to tek on as many men as 'e could and seemingly, from wot this chap my Ronnie was talking to had to say, there weren't an inch of space left on board.

'He were lucky, 'cos he and his mates were up on deck and saw this bomb coming for them, so he shouted to his mates to jump. Three days he were in the water before he got picked up, but, like 'e said, he were lucky. He had me, aye, and my Ronnie as well, in tears when he told us about how them as couldn't get off could be heard singing "Roll Out the Barrel". Then he said they 'eard them singing "There'll Allus Be an England" as she went down.'

Silence filled the small kitchen.

Frank was holding June's hand, and tears were rolling down her face.

'Poor sods,' Frank said thickly.

'Anne's brother, Richard, and his friend are in the RAF and they were stationed at Nantes,' Molly told them, white-faced. 'I know how much she's bin worrying because they haven't heard anything yet.' She turned to look at Frank. 'Do you think I should . . . ?'

He shook his head. 'Best not,' he told her quietly. 'If he were there, she'll be hearing soon enough, I reckon.'

'We heard as how the families aren't goin' to be told properly what happened,' Sally told them unhappily. 'There's to be a D-notice put on, and, like I said, them as were there have been warned not to say anything. Ronnie says one of the men told him that they reckon there was over four thousand men on board – and not just men either.' She paused. 'There were women and kiddies too, being brought home to safety.'

Molly bit down hard on her bottom lip, whilst June gave a small gulping sob.

* * *

Molly and Anne were on duty at Mill Road Hospital that night, and Molly knew the moment she saw her friend's face that she had received bad news.

'It's Richard,' Anne told her wretchedly. 'We had a telegram this morning: "Missing feared lost in action." Oh, Molly . . .' Anne collapsed into her friend's arms.

Molly felt sick inside. She desperately wanted to tell Anne what she had heard from Sally, but what if Richard had not been on board that ship? It would be wrong of her to go upsetting Anne with such a horrific story, especially if the Government were planning not to reveal the details of what had actually happened. For Anne's own sake it was best that she didn't say anything, Molly reasoned, even if that did leave her feeling uncomfortable and guilty. All she could do was hold her friend's hands tightly in her own, and share her tears.

Later that evening, in the small kitchen of number 78, she stood with her father, June and Frank, Frank's mother and Sally, as they all listened to the news.

'Mr Churchill reported to Parliament today on future prospects,' the newsreader announced. 'Britain now fights on alone.'

Molly could hear her indrawn gasp echoed by those of the other women as the newsreader paused to clear his throat. Molly reached for June and Sally's hands, holding them tightly. Frank was holding June's other hand and his mother's, whilst Albert stood straight as a ramrod, listening intently. June and Doris had put aside their differences, if only for the time being, sharing the same shocked grief that had swept the whole nation.

'In stirring words,' the newsreader continued, 'Mr Churchill told Members of Parliament, "Let us brace ourselves to do our duty, and so bear ourselves that if the British Commonwealth and Empire lasts a thousand years men will still say, '*This* was their finest hour.'"'

They all looked at one another, the men's as well as the women's eyes brimming with tears.

'I just hope that hour comes soon,' Molly sniffed, reaching for her handkerchief, 'before more brave men have to die.'

'That's war, lass,' her father told her sombrely. 'Brave men dying.'

TWELVE

'Molly, I've had news of Philip. I wrote to his parents to . . . to tell them about Richard, and I've had a letter back from his mother. She says that Philip is in a military hospital down south, but that she hasn't been able to go and see him because she can't leave his father. They live in Scotland and Philip's father has a weak heart.'

Anne's face showed the strain of the last few weeks. A memorial service had been held in the local church for those young men who, like Richard, had been deemed 'lost in action'. The service had been so well attended that some people had had to stand outside, but, as Anne had confided to Molly, her parents were still refusing to accept that Richard was dead, waiting nervously each day for the postman, hoping he would bring some word of their only son's fate.

'Oh, Anne!' Molly reached for her friend's hands.

'It's bad news, Molly,' Anne told her bravely.

359

'Philip was very badly injured and his mother says that at first they didn't think he was going to live. He was unconscious for over a week and even now . . .' Tears filled Anne's eyes and rolled down her cheeks to splash onto Molly's hand. 'They've had to amputate both his legs,' she almost whispered, as if saying the words made the situation even more horribly real.

Wordlessly, Molly hugged her friend with fierce compassion.

'I want to go and see him but when I wrote to the hospital they wrote back to say that only close family were allowed to visit. I've written again to tell them that I'm Philip's fiancée. I'm not going to wait for them to write back to me, Molly. I'm going to go down and see Philip, and nothing and no one is going to stop me. I'm going down there, to Aldershot, tomorrow.'

'Will you be all right going on your own?' Molly asked worriedly.

'I'll be a lot better knowing that I'm going to be seeing him than I am stuck here worrying about him,' Anne told her firmly.

'I can't believe the cheek of that Hitler, sayin' as how he's going to destroy London,' Sally was announcing fiercely as Molly walked into the kitchen after going to see Anne off at Lime Street station. But Molly could hear the anxiety in Sally's voice, and it was a worry that the rest of the country shared. 'Hasn't he learned anything from our lads showin' his blummin' Luftwaffe what's what?'

'Well, it seems it hasn't put him off doing his best to make a mess of Liverpool,' June pointed out sharply. 'Three times in the last week I've had to get up out of me bed and go down to that blummin' air-raid shelter on account of him bombing us. It's more than a body needs in my condition.'

Although June refused to say as much, Molly knew how relieved her sister was to know that Frank's mother was close at hand to help her through the birth.

Buying new things for the coming baby was impossible. Every scrap of material that could be used to forward the war effort was being utilised, even if that meant melting down park and house railings, and people having to endure utility goods as well as food rationing. But neighbours had promised to lend what they could, and Molly had spent every spare minute she had knitting and sewing for the baby, using fabric and wool salvaged from old clothes.

Both Frank and Ronnie were now overseas again, fighting for their country.

'Here, you'll never guess who I saw the other day,' Sally said. 'That Johnny Everton. Seems that he's been invalided out of the army now and he's training up to join that Home Guard they're going to be havin'. Asked after you most particular, he did, Molly,' she added meaningfully.

Molly could feel herself blushing. 'I knew he was back in Liverpool,' she admitted.

'Oh, you did, did you?' June chimed in. 'Well, you never said anything to me about that!'

'He was at Dunkirk,' Molly told her quietly. 'I was on duty at Lime Street when he came off one of the trains, and then I saw him again later in hospital. He said then that he didn't think he'd be going back to active service.'

'Well, I reckon he's still sweet on you, Molly,' Sally teased her.

'Me and every other girl in Liverpool,' Molly laughed. 'Are you all right, June?' she asked worriedly, seeing her sister suddenly wince.

'My back's giving me some gyp,' June complained, trying to ease herself into a more comfortable position. 'Bin aching all night, it has.'

'I've got to go,' Molly told them both, after she had sympathised with her sister, 'otherwise I'm going to be late for WVS. All the voluntary services for our area will be there, on account of this meeting that was held up at the Police Training School on Mather Avenue earlier in the week after the bombings.'

'Just as well Jerry didn't know about that, otherwise he'd have bin bombing the Training School, and killed them wot's supposed to be sortin' the rest of us out, and then where would we be?' Sally said.

'We've got extra air-raid training tonight,' Molly told them, 'and I've got to be there as I've been put on the emergency services driving list.'

'I wish you weren't doing that, our Molly,' June said worriedly. 'Not now that Jerry has bin dropping his ruddy bombs on us, damaging the overhead railway, aye, and killin' them poor lads in Walton Prison.'

For a few seconds they were all silent.

'That was a right shame, but the rest of the bombs didn't hit anything, thanks to our own lads on them ack-ack guns,' Molly reassured her. 'Mind you, I'm not saying that I don't wish that you and Sally would go and stay with our Auntie Violet, like she's said that you can do,' she added.

'Oh, yes, that'd be a fine thing, wouldn't it, me and Sally having our babies there, when we've got Doris all sorted out to deliver 'em here,' June derided her. 'And what if my Frank gets leave? By the time he gets out to Nantwich it will be time for him to go back again. No, Jerry can do his worst. I'm staying here in Liverpool.'

Given that the meeting Molly was attending tonight was a joint meeting between the WVS, the Home Guard, the ARP and others, to update their combined plans of action, she was not altogether surprised to see Johnny there. He was standing with a group of men by the doorway into the hall, smoking a cigarette, and as soon as he saw Molly he came over to her, offering her one.

Shaking her head, she refused it.

'Still no bad habits then?' Johnny teased her. 'Or are you keeping them as a secret?'

'You were right first time,' Molly told him firmly, trying not to laugh.

'Quickly now, Molly,' Mrs Wesley commanded, catching sight of her. 'I want you there whilst we're talking about the driving roster for the mobile kitchens.'

'I've already been put down to drive for the emergency services,' Molly reminded her superior.

'Yes, I know. That is why I want to check the rosters,' Mrs Wesley told her briskly.

'So you're a driver now? Well, I never.' Johnny grinned admiringly at Molly, catching up with her as she left the hall after the meeting had finished. 'Who would have thought it! Little Molly Dearden, a driver.'

'That's enough of your cheek, Johnny Everton,' Molly told him severely.

'I'll walk you home,' Johnny offered, adding before Molly could refuse, 'Seeing as I'm going that way anyway.'

It was too dark to see the barrage balloons hanging low on the skyline down by the docks, but Molly was still acutely conscious of them and the reason they were there. The bombing raids Jerry had already made hadn't done much damage, but they had changed the mood of the people of Liverpool, leaving everyone feeling slightly on edge.

'How's your hand?' Molly asked Johnny politely

as they walked up through the city together, heading towards Mill Road Hospital.

'See for yourself.' He slipped his hand into her own and clasped it before she could stop him.

'That's enough of that, Johnny Everton,' Molly protested, trying to tug her hand free but he was holding it too tightly for her to do so.

'I still miss yer, Molly,' he told her softly.

Molly couldn't see his face in the darkness of the blackout but she didn't need to.

'Oh yes? Well, you didn't look like you was missing anything the other Saturday when I saw you down at the Grafton, dancing with that red-head,' she told him forthrightly.

'Jealous, were yer?' he laughed, squeezing her hand.

'Course not,' Molly denied truthfully.

'Pity . . . Walking out wi' anyone yerself, are yer?'

'No.' She had been asked out several times in the months following Eddie's death, but she hadn't got the heart for it.

'What are you looking for?' she asked him curiously as he kept pausing to glance up at the sky.

'I'm hoping that Jerry will send them bombers of his over,' he told her. 'Then you and me will have to find the nearest shelter, and spend the night there.'

'Give over, do,' Molly chided him, but she couldn't help listening out for the now increasingly familiar sound of the air-raid siren, even though she knew he had only been flirting with her. He was the kind of lad who would try it on with any girl.

They had reached Edge Hill, the noise from the goods yard spilling into the darkness as they walked past.

'Yer dad still working at the gridiron?' Johnny asked, with a nod in the direction of the yard.

'Yes. They're doing twelve-hour shifts now, on account of all the munitions stuff from Napiers and the rest.'

They were almost at the turn-off for the cul-de-sac, but instead of leaving her there as she had expected him to, Johnny kept a firm grip on her hand and guided her across the road.

'I can make me own way from here,' Molly told him.

'What's up? Scared of being on yer own in the dark wi' me, is that it?'

Molly's eyes were accustomed to the darkness now and she could see the brief flash of his teeth as he grinned.

'If I was, then I wouldn't have walked back with you,' she answered him smartly. 'You're a flirt, Johnny Everton, and no mistake,' she added for good measure, 'but you're wastin' your time flirting with me, 'cos I'm not interested in that sort of thing.'

'Maybe it's different wi' you and I'm not just flirtin',' Johnny said softly, purposefully backing her up into a shadowy corner before she realised what he was up to.

'Johnny . . .' she started to protest, but it was already too late. He had her firmly in his arms and was kissing her before she could finish saying his name.

Funny how things could change, Molly thought dizzily. Because now, instead of disliking the knowing intimacy of Johnny's kiss, as she had done before, she discovered that she actually did quite like it.

It was such a long time since she had felt a man's strong arms holding her close, and a man's lips on her own. Johnny wasn't her dear sweet Eddie, and she felt none of the tender sweetness and longing with Johnny that she had felt with Eddie, but he was quite definitely doing something to her, Molly admitted, giving him a small push to free herself as she felt his hand moving up from her waist towards her breast.

'There'll be none of that, thank you very much,' she told him primly, and meant it, even though the effect was slightly spoiled by the breathlessness in her voice.

'I've allus had a bit of a fancy for you, Molly. There's sommat about yer that's got right under me skin,' Johnny admitted, his own voice gruff. 'Come out wi' us to the Grafton on Saturday night?'

Molly shook her head. 'Folks'd be talking fifteen to the dozen if I did that, and you know it.'

'So what if they do? Who cares?'

'I do, and so would me dad and our June,' she

answered him. 'They think you're a right bad lot and no mistake, leaving that poor girl the way you did.'

'I've told you that kiddie isn't mine,' Johnny protested.

'Well, she says it is. Anyway, it isn't just that,' she admitted honestly as they started to walk down the cul-de-sac together. Johnny wasn't touching her but he was walking closer to her now than he had been doing before, and yet she didn't really feel inclined to move away.

'So what is it, then?' he challenged her.

'There's my Eddie, for one thing,' she informed him. 'He's not been gone a year yet and it wouldn't be proper for me to be walking out with anyone else.'

'It's different when there's a war on,' Johnny answered grimly. 'We could be dead usselves ter-morrer.'

'Johnny, don't say that,' Molly protested shakily.

'You heard what we was being told tonight,' he persisted doggedly. 'Hitler's already started sending them bombers of his over, and there's a lot of 'em going to be headin' for Liverpool on account of the docks.'

'We've got the barrage balloons, though, and the army's anti-aircraft guns, and them search-lights. And then there's the RAF, as well, right close by Speke, never mind them at Cranage, and Tern Hill and the rest,' Molly reminded him stoutly, refusing to be afraid.

'Aye, well, if yer want my advice you'll get your-self into the nearest shelter you can find when them air-raid sirens go off.'

'We can't do that if we're on duty,' Molly protested.

They had virtually reached number 78 now, and she turned to him, putting her hand on his arm as she begged him, 'Let's just be friends, that's all, please, Johnny.'

He looked at her, shook his head and then said gruffly, 'Go on then, all right, but mind, I'm not promising never ter kiss yer again, 'cos I know it's a promise I just won't be able to keep, not wi' them lovely lips of yours, Molly.'

'Cheeky blighter,' Molly murmured to herself as she hurried up the path, but she was smiling in the darkness.

'Gawd, it's 'ot,' Ruby protested. 'Open us one of them winders, will yer, Molly?'

'They're jammed shut, remember?' Molly told her as she wiped the perspiration from her own forehead, before turning back to her sewing machine.

In addition to making uniforms, they were now making parachutes as well, and the air in the work-room was stiflingly hot and smelled of fabric dye and parachute silk.

'At least we didn't have no ruddy air-raid siren going off last night,' Sheila reminded them, stifling a yawn, before adding, ''Ere, I heard the other day that Hitler bombed Walton Prison 'cos he thought if he freed them in there they'd start fighting for 'im.'

'And how are they supposed to do that when they're bleedin' dead?' Mavis scoffed unkindly.

'He didn't mean to kill 'em, did he? He just wanted to help 'em to get out, like.'

'Aye, well, he certainly knew what he was doing when he bombed the overhead railway tekkin' stuff to the docks. Your dad works on the railways, doesn't he, Molly?'

'Yes, up at the gridiron on Edge Hill. He said this morning that the damage to the overhead wasn't too bad, and that it's not stopping supplies getting to the docks for our lads.'

'Speaking of our lads, we'd better get crackin' with these parachutes,' Iris reminded them briskly, 'otherwise they'll be 'aving to jump out of their planes wi' nowt to help 'em other than a few pairs of silk bloomers. How's your June, by the way, Molly?'

With June's baby due shortly she had been given leave from work.

'She's bin feeling the heat, and worrying about having to run to the shelter if there's an air raid. And she's missing her Frank, of course.'

Despite the lack of sunshine there was a muggy stickiness in the air that made Molly drag her feet a bit on her walk home from work. At least June would have a bit of tea ready for her, a luxury for Molly. She felt strange going to work without her sister and she missed her company, even though she got on well with the other girls. No friend, however close, could ever take a sister's place, Molly acknowledged.

The back door was wide open, and the strong smell of carbolic coming from inside the house made Molly's nose wrinkle.

Her sister was on her hands and knees, scrubbing the kitchen floor furiously as though her life depended on it, her face red and strands of hair escaping from her headscarf.

'June,' Molly protested, rushing into the kitchen, 'you shouldn't be doing that in your condition.'

'I don't know what it is but I just got this urge on me to start scrubbin',' June told her, panting slightly, as Molly helped her to her feet, and then wincing, her face suddenly paling.

'What is it? Did the baby kick?' Molly asked her.

'Kick? It felt more like he were tying knots in me guts,' June answered her forthrightly, gasping and clinging to Molly's arm as she panted. 'Bloody hell, he's doin' it again.'

'Come and sit down and let me put the kettle on,' Molly told her, guiding her over to a chair and then going back to remove the bucket and scrubbing brush, before hurrying over to the sink to fill the kettle.

June was still complaining that the baby was giving her bellyache an hour later when their father came home.

'Scrubbin' floors, is it?' Elsie commented knowingly when she popped in for a gossip later on in the evening. 'Sounds to me like you're goin' to be needing Frank's mam before too long.'

'Give over, Elsie,' June protested. 'The baby isn't due for another three weeks yet.'

'Mebbe, but does 'e know that?' Elsie quipped. 'He'll be here before the end of the weekend, I reckon. You mark my words.'

'Perhaps I should run round to Frank's mam's, June, and tell her what's happened,' Molly suggested worriedly. 'I know she's helping out at Mill Road Hospital on some shifts and it's better to be safe than sorry.'

'I'm all right. It's just a bit of wind, that's all. And as for me scrubbin' the floor, I've bin meaning to do it all week, but what with us having our baths last weekend and having to watch how much water we use, this was me first chance.'

Molly watched her sister sympathetically as June tried surreptitiously to massage her swollen belly. She suspected that June, for all her bravado, was secretly worrying about having her baby. This was one of those times when they needed their mother to turn to, Molly acknowledged.

Her own anxiety increased later on when her father came into the kitchen and closed the door to say quietly to her, 'Don't say anything to June, lass – there's no point in worrying her – but I reckon it might be a good idea to run down to Frank's mam's and just give her the nod, like.'

'I'll just dry me hands and go down now,' Molly agreed.

THIRTEEN

Frank's mother had obviously just been on the point of going to bed when Molly knocked. Doris's hair was in curling rags and she was wearing her dressing gown, and from the look of her face Molly suspected she had taken her teeth out.

'Scrubbin' floors and holding her belly, is she?' she repeated when Molly had told her what was happening. 'Well, it's a fact that there's many a woman bin scrubbing her floor when she had her first labour pains but your June has another three weeks to go, and her waters haven't broken yet. Added to which, she's a bit mardy.'

It was a statement Molly couldn't deny, but she still said stubbornly, 'It was me dad who said I should run down and tell you.'

'Did he? Very well then, you go back home, Molly, and I'll pop over and have a look at her in the morning. If yer think yer need me during the night, though, you come right over and knock me up, mind. I don't want nothing 'appening to my Frank's baby.'

Molly had just reached number 78 when she heard the thin shrill wail of the siren. She met her father and June at the door. Her father's arm was round June's shoulders as he tried to help her. All around them doors were opening and families were making a run for the shared shelter at the bottom of the cul-de-sac.

'I've forgotten me bag,' June wailed as Daisy hurried past with hers.

'Dad, you get June down to the shelter, I'll get the bags,' Molly called out, leaving her father to help her sister as she darted into the house to retrieve the bags everyone was supposed to keep ready for air-raid emergencies.

She caught up with her father and June a few yards short of the shelter. The siren was still going, and down by the docks the night sky was beginning to glow red from the fires from the incendiary bombs and the shells from the ack-ack guns.

'Gawd, will yer listen ter the noise of them,' Elsie said to Molly as they helped June down into the shelter. 'There must be hundreds of the buggers coming. Look at them parachute bombs.'

There was silence, and then a sudden explosion, over by the railway sidings, had them all ducking for cover and then hurrying into the shelter.

'Ooo, me belly,' June moaned, clasping her stomach as she was helped to a seat.

'I 'ope this bloody air raid doesn't last long,

'cos I've left our George sitting on the lav,' Pearl announced, whilst the mothers set about getting the children tucked into their sleeping bags.

'Are you all right, June?' Molly asked her sister anxiously, studying June's pale sweaty face.

'No, I'm bloody not,' June answered her, beads of sweat gathering on her face. 'I . . .'

What she said was drowned out by the sound of a bomb exploding.

'Blimey, that one were close,' someone protested nervously, whilst one of the smaller children started to wail in fear.

'Gawd knows how many planes Hitler has sent over this time,' one of the men muttered, 'and by the sound of it they're still coming. I reckon he means business tonight.'

Everyone exchanged worried looks.

'It'll be the docks and Birkenhead they're after, not us up here,' another man tried to comfort them, 'and our lads will soon sort them out.'

'Mam, I feel sick,' one of Daisy's boys announced.

'Anyone fancy a game of cards?' her husband asked, removing a pack from his pocket.

'Put them away. We don't want no bloody gambling in 'ere,' Daisy told him sharply.

Whilst she listened to everything going on around her, Molly was still concentrating on what was happening outside, and she knew from the looks on her neighbours' faces that she wasn't the only one.

'That's the last of Jerry's planes now,' Jim Fowler announced. 'I've been counting and it's bin nearly a minute since I heard one.'

No sooner had he spoken than they all heard the roar of a plane's engines, so loud and low that Molly wasn't the only one to duck, fearing it might actually hit the shelter.

'Sounds like our lads have got that one.'

'Sounds to me more like *it's* gonna get *us*,' Daisy muttered, giving a small scream at an explosion close at hand.

'Well, that's one as won't be going back tonight,' Jim announced with satisfaction.

'Molly, I got ter get out of here,' June moaned. 'I feel right poorly, I really do.'

Molly reached for her sister's hand and held it tightly. 'It won't be long now before the all clear goes, June,' she tried to comfort her, but the truth was, as they all knew, the bombing raid was only just beginning.

'No . . . I can't stay here any longer,' June told her, pulling away and standing up, her eyes widening as she looked down at her feet, her face suddenly bright red.

'Mam, June's peeing.'

'It's all right, June,' Elsie tried to comfort her. They could all see how distressed and embarrassed poor June was. 'It's just your waters breaking, that's all.' She patted June's hand but Molly could see the concern in Elsie's face, and her own stomach tightened with fear.

''Ere, June, you can't go into labour now, in here,' Daisy protested.

'Aye, June, you tell Mother Nature that she's got ter wait for Jerry to go home,' one of the other women joked, whilst Elsie said firmly, 'We'd better see what we can sort out, just in case.'

They could all hear the sound of bombs exploding and planes overhead, their flight paths tracked by the ack-ack gunners, and all of them knew that it could be several hours before they heard the all clear.

'I can't have me baby here,' June protested weepily. 'My Frank wouldn't like it . . .'

'There there, June. Don't you go upsetting yourself. Let's have a cup of tea,' Daisy suggested, adding ruthlessly, 'You men tek yourselves off ter the back of the shelter, will yer?'

'Oooh . . .' June put her hand on her belly, groaning in obvious pain. 'Oh, Molly, I'm that scared,' she whimpered, tears flooding her eyes as she reached for Molly's hand.

'Come and lie down over here, June lass. Happen you'll feel a bit more comfortable then,' one of the other women offered sympathetically, whilst another mother herded the children out of the way.

'How often are yer having yer pains, June?' Elsie asked practically.

'I don't know,' June groaned. 'I . . .'

They all tensed as the door to the shelter was suddenly pushed open.

'I couldn't sleep so I thought I might as well get meself down here just in case, seeing as it looks like we won't be hearing the all clear for a good while,' Frank's mother said breathlessly.

Molly could have kissed her, and even June looked relieved to see her mother-in-law.

'Her waters have broken, Doris,' Elsie informed her importantly.

'Have they, an' all!' she responded. 'Give us a hand, will yer, Molly?'

In the large bag Doris had brought with her was a sheet, which she handed to the other women, who used it to make an impromptu screen to provide June with a bit of modesty whilst the men were instructed to start a singsong – 'Mek as much noise as yer can,' Doris told them, adding to Daisy, 'We don't want the kiddies scared to death if June starts yellin'.'

'My two have heard it all before,' Daisy told her matter-of-factly.

'This is going ter kill me, I know it is,' June sobbed.

'No such thing,' Doris told her sturdily. 'Perfect hips you've got for childbirth, June, and I should know, seein' how many I've delivered in my time. Molly, be a good lass and come an' give me a hand. You can remember how it was with Sally, can't you? Elsie, get someone to boil us up some water, will yer?'

'No, Molly, don't go,' June cried, grabbing hold of Molly's hand when Molly started to move away to make room for Doris to examine her sister. 'Oh . . .'

'That's right, June,' Doris instructed briskly. 'No pushing yet.' Molly could feel June's nails biting down into her hand. Her sister's face was an eerie colour in the faint blue glow of the shelter's lights, and filmed with sweat. Molly knew that she had been there when Sally had given birth, but now was different, because this was her own sister, and this was no siren practice but a real air raid. Another bomb exploded somewhere near at hand.

'Come on now, June, that's enough fuss,' Doris was saying calmly, her voice raised so that June could hear her above the sound of her own moans and the staccato noise of the busy ack-ack guns.

The minutes and then the hours ticked slowly away whilst the Germans bombed the city and June struggled to give birth. The air inside the shelter, never fresh, was now fetid with pain and fear.

As Doris had instructed her to do, Molly kept wiping the sweat from June's face, offering her sister what comfort she could as June cried and clung to her hand.

'How's she doin', Doris?' Molly overheard Elsie asking in a whisper.

Women died in childbirth – Molly knew that. Suddenly she was filled with fear for her sister.

'You're doin' fine, June,' she heard Doris saying. 'Soon be over now, but don't push until I tell yer.'

'It's killin' me,' June moaned. 'I can't . . .'

'Yes, you can. Take deep breaths. Now you can start to push . . .'

'No, I can't . . .' June wailed. 'It hurts too much . . .'

A cluster of bombs suddenly exploded in an ear-splitting volley of noise that seemed to go on for ever, and it was only when the noise had finally died away that Molly realised that June's baby had been born.

'It's a girl, June,' she heard Doris announcing as the new arrival gave her first cries.

Miraculously, at least to Molly, suddenly June was all smiles of triumph.

'By, but you were lucky. That was one of the easiest labours I've ever seen,' Doris told June matter-of-factly. 'Here, you hold the baby for a minute, Molly,' she demanded, handing Molly her niece whilst she attended to June.

Tears of relief filling her eyes, Molly took the baby. High above them in the night sky, she could hear the sound of the bombers leaving the city, the danger over for another night.

The baby was so perfect, and so beautiful. Molly blinked away her tears of wonderment as the baby stared up at her with an unwavering dark blue-eyed stare. She could actually feel a small tug on her own womb as she looked back at her. A feeling of such intense love filled Molly that she could hardly bear to hand the baby back to Doris to give to June.

On her sister's face was a look of such softness

and pride that Molly's throat tightened with envy as well as with joy. It was hard not to think about Eddie and the children she would never have.

'She's my Frank all over again,' Doris pronounced proudly. 'I could see that the moment she was born. A real Brookes, she is, and no mistake.'

'Dad,' Molly called, lifting the sheet and smiling emotionally at her father. 'Come and have a look at your granddaughter.'

'By, but she's the image of yer mam, our June,' he whispered chokily as the baby looked up at him. Tears ran freely down his face as he reached out and touched the baby's cheek with one finger. 'Aye, the image of my Rosie, she is.'

The baby yawned and blinked. The all clear started to sound and Doris went to summon some of the men to carry June back to her own bed on the shelter's one and only emergency stretcher.

PART THREE

October 1940

ONE

'Of course, you would choose to have your baby the night Hitler decides to send a hundred and sixty bombers to Liverpool. You've allus been an awkward bugger,' their Uncle Joe teased June just over a month later, as she sat in the rocking chair Doris Brookes had sent round for her, nursing baby Elizabeth Rose, as she had decided to name her and Frank's daughter.

'After the little princesses and our mam, bless 'em,' she had told Molly and her father.

'It weren't my fault,' June protested indignantly, but she was still smiling.

Molly watched her sister a little sadly. Since the birth of her baby, June had been so wrapped up in her that she scarcely had time for anything or anyone else, and Molly was beginning to feel rather shut out of her sister's new life as a mother. It seemed to Molly now that June preferred Sally's company to her own, especially now that Sally had had her own baby, another little boy, and

385

although she tried not to do so she couldn't help feeling hurt and slightly resentful at the way Sally seemed to get to spend more time with little Elizabeth Rose than her adoring Auntie Molly. June even seemed to prefer Frank's mother's company to her own now, June very much the watchful mother as Doris Brookes joined her in adoration of the newest member of the Brookes family.

'Frank's written to say that he's hoping to get leave in November, so we'll have the baby christened then, providing Jerry doesn't go and bomb our church like he's done the Cathedral.'

'Aye, and he got them kiddies in that convalescent home in Birkenhead, damn him,' Joe added soberly. 'Poor little blighters didn't stand a chance. Half of them couldn't even walk, never mind run.'

'Stop it – I can't bear to hear about those little bairns,' June told their uncle sharply. 'And I keep telling our Molly that she's worryin' me half to death going out driving them ambulances. It's bad enough me not sleepin' on account of baby, and Jerry bombers coming over, but then I've got our Molly coming in at all hours, wakin' me up when I do get off.'

'I've offered to sleep downstairs when I'm on ambulance duty,' Molly reminded her stiffly.

'Don't go on at the poor lass, June,' Joe protested, giving Molly a warm smile. 'Where'd the rest of us be wi'out the likes of her? I'd have volunteered to do a bit more meself if we weren't on twelve-hour shifts now.'

'Aye, well, it's us mothers who have the worst of it, worrying ourselves sick about our kiddies,' June retaliated stubbornly.

'Auntie Violet has already offered to have you and Sally and the children at the farm, June,' Molly pointed out quietly. 'And it'd be safer for you there as well, what with Liverpool being bombed every other night.'

'What, and have our auntie making me and Sally work our fingers to the bone doing farm work, 'cos that's what will happen, I reckon. She's allus complaining about them not having enough men to do the work.'

It seemed to Molly sometimes that instead of being happy because she had such a beautiful baby, June was constantly worrying and getting upset. It was the war that was making everyone's temper wear a bit thin, she reasoned, what with the relentless pressure of Hitler's bombing campaign night after night, depriving people of much-needed sleep and wearing down their nerves. Molly was now doing a full day's work at the factory, and her WVS work as well, plus driving when it was her turn on the rota. Mr Harding had told her that any time she needed to come into work late because she had been driving the previous night she was free to do so, but Molly's pride wouldn't let her take advantage of his offer when she knew that others were turning up for work after doing voluntary service at night.

Sometimes it seemed to Molly that she was closer now to the other people on the emergency services team than she was to her own family, and one member of that team was Johnny Everton.

'How come you've got transferred to this lot?' Molly had asked him suspiciously when he had suddenly appeared amongst them one night, announcing that he had been included in their team because they were a man short.

'Had a word with a friend of a friend and said as how I fancied transferring,' Johnny had told her meaningfully, before adding, 'Nod's as good as a wink, if you know the right lads, and there's a chap in charge whose brother was in the same unit as us. Aren't you going to ask me why I transferred then?' he had teased her.

'Why should I? It isn't any business of mine,' Molly had answered.

'No? Well, that's where you're wrong, Miss Know-it-all, 'cos the only reason I asked to be part of this lot was on account of you,' he had told her softly. 'I should never have given you up, Molly, and if I had me time again . . .'

Her heart thudded unevenly now, remembering the way he had looked at her when he had said those words. She wasn't in love with him – not like she had been with Eddie, she knew that – but there *was* definitely something about Johnny that made her heart race that little bit faster.

*   *   *

'Anne!' Molly exclaimed in delight as virtually the first person she saw when she arrived at the church hall for WVS was her friend.

'When did you get back?'

'Last night.'

'How is Philip? Did you see him?' Molly asked her urgently.

Anne nodded. 'He's very poorly, though, Molly. He won't talk about what happened. At first he wouldn't talk to me at all. He said he didn't want me there because I pitied him. But I don't pity him, Molly, I love him. He's still Philip, even if he has lost his legs, and he's still the man I love. I hated having to come back and leave him. The nurses are wonderful but they are so busy, and when Philip is having one of his bad days . . . I just wish he would talk to me properly, Molly.'

Molly listened sympathetically. She could understand how Anne must feel. She would have felt the same if it had been Eddie who had been hurt.

'It must have been dreadful for you,' Molly whispered as they helped to hand out cups of tea to the queue of people now coming in through the doors. Most of them were now homeless, having been bombed out, and they had come to the WVS centre for advice and help.

'No, no such thing,' Molly reassured an anxious young mother concerned that her children would be taken from her and packed off overseas.

'I'm joining the ATS,' Anne announced abruptly.

389

Molly almost dropped the cup of tea she had just poured.

'I can't bear not being with Philip, Molly. And it's so awful at home,' Anne told her sadly. 'My parents can't get over losing our Richard. It's like life stopped for them the day he died. I feel guilty sometimes 'cos it's him that's dead and me that's alive. Don't get me wrong, I miss him too and I always will, but . . .' Anne heaved a heavy sigh and then continued, 'I sorted everything out whilst I was down there. I'll be leaving for Aldershot at the end of the week. I'm going to be based there, which means I'll be able to do my bit for the war effort and be close to Philip, for when he comes out of hospital.'

Molly shook her head. Her friend's news was so unexpected she didn't know what to say, other than a gruff, and truthful, 'I'm going to miss you, Anne.'

'I'm going to miss you too, but I know it's for the best. Philip needs me and I want to be with him more than anything.'

The two girls exchanged mutually understanding looks.

'Promise me you'll write to me,' Anne begged.

'You know I will,' Molly assured her emotionally.

TWO

'Quick, you're to get t'ambulance over to Durning Road, Edge Hill, as fast as you can.' The young Civil Defence cadet was red in the face from pedalling frantically through the smoke-filled streets, or at least what you could see of his face was red in the flare of the fires still burning from bombs that had been dropped earlier in the evening, Molly corrected herself, as he delivered his message to the nearest warden. 'There's bin a bomb dropped on the Junior Technical College, right on top of t'shelter there. There's a message gone out for as many ARP wardens, fire engines and ambulances as can get there.'

With that he was back on his bike, pedalling furiously in the direction of the nearest ARP station.

They had just finished evacuating the occupants of a street down by the docks where one of the houses had taken a direct hit from the new parachute mines Hitler's bombers were dropping on the city. Fortunately no one had been hurt.

'Did you hear that?' the senior warden asked Molly curtly.

She nodded and started the ambulance's engine.

'Come on, lads,' she heard him call out to his men. 'We'll leave this for now. We've had an emergency call at Durning Road.'

Durning Road – there would be people in that shelter she knew, Molly thought. She couldn't help exchanging a worried look with Johnny, though, when he swung himself up into the ambulance to take the seat beside her.

'Your mam and your sisters won't be up there, will they?' she asked him tersely.

'I doubt it. Me mam won't leave the house when there's a warning. She says she reckons she is safest under her own stairs.'

'Them seats you're sitting in are supposed to be for medical personnel,' Molly reminded Johnny.

'That's all right then. Done me first-aid training now, I have,' he told her with a grin.

Molly laughed.

She had come to know every short cut in the city during these last few weeks, and now she set off, expertly driving up what looked like an impossibly narrow street, which she knew would take them right up to Durning Road.

After London, Liverpool had suffered the worst of Hitler's bombing raids, although, unlike London, the attacks on Liverpool by Jerry bombers had not been mentioned in the news. So far, Liverpool had suffered over two hundred air raids, but tonight's was the worst so far, Molly decided, as she cut through a back alleyway using the pavement, causing the men crammed into the ambulance cab with her to start making jokes about women drivers.

'Don't you pay them no attention, Molly,' one of the nurses defended her stoutly.

'Gawd, look at that,' Johnny whistled as up ahead of them, low in the sky, they saw the unmistakable outline of a German plane and, below it, the parachute mines it had just dropped drifting slowly down to earth.

All around them they could see fires burning, casting an orange glow through the choking smoke.

'I heard as how one of Jerry's bombers chased a corporation bus all the way up Neddy Road the other night. Thought they was gonna be goners, all the passengers did, when he started strafing 'em. One poor woman lost her little kiddie. Only six months old, got killed by a piece of shrapnel,' one of the men announced.

Listening to him, Molly winced, and then turned into Durning Road. Up ahead of them they could see where the parachute mine had landed and the devastation it had caused. Several fire crews were trying to put out the blaze.

Other rescue workers were already on the scene, and everyone inside the ambulance fell silent as they saw how bad the damage was.

Molly pulled up next to a couple of other

ambulances that had arrived ahead of them. Everyone bailed out of the ambulance, including Molly.

'Wait here,' the senior ARP warden told them. 'I'll go and find out what's happening.'

He was back in less than five minutes, his face set and pale.

'The shelter underneath the school collapsed when the mine hit the school. They're starting to bring folk out now. There's no knowing yet how many injured there'll be. Come on, lads,' he told his men. 'Let's go and get started.'

At the site, rescue workers were digging frantically, some with just their bare hands, to try to reach those trapped inside the shelter. Suddenly Johnny realised that Molly was with them.

'What are you doing here?' he demanded. 'Get back to the ambulance, Molly. Bloody Jerry might come back and finish what he's started.'

'Well, and if he does, all the more reason for me to be here helping, to get them as is trapped out before he drops any more bombs on them,' Molly answered him firmly.

A pall of brick dust and smoke hung over the bombed building. Horrifically, mingled with the sounds of people using everything they could to remove the debris, interspersed with mono-syllabic commands from those in charge, could be heard quite plainly the tormented cries and pleas for help of those trapped inside the building.

Molly had been digging for nearly ten minutes, working side by side with Johnny, driven by the thin unremitting wail of a young child, when abruptly it ceased, causing bile to rise sourly in her throat. She didn't stop working, though, not even to look at Johnny.

'Watch out,' Johnny warned her, making a grab for her arm and hauling her out of danger, as the ground suddenly gave way beneath her.

'You'd best get back to your ambulance, Molly. They're bringing some of them out now,' one of the ARP men hurried over to tell her.

'How bad is it?' Molly asked him anxiously.

'It's bad. It seems like the central heating system's bin damaged and there's boiling water and gas pouring into the ruddy shelter.'

A woman being helped to safety, her hair and clothes almost burned off her and blood oozing from her cuts, kept asking over and over again, 'My little lad, where is he? He were sitting on me knee. Only four he is . . .'

'Calm yerself, love. Let's get yer cleaned up a bit, then we'll see about your lad,' Molly said gently, going to help.

The rescuer who had helped her free gave Molly a meaningful shake of his head and told her quietly, 'Her kiddie's bought it – lying dead in her arms, he were, but she wouldn't let us take him. She didn't want to believe that he were dead, see.'

On the ground beyond the devastation an

ominous number of unmoving bodies were being lined up by the rescuers, some of them so small that the sight of them made Molly's eyes sting with anguish.

It was two o'clock in the morning, and Molly was due to go off duty, but she knew that, like the others, she would keep on working until everything that could be done had been done.

It was just gone four when someone digging alongside her into the rubble, which they did sometimes with their bare hands if they thought they might be close to reaching a trapped person, nudged her in the ribs and said, 'There's the all clear.'

Numbly, Molly listened. The all clear signalled the end of another night's bombing and the coming of a new day, but, to those who mourned the victims of this terrible night, it could only emphasise that the tragedy of what had happened to them and those they loved could never be set aside.

Molly looked tiredly at the back door to number 78. After driving her ambulance back to its base, she had then walked home through the grey smoke-hazed chill of the late November morning, not even pausing to look at fresh bomb sites in appalled horror as she had done in the early days of the air raids.

Small groups of people huddled outside some of the newly bombed houses, clutching bundles of belongings. By the time it was properly daylight the bomb sites would have been picked over by looters searching for anything of value the house-holders might have left behind.

Already, straggling lines of trekkers were returning to the city, having spent the night wher-ever they could find a bed, usually a church hall or other place of temporary accommodation for the homeless in the villages on the outskirts of Liverpool, some because they no longer had a bed of their own and some because they were too afraid to risk staying in their own beds any more.

Wearily Molly opened the back door, always left unlocked now, and then shut it again, leaning on it and closing her eyes as she willed herself to gather up her strength. June would want to know where she had been and why, and she knew how much what had happened would upset her sister.

Whilst she was still leaning there with her eyes closed, a gentle but firm hand touched her shoulder and a kind voice commanded, 'Come on and sit down. I've bin waiting for you to get in safely, and I've got the kettle on.'

'Frank!' Molly stared at her brother-in-law. 'When did you get back?'

'Last night. Come on,' he repeated, reaching to take hold of her arm.

'I'm filthy,' Molly warned him. 'There was a bomb dropped on the college in Durning Road.' She gave a small shudder.

'Yes, I know. I thought you might be there,'

Frank told her quietly. 'Mam was sent for to go and help out at the hospital. We heard that it was a bad 'un.'

'Yes,' Molly agreed bleakly. 'There's bin a lot killed, some of them kiddies . . .' She started to shake, tears pouring down her face. 'There was this poor woman, Frank, still holding on to her kiddies, even though they was dead . . .'

Suddenly she was in Frank's arms and he was holding her firmly, his hand cradling the back of her head, whilst he ignored her tearful almost incoherent protests that she was all smoky and dirty, and her tears soaking into his shirt.

THREE

What time was it? She could see light coming in through the curtains, and she could hear voices from the room down below so it must be early morning.

Her eyes felt sore and gritty and her throat felt raw from the smoke of last night's bomb.

Last night! Molly sat bolt upright in her bed, and then reached for her watch. The pain of Eddie's death had softened enough for her to be able to wear it now without being filled with misery, but she still thought of him every time she put it on. It had been so typical of him that he had thought to make sure she had her birthday present even though he had known he wouldn't be there to give it to her.

It was half-past one, gone dinner time. She pushed back the bedclothes. The gold satin eiderdown hadn't even shifted from its position on top of the matching bedspread, a sure sign of how deeply she had slept. She could not even remember getting undressed. All she could remember was the hell on earth that had been the scene at the college – that and coming home to find Frank waiting for her.

A thin wail pierced the muted adult voices downstairs. Baby Elizabeth Rose was obviously awake and hungry.

'No, Frank, don't pick her up, you mustn't. Dr Truby King says it will spoil her if we pick her up every time she cries,' Molly heard her sister cautioning her husband crossly. As Molly walked into the kitchen she sighed. Elsie had said how much she regretted giving June the book, which now seemed to rule her life.

'Oh, there you are,' June commented. 'I suppose you're going to want some breakfast now, are you, and me having only just finished cleaning up the kitchen?'

'I'm not really hungry, June,' Molly answered her quietly, unaware of the look Frank was giving her. 'I'll just make meself a cuppa and then I'd better get off to work, otherwise Mr Harding will be wondering what's happened to me.'

'You can sit yourself right down here, Molly,' Frank announced firmly. 'You're not going anywhere until you've got some food inside you.'

'Oh, do stop fussing, will you, Frank?' June demanded waspishly. 'Some of us didn't get a wink of sleep last night, what with them bombs, and folk coming in at all hours of the night, and then staying in their beds all morning whilst the rest of us have had to just get on wi' it.'

'I don't need any breakfast, Frank, honest,' Molly assured her brother-in-law quietly.

The truth was that she didn't think she could eat anything. A leaden weight of dull misery filled her chest every time she thought about the previous night. Just looking at Elizabeth Rose, lying so pink and healthy in her pram, made Molly's heart lurch against her ribs as she remembered the tiny bodies that had been brought up out of the shelter. Not that she would say anything like that to June, of course.

'Here you are, Molly lass. Drink this.'

She looked up at Frank in surprise. She hadn't even heard the kettle boil and now here he was holding out a mug of tea to her.

As she took it from him she realised that she couldn't quite bring herself to look directly at him. Because of last night? Because for a few minutes he had held her in his arms? As a brother, that was all, Molly reminded herself sharply. That was how Frank had held her and that was all he was to her. That was all she wanted him to be to her.

'I'll be off to work as soon as I've drunk this.'

'Are you on duty again tonight?' Frank asked her quietly.

Molly nodded.

'In that case I'll come along with you,' Frank told her, earning himself a scathing look from June.

'And why would you be wantin' to do that?

You've only just come home on leave, and if there's anyone needs a bit o' help it's me,' she told him sharply.

'Last night you said I was upsettin' the baby on account of her not knowing me, and keeping you awake into the bargain,' Frank pointed out gently. 'Besides, with Jerry bombing Liverpool the way he is, the emergency services need all the help they can get. I feel so helpless staying at home when people need support.'

'Some help you'll be if you go and get yourself hurt,' June sniffed disparagingly. 'You're a soldier, don't forget, Frank, and you're entitled to have a bit o' leave and spend it wi' your family.'

'It's really kind of you to offer to help, Frank,' Molly put in placatingly, 'but June's right, you've come home to see her and Elizabeth Rose, not go out working.'

'We're all in this together,' Frank said quietly, 'and from what I've heard about the bombing Liverpool's bin suffering; another pair of hands wouldn't go amiss.'

'Aye, well, another pair of hands wouldn't go amiss here neither, if it comes to that,' June informed him crossly, adding in an even sharper voice, as the baby started to cry, 'Oh, look now what you've done, and I'd only just got her off to sleep, an' all.'

Molly could see the way Frank's face was reddening from June's rebuke. Discreetly she looked away. June had refused to go to Doris's.

'Why don't I wheel her down to me mam's for a bit o' fresh air? A ride in the pram might send her off,' Frank suggested.

'Take her out in this perishing cold weather? Are you mad?' June objected. ''Sides, your mam will be wanting to pick her up like she allus does and if I've told her once I've told her a hundred times that Dr Truby says babies mustn't be picked up except at feeding and changing times. You go on yer own if you want to go and see yer mam.'

To Molly's relief there was a knock on the door.

'It's only me,' Elsie announced, bustling in. 'Oh, you're still here then, Molly. I'd heard as how you was wi' them down at Durning Road last night. Poor things. They was saying in the grocer's that there's upwards of three hundred bin killed and more to come. Aye, and some of them kiddies as well . . .'

'If you ask me, none of them shelters is safe,' June announced. Since giving birth to her baby, June had developed a dislike of air-raid shelters, insisting that she felt safer inside her own house, and Molly had learned not to try to convince her otherwise, even though the Government had said that people would be safer inside the shelters than their own homes.

'That'll be Sally,' June announced when there was a second knock on the door.

'I've just come round to see if there's anything else you want me to do to help with the christening,' Sally smiled, as she kneeled down to release her toddler from his leading reins, whilst expertly rocking the pram with her foot.

'Let me help,' Frank proffered, but immediately June snapped, 'Don't listen to him, Sally, he's useless. Elizabeth Rose screams her head off every time he goes near her.'

'Well, she hasn't had time to realise that he's her dad yet, has she?' Sally offered pacifically, before adding, 'I expect you've heard about the Durning Road bombing last night?'

'Our Molly was there,' June answered her. 'Weren't you?'

Elizabeth Rose had started crying again, drowning out Molly's reply.

'I don't know what I'm going to do with her, Sally,' June said tiredly. 'She just won't stop crying and her nappy rash is that bad . . .'

'She sounds hungry to me,' Sally proffered.

'Hungry? She can't be. I've bin feeding her dead on time.'

'June . . .'

'No, it's her nappy rash that's upsetting her.'

Her sister sounded so harried that Molly couldn't help feeling sorry for her.

'Put plenty of Vaseline on her when you change her. That's what I do,' Sally confided. 'Mr Smithers up at the chemist's on Edge Road will sell yer some if you tell him it's for yer baby,' she promised, obviously anticipating June's next complaint that you couldn't buy supplies like Vaseline for love nor money.

It was nearly three o'clock and Molly was on duty again at seven. As though he had read her mind, Frank turned to her and said quietly, 'If I was you, Molly, I wouldn't bother goin' into work. Not today. I'll go along and have a word with Mr Harding, if you like. I'll explain to him where you was last night and what you was doin' and then I'll call at me mam's on the way back. She was expecting June to move in with her whilst I was home, and I'll have to explain to her that June doesn't want to in case it upsets Elizabeth Rose's routine.'

Frank was avoiding looking at her as he spoke and Molly's heart went out to him. She had over-heard the argument between him and June when June had announced that she was staying at number 78 instead of joining Frank at his mother's.

'Oh, Frank, you don't need—' Molly began, but he shook his head and gave her a gentle smile.

'You'd be doing me a favour – aye, and your June as well. I reckon she'll be glad to get me out from under her feet.'

It was said mildly enough, but Molly could still see that June's behaviour was upsetting him. Worriedly, she watched as Frank went to get his coat whilst June ignored him. What was wrong with her sister? Surely she must be delighted to have her husband home, and yet she was behaving as though she could hardly bear the sight of him. June hadn't been herself at all these last few weeks and Molly was concerned about her. But every time she tried to say so, June refused to listen to her, claiming that Molly was making a fuss about nothing and that it was only natural that she should feel tired and out of sorts.

'I'm off now then,' Frank called out.

'Aye, well, think on, Frank. I do not want you coming back tellin' me how your mam thinks I should be bringing my Elizabeth Rose up,' June warned him, 'and I do not want you coming in after I've got her settled neither and waking her up like you did last night.'

''Ere, June, you was a bit hard on poor Frank,' Sally protested as soon as he had gone.

Molly was glad that it was Sally who had spoken out, even if she was thinking the same thing. June certainly didn't look very pleased by her friend's comment.

'I dare say you'd feel like being hard on your Ronnie if he was to come bursting in and upsetting your two's routine,' June snapped. 'I'd just about got Elizabeth Rose settled to a proper routine, an' all, and now there's Frank waking her up when she should be sleepin', with never a thought for me. Downright selfish, he's being, and I've told him so. It's bad enough with our Molly coming and going at all hours.' June's face had become as heated as her voice.

Sally was looking startled and Elsie had opened her mouth, obviously about to put in her own twopennyworth when the back door opened and Frank walked back in – accompanied by Johnny.

'Look who I just found on the doorstep,' Frank grinned with a twinkle in his eyes. 'I wonder who he could be coming to see?'

Molly could feel a warm blush creeping up her whole body, beginning at her toes.

'He's got no business visiting anyone in this house, and if it's our Molly he's after—' June began.

'Cut it out, June,' Frank stopped her sharply.

Molly was shocked. She had never heard Frank utter a sharp word before in her life.

'Don't you go talking to me like that, Frank Brookes,' June retaliated. 'You might be a corporal, but this isn't the army.'

'Nipper playing yer up, is it, June?' Johnny cut in easily. To Molly's amazement he gave her sister a sympathetic smile. He'd always said that he thought June was a right old bossy boots. And to her even greater amazement, instead of snapping at him, June actually returned his smile.

'See, Frank Brookes,' she tossed her head, and nodded towards Johnny, 'some men understand how it is when you've got a baby keeping you awake all hours.'

'Pretty little thing,' Johnny commented, looking down at the baby. 'Teks after her mother, she does, June.'

June started to laugh. 'Go on with yer, Johnny, and less of yer nonsense. And what brings you round here?'

'You was right the first time,' Johnny answered

her cheerfully. 'I've come round on account of your Molly.' He turned to her. 'Just to see if you was all right, like, after last night.'

'I'm fine, Johnny, thanks for asking,' Molly answered swiftly.

'That's good then, only I was a bit worried when they said you hadn't bin into work.'

'You've bin to Hardings?' Molly demanded.

'Aye. Just in case she hasn't told yer yet,' he continued, turning back to June and the others, 'your Molly deserves a medal for what she did last night. A real heroine, she is, and no mistake. Wi'out her help there's a fair few from last night who wouldn't be alive right now.'

'Give over,' Molly protested self-consciously. 'I was only doing me duty, same as the rest of us.'

''Ere, if yer not doing anything this Saturday how about comin' wi' me to the Grafton?' Johnny asked guilelessly.

'By, but you've got your cheek, Johnny,' June breathed sharply. 'But you're wastin' your breath because our Molly will be helping me get ready for baby's christening on Saturday night.'

'It's kind of you to come round, Johnny,' Molly told him, standing up determinedly. 'I'll see you out.'

'Sure you don't want to change your mind and come to the Grafton wi' me on Saturday night?' Johnny coaxed her as she stood politely on the doorstep, waiting for him to leave.

'You heard what our June said. It's Elizabeth Rose's christening on Sunday.'

'What about the Saturday after, then?' Johnny asked.

All Molly could do was shake her head and try not to laugh. No matter what happened in the world, Johnny Everton would always be up to his old tricks.

'I hope you're not encouraging him, our Molly,' June told her as soon as she returned to the back room. 'I would have thought you'd have learned your lesson last time.'

'We're just friends, that's all,' Molly defended herself, thinking how June was an expert at rewriting history – she'd pushed her into the engagement with Johnny! 'Both of us working together on the emergency services means we bump into each other from time to time. Anyway, it was you that wanted me to go out with him in the first place,' she reminded her sister.

'That were then,' June told her firmly, 'before I knew what he were really like. I thought you said you was going down to your mam's, Frank?' she prodded her husband. 'If you go now, happen she'll do yer a bit of tea and that'll save me the trouble.'

'Wait on a bit, Frank,' Sally begged him as he reached up to the row of coat pegs by the back door for his coat. 'I'll walk back wi' yer. I've got to go past yer mam's on me own way home.'

'Aye, I'd better be getting back, an' all,' Elsie agreed. 'My two will be coming in wanting their teas any minute.'

Molly could see how desperate everyone was to leave the uncomfortable atmosphere of the house, but there was something she had to say to Elsie, so she went to the door with her, pulling it to behind them, and then saying quickly, 'Elsie, I know how it must look, with Johnny coming round and going on like he did . . .'

Elsie shook her head. 'There's no need for you to go explaining anything to me, Molly. I've got eyes in me head and I could see plain enough that you was head over heels in love with our Eddie and him with you. Eddie was me nephew, and what happened to him were a cruel thing, but you're as close to me as a daughter, Molly. Nothing can bring our Eddie back, and the last thing he would want is for you to spend the rest of your life grieving for him. I know you'll allus hold a special place in your heart for him, Molly, an' there's nothing wrong in you goin' out and havin' a bit o' fun.'

'Oh, Elsie . . .' Tears of relief and gratitude filled Molly's eyes.

'There, lass,' Elsie comforted her, putting her arms around her and giving her a hug.

'June, what's wrong?' Molly asked her sister worriedly.

'I'm sure I do not know what you mean,' June responded, scowling.

'Yes, you do,' Molly persisted. 'I'm talking about the way you've bin with poor Frank, and—'

'Oh, so it's "poor" Frank now, is it? Well, I should have known as how you'd side with him. You've allus had a bit of a soft spot for him, aye, and so has he for you.'

'It isn't anything to do with that,' Molly denied. 'It's you I'm worried about. You've bin proper nasty with your Frank ever since he came home. Why didn't you go back to his mam's with him?'

'Back? I'm not going round there and having her tell me how to bring up me own baby. No, thank you.'

'So where are you and Frank going to be sleeping then whilst he's home on leave?' Molly challenged her.

'Frank can sleep where he likes. I'm staying here. He's got two choices – either he can go to his mam's or he can sleep on the settee in the front room here, like he did last night.'

Molly tried not to show how disturbed she was by June's remarks. Admittedly she wasn't married with a young baby but she would have thought that after such a long period of absence June would be eager to have her husband home on leave, instead of behaving as though she resented him being here.

'I thought he must have gone to his mam's after I saw him really early this morning – that he'd only just returned. You never made him sleep on that, June?' Molly protested. 'Not after what he's bin through with Dunkirk.'

'And what about me? What about what I've bin

through? I thought I were goin' to die in that air-raid shelter, when I was having Elizabeth Rose. Frank can sleep where he likes, but I'm staying put here in me own bed.'

'June, Frank is your *husband*. I know that whilst he's bin away you and me have bin sharing our old room, but now that he's home on leave . . .'

June looked at her defiantly. 'Now that he's home on leave what?'

This wasn't the June Molly thought she knew, and it certainly wasn't the June who had returned from honeymoon so happily excited about being married to Frank. 'I thought you said that it had bin decided that when Frank came home on leave you'd move back into Frank's old room at his mam's.'

'And what's that going to do to Elizabeth Rose? I don't want to go unsettling her by carting her off to Frank's mam's and making her sleep in a strange room.' June looked aggrieved.

'Lillibet's only tiny – she won't even notice the change,' Molly replied. 'Besides, Doris is her grandmother – the only one she has.'

'Yes, and I am her mother. And I'll thank you not to call her Lillibet. How many times do I have to tell you, our Molly, that Dr Truby says you 'ave to call baby by her proper name?'

'Well, if Lillibet is good enough for the Queen . . .' Molly responded promptly, immediately wishing she hadn't when she saw June's scowl. 'Look, June, don't let's fall out,' she begged her. 'Listen, why don't I ask Sally if I can stay with her whilst Frank's on leave and then you and him can share our room. I know it's only got single beds, but—'

'What, and have *him* coming in waking up baby at all hours, instead of you?' June gave a dismissive shrug. 'No thanks!'

What had happened to the giggling girl who had blushed and laughed as she had talked about the honeymoon she and Frank had spent in Blackpool, Molly wondered unhappily. She was sure that in her sister's shoes she would have been only too eager to be with her husband. But, unlike June, she did not have a baby to think about, she reminded herself, careful not to be critical of her sister. Even so, she couldn't help reminding her gently, 'Only last week you were saying how much you wanted Frank to come home.'

'I wanted him to be here for the christening, yes,' June snapped. 'But I don't want—' She broke off as the back door opened and their father came in. He was carrying a copy of the *Liverpool Echo* under his arm.

'Eeh, lass,' was all he said as he looked at Molly, shaking his head sadly. 'The *Echo* says there was over three hundred killed at Durning Road last night.'

Molly said nothing. How could she when she was thinking it was surprising the death toll had not been higher?

'Ruddy German bombers!' It was so unlike her

father to swear, but she could understand why he had done so. Who could have been there last night, seen and heard what the rescuers had seen and heard, held the lifeless but still warm bodies of young children in their arms and not felt like damning the people who could commit such an atrocity?

'I can't pretend I wasn't lying in me bed worrying about you last night, lass,' her father said quietly. 'When we was in the shelter we heard them bombers coming over and I 'ad a feeling it were going to be a bad night. Then we heard the bombs going off and, of course, Pearl Lawson's George had to start piping up they was close, as if the rest of us couldn't hear that just as good as he could,' Albert snorted derisively. 'Some folk don't know how to handle themselves in a crisis, I tell you. Women and young kiddies in that shelter, there was – he should have been keeping his gloomy thoughts to himself.'

'Well, you won't get me going in one of them shelters again,' June broke in vehemently. 'Not after what happened to them at Durning Road. Me and Elizabeth Rose are going to be staying right here.'

Molly was horrified. She knew how much her sister disliked going into the shelter but this was the first time June had voiced an outright future refusal to do so.

'June, you can't mean that,' she protested. 'It wouldn't be safe for you to stay here.'

414

'Well, you would say that, wouldn't you, on account of your working for the emergency services, but I've heard that there's plenty of people staying in their homes. Under the stairs is where I'm going to be in future, and that's that.'

Molly and her father exchanged anxious glances, but Molly knew from her father's small shake of the head that, like her, he knew it was pointless trying to argue with June in her present mood. The old sharp-tongued June, whom Molly had thought softened with her marriage to Frank, was back with a vengeance.

'Where's Frank?' Albert asked.

'He's gone round to his mam's, Dad,' Molly answered when June didn't do so.

'Tell you what, June,' their father offered warmly, 'why don't you go upstairs and change into sommat pretty and get your Frank to tek you out dancing or to the pictures? Do you the power of good, it will. And me and Molly will look after little Libby for yer.'

'Power of good! Get meself bombed, more like. No,' June shook her head, 'I'm not goin' anywhere. I'm staying right here with my little precious.' Only now did her face soften as she looked down at her baby.

'You go and get cleaned up, Dad, and I'll make a start with the tea,' Molly offered. 'What is it we're having tonight, June?'

With both their father and Molly working full time, and Molly doing voluntary emergency work and her WVS work as well, June had taken over all the domestic chores, including the cooking and most of the shopping. The increasingly long queues brought about by the rationing meant that buying food, even when it was on ration and available, took a long time.

'I was going to make some Spam fritters, but what with you keeping me awake most of last night, and then Frank getting baby upset, I never did them. There's a bit of that soup left, though.'

'You have that, Dad,' Molly smiled at their father. 'It's WVS later and I can probably get a bit of sommat there.'

'A nice juicy meat pie, that's what I fancy,' June murmured tiredly.

'Aye, well, you'll not be getting one of those until this war's over,' their father prophesied grimly.

'War, war, war – that's all anyone ever talks about,' June exploded. 'Well, I'm sick of it. If it's not Jerry bombers and them air-raid sirens, it's them ack-ack guns.'

Molly looked over to her father's chair, where he had left the paper. The grainy photographs on the front page didn't reflect the full horror of last night, but what they did show was enough to reawaken the feelings of helplessness and despair she had felt as she listened to the cries for help and screams of pain coming from those trapped underground. June didn't know how lucky she was.

One woman had gone into the shelter with five children and had lost all but one of them. Molly knew she would never forget the sight of her sitting there in complete silence after she had been rescued, staring numbly at the bodies of her children.

Another mother had screamed and gone on screaming, refusing to accept that the small bundle the rescuers had removed from her arms was dead.

'Poor little sod's head was smashed in,' Molly had overheard one of the other men telling Johnny, 'but we covered it up so she couldn't see.'

Amongst those who had survived there had been some horrific injuries, dreadful burns from the blast and the boiling water, a man whose leg had had to be amputated in order for them to remove him from the wreckage; a woman whose arm had been so badly mangled Molly had felt sick when she saw it, not even recognising what it was at first.

There had been so many bombs now and so many deaths, but this had shocked Molly more than all the others put together. But she couldn't say anything – not to her dad, who she knew was worrying already about her being hurt in the course of her voluntary work; and certainly not to June, who thought only of herself and Lillibet. Not that Molly could truly blame her sister. It was only natural that she should want to protect her baby. Molly couldn't help wondering if the loss of their own mother might be preying on her mind now June had a child of her own.

She could have told Frank, though, and he would have understood. Molly looked towards the back door. Frank was June's husband, even if June herself no longer seemed to want him, nor seemed to realise how lucky she was to have a man like Frank. Molly would have given anything to have her own Eddie back and to know he was safe. He was never far from her thoughts, even if her pain was easier to bear.

FOUR

'What's up, Molly? You've hardly said a word all morning,' Irene chivvied.

'Leave her alone, Irene,' Ruby defended her. 'It was only t'other night that she was down helping them bombed at Durning Road. Our Hilda told me she'd seen you there,' Ruby explained. 'Said as how you and the others were proper heroes, that them as hadn't got no shovels nor nothing was digging into the wreckage with their bare hands. Over three hundred gone and more dying every day in hospital from their wounds is what I've heard,' she added almost ghoulishly.

'Put a sock in it, will yer, Rube?' Irene demanded, nodding in the direction of one of the new workers, a pale-faced girl who was working away with her back to them. 'Lily there's sister were in that shelter. Up at Mill Road she is now, and in a right bad way,' Irene added in a low voice. 'Carryin', she was, but she's lost the baby.'

Everyone made sympathetic noises and eyed the girl's ramrod-straight back.

'It's your June's little 'un's christening this Sunday, isn't it, Molly?' Irene changed the subject. 'I'd heard as how her Frank's back on leave, an' all. She must be right pleased about that.'

Was Irene merely making idle conversation or had she heard about June's refusal to move into Frank's old room at his mother's whilst Frank was home on leave? Gossip spread fast in their area, never more so than in wartime. Knowing Irene, and how she always managed to have all the latest gossip, Molly would have been surprised if she *hadn't* somehow got wind of what had happened.

'Well, I believe in doing me best by my own kiddies,' Molly could hear Daisy announcing virtuously as she stood with several other women from the close who had come to the church to witness Elizabeth Rose's christening, 'but there's times when it's your 'ubby you has to think about, and if you ask me, sending him to stay on his own at his mam's when he's just come home from fighting on the front line, then . . . oh, I didn't see you there, Molly,' she stammered, embarrassed.

Molly didn't say anything. What could she say to defend her sister, when her own feelings were so similar to the ones Daisy had just been so vigorously stating?

Unwillingly Molly started to make her way to June's side. Her sister had been snappy with everyone these last few days, but Molly felt that she had been singled out for some of her sharpest criticisms. Although not as many as she flung at poor Frank.

Molly could hear June's voice now, raised and angry, as she demanded, 'No, Frank, you're not holding her right. Give her to me.'

'Leave him be, June,' Uncle Joe told her. 'Poor lad's only doing his best. It ain't his fault if he don't know one end of a baby from t'other,' Joe joked, causing everyone around them to laugh and June's face to become red with increased anger.

'It's all right for you to go making a joke about it, but it's me as has got to get Elizabeth Rose sorted out when he's bin and gone and upset her. Scared to death of him, she is . . .'

'Scared to death of Frank or sick to death of the sound of June's voice?' Molly heard John Fowler mutter to Elsie. 'I know I would be.'

'Oh, there you are,' June greeted Molly sharply when Molly had made her way to her side through the crowd outside the church. 'I want to get back to the house. It's nearly time for Elizabeth Rose's feed.'

'Mam hasn't had a chance to hold Libby yet, June,' Frank protested.

'Didn't you hear me, cloth ears? I've just said it's time for her feed, and if I've told you once I've told you a hundred times, her name is Elizabeth Rose and not Libby.'

'That bloody book,' Frank suddenly swore, his

normally soft voice hardening. 'It wants throwing out and—'

'You'll not touch my book, and if anything wants throwing out of the house, then it's you, Frank Brookes,' June told him fiercely, spinning round on her heel, clutching Elizabeth Rose to her as she started to hurry towards the church gate.

Elsie, who was standing next to Molly watching her, shook her head. 'Eeh, Molly, you don't know how much I wish now I hadn't brought June that book wot Mrs Simpkins was throwing out.'

'It's not your fault, Elsie,' Molly quickly reassured her, and indeed Molly genuinely believed that that was the truth, even if June was driving everyone up the wall with her determination to follow Dr Truby King's instructions on how to bring up a baby.

'I don't know what's come over your June, turning on poor Frank like that,' Elsie continued. 'She doesn't know how lucky she is to have him – aye, and in one piece, an' all.' They exchanged sorrowful smiles, thinking of Eddie.

Molly wished she was brave enough to say something to June about what was going on, but she didn't want to risk having her sister fall out with her. Perhaps if she were to have a word with Sally, she might speak to June. They weren't as close as they had been, but surely as a new mother June would be more inclined to listen to Sally than she would to her unmarried and childless younger sister. Her mind made up, Molly waited until Sally was on her own with her two children before hurrying over to her.

'What's up with your June, Molly?' Sally demanded, echoing Elsie's comments. 'She's done nowt but get at poor Frank since the moment he came home.'

'I don't know. In fact, I was just about to ask you if you would have a word with her and see if you can find out what's wrong with her,' Molly admitted.

'It wouldn't do any good,' Sally said. 'I've already had a bit of a fall-out wi' her over the way she's bin. Catch me getting away wi' treating my Ronnie the way she's done her Frank! But then Frank has always bin a bit of a softie. But he is still a man, for all that, Molly, and a good-looking one, an' all. And I can tell you now, there'll be plenty of lasses willing to keep him company and give him what your June is refusing him, and you mark my words, she'll end up finding that out the hard way if she doesn't watch out.'

'Frank would never do anything like that,' Molly protested, genuinely shocked at Sally's words.

'He's a man,' Sally insisted, 'with a man's needs,' she emphasised pointedly. 'I've seen them down at the dance hall when I'm working there, Molly: men who are hungry for a bit of female company and a smile. I must admit, though, I never thought your June would be one of them women wot changes the moment she gets a wedding ring on her finger.'

'She isn't,' Molly defended her sister. 'It's only since she's had Elizabeth Rose that she's bin like this. I think she's worrying about something and not wanting to say anything.'

Sally's expression softened slightly. 'You're a good sister to her, Molly, and happen you've got a point. It upset her real bad, her giving birth in that ruddy shelter like that. But that's no reason to go round being right nasty to folk. She really snapped my head off the other day when I told her that if I was her I wouldn't keep on waking Libby up to feed her just because some ruddy book said I had to. As good as told me I weren't a good mother, she did,' Sally continued indignantly.

'I'm sure she didn't mean that, Sally,' Molly tried to calm her.

'Mebbe not, but she's got a few backs up in the close, I can tell you. If she doesn't watch out she's not going to have any friends left,' Sally warned.

'Just listen to that lot in there,' Molly laughed, jerking her head in the direction of the parlour whilst she finished washing up the tea cups, sherry glasses and sandwich plates their family and neighbours had used.

'It's a pity you encouraged them to come back, if you ask me, Molly. And our Uncle Joe's the worst of the lot,' June grumbled. 'Haven't they got any homes to go to? I had to wake Elizabeth Rose to give her her feed, and now with all this racket going on I'm never going to get her off again, she's that grizzly.'

Molly took a deep breath and turned round to face her sister. It was now or never.

'I know it's none of my business, June,' she began hesitantly whilst June stiffened and watched her warily, 'but there was a few saying at the church today how tired you was looking.' Molly was trying her best to be tactful. 'And I was just thinking,' she hesitated and then plunged on desperately, 'well, what I mean is, June, when Libby – I mean Elizabeth Rose – is sleepin', do you really have to wake her up to feed her? Only it seems to me that if you were to just let her sleep and then—'

'It's Frank's mam who's put you up to this, isn't it?' June interrupted angrily. 'I saw how the two of you was thick as thieves before we went into the church. Well, you're right about one thing, Molly: it isn't any of your business – nor hers neither.'

Molly fervently wished she hadn't started this conversation but since she had, she'd better have her say.

'But, June, the poor little thing looks so tired sometimes, and I've seen her falling asleep whilst you're trying to give her her bottle, and then she wakes up in the night . . .'

'Oh, I get it now. It isn't me you're worried

425

about but yourself. Well, I'm sorry if you don't want us here—'

'June, that's not true. I *do* want you here,' Molly interjected.

'So what are you complaining for then?'

'Well, it's just that people have bin saying . . . that is, they've been asking . . . well, it's this routine of yours, June. Even Elsie said today that she wished she hadn't given you that book.'

'Let them say what they like. I don't care,' June told her defiantly.

Molly took a deep breath. She had come this far – she must continue otherwise her sister's marriage, not to mention her friendships and sanity, would be in jeopardy.

'It isn't just that, June. People have been talking about you and Frank and saying things.'

'What kind of things?'

Why on earth had she started this, Molly wondered uncomfortably. Here they were with a houseful of visitors who could walk into the kitchen at any time, and June looking like she was about to murder her.

'Well, they've seen how your Frank's bin staying at his mam's whilst you're sleeping here,' Molly told her. 'Why don't you go back with him tonight, June? Ten to one Libby won't wake up now until morning and you can leave her here with me if you want, or put her in her pram and take her with you.'

'I'm not going anywhere and neither is she. Oh,

Molly, please don't go on at me. I've got enough to cope with, what with Elizabeth Rose.' To Molly's dismay June suddenly burst into tears.

'Oh, June, don't,' Molly begged her, hurrying to comfort her. 'I didn't mean to upset you. Please don't cry.'

'I can't help it, Molly. I keep thinking about the bombs and being trapped in the shelter like they was in Durning Road. If anything was to happen to Elizabeth Rose . . .'

'Nothing is going to happen to her,' Molly tried to reassure her, handing June her own clean handkerchief so that she could dry her tears. 'You mustn't get yourself upset like this, June.'

'I can't help it,' June repeated. 'Everything's getting on top of me, what with this war, and I worry that much.' June sniffed. 'Oh, Molly, what's to become of us all?'

'The war will soon be over, June,' Molly told her firmly. 'You just wait and see.'

A small smile touched June's mouth. 'Just listen to you. Anyone would think as you was my big sister and not the other way round.'

''Ere, Molly, is all that beer gone? Oh . . .' Their Uncle Joe stood in the doorway looking from Molly's face to June's, but to Molly's relief, before he could say anything, they all heard the thin wail coming from the room upstairs.

'Oh, there's Elizabeth Rose crying again,' June sighed. 'I'd better go up to her.'

* * *

'It's nearly midnight, Frank,' Molly said gently. The others had all gone home long ago, and Albert, like June, had gone up to bed over an hour ago. Molly had stayed downstairs to finish cleaning up.

'Come on, let me give you a hand finishing up wi' this lot first,' Frank insisted, rolling up his sleeves.

'There's no call for you to do that,' Molly said. 'I'm finished now anyway. At least it doesn't look as though we're going to have Hitler's bombers coming over tonight. They're normally here by now. Mind you, I wasn't really expecting them tonight. They seem to come every other night. Not that it's a good idea to rely on that. Jerry likes to try to catch us out, if he can.'

Frank gave her a thoughtful look and Molly knew that he wasn't deceived by her pretence at needing to stay up to tidy up, and that he understood she was still downstairs in case she was called out to help with an emergency.

'You're as bad as me mam, you are – allus worrying about other folk more than you do yourself,' Frank chided her gently.

'Well, if they had come over, I'd have been able to help June get into the shelter, with Libby.'

'I was hoping June might come back down. I wanted to talk to her,' Frank told her.

'She's probably asleep now, but you can go up and see,' Molly offered, feeling sorry for him. Far from recuperating at home after his ordeal at the front, he looked even more broken and defeated than when he'd first come back.

'I'd better not do that. I'd probably wake the baby up and then I'd be in worse trouble than I am already.'

'You know June only worries about keeping her to her routine on account of this book she's been reading. She's trying to be the perfect mother and it's taking its toll on her, especially at such a time.' Molly felt honour-bound to defend her sister.

'Aye, I know. Showed it to me, she did, and said as how I were making her do things all wrong, what with wanting to pick up our Libby. By, but she's a bonny baby, Molly,' Frank beamed proudly. 'Pretty as a picture wi' them dark curls.'

Molly couldn't help but smile in agreement. Her niece was the most beautiful baby she'd ever seen – she was happy to admit it. 'Dad says that she's got a real look of our mam,' she told him.

'That's funny, *my* mam says she's got me dad's curls,' Frank told her straight-faced, but when Molly looked at him she could see the laughter gleaming in his eyes. He had always had a good sense of humour, had Frank. 'Not that I'm getting to see much of her,' Frank added, his smile fading. 'Every time I go near her June complains about sommat or other.'

'She doesn't mean anything by it, Frank,' Molly tried to comfort him. 'It's just that she worries, what with the war, an' all.'

'Aye . . . she's said, and she's said too about her

giving birth to Libby in the air-raid shelter. It really upset her, that did.'

'Yes,' Molly agreed. 'Look,' she suggested quietly, 'why don't you go up to her, Frank? And . . . and stay the night? I can sleep down here tonight, and if it helps . . .'

'There you go again, thinking of others and not yourself,' Frank told her gruffly. 'It's a kind thought, Molly, but I don't see as how it would do any good. Your June agreed last time I was home that when I was on leave the two of us would stay at me mam's. Now she says that she can't stay there on account of Libby's routine.'

Anger, confusion, defeat – Molly could hear them all in his voice and her heart ached for him. She reached out across the table and put her hand over his. 'You and June are married, Frank. You need to spend time together. She's your wife.'

'You'd never think it from the way she's behaving,' Frank retorted grimly. 'Not that I'm wanting to press her to do sommat as she doesn't want,' he added awkwardly, blushing slightly, before emphasising, 'What I was meaning is that I wouldn't want to be forcing meself on her or anything like that. But when a man's bin away living wi' other men, when he comes home he wants . . . well, I don't want to get personal, like, Molly, but there's some nights as I'd give a lot to have someone to hold.'

'I know what you mean,' Molly assured him in a low voice. And it was true she did. 'I know it's not sommat as I should say, but I can't help wishing that me and Eddie had . . . It would have given me something to remember if we'd bin together properly, like.' Her colour was high but what she had said was the truth, even if Frank was the first person she had felt able to admit it to. 'I suppose you think badly of me now for saying I feel like that, me and Eddie not being married, an' all.'

'I could never think badly of you, Molly,' Frank told her thickly, lifting his hand from beneath hers and giving hers a small squeeze.

'We didn't do anything as we shouldn't have done,' Molly said, adding proudly, 'My Eddie wasn't like that. But sometimes I wish . . .' They both looked up towards the ceiling as they heard a door opening upstairs.

'That will be June getting up to come down and do Libby's feed,' Molly told him. 'Why don't you have another word with her, Frank,' she coaxed, 'and try—'

It shocked her to see him shaking his head. 'It's no use, Molly. She's changed,' he told her helplessly. 'She's not the June I married any more, and that's a fact.'

FIVE

'There's a letter come for you, Molly,' June announced when Molly came in from work. 'I've put it on the mantelpiece.'

'It's from Anne,' Molly told her. The two friends had been writing regularly to one another, exchanging news, and although Molly had worried about her friend at first, as well as missing her, she had been reassured by the cheerful optimistic tone of Anne's letters. She could, of course, fully understand that Anne wanted to be with Philip. She would have felt just the same in her shoes. She opened the letter, quickly scanning it, her face breaking into a wide smile.

'Listen to this, June,' she announced excitedly. 'Anne says she's bin given leave so she's coming home for Christmas, and she's bringing Philip with her.'

Making herself a cup of tea, Molly went to sit down and read Anne's letter more thoroughly.

'Philip is so very, very brave, Molly,' Anne had written.

He has so much to bear, but as he says, there are others who are worse off than him. He has been told that he will be fitted with artificial legs just as soon as he is strong enough, and although he has told me that he doesn't want to hold me to the promises we made to one another before he left for France, I know he is the one for me and that no one could ever take his place. Besides, I've told him that he can't refuse to marry me now, since my parents say that I've totally disgraced myself by moving down to Aldershot to be with him. Not that I would ever hold him to a promise he didn't want to keep, but I know he is simply being honourable in offering to release me from our 'unofficial' engagement.

It was a surprise and a relief when my mother wrote to suggest we should come up for Christmas. I was afraid that they would never be able to forgive Philip for being alive when Richard is dead. I am so looking forward to seeing you. I have missed you so much. I have told Philip what a tower of strength you were for me when I first heard that he was so badly wounded.

Molly sighed as she finished reading Anne's letter. Life wasn't going to be easy for Anne if she and Philip did marry, but at least they would have one another. She folded the letter and put it back in its envelope. It was her turn on night duty with the emergency services team and she had to be down at the depot in half an hour.

The heavy bombardment Liverpool had been suffering might have eased off a little but the results of it could be seen everywhere. The streets of Liverpool now looked like the mouth of a very elderly person, Molly reflected, with cavities and gaps where healthy teeth had once been, or in Liverpool's case where buildings had once stood. In the centre of the city hardly a street remained without a gaping hole in it, and the closer one got to the docks the worse the devastation was, with literally whole streets flattened by Hitler's bombers. One of the new girls at the factory had arrived at work one morning to say that their house had been destroyed the previous night and that she and her parents had had to move in with her father's cousin. At least they were alive. One of the other girls had reported that half the street next to her own had gone, taking the lives of three families who had lived there. Now at night there was an eerie silence in the worst affected areas, deserted by those who had once lived there, either because their homes had been destroyed, or out of fear that theirs would be next.

Files of trekkers left the city every night, and in Knotty Ash and Aintree, and the villages closest to the city, the local inhabitants were complaining that the trekkers coming in every night and occupying what shelter there was were depriving them of shelter space, should they need it.

Like all the other WVS volunteers, Molly had done her bit helping to hand out hot drinks and food to those bombed out of their homes.

It was pitiful to see elderly folk frightened and confused, crying over their smashed treasures as they stared at the wreckage, but what was even worse was those times when the volunteers had to try to comfort those whose loved ones lay beneath the rubble of beams and bricks.

Molly had almost reached her destination when she heard a sound that made her whole body stiffen in dreaded recognition. Everyone in Liverpool now knew the differing engine sounds of the enemy planes coming in: the droning heaviness when they were still laden with bombs, and then the screaming whine of the bombs themselves, followed by silence just before they exploded.

This plane was different, though. Its engine sounded lighter somehow – and faster. Up ahead of her in the darkness, she could just about make out the shape of a corporation bus crawling along the road, its windows blacked out in accordance with the law. Although she didn't have much further to walk, suddenly she didn't want to be alone. If she ran she might be able to catch the bus.

The noise from the plane was growing louder. Instinctively she ducked into the shelter of a doorway and then looked up cautiously. To her shock the plane was even lower than she had thought – not a bomber surely, but a small fighter plane that was almost touching the chimneypots. The bus driver had obviously already seen it too because he had put his foot down and was driving at full pelt as he tried to escape from it. But he hadn't got a chance; Molly could see that. As she watched, helpless to do anything, the fighter opened fire on the bus, raking it with a staccato burst of gunfire that briefly illuminated both the bus and the road.

As the noise died away and the plane disappeared, Molly could hear the wounded and dying screaming, trapped inside the bus. In front of her horrified gaze, people were staggering off the bus, their clothes on fire, but as she started to run towards them the bus itself exploded with a dull boom.

The auxiliary fire service was on the scene almost as fast as she was, but there was nothing they could do.

'You're late,' Mrs Wesley told Molly sharply half an hour later when she walked into the hall where they were on duty to hand out tea and blankets.

'There was this plane,' Molly told her slowly, still gripped by the shock of what she had seen. 'Not a bomber, a fighter. It got a bus. I think it was a number 83. I went to help but there was nothing . . .' She swallowed hard. For the rest of her life she knew that she would remember the smell of burning flesh and the sound of the screams of those who had not been lucky enough to be killed in the initial blast. 'I'm sorry I'm late . . .'

To her surprise Mrs Wesley had taken hold of her arm and was leading her towards a chair, calling over her shoulder as she did so, 'Aileen, bring Molly a cup of tea, will you?'

'It's all right. I'm all right,' Molly tried to say, but to her own astonishment the words just wouldn't come, her lips were trembling so much. In fact, she was shaking all over.

'It's all right, Molly. You're in shock, dear. Now come on and drink this tea. It will help you feel better.'

Molly stared at her. Could this really be Mrs Wesley talking to her so gently? That thought alone was enough to make Molly take a deep breath and insist firmly, 'I'm all right now, Mrs Wesley,' before determinedly standing up.

Mrs Wesley gave her an approving smile. For good reason was Molly one of her star girls. Underneath her sweet, innocent demeanour lay a tough and resilient woman. Mrs Wesley knew she had suffered so badly when her young man had died and for weeks had seemed upset and angry at the world, but she had pulled through admirably. Mrs Wesley prayed that once this awful war was over she would find happiness again. Not that she could ever tell Molly that, of course – it wouldn't do for Mrs Wesley's no-nonsense attitude to be seen to be crumbling.

'Now, you go and help Aileen tonight, Molly.

We're expecting a lot to be coming in and we're running short of blankets.' She gave a small sigh. 'It would help, of course, if people handed them back in the morning instead of going off with them.'

Shelters such as the church hall, provided by the council and manned by the voluntary services, were only supposed to be for overnight emergency accommodation for those who had nowhere else to go, but increasingly Molly and the others were recognising regulars.

'Well, it's so much better here, duck, than down them dirty shelters,' one elderly lady had confided to Molly when Molly had tried to point out to her that she wasn't really supposed to come to the hall every night. 'If you go in them shelters you've got to use them nasty lavvies and you don't get no nice cuppa like you do here. Pity there's no sugar, though.'

Molly thought about this lady now and asked Aileen ruefully, 'Where's Mrs Marshall? She's normally here by now.'

'Haven't you heard? She got bombed out the other night. The whole street's gone. Just like that. Oh Gawd, look at this little lot,' Aileen protested glumly, as several people came in, their faces and clothes black with chimney soot. Molly and the others were familiar now with the sight of soot-blackened victims of Hitler's bombing campaign.

'Two sugars, please, and I'll have a Mars bar, an' all, if you've got one.'

438

'Johnny,' Molly laughed, as she looked up from filling cups with tea to see him grinning down at her. 'What are you doing here? You'll be in trouble if Mrs W. sees you.'

'That's all you know, Molly Dearden. Glad to see me, she was, I can tell you.'

Molly gave him a suspicious look. 'If this is one of your jokes . . .'

'No. Cross me heart and hope to die.' Johnny clasped his hand to his chest. 'I've just brung a load of blankets in for her,' he explained, 'and I thought that whilst I was here I might as well do the gentlemanly thing and wait for you so that I can see you home safely.'

'Since when did you want to see any lass home *safely*?' Molly challenged him, but secretly she knew she would be only too glad to have his company on the long walk back home after what had happened earlier. One thing she had to admit about Johnny was that, somehow or other, he always managed to make her smile. She felt so much better about sharing a laugh and a joke with him now that she had spoken to Elsie. Her neighbour's kind words had removed the burden of guilt she had been carrying. It was as Elsie had said: she would never ever forget her dearest Eddie, and no one could ever take the place in her heart and her memories that was his alone.

'Made any plans for Christmas yet?' Johnny asked half an hour later as they stepped out of the hall into the cold dampness of the December night.

'Only if you was free one night, how about coming dancing wi' me?'

'I'll think about it,' she replied automatically, and then wondered if she had gone mad. What on earth had made her say that? 'But I'm only thinking about it, mind,' she warned him, just in case he got the wrong idea. 'I'm not saying that I will.'

'Come on, quick, there's a bus. If we run we can catch it.'

'No!' Molly stood stock-still in the street.

'What? Aw, it's gone now; we've missed it. What's to do with yer?' he demanded, as he turned round to see her trembling violently.

Molly shook her head; she couldn't speak – not even to tell Johnny to let go of her when, quick as anything, he took her in his arms, holding her tightly.

Something about the warmth of his strong male body against the softness of her own seemed to calm her down.

'That's better,' he told her. 'What's to do?'

He was still holding her, and her voice was muffled by his coat as she told him what had happened earlier. 'I saw them, Johnny. Them that wasn't killed came staggering off the bus screaming and in flames. I could smell their flesh.' She buried her face further into his coat and let him comfort her as she wept for the death and destruction, and her own horror at the sight of it.

'When is it all going to end, Johnny? And

440

how many of us will still be alive when it does?'

'I don't know,' he told her truthfully, 'but what I do know is that I'm damn well going to live whilst I can. Life's too precious to waste. Fancy doing some living wi' me, Molly?'

He was the eternal flirt, she decided ruefully, always ready to try it on, and yet she could not help smiling as she listened to him say all the things he wanted to do and how he wouldn't let something so trifling as war stop him.

He had only partially released her from his arms, so that as they walked along the pavement he had an arm around her shoulders still, keeping her close to him. Not that it really mattered. There was no one about to see them, even though the all clear had gone over an hour ago.

'You know sommat, Molly?'

'What?' she asked him unsuspectingly.

'I really do think I'm going to have to kiss you.'

They had stopped walking. Indignantly Molly looked up at him. 'What? You . . .' she began to protest, her words softening to a dizzy 'Mmmm', followed by silence as he kissed her tenderly and achingly slowly.

Molly opened her eyes and blinked. 'You shouldn't have done that,' she said gravely. But there was more softness than accusation in her voice and she didn't object when he gave her a hug and deposited a swift kiss on the tip of her nose.

*　　*　　*

Well, wasn't life just the funniest thing, Molly reflected tiredly as she tiptoed towards her bed, determined not to wake either Lillibet or June. Who would have thought that she would actually enjoy being kissed by Johnny Everton? But she had, she admitted. As she snuggled down under her eiderdown, she touched the ring Eddie had given her, which she still wore. Sudden tears blurred her eyes. What would he have thought about Johnny kissing her? Would he have understood that even though she would give anything for him to be alive, there were times like tonight when she needed to be held in a pair of strong warm arms? This war was changing so much about the way they all lived their lives.

'Has anyone heard anything from Aggie? Only I heard as how her street got it last night.'

'I haven't heard nothing,' one of the girls responded to Irene's query as they all hurried to remove their wet coats and get out of the small, damp, cold cloakroom with its smell of wet wool, and upstairs into the relative warmth of the machine room.

'What about you, Molly?' Irene called out. 'You was on emergency services duty last night, wasn't you?'

'Yes, but not down that end. We were on a call down by the docks,' Molly answered her tiredly.

The visible pall of smoke and soot that hung over Liverpool from the devastation of its buildings was partnered by the invisible pall of misery that was engulfing its people. Not that anyone was going to say they were miserable – not likely, when so many were suffering far worse than they – but it was there in their faces all the same.

'Ten to one if her street has bin hit, she'll have gone to that aunt of hers wot lives out Chester way,' Lettice Rooney, one of the new girls, told Irene. 'She was only saying t'other day that she was sick to death of Jerry and his bombs.'

'Huh, wot makes her think it's any different for the rest of us?' Irene asked sharply. 'But you don't see us tekkin' off to blummin' Chester. 'Oo the hell does she think is goin' to mek parachutes for our lads if we all tek ourselves off out of harm's way?'

'Will your hubby be home on leave for Christmas, Irene?' Molly asked, wanting to change the subject before it developed into a full-scale row. Irene, like Molly and one or two of the others, didn't live right down in the dock area, where most of the girls, including the missing Aggie, lived, and where they had endured the worst of the almost nightly bombing, with whole streets reduced to rubble and whole families wiped out in one bomb blast.

Molly stood by Irene as the other girls slid into their seats and started up their sewing machines. Once they were working it was almost impossible to hear what anyone said over the noise.

'No such luck. Not where he is,' Irene answered grimly. 'He's not like some who dropped lucky and got posted on home duty.'

There was a small silence whilst the girls avoided looking at one another. Every regiment in the British Army consisted of two divisions, one of which was traditionally always kept 'battle ready' whilst the other provided backup. Now, with the country at war, every regiment had one half of its men on active overseas duty whilst the other half remained at home to guard the country. If you were lucky enough to have your menfolk stationed on 'home duty', even if that meant they were living at the opposite end of the country, you could consider yourself to be very fortunate indeed.

'Just because my Bobby's posted on home duty doesn't mean he isn't doing his bit,' one of the other girls defended her own husband now, her face flushed.

'Did I say that he weren't?' Irene retorted angrily.

The machines started to whirr, cutting off whatever response might have been made, but it was plain that Irene hadn't finished having her say, because ten minutes later, she stopped her own machine and said loudly, 'I'm willing to bet, though, Nancy, that your Bobby is coming home on leave at Christmas?'

Nancy White stopped her own machine, tossing her turbaned head as she answered back smartly,

'Well, that's where you're wrong, because he isn't.'

It was dinner time before the matter was referred to again.

Molly, who was eating her cheese sandwich as slowly as she could to make it go further and trick her stomach into believing it wasn't hungry, heard Nancy White giggling as she confided to her friends, 'A right bossy so-and-so that Irene is. I'd have given a week's wages this morning to stand up and tell her that the reason my Bobby is not coming home this Christmas is because I'm going down to Aldershot to see him. He says as how they'll be havin' a right good knees-up at the Naafi canteen, and no need to worry about rationing. And he's got me a room at some lodgings down there, so as we can spend a bit of time together, you know, private, like.' She giggled again. ''Oo knows, I might come back wi' sommat in me belly instead of me Christmas stocking.'

'Wot? And how will you go on then,' one of the others derided her, 'your husband in the army, and you with a kid to look after? There'd be no going out dancin' every weekend then.'

Nancy pulled a face. 'No, and I wouldn't have to come workin' here neither, and have to listen to old misery guts every day. 'Sides,' she added, tossing her newly peroxided hair, 'like as not me mam will look after the kiddie for us.'

'It's all right for some,' one of the other girls sniffed.

And as Molly folded up the greaseproof paper

that had held her sandwiches she couldn't help but silently agree, when she contrasted her sister's increasing anxiety over her baby's routine with the casual attitude of girls like Nancy White.

'Where are you off to then?' June demanded when Molly came downstairs dressed to go out.

'I had another letter from Anne yesterday. She's coming home today and I thought I'd go down to Lime Street to meet her. She's bringing Philip with her and she'll have her hands full, what with him being in a wheelchair.'

'Oh, I see, you're going meeting *Anne*, are you? Well, that explains it then,' June said bitterly.

'What do you mean?'

'It's obvious what I mean, Molly Dearden!' June replied sharply. 'Anyone can see that she's more important to you than I am. I could see that before she went off to Aldershot, but then, of course, I'm only your sister, and why should you stay in and keep me company when Anne's coming home?'

'June, it isn't like that, and besides, I thought you'd be going round to Sally's tonight, seeing as it's her night off.'

'What, and have her going on at me, saying that I'm not doing right by my Frank?' June sniffed disparagingly. 'Much room she's got to talk, with her going working at the Grafton four nights out of seven and mixing with all sorts. Catch me doing that!'

'Sally needs the money, June, you know that.

She's got those two kiddies and the rent to pay, and all she gets is what the Government gives her on account of her Ronnie being in the army.'

Molly didn't want to aggravate her sister any further by pointing out that June lived rent free under their father's roof, as she did herself, and that with both their father and Molly working there was no need for June to have to work as well. Things might be a bit tight but they managed, and it was understood that June kept the money the Government paid to all service wives for herself and Libby. Sally, on the other hand, had no family to help her; no parental roof under which she could live, and she had two children to support.

'She could work days, and put the kiddies in one of them new crèche things the Government has provided so as women can go and do war work,' June defended her criticism determinedly.

'What, work at one of them armaments factories?' Molly asked her dubiously. 'You know all sorts goes on there, June, with thieving and that, and they have to work twelve-hour shifts without a day off. Sally told me herself that with her tips and that, she earns enough at the Grafton for her to need to work only four nights a week, even after she's paying for someone to sit in with the kiddies for her.'

'Lucky her, that's all I can say, but I wonder if her Ronnie thinks it's so lucky, seeing as what she might have to be doing to get them tips.'

'June!' Molly protested, scandalised. 'How can you say such a thing? Sally isn't like that, and you know it.'

'Huh, how am I supposed to know what she's like now, seeing as I hardly ever see her, and when I do all she does is go on about Frank's mam and "poor" Frank?' Suddenly, to Molly's distress, June's eyes filled with tears.

'Oh, Molly, this time last year I were looking forward to me and Frank getting wed and now look at me.'

'June, what's wrong?' Molly begged as her sister dropped her head into her hands and began to cry as though her heart was breaking.

'I don't know,' June admitted. 'I just feel so . . . so all churned up inside sometimes, Molly, what with all the worry of looking after Elizabeth Rose, and her crying that much. Do you know, Frank's mam had the cheek to tell me that she thought my little Lillibet were hungry. As if I wasn't feeding her regular.'

Molly didn't know now what to say. She had noticed herself how greedily Lillibet sometimes took her bottle, only to reject it and then start to scream as though she were in pain. She was a small baby, delicately made, June liked to say, like their own mother.

'Frank even told me that his mam said that Lillibet had colic and that it was my fault for keeping waking her up to feed her,' June confided angrily.

'I expect he thought he was helping you, June,' Molly tried to placate her, but June was having none of it.

'Help me! Hinder me, more like. This is not what I thought it were going to be like when I wed him, Molly, and if you want the truth, I'm beginning to wish that I hadn't.'

'June, you can't mean that,' Molly protested, but June wasn't listening. Instead her face was taking on a weary resigned expression as they both heard the wailing coming from upstairs.

'I've got to go,' Molly told her hurriedly, 'otherwise I won't get to Lime Street in time to meet Anne's train.'

She was wishing now that she hadn't arranged to meet her friend and that she could stay with June, whose comments had left her feeling very anxious. June couldn't have meant what she had said about wishing she hadn't married Frank, surely?

SIX

Molly spotted Anne before her friend saw her. They were almost the last off the train, Anne, in her smart ATS uniform, drawing envious looks from some of the women passengers, and wary ones from others. The ATS girls had begun to get a very racy reputation in certain quarters, and Molly had read that some parents were refusing to let their daughters join up, fearing for their moral welfare.

The man in the wheelchair she was pushing had to be Philip, and there seemed to be some good-natured repartee between those who had helped them to get the wheelchair out of the guard's van and Philip himself, to judge from the laughter Molly could hear.

Her spirits started to lift. She couldn't help worrying about June, though. Although her sister would never admit it, Molly guessed that June was missing seeing Sally. Perhaps if she called round at Sally's and had a word with her . . . ? Her mind busy with plans, she waited until the crowd of people leaving the train had thinned out a little before hurrying along the platform towards Anne.

'Molly!' Anne exclaimed happily. 'You look wonderful. Look, Philip, here's Molly.'

'Hello, Molly. Forgive me for not standing to greet you.' He nodded towards the arm of the wheelchair briefly. He was smiling but Molly could sense his tension. His face looked thinner and drawn with pain.

'Hello, Philip,' Molly responded. 'I can't believe it's been almost a year since I last saw you!'

'Last Christmas. Christ, is that only when it was? So much has happened since then. It feels like another life.'

'Molly, you're going to be the first to know,' Anne broke in excitedly, extending her hand so that Molly could see a lovely diamond ring glittering. 'Me and Philip are formally engaged now.'

There was no need for Molly to ask if Anne was happy. Her friend was positively glowing with delight as Molly admired the ring and congratulated Philip.

'Have you decided on a date yet?'

'We wanted to talk to Mum and Dad first. I want them to be pleased for me, but I intend to marry Philip no matter what they say. It isn't Philip's fault that Richard's dead and he's alive,' Anne told her, her glow dimming slightly as she added quietly, 'We want to get married as soon as possible. Philip will have to move to a new hospital

451

in the New Year, and it could be that he would be moved so far away that I wouldn't be able to visit him. But once we're married, I could leave the ATS and look after him myself.'

'Rubbish. You aren't giving up your own life to nurse an invalid,' Philip told her sharply. 'I won't have it.'

'But you won't be an invalid once you've get your new legs, darling,' Anne protested in a low voice, and Molly guessed that this was an argument they had had many times before.

'They're not new legs, Anne, they're artificial limbs,' Philip corrected her. 'Pieces of metal, that's all. I shall still be an invalid, just an invalid with a pair of artificial legs.'

'You aren't an invalid. You're the man I love,' Anne said softly.

'I haven't got any legs – that makes me an invalid,' Philip argued grimly. 'And I'm not going to let you sacrifice yourself for me.'

'We've already been through all this, Pip. It isn't a sacrifice, it's what I want to do. I love you and . . . and I want to spend every minute I can with you.'

Molly was beginning to feel uncomfortable. She could see the love between them but she could also see Philip's frustrated bitterness.

'Philip!' Anne begged emotionally.

Remorsefully he reached out and took hold of her hand. 'I'm sorry, sweetheart. I suppose I'm just feeling a bit anxious about how your parents are going to react to the fact that their lovely daughter is throwing herself away on a cripple.'

'We've had some pretty bad bombing raids since you left,' Molly told Anne, tactfully changing the subject. 'You heard about the one at Durning Road?'

'Oh, yes, that was dreadful. Over three hundred killed, I heard.'

'Yes,' Molly agreed. 'It was a terrible night.'

'There were *three thousand* killed when the *Lancastria* went up,' Philip cut across their exchange bitterly.

Anne gave Molly an uncertain look that was part anxiety and part plea.

'Darling, I don't think—'

'You don't think what? You don't think I should talk about it? Why not? Because the bloody Government doesn't want this country to know how three thousand men lost their lives – men like your brother. He would have been alive today but for us getting on that ruddy ship. Plenty of room, they told us, saving it for you RAF lads, they said, go and get yourselves something to eat, we'll be sailing soon. For hours we were on board her, packed in like sardines – worse than sardines – women and kiddies as well. It's a wonder the damn thing didn't sink. Do you know how many she was registered to carry? Not even half of that, and three thousand is only them as they counted. If you want my opinion there was damn-near twice that many on board.'

'Darling, please don't. You'll only get yourself all upset,' Anne was pleading.

'Anne, let me give you a hand pushing Philip's wheelchair,' Molly suggested.

'Oh, I hadn't realised it would be as bad as this!' Anne exclaimed as they walked up through the city, both her expression and her voice revealing her shock at the bomb damage as the two girls took it in turns to push Philip's wheelchair.

'Jerry's trying to put the docks out of action, but it's the streets down by the docks that have suffered the worst of it. Thousands have been made homeless, and hundreds killed and injured. There's bad feeling up here on account of us not getting any mention in the papers. Folk are saying that every time you open them it's all the East End this and the East End that, and never a word about Liverpool and what we're having to put up with.'

'Perhaps it's because the Government doesn't want the Germans to know how much damage they've caused,' Anne suggested.

Molly nodded. Maybe she was right.

The grey December afternoon had already given way to a dirty damp darkness and the kind of cold that seeps sourly into the bones. Anne shivered and huddled deeper into her coat, admitting wanly, 'I'd forgotten how cold and damp Liverpool can be.'

Molly smiled at her, puffing slightly as she pushed the heavy chair up the long hill towards

Edge Hill Road. Philip hadn't said a word since they'd left the station.

'Here, wait a minute,' Anne protested, going to the front of the wheelchair to fuss round Philip, making sure he was well wrapped up whilst Molly stood behind it to check it didn't start to slide backwards.

'There's no point in you doing that,' Philip snapped sharply at Anne as she kneeled down to wrap the tartan rug round his lower half.

Watching them, Molly thought how very hard it must be for both: Anne constantly apologetic because she was healthy and whole, and Philip angry and resentful as any man would be at the loss of his freedom; perhaps resentful too of his dependence on Anne.

It wasn't her place to question their relationship, Molly knew, but all around her now she could see the evidence of the way war was affecting relationships between men and women.

'Nearly there now,' Anne told Philip cheerfully.

'For God's sake, stop treating me like a child. I was a bloody navigator, for God's sake, Anne. I know we're "nearly there".' Almost immediately he reached for her hand and said apologetically, 'Sorry, sweetheart, that was bloody rude of me. It's just this damn leg is giving me such gyp at the moment. Funny old thing, having an amputation: the bloody leg still aches even though it isn't there.'

Anne gave a small, slightly forced laugh, and

Molly managed to join in, even though inside she was filled with pity for them both.

'You don't need to come any further with us, Molly,' Anne told her as they stood together under the Picton Clock where they had met so many times in the past. 'We'll be fine from here. It's all downhill. I'll see you tomorrow.'

Giving her friend a quick hug, Molly stood and watched them until they were safely across the road, before turning to make her own way home.

She was tired and hungry. 'It's corned beef hash tonight, like it or not,' she warned her grumbling tummy. Feeling hungry was just one of the things they were all having to get used to now, but what was a bit of hunger when you looked at men like Philip, Molly asked herself grimly.

As she turned into the close, on a sudden impulse she hurried over to Sally's house, making her way up the alleyway between it and the next pair of semis, and then going in through the gate to the small back garden so that she could knock on the back door.

'Molly!' Sally exclaimed as she opened the door. 'Now there's a surprise! Don't stand on the doorstep. Come on in.'

'I don't want to disturb you if you're busy,' Molly protested.

'No, I've given the kiddies their bath down here in the kitchen. It saves on water, like the Government says we have to, and it's warmer here than in the bathroom. They're in bed now.'

'It's about our June,' Molly began.

It made her feel disloyal to be standing here, in Sally's kitchen, discussing her sister with her behind her back, but it was for June's own sake that she was doing this, she comforted herself.

'I'm worried about her, Sally. She's not bin herself just recently.'

'You can say that again,' Sally agreed vehemently. 'Nearly snapped me head off, she did, when I told her she was being too hard on her Frank. I thought that her and me was good friends, but the way she's bin behaving, I don't know now as she's someone I want for a friend.'

'Oh, Sally, please don't fall out with her,' Molly begged.

'Me fall out with her? It's her as is doing the falling out,' Sally told Molly sharply. 'Allus going on about that bloomin' Dr Truby and that ruddy book. And then for her to go and treat her Frank the way she did when he came home . . . I know she's your sister, Molly, and o' course you want to help her, but if you want my opinion, your June needs to get herself sorted out. We're all in this war together, and she's not the only one with a little 'un to worry about. I've got two of me own, and no family to help out. I don't know what I'd have done without Frank's mam showing me how to go on. Your June ought to be thankful she's got such a good ma-in-law instead of being the way she is wi' her. Aw, don't look like that, Molly,' Sally sighed when she saw

Molly's face fall, crossing the small kitchen to give her a hug.

'It will all come out in the wash, you see if it doesn't. Your June needs to come to her senses, that's all. Look,' Sally proffered after a small pause, 'I'll call round and see her tomorrow – how does that suit you?'

'Oh, Sally, would you? Thank you!' Molly beamed with relief.

'I hope we don't get Jerry coming over again tonight,' Molly heard one of the other WVS women saying tiredly as they all hurried into the hall. 'Three times this week already we've had to spend the night in the air-raid shelter. My youngest was falling asleep over his breakfast this morning – what there was of it.' She sniffed disparagingly.

'Aye, so were my two,' another woman joined in, 'and you'll never guess what one of the little buggers did the other day. He only came home with a ruddy great piece of shrapnel he'd found. Said he was collecting it to exchange at school and that some lad had told the others he'd found a bomb and that he'd only tell them where it was if they gave him a penny each. Things they get up to! If I've told my lot once I've told 'em a dozen times to keep away from bomb sites in case they have an accident.'

Molly was just starting to inch past the chatting women when she saw Anne coming in through the door. She hurried to make her way towards her, hugging her warmly and exclaiming happily, 'Anne, how lovely! I didn't expect to see you here tonight.'

'No. It was a bit of a spur-of-the-moment decision, really. Mum and Dad have been getting on so well with Philip; after I'd worried myself sick about them still resenting the fact that he's alive and Richard is dead. You could have knocked me down with a feather when my father started talking to him about Richard.'

'I expect at first they were too shocked and upset by Richard's death to think straight. You don't when it first happens,' Molly answered.

Anne reached for her hand and squeezed it gently. 'I haven't had a chance yet to ask how you are. I know how lucky I am to have Philip, Molly, and how hard it must be for you.'

'I'll never forget Eddie. I think about him every day, but it isn't as bad as it was,' Molly said matter-of-factly.

'I have missed you, Molly, and I've missed all of this as well.' Anne glanced round the busy room. 'That's why I telephoned Mrs Wesley and asked if I might come along.'

Molly privately suspected that Anne needed some precious time away from Philip and his erratic moods, but didn't want to upset her friend by saying so.

'I'd better get over to the tea wagon,' Molly said. 'Come with me so that we can chat.'

Anne's smart khaki ATS uniform stood out

sharply against the more old-fashioned dullness of the WVS uniforms, and Molly could see the sideways looks she was attracting.

'I reckon that every woman in here who isn't married is envying you your uniform,' she teased Anne.

Anne pulled a small face. 'You should hear the comments we get – "All those soldiers . . ." is just about the most polite of them. We have an important role to play in this war, but to listen to some people you'd think the only reason we joined up was to have fun,' she complained as they reached the tea wagon, continuing ruefully whilst Molly took off her jacket and pulled on an overall, 'Of course, there are those girls who *have* joined because they think it's going to be a bit of a lark, living away from home amongst thousands of soldiers. But I can tell you, Molly, they soon get to realise that what they're in for isn't a good time but really hard work.'

'You're enjoying it, though?' Molly smiled. Her friend seemed tired and drawn but also more grown up and confident – yet another of the contradictions war had brought with it. While the bombs fell and people suffered, girls like her and Anne were discovering whole new aspects of themselves.

'I'm enjoying being so close to Philip,' Anne corrected her firmly. Her smile disappeared as she added, 'But like I told you, he won't be able to stay where he is in the army hospital for very much longer. They want to move him to St Mary's Hospital in Roehampton. That's where he'll be fitted with his new legs and be taught how to use them. It's about thirty miles from Aldershot. That's one of the reasons we want to get married as quickly as we can,' she reminded Molly, 'so that I can apply to live out and we can be together.'

'At least things are looking up with your parents.' Molly knew they must be worrying about their daughter, living away from home for the very first time, especially as she was their only surviving child.

'Oh, yes. They'll never get over losing Richard – none of us will – but they want me to be happy. They couldn't ask Philip enough about the time he and Richard were in Nantes together.' She shook her head ruefully. 'After all the worrying I'd been doing that Dad would refuse to even speak to Philip. That's another of the reasons I've come here: I could see that both of them, but especially Dad, wanted to get Philip to themselves, to talk about Richard. They were together right until the last. Philip feels guilty because he survived and Richard didn't but I've told him that he mustn't. He isn't to blame for what happened. He gets such low moods sometimes, Molly. But they've told me at the hospital that that happens to a lot of the men.'

Molly touched Anne's arm sympathetically. 'Our brave boys see such dreadful things, Anne. All we can do is help them as much as we can.'

'Call this tea?' a stout woman in a grubby-looking coat complained as she took the cup Molly handed to her. A clawlike hand with dirty nails curled round it. 'Cat's pee, more like.'

'Go on with you, Mrs T.,' Molly smiled. 'You won't get a better cuppa anywhere.

'She's one of our regulars,' she whispered to Anne as the elderly woman turned her back on them to slurp her tea noisily. 'You watch, she'll be back at the end of the queue just as soon as she's finished that one.'

'Is she one of those trekkers?' Anne asked.

'No, poor soul was bombed out of her house down on Pilcher Street. According to her neighbours she lived alone with her son, and he's disappeared. The council have offered her alternative accommodation but she won't take it. Says she's not going to let Jerry bomb her out a second time so she spends all her time walking round Liverpool. But tell me about the ATS and Aldershot – is it exciting?' Molly demanded, changing the subject.

Anne laughed and teased, 'Why? Are you thinking of joining up?'

'No, I couldn't leave our dad and June.' Molly's eyes momentarily clouded at the thought of her sister.

'Mmm, and what about that chap who was chasing you around? Johnny?'

Molly blushed and laughed, then admitted, 'He keeps asking me out but June doesn't approve.'

Leaning closer to her so that she couldn't be overheard, Anne told her fiercely, 'Well, never mind your June, Molly. We only get one shot at life, and as you and me both know some folks don't get much of a shot at it at all, so we've got to make the best of things whilst we're still here. Leastways, that's what I think now. That's why me and Philip are getting married as quick as we can. Besides,' she fiddled with her engagement ring and then confided in a rush, 'I wouldn't say this to anyone else but you, Molly, it's important we get married just as soon as we can now, just in case, like . . . if you take my meaning. Not that we've done anything that lots of other unwed couples aren't doing,' she defended herself hastily when she saw Molly's eyes widen slightly.

Anne and Philip were sharing the intimacies of a married couple? Molly knew she ought to be more shocked than she actually was, but the truth was that a part of her still mourned the fact that she and Eddie had not shared those intimacies. She was happy that Anne and Philip could still enjoy intimacy with Philip's terrible injuries. And they wouldn't be the first couple to be pushed by this war into the kind of behaviour that they would once have shunned, Molly knew. Lying in bed at night not knowing if you would live to see another morning made a person anxious to take what happiness they could find, instead of putting off the opportunity to enjoy it for a future they might not have.

* * *

'Phew, I'm glad that's over,' Anne sighed when Molly had finished her stint at the tea wagon and the two young women were free to leave. 'I'd forgotten what hard work WVS is.'

'The queues get longer every night,' Molly told her soberly. Because she was working at the factory, Molly didn't work all through the night unless she was on emergency duty, but it was still gone midnight when she and Anne left the shabby hall and started to make their way home. The long days were taking their toll and only this morning Molly had had to use some of her precious Cyclax on the circles under her eyes, which seemed to be a permanent fixture of her face these days.

'No bomber's moon tonight, thank heavens,' Molly said tiredly as they linked arms and set off through the rundown streets.

'I'm glad we've got a bit of time to ourselves, Molly,' Anne began awkwardly. 'The thing is that if things had been different, you would have been the first one I would have wanted to be my bridesmaid, but me and Philip have decided to get married down in Aldershot, not knowing how fit he'll be to travel up here, and it being easier to get everything sorted out down there. My parents will travel down to see us married, but I'm not asking anyone else, what with it being so close to Christmas and everything.' She paused and then said in a low voice Molly had to strain to hear, 'I had no real idea what it was going to be like when I decided to leave Liverpool so that I could be nearer to Philip. It was such a shock when I first went to visit him.'

'It must have been,' Molly agreed gently 'Seeing him so badly wounded when—'

'No, it wasn't that.' Anne shook her head impatiently. 'It was what he told me about how he came to lose his legs and how our Richard was killed. Lost in action was what we'd been told, as you know, but according to Philip . . .' She paused and then said chokily, 'You heard all that he was saying about the *Lancastria*. It preys on his mind all the time. The Government lied about Richard being lost in action. It was no such thing. Bombed, they were, like sitting ducks, trapped in this ship. The *Lancastria* that was supposed to be bringing them home to safety when the Germans invaded France. Everyone knows about Dunkirk. The papers were full of it and how all those men were rescued from Jerry, but no one has said a word about this St-Nazaire and what happened there; how men like Richard died. Thousands of them, Philip said there were, bombed and killed and drowned, and not a word of what happened told to anyone.'

Tears were pouring down Anne's face. Molly turned to her and gave her a fierce hug. 'Yes, I know. We heard what had happened from Sally. Her husband was in hospital down south when some of the survivors were being brought in and he told her about it, and how the Government was putting a D-notice on it so that it was all to be kept a secret. Frank said he reckoned it was because Mr Churchill thought the country had enough bad news to cope with with Dunkirk, without there being any more.'

'What?'

Molly could hear the shocked anger in Anne's voice as she pushed her away. 'You knew and you never said a word to me, even though you must have known our Richard . . . ?' Anne couldn't go on.

Her friend's reaction was so unexpected that Molly didn't know what to say. Feeling guilty and wishing she hadn't said anything, she groped for the words to explain, and put things right.

'When we heard the news I didn't know what to do, Anne. We'd been told not to talk about it. I only knew that some of the men involved were from the RAF base at Nantes. Sally said that Ronnie had told her that some of the men had been taken off by other ships. I didn't want to upset you when Richard could have been saved.'

Anne had turned towards her and Molly could see the anger in her eyes. 'But he wasn't and you knew what had likely happened to him, and yet you never said a word, not even when I told you we'd had that telegram saying he was presumed lost, and we were hoping and praying . . .'

Tears were running down Anne's face and Molly longed to comfort her but the moment she stepped towards her, Anne stepped back.

'Anne . . .'

'I thought you and me were friends, Molly

Dearden, but some friend you are when you didn't even tell me about what happened to my own brother.'

'I just wanted to spare you,' Molly began, but Anne was having none of it.

'Spare me what? Spare me from knowing the truth that I had a right to know?'

'Anne, there'd been a D-notice . . .'

Anne ignored her. 'How would you have felt if Richard had been your brother? Wouldn't you have wanted to know the truth? Wouldn't you have felt you had a right to know the truth? Didn't you want to know every last bit about your Eddie?'

Molly was filled with guilt and shame. Anne was right, she should have told her the truth. Frank had meant well when he had advised her to say nothing, but Frank was a soldier, and a man. She was a woman and Anne was her dearest friend. They had shared special confidences and supported one another. She only had to think how she would have felt if Anne had withheld such information from her to recognise her own guilt.

'You've spared me nothing, Molly, 'cos I know it all now. I know what happened to our Richard and I know what a bad friend you've been. I'd thought better of you than that.'

She was already turning away, and Molly had to run after her and catch hold of her arm. The thick, stiff fabric of Anne's greatcoat slipped through her fingers as she pulled away from her.

'Anne, please don't be like this. Please don't let's fall out.'

'Fall out! I'm not falling out with you, Molly. I just don't want to see you again, that's all. I thought I could trust you and that you and I were friends. But I can see now that you're not my friend – you're anything but! And to think I was upsetting myself because I couldn't ask you to be my bridesmaid.'

She had gone before Molly could stop her.

The speed with which the whole thing had happened left Molly feeling too shocked and upset to do anything other than blink away her tears.

She had never meant to deceive Anne. All she had wanted to do was to spare her the pain of worrying that Richard had been on the *Lancastria* before her family received official notification of his whereabouts. And then afterwards, once Anne had told her they had received news of his death, it hadn't seemed right to tell her what she herself already knew.

But it was too late now, though, to wish she had acted differently.

'I want a word with you,' June announced ominously.

She was standing in the kitchen with her hands on her hips whilst Molly removed her outdoor coat. She had been working for the WVS all evening and her fingers felt so numb from the freezing cold that she could scarcely manage to push the buttons through the buttonholes. It had been that kind of raw coldness that seemed to get right into your bones, and she shivered in the meagre heat of the kitchen. Everyone had been told to cut down on the amount of fuel they burned, and much as she wanted to do her bit, Molly longed for the warmth of a roaring fire so that she could toast her cold hands and feet. Now what had she done, Molly wondered tiredly as she heard the harsh note in her sister's voice. She didn't have to wait long to find out.

'Sally were round here tonight,' June informed her.

Molly had finally managed to unfasten her coat. She blew on her cold fingers, wincing as the blood returned to them and they started to sting with pain.

'She said as how she'd come because you'd been round there begging her to see me and saying how you was worried about me and Frank.'

Molly's heart sank. 'June, I just wanted the two of you to be friends again,' Molly told her.

'Friends? Some sister you are, Molly, going round there after what she's done. I'll thank you to mind your own business from now on, and not go round telling folks about me and my Frank's private business.'

Molly felt more miserable with every word June said. What was happening to everyone? First Anne and now June was having a go at her, and all she had done was try to act for the best. A lump of misery rose up in her throat and tears weren't very far away.

'June . . .' she began, but before she could say anything the rising wail of the air-raid siren interrupted her.

'Quick, June,' she instructed her sister, reaching for her coat again, not wanting to waste time going upstairs to get the thick warm men's dressing gowns that she and June had found at a jumble sale and pounced on with delight. It might have taken three washes to get rid of the smells of hair pomade and tobacco smoke, but there was no doubt that they were proving their worth now on the freezing winter nights.

Her coat already on, Molly snatched Lillibet up out of her pram, covers and all.

'I've got the baby and I'll get the bag. You get your coat on and hurry,' she urged her sister.

'I'm not going anywhere,' June told her fiercely. 'I'm . . .'

The heavy drone of the bombers almost directly overhead drowned out the rest of what she was saying.

'Well, we are.'

'You can't take her,' June objected. 'She's mine! Leave her here with me.'

Ignoring her demand, Molly headed for the hall where the bags they were all supposed to keep packed for the air-raid shelter were waiting, trying to comfort Lillibet above the noise of the AA guns.

'Molly, you're not to take her,' June was screaming, but Molly stoutly ignored her.

'We can't stay here. It's not safe.' She flung open the front door, shuddering at the noise outside the house. The windows were rattling with the gun-fire, and above her head Molly could hear the steady throb of German engines. Down towards the docks, shells exploded, briefly illuminating the night sky. Holding Lillibet tightly, Molly ran for the air-raid shelter, praying that June would follow her.

As the door to the shelter opened and willing hands pulled her in, she looked over her shoulder and saw to her relief that her sister was only a few yards behind her.

'Don't close the door yet; June's coming,' she warned John Fowler.

'What about yer dad?'

'Dad's doing a late shift down at the gridiron.'

June finally reached the shelter and was hauled in unceremoniously, and the door pulled shut, enclosing them all in the small airless space with its smell of sweat and urine and fear.

'Here, June, you sit down here,' Molly coaxed her sister, offering her her own seat close to the door, but still keeping hold of Elizabeth Rose. A fine thing it would be if June took it into her head to run out with the baby whilst German bombers were flying so low overhead that she could be seen. There were stories circulating of people being shot at from the bombers, some of them flew in so low, although the authorities dismissed them as non-sense.

'I told yer we should have made this ruddy shelter twice the size it is,' someone grumbled, as Daisy's two sons started to fight, whilst someone else coughed and set off half a dozen more in the rank air.

'I've brought a flask and some sandwiches,' Elsie whispered to Molly. 'I saw you'd only just got in when the siren went off, so you can share wi' us, if you like. How's your June keeping?' she continued, still whispering. 'Only there's bin a few folk asking, the way she were carrying on when her Frank were home.'

June had her back to them and was sitting rigidly still facing the door, but Molly didn't want to take the risk that she might overhear them, not with what had happened earlier on her conscience, so she simply said quietly, and untruthfully, 'She's fine.'

Elsie looked disappointed as she handed Molly a cup of tea. However, when Molly asked June if she wanted one, her sister refused to answer her, pulling her arm away and keeping her back turned towards her.

It was going to be a long night, Molly reflected.

SEVEN

'So how about it then? Are you going to let me tek you dancing this Christmas, Molly?' Johnny demanded as Molly negotiated the heavy emergency services vehicle round a tight corner.

Without taking her eyes off the road she told him, 'I might . . .'

There was a cheer from the others in the van, accompanied by a spontaneous burst of hand clapping and whistles, all of which made Molly colour up, but she still didn't take her eyes off the road.

They had received the call-out five minutes earlier, along with the terse warning that it 'looked like a bad one'. They were a few days away from Christmas, and already at number 78 the carefully preserved decorations had gone up. Somehow or other a small if somewhat lopsided Christmas tree had found its way from Nantwich to the close, and had been ceremoniously propped up in a corner of the front room, in a bucket full of soil from the allotment. The bright shiny clip-on candle holders Molly remembered from her childhood had been carefully fastened to the branches and, thanks to their foresight, there would be enough left of last year's candles for them to light on Christmas Day for Elizabeth Rose.

This year some of the families in the close, including the Deardens, had decided to get together for Christmas dinner and share their rations. All in all there were going to be close on twenty adults and nearly as many children filling Pearl Lawson's small house on Christmas Day. Only the other night in the air-raid shelter, everyone had given a cheer when Molly's father had announced that his sister had promised to send a turkey.

Pearl's husband, George, had rubbed the side of his nose and said knowingly that he wouldn't be surprised if he could come up with a few tins of peaches and the like for the trifle, and another cheer had gone up when he had added that he wasn't promising but there could be a bottle of beer mysteriously appearing for them as wanted one.

But it wasn't Christmas Day yet, and some folk might not even make it to then if Jerry had his way, Molly reflected darkly, as she changed gear ahead of another corner.

Up above them she could hear the noise of the bombers. In a street to the right, a bomb suddenly exploded, showering the cobbles with shrapnel. Gritting her teeth, Molly put her foot down on the accelerator.

'Left here, Molly,' Johnny told her tersely, without lifting his hand from her knee, where he had placed it earlier when he had asked her out.

'I know.' She didn't bother to remove his hand. In truth it felt quite comforting to have it there and she knew he was not going to try anything on with the others crowded into the van with them.

Over the weeks a camaraderie had built up between all of them that was almost that of a close-knit family unit. Sometimes she felt more comfortable in their company than she did in June's, Molly decided as she turned left.

Up ahead of them they saw where half the buildings in the narrow street had been flattened by the bomb that had dropped on them.

Johnny was out of the van almost before it had stopped, leaving the others, and Molly, who parked the vehicle safely out of reach of the sparks from the burning roof timbers, to follow him. Without it being formally said, Johnny seemed to have taken charge of their small unit, and Molly for one was glad that he had done so. For all his flirty ways, Johnny had an air of experience and authority about him that others responded to. The war had matured him, Molly recognised. He was a man now, and just thinking that caused her belly to tighten in a way that told her that she would be accepting his invitation.

Automatically, as she ran to join the others she reached for the locket Eddie had given her, touching it with loving fingers. She wore her ring on the same chain now – like everyone else she had lost weight on the reduced diet rationing had forced on them all, and she was terrified she would lose it clawing through the rubble if she kept it on her finger – and she said a small prayer in Eddie's name for the lives of those who had been in the burning houses. A fire engine pulled up alongside, men jumping out and starting up the pumps. Through the smoke and dust Molly could see the familiar tin hat of the local air raid warden. It was one of his duties to keep a list of the names of everyone living in each house.

'Any inside?' Johnny called out to him.

'Yes. I dunno how many, though. The ruddy bomb dropped almost as soon as the siren went off. They wouldn't have had a chance,' the warden added bitterly. 'I've sent a lad down to the shelter to check and see who's down there but, like I said, they wouldn't have had much chance to get out. There's at least six houses have caught it, I reckon, and families in every one of them. Some of them had taken relatives in who had been bombed out from down by the docks, and we hadn't had time to list 'em all. They only arrived last night. I've heard as how there's bin a direct hit on one of the big air-raid shelters as well.'

The ARP warden led the way to the tangle of burning timbers and soot-blackened bricks that had once been half a row of terraced houses.

Either side of the bombed homes, people were standing dressed in their night clothes, looking dazed, mothers clutching their children, whilst they stared in disbelief at the wreckage of their neighbours' houses.

'I can't believe it . . .' one woman started to sob. 'I only spoke to Sandra from next door at tea time and now like as not she's dead and her kiddies wi' her.'

Down over the docks searchlights still raked the sky whilst the AA guns pounded the incoming bombers.

Molly took hold of the woman's arm and asked her where the nearest shelter was.

'Down on Ducie Street.'

'I'll see they get to the shelter,' a slender young woman wearing a WVS uniform offered, coming across the street to join them.

Molly nodded in relief. She couldn't leave the van, being its driver, but her instincts told her that the children standing around watching should be in a shelter. She winced as another bomb exploded by the docks, and then hurried to join the men who were clearing the debris and searching for survivors.

'So you don't know who might have been in here?' she heard Johnny saying curtly to the ARP warden.

'No. There hasn't been time to register them wot moved in last night. In fact I was on me way over to do that when the ruddy bomb dropped. There can't be many as have survived this lot, though,' he pronounced.

'Well, we can't leave until we've made sure. Did any of them have shelters set up inside? If so, we'll check them houses first.'

'I dunno . . . If they did they never said.' The ARP man looked uncomfortable. 'I've only just tekken over here, see, on account of the ARP chap they had having had a bad fall.'

Molly was working alongside two of the men. One of them stopped digging and pointed to a limp hand sticking up out of the bricks.

'Looks to me like it's bin blown off,' the other man opined matter-of-factly, but we'd better tek a butcher's just in case.'

Molly swallowed hard on the saliva of horror thickening in her throat. This was no time to start acting like a girl. Determinedly she followed the two men, picking her way over the unstable mound of bricks, beyond which lay the crater made by the bomb.

One of the men had reached the hand. He leaned down towards it, sliding his own hand into it. 'Cold as a piece of wet fish,' he proclaimed, whilst his companion started to remove the bricks around it.

Quickly Molly went to help. Beyond the hand was an arm, blue-veined and slender. A woman's arm. A woman probably just like her. Stoically she worked on, taking the bricks from the man lifting them and passing them back through the human chain that had formed behind her, all the while unable to stop glancing at that pale white arm.

Another half-dozen bricks were passed back, then a dozen more, the arm grew longer and Molly's hopes rose, and then just as she turned away to pass on yet another brick she heard the man holding the hand exclaim in disgust, 'There, I knew it.'

She looked back just in time to see him removing a severed arm, its elbow neatly crooked.

She wasn't going to be sick, no matter how much she wanted to. That would be letting the side down and she wouldn't do that, not for one moment.

'Quick, over here. I can hear someone.'

Abandoning the pile of bricks they had been moving, the whole team hurried to where Johnny was crouching, his ear pressed to the rubble.

'I can't hear anything,' one of the men told him.

'Molly, you come and listen,' Johnny commanded.

As Molly kneeled down beside him he reached out his arm and drew her close to his body. She could feel the strong beat of his heart against her own flesh and smell the hot male scent of him through the smoky dampness of the winter night. It gave her an odd feeling to be so close to him. Hastily she pushed it away from herself, and concentrated instead on listening, her ear pressed to the filthy rubble.

She was just about to shake her head and move away when she heard it – the faintest of sounds.

It wasn't a sound she could identify like a cry or even a gasp, but somehow immediately she knew it was human.

She looked at Johnny and, without her having to say anything, he called back over his shoulder, 'Get as many men as you can over here. There's someone down there.'

Within seconds the heap of rubble was surrounded by willing volunteers, working to remove the tangle of roof slates, bricks and beams.

'Wait up,' one of the men shouted. 'There's a bloody great beam under here.' As he spoke, the rubble suddenly shifted beneath their feet, sending bricks skittering across the wet cobbles in a shower of plaster dust.

'Keep still, Molly,' Johnny urged her, reaching out to steady her.

'Get Charlie over here,' one of the firemen, putting out the blaze from a ruptured gas pipe several yards away, called back to the men working the pump. 'He were a civil engineer afore he retired,' he yelled to the rescue party above the relentless thud of the AA batteries. 'Knows a thing or two about buildings, Charlie does. Here, Jeff, where's Charlie?'

Searchlights arced and wheeled overhead, looking for the intruders, briefly patterning the scene in ghostly flashes of stark white. The sudden warning whine of a falling bomb caused the fireman to break off and curse as the emergency service workers all ducked and then waited.

'Close,' Johnny exhaled as they heard the heavy thud of the explosion, 'but at least it missed the docks.'

A small wiry-looking man was making his way towards them, picking his way over the rubble.

'There's someone alive in there,' Johnny told him quickly.

Ignoring Johnny, he crouched down and put his own ear to the mass of rubble.

'Kiddie, by the sound of it,' he grunted.

'How can you tell?' Molly asked.

Under the searchlights she could see beneath the grimy soot of the bomb site the lines that time had carved in his face, as he poked around amongst the rubble.

'Breathing's too light for an adult. I doubt you'll get it out, though,' he announced as he stood and kicked a piece of protruding timber sending up a shower of soot and plaster dust, and then brushed the dust off his hands.

Molly stared at him uncomprehendingly.

'Whole ruddy lot is going to collapse. See this?' He put his toe on a piece of timber. 'One of the main roof beams, this is. Now watch this . . .' He used his foot to rock the wood, sending bricks and dust tumbling into the street below. 'It's unstable, see, and just about balancing on sommat under-neath. You start shifting this stuff on top of it and the whole lot could cave in.'

Silence.

Molly looked imploringly at Johnny whilst one

of the men shifted his weight uncomfortably from one foot to the other, and, as though in confirmation of what Charlie had just told them, a trickle of debris started to gather force to become a small avalanche.

'We can't just leave them there,' Molly protested. The men were avoiding looking at her, shuffling their feet. She turned to Charlie. 'There must be some way.'

He gave a small shrug. 'Aye, well, the best way would be to try to tunnel under this lot. I reckon what's happened is that whoever's down there were under the stairs, the blast has brought the house down on top of them, but there's bin a beam got wedged somehow that has kept the worst of it off of them. If we move this stuff from on top of it we'll risk the beam tipping and crushing them, so the only way to do it would be to try to tunnel in.'

'How do we do that?' Johnny asked.

They all looked at Charlie whilst he sucked on his teeth and walked round the mound of rubble.

'See this here?' He directed their attention to a small gap between a broken window and the ground. 'I reckon we could start here. The beams will have fallen, crosswise, see, and this would be the quickest way between 'em. You'll have to shore up the tunnel as you work, mind.'

One hour passed and then another, as they worked laboriously to carve out a narrow passageway through the rubble. Overhead a second wave of bombers came in, dropping a clutch of bombs over the dock area. It had started to rain, but Molly was oblivious to the discomfort of her cold wet body and her bruised and bleeding fingers as she worked alongside the men, all of them taking it in turns to wriggle into the narrow tunnel they were excavating and carefully drag back more rubble.

It was Johnny, lying on his back, who put in place the wooden staves and rescued pieces of corrugated iron in order to keep the narrow tunnel safe from falling debris, but it was Charlie who, to Molly's admiration, insisted on crawling into the darkness to investigate the barrier they had hit.

'It's a door, but there's a space,' he called back to them. 'Come on, sweetheart . . .' they could hear him saying in a softer voice. Molly's heart turned over. All of them had stopped working, and were waiting motionless, straining to listen. Then abruptly they all heard Charlie swearing loudly – 'Bloody hell' – followed by the sound of small pieces of falling debris and then something small and dark shot out of the tunnel.

'What . . . ?'

'It's a cat.'

'A cat?'

The animal had already disappeared, and in the light of their torches, Molly could see Charlie backing slowly out of the tunnel.

'Was that all it was?' she asked him tiredly. 'A cat?'

Glancing upwards briefly to listen to the drone of the first wave of homeward-bound bombers, in the glare from the searchlights Molly could see patches of paler bloodied flesh on Charlie's face where the debris had rubbed against his skin.

'No,' he told them all wearily, 'there's two kiddies in there; and their mam's wi' them as well but I reckon she's a goner. A door's fallen, trapping them in what's left of the under-stairs. There's a gap there, and it may be big enough for them to crawl out. I could just about get me head inside.' He grimaced. 'Thought for a moment I weren't going to be able to get it out again, though – at least not wi'out cutting off me ears.'

The men laughed but Molly shuddered.

'The trouble is, the two kiddies are that scared they won't try to get out. I reckon one of them's still only a babby, perhaps can't even walk proper, like. T'other one said sommat about their ma telling them not to go talking to strangers in case they was Germans. I daren't lift the door in case it brings the whole lot down on top of them.'

There was silence as the rescuers considered what to do.

'See, this space is big enough p'haps for them to get out, but they won't come out. But it's too small for us to get inside and get them out . . .'

Molly took a deep breath and said quietly, 'Maybe I could try.'

She felt the hiss of Johnny's breath on the back

of her neck, as his hand curled restrainingly round her arm.

'I'm smaller than the rest of you,' she pressed on doggedly, 'and perhaps if I took off me coat, I could—'

'No, Molly. It's too much of a risk,' Johnny protested.

'The lass might have a point,' Charlie said bluntly. 'If'n she's willing to do it . . .'

Willing to do it? She was terrified, but she knew she could not walk away and leave those children there to die alongside their mother.

'I'm willing,' she announced with more conviction than she felt.

Charlie nodded. 'Right, you go in slow and careful, like, and you don't touch nothing. Go and bring us a good length of rope from off the engine, will you, Danny?' he called out to one of the men.

'What's that for?' Molly demanded when Danny came hurrying back with a coil of shipwright's rope.

'We'll tie it round your ankles,' Charlie told her. 'Just in case, like. If anything does happen and the tunnel starts to cave in, we can pull you out faster that way than if you was to crawl backwards.'

Molly started to tremble, imagining the situation he was describing so graphically, and then wishing she had not done.

'Molly, you can't do this,' Johnny told her fiercely. 'I won't let you.'

Molly stuck out her chin. 'And who are you to

tell me what to do, Johnny Everton?' she challenged him, but secretly, deep down inside, a part of her wished that he did have the right to stop her. She felt icy cold with fear and yet at the same time she was burning up with nervous heat.

'You go in slow, like I said,' Charlie told her, 'and if you manage to get hold of one of them, then you give a small kick – just a small one, mind – and we'll have you out of there faster than a grease monkey down a four-masted rigger.'

Molly took off her heavy coat and the jacket she was wearing underneath it. She had never ever felt so scared of anything. She had been in the tunnel earlier in the evening, but not on her own, and not under circumstances such as these.

'Molly . . .'

She could hear the urgency and the emotion in Johnny's voice, but she dared not let herself look at him. If she did she knew she wouldn't be able to do what she had to.

She kneeled down and then lay full length on the rubble in front of the tunnel mouth, waiting for Charlie to tie the rope to her.

'No, let me do it,' she heard Johnny saying.

The touch of his fingers on her calves felt oddly comforting and for some reason it made her want to cry.

'All set?' Charlie asked.

Molly nodded.

Keeping the small torch Charlie had given her firmly in her hand, she started to wriggle her way down the tunnel. The fetid closeness of its air seemed to suck the oxygen from her lungs instead of replacing it. When her body blocked off what little light there was from outside, panic hit her. The impulse to try to sit up and turn round jerked through her body in a frantic desperate reflex. Her heart was pounding and she was shaking from head to foot, her body drenched in sweat. She had to get out of here, she had to. And then she heard a child's voice whispering in fear.

'Mummy, please wake up.'

Molly's head jerked up and banged against the top of the tunnel, immediately dislodging a small stream of dust and crushed brick. She must keep going.

It wasn't much further; she could see the gap Charlie had described to them. It looked frighteningly narrow and unstable. She could taste brick dust on her tongue. It was clogging her mouth and making it difficult for her to breathe. But she was nearly there. Another wriggle and she would be able to reach out and put her hand inside the gap.

She had her hand on the splintered wooden door.

'Hello there.' She tried to make her voice sound as relaxed and calm as possible. 'My name's Molly. I've come to help you out. Which of you is going to be first?'

Silence . . .

A cold sweat poured from her. What if she was

too late? What if she had risked her own life to no purpose?

'I know,' she continued, 'why don't I count to ten first and then one of you—'

'Are you a German?'

Her whole body sagged in relief, and to her astonishment she actually wanted to laugh. 'No, sweetheart, I'm not. How many of you are in there? If it's just the two of you, why don't I take baby out first . . . ?'

'Our mam says as how we aren't to talk to strangers . . .'

Molly's back ached, and the slow trickle of silt coming in through the ceiling of the tunnel was forming a heavy weight now right in the middle of it. 'I'm not a stranger.'

'Who are you then?'

'Your mam asked me to come over and see if you was all right if there was any bombing.' Molly could hear the sound of cautious movement from behind the barricade. And then the light of her torch illuminated the face of a small child. A girl, Molly saw, fresh blood seeping from scratches on her skin.

'Our mam's in here with us,' she told Molly slowly.

'Yes, I know. Can she say anything?' Molly swallowed hard as she forced out the words.

The child shook her head. 'No, she's lying down and she's gone to sleep. She feels all cold.'

Something fell on Molly's face and crawled over

488

her cheek. She dropped the torch and only just managed to stop herself from screaming. She could hear the rattle of the torch falling inside the space and then the more ominous rattle of falling bricks.

'Your torch has gone out.'

'Oh dear, never mind. Give it back to me, will you, sweetheart?'

One second. Two . . . ten, and then she felt the torch being thrust back into her hand. Her own fingers closed round the thin wrist. All she had to do now was kick and she and this child would be pulled free. This child . . .

'So it's just you and your sister in there, is it?' she asked.

'Me bruvver. He's only a baby, though, and can't say nuffing yet. Stinks, he does, 'cos he's messed his nappy.'

Molly's heart dropped. There was no chance then of her coming back and persuading the other child to come to her.

'What's your name?' she asked the little girl.

'Fanny.'

'Well, Fanny, here's what I want you to do. We need to get your brother out so as we can change his nappy, don't we? So why don't you pass him to me . . .'

'He's too heavy for me to lift 'im. A right little bruiser he is, our mam says.'

Molly was beginning to feel faint with exhaustion. She edged a bit nearer. Perhaps if she could manage to squeeze her head into the gap . . . Fear

489

crawled through her stomach and erupted, driving her heart right up into her throat.

'Can you push him to the gap, Fanny?' she asked.

'I'll try.'

She could hear the sharp angry wail of the baby and the heavy panting of the little girl. 'Here you are,' she told Molly, 'but you'll not get 'im through there. A right fat little bugger, he is.'

Very carefully Molly reached into the gap. She thought quickly. They couldn't have much time left – already she was gasping for proper air. Keeping her hands closed over the baby's head to protect it, she said firmly, 'Fanny, I'm going to pull the baby out now and I want you to hold on to his feet and not let go. No matter what, you must hold on to him, do you understand?'

'Our mam will kill me if I pulls his legs off,' Fanny told her in a small voice.

'You won't do that. Now hold tight . . .'

Her heart felt as though it was going to burst out of her chest as she raised her legs and gave a small kick. But that was nothing to the fear that gripped her when there was no response.

What had happened? Had the rope somehow come loose? Was she destined to die in here with the children? Was she . . . ?

'Our Georgie's peeing himself, miss, and it's coming down his legs.'

'Never mind, Fanny. Just keep holding on,' Molly told her. And then miraculously she felt it:

the small but unmistakable movement of her own body backward.

Could she get the baby safely through the gap? She winced as she felt the splintered wood ripping at her hands, but then suddenly his head was safely through and she was able to reach further back to grasp his body, and then his legs, and then Fanny's hands.

Thinner than her brother, Fanny slipped neatly through the gap, clinging on to her brother as Molly had instructed.

Slowly, inch by inch, for what seemed like a lifetime, Molly was pulled back the way she had crawled, every now and again debris showering down on them.

'I'm scared, miss,' Fanny protested. 'I want me mam.'

'Not much further now,' Molly promised her, and then suddenly she really knew that it wouldn't be, because she could feel cold air on her legs and someone grabbing hold of them and tugging her forcefully out of the tunnel.

She could hear the baby crying lustily, then Johnny's voice, and the voices of the others, but somehow she couldn't summon the energy to reply. Someone had taken the baby from her and she could hear Fanny protesting sturdily, 'Hey, mister, put me bruvver down.'

Instinctively she knew it was Johnny who was crouching down beside her, helping her to sit up and offering her some water.

'Bloody hell, but I reckon that's the bravest thing I've ever seen,' she heard a male voice exclaiming admiringly, close at hand.

Automatically Molly looked round to see who he meant, and then realised that he meant her.

EIGHT

'Sure you're OK?' Johnny shouted to Molly above the noise of bombers flying low over the city as they headed back to Germany.

They were standing on Edge Hill Road, and they were on their way home. The children had been taken off to Mill Road Hospital to get checked over, and a heavy rescue team had been called in to remove the rubble of the houses and excavate the bodies of those who had died in them.

Molly looked up at the night sky. It was four o'clock in the morning and heavy rain slanted down on them.

'It's all right, they've gone now,' Johnny told her comfortingly.

'For tonight,' Molly agreed, 'but they'll be back.' Tears brimmed in her eyes and suddenly she was sobbing. 'Oh, Johnny . . .' She was in his arms and he was holding her and patting her back, ignoring her dusty hair and grubby face as he comforted her. 'That poor woman and them kiddies.'

'They've a lot to be grateful for. You saved those kids' lives. Real pluck, that's what you've got.'

She stopped crying and looked up at him, and right there and then, in the middle of the street, he bent his head and kissed her.

She could taste the cold night air and rain on his lips. She wondered dizzily if he could taste dust and death on hers, and then she stopped thinking about anything as he tightened his hold on her and drew her so close to him that she was leaning right into him as bold as brass, and not caring one single jot about it; not caring about anything at all but how good it felt to be held and kissed by him.

She was trembling when he finally released her.

'I'd give anything right now for a bath, but I daren't risk waking our June up,' she told him, striving to sound normal.

'Come back wi' me then, and share mine.'

Molly laughed. 'Oh, yes, your mam and sisters would love that.'

'I don't live with them any more; I've got me own place now.'

Molly's heart pounded against her ribs.

'I'll even let you have the water first,' he told her, adding softly, 'unless, of course, you want to share it with me.'

'Give over, Johnny. That's enough of your joking,' Molly told him, trying to sound dismissive and uncaring, but her voice was giving her away.

'Who says I'm joking?'

They stood looking at one another in the darkness without touching. If she went with him now she knew what would happen, what she was agreeing to. There had been so much death and destruction, so much pain and despair, and something within her yearned for the warmth of Johnny's touch.

'Come with me,' he whispered.

Silently, she reached out and put her hand in his.

He pulled her into his arms so fast and kissed her so passionately that she didn't have time to resist, or change her mind.

'You'll be covered in dust,' she protested against his mouth.

'I don't care,' he told her thickly. 'I don't care about anything or anyone, only this and you, Molly.'

The house he was renting was a small end terrace tucked down a maze of backstreets. They sneaked down the back alleyway to it like two children playing hooky from school, but the laughter died out of Molly's eyes when Johnny opened the door and stepped back to let her in. She couldn't help thinking of the time when she and Eddie had found it almost impossible to resist each other. It seemed like a lifetime ago, but in fact it was barely a year. Was she being disloyal to the memory of her beloved Eddie?

'You don't have to if you don't want,' he told her.

Her mouth had gone dry. She thought of Eddie, and of June and of her father, and of all those who would not recognise the Molly who was standing here now. *Their* Molly knew nothing of death or destruction, or other people's pain, or feared that there might be no tomorrow.

This Molly knew all of those things and *this* Molly shared that knowledge with Johnny.

Their Molly would run a mile rather than hold out her hand to Johnny the way this Molly was doing, and when he took it and led her inside the door he was holding open, then their Molly could easily be gone for ever.

Earlier, lying in that tunnel, desperately afraid that she might be trapped there, torn between her longing to escape and her stubborn determination not to leave those children behind, she had felt as though death was hovering over her and she could feel its fearful icy breath.

She had escaped from it and she was alive, and now she wanted desperately to live – to live every bit of her life in every single way she could, starting now with this and with Johnny.

'I want to,' she answered him and, shockingly, she knew that it was true.

It was a shabby house that smelled slightly of damp, but Johnny had got it spotlessly clean, she noticed approvingly as he ushered her into the kitchen.

'Sit down, whilst I light the geyser for the hot water,' he told her, indicating the oilcloth-covered kitchen table with its two chairs.

Molly pulled a face. 'I'd better not. I'm filthy,' she told him, shivering slightly, and then frowning as he said, 'Hang on here a tick,' and then opened the back door. When he came back he was carrying a tin bath.

'And where are you going to put that?' she demanded warily.

Johnny grinned. 'Why, right here in front of the fire, of course.'

'What? You're expecting me to bath meself here, with no lock on the door, where anyone could see me?' she demanded, scandalised. They both knew that by 'anyone' she meant him.

'I'll stoke up the fire for you,' Johnny offered. Without waiting for her to answer him, he added, 'Wait on whilst I go upstairs and bring down some towels.'

She could leave now, Molly told herself as she heard his feet thumping on the stairs. Did he really expect her to take a bath in a tub in the kitchen? She would do no such thing! The geyser was starting to bubble. Automatically she went over and switched off the gas. By the time she had done so, Johnny was back carrying an armful of unexpectedly good quality towels.

'Fell off a lorry,' he told her with a big grin as he put them on the table, and then stirred up the banked-down fire and added some more coke to it.

'I'm not having a bath in that,' Molly began to protest, but Johnny ignored her, carefully placing two towels on the floor and then putting the bath onto them before connecting a piece of hose from the geyser to the bath.

Steam rose from the tin bath as the piping-hot water flowed into it.

'I'll put some cold in whilst you're getting undressed and then I'll get the geyser going again.'

He made it all seem so matter-of-fact, but Molly had never undressed in front of anyone other than her sister, much less a man.

'What's up?' Johnny began when she didn't move, and then he grinned and said, 'Oh, I get it. Hang on, then.'

Molly heard him moving around in the scullery and when he came back he was carrying a wooden clothes maiden, which he opened out and placed between the bath and the rest of the kitchen, solemnly hanging the other towels on it to provide her with a small screen.

'You'll have to turn your back,' Molly told him, 'and keep it turned.'

'OK.'

She took off her coat first, and then her jacket and then, making sure he was not looking, she scurried behind the makeshift screen and quickly tugged off her skirt, and then unclipped her suspenders so that she could roll down the thick lisle stockings that were part of her uniform. Her blouse came off next, and then, after a quick look

498

to make sure that Johnny wasn't watching, she hurriedly unfastened her brassiere and removed the rest of her underwear.

Parts of her body were bruised and scraped, but Molly ignored them, quickly stepping into the tub and then exhaling as she felt the welcome warmth of the clean warm water against her skin.

'Forgot to give you the soap.'

'Johnny!' Molly squeaked indignantly, as she heard his voice coming from behind her, her face bright red as she drew up her knees and covered her naked breasts with her hands. She didn't dare to turn round and look at him.

'Johnny what?' he asked her softly. 'I just thought you might want a helping hand, that's all.' And then to Molly's shock she could feel him soaping her back with a surprising tenderness.

The coke crackled and burned, sending a warm glow over the room, whilst the sensation of Johnny's hands on her bare back was sending an equally warm glow shooting through her body right down to her toes. And once she had begun to get over her apprehension and embarrassment, the sensation was, well, rather nice. Even so, she felt obliged to protest shyly, 'Johnny, don't.'

'Don't what?' he demanded softly, his breath tickling her neck and making her shiver deliciously, and then shiver again when she felt him kissing where his breath had touched. His fingertips trailed down her bare arm, making her gasp and quiver. 'Stay there.' She could hear the laughter in his voice and something deeper and darker as well, which made her heart bounce. 'I'll get you a towel.'

He was back before she could think of anything to say, standing beside the bath, holding the towel open for her.

'If you think I'm going to step out of this bath naked . . .' Molly told him, trying to sound non-chalant, but instead blushing so hotly she felt as though her face were on fire.

'Well, we've only one bath and one lot of hot water, and it's my turn now, but you stay there if you want,' Johnny told her, grinning.

'Johnny, don't you dare get in this bath,' Molly commanded ineffectively. When he dropped the towel and advanced on the bath she squeaked and used her hands to send a showery deterrent in his direction. It hit his shirt, soaking him to his skin, so that in the firelight she could see the broad plane of his torso roped with hard muscle.

'Right. That's it . . .'

'No, Johnny, don't you dare come any closer. Don't you *dare*,' Molly objected.

Of course he ignored her, and so Molly splashed more water over him in an attempt to keep him away, and then laughed to see how wet he was, and was still laughing and protesting several seconds later when he braved her watery onslaught, ignored her attempts to deflect him, and simply scooped her out of the bath, quickly wrapping her in a towel, and then sliding her to her feet in between her giggles and his own laughter.

Almost sliding her to her feet, Molly recognised dizzily, her giggles and his laughter fading into silence as he held her close to him, still wrapped in the towel, and then bent his head and kissed her, very slowly. And then when she sighed in pleasure he kissed her again, much harder this time.

'Oh, Johnny, I don't think . . .!' Suddenly she felt shaky and unsure of what she was doing, and afraid of her own feelings.

'We could be dead tomorrow,' Johnny told her, almost roughly.

Molly shuddered, all too aware of the truth of what he was saying. 'Yes.' Then she kissed him shyly, and they both knew exactly what she was agreeing to.

'Did you and Eddie ever?' Johnny asked her thickly when he had stopped kissing her.

'No, never,' Molly answered, her face burning afresh.

'So you're still a . . .?' Johnny probed.

'Yes, yes,' Molly agreed hurriedly, embarrassed.

There was a small silence. Then Johnny asked her slowly, 'Are you sure you want to?'

Did she? All Molly knew was that having come so far, she didn't want to turn back. She might not love Johnny like she had Eddie – she would never love anyone else like that ever again, she knew that – but she liked it when he kissed her, and if she walked away from him now she knew that a part of her would always regret doing so.

'I'm sure,' she told him firmly. 'I don't want to die without knowing what it feels like, Johnny.'

Rather than think what she was doing was wrong, as she would have done before, after what she had seen tonight, it suddenly seemed so right and so very, very necessary.

Could there be anything more comforting than this, Molly reflected sleepily as she lay tucked up next to Johnny, her body savouring the warmth of his whilst he held her close. She was a woman now and there was no going back, but she didn't regret what had happened. It had been neither as bad as she had dreaded as a young girl, nor as good as she had dreamed lying alone in her bed thinking of Eddie, the excitement generated by Johnny's passionate kisses fizzing so impatiently inside her somehow but not quite reaching what she had sensed might be its potential. But if the pleasure hadn't been as intense as she had secretly dreamed, then neither had the pain been anything like as bad as she had heard other girls at the factory describe.

'All right?' Johnny asked her.

She could hear the tenderness in his voice, and nodded. 'I have to go home,' she reminded him. June and her dad were used to her being out all hours with the WVS but she knew she should get back before dawn arrived.

'Not yet. The all clear's only just gone.' He kissed her forehead and Molly relaxed into the comfort of his hold, only too willing to stay in his embrace.

Did she look any different? Would those who were close to her, like her sister, be able to see any difference in her face, Molly wondered, stepping into the kitchen of number 78, hearing June's slipper-shod feet on the stairs.

She hadn't let Johnny come into the house with her, nor had she let him kiss her goodbye on the doorstep as he had obviously been intending to do, and yet for all her fierce determination not to do anything that would publicly link them together as a couple, she could not and did not regret what had happened, she admitted.

'You're back! Thank goodness. I've hardly slept a wink, what with Elizabeth Rose crying, and them bombs going off all the time,' said June, giving her a quick hug and then hurrying to fill the kettle. Molly was surprised and touched by her concern but also worried that June would smell Johnny's scent on her and quickly released herself from June's embrace.

'Where was you anyway?'

'We were called out to one of the streets down near the docks. There'd been a direct hit and half of the houses had gone.'

Something in her voice must have given her away, Molly realised, because June stopped filling the kettle and waited.

'Two kiddies were trapped, but we managed to

get them out,' Molly answered June's unspoken question, making a heroic effort to smile and sound relaxed.

'What about their mam?' asked June.

Molly's throat had gone dry. Her eyes felt itchy and sore. From the dust in the tunnel? From the tears she had cried in Johnny's arms for the two children now without a mother and for the young woman whose whole life should have been ahead of her? Molly didn't know. What she did know, though, was that she didn't want to upset her sister.

'They hadn't found her when I left,' she said. It was, after all, technically the truth in the sense that the young mother had still been sealed in the tomb of her destroyed house.

'It's nearly Christmas,' said June in a low voice, 'but how are we supposed to want to celebrate it with all that's going on?'

'We've just got to do our best, June,' Molly answered her. 'There's nothing else we can do. Your Frank would want you and Lillibet—'

'My Frank?' June cut across her. 'I dunno that he is mine any more, Molly, nor if I want him to be. Us getting married and all that seems ever such a long time ago now. When he came home for Elizabeth Rose's christening it were like I didn't really know him any more.'

'June, don't say that,' Molly protested, her voice muffled by tiredness and despair.

June started to cry so Molly went to put her arms around her, trying to comfort her. 'It's just

504

this war, June. Frank loves you and you love him
and—'

'No.' June shook her head. 'I don't know as I
do any more, Molly. In fact, sometimes I think I
hate him for leaving me with Elizabeth Rose to
worry about and him not being here. It's all right
for him, all he has to do is come home once in a
while and everyone thinks he's wonderful, but it's
me as has to cope with everything, not him. Molly,
if anything was to happen to me I want you to
promise me that you'll bring my Elizabeth Rose
up as though she were your own.'

'Nothing's going to happen to you,' Molly stressed.

'You can't say that – no one can. That woman
last night whose kiddies you rescued – that could
have bin any of us. And if it were to be me, Molly,
I don't want my little girl being brought up by
Frank's mam, and I do not want her being like
you and me neither, having to grow up without
her mam. If I wasn't to be here then you're the
nearest thing she's going to have to a mam of her
own, Molly, and I want you to promise me that
if owt does happen to me, then you'll love her and
look after her like she was your own.'

'June . . .'

'Promise me,' June insisted, her grip on Molly's
arm so tight that her nails were digging into
Molly's flesh.

Tears stung Molly's eyes. 'You don't have to ask
me to promise anything, June. You know that I
already love her like she was my own.'

505

'But promise me all the same.'

June's face was grey with tiredness and strain in the dull late December light grudgingly seeping into the morning sky. Molly's heart turned over inside her chest as she looked at her sister. When had the lively and vivacious June grown so gaunt and desperate-looking? So much as though something were eating her up inside and destroying her warmth and spirit.

'I promise,' Molly told her. There could be no exchange of confidences now from her to June, telling her about last night and Johnny, Molly realised. The June with whom she might once have had that kind of exchange had gone and been replaced by someone Molly was frighteningly aware she hardly recognised.

'There she is, crying again,' said June, looking up towards the ceiling.

'I'll make her a bottle and take it up to her, if you like,' Molly offered.

June shook her head. 'She's not due a feed for another hour yet,' she told Molly sharply.

'Surely it wouldn't do her any harm to feed her now. She sounds so hungry, and then you can go back to bed and have another hour yourself, seeing as how the bombers kept you awake,' Molly coaxed, hardly daring to breathe as June frowned and seemed to consider. But then just as she looked about to accept, her shoulders tightened as though she were preparing herself to carry a heavy burden, her mouth tightening as she shook her head again.

'I'm not going against what Dr Truby says to do,' she informed Molly fiercely. 'So you can stop trying to persuade me.' Her expression changed, tears filling her eyes and her voice wobbling slightly as she exclaimed woefully, 'Oh, Molly, I don't know what's happening to me sometimes. I feel that mytherated and cross wi' meself, you and me shouldn't be falling out – you're me sister.'

'We aren't falling out,' Molly tried to comfort her, giving her a hug. 'Like you said, we're sisters, you and me, June, and nothing can ever come between us,' she added stoutly, and meant it.

'Oh, I know what I meant to tell you,' June sniffed, trying to regain control. 'You know them tins of fruit Pearl Lawson's hubby were supposed to have got for Christmas Day?'

Molly nodded, relieved to see June behaving like the June of old, for now at least.

'Well, it seems that Marjorie Gladdings from number 53 opened a tin t'other day, expecting to find peaches and that inside, and instead it were full of carrots. Went mad, she did, running across to Pearl's, yellin' her head off that she'd bin robbed on account of paying George under the counter for them, and saying as how it were all a con, and that George were as bent as a nine-bob note.'

When Molly had finished laughing, more out of relief than mirth, she hugged June again.

'What's that for when it's at home?' June demanded.

'Nothing,' Molly answered her, still smiling, 'exceptin' that you're my sister.'

She couldn't remember a time she had last felt as sick with nerves as this, Molly admitted as she stood outside the front gate of the neat semi-detached house. With every step she had taken down the tree-lined avenue she had wondered if she had the courage to go on. This part of Wavertree, with its smart houses and its tennis club, was a world away from her own home in Chestnut Close. The palms of her hands felt sweaty inside her gloves, and her stomach was churning. But this was something she had to do. She had made up her mind about that. She just hoped that Anne would listen to her and that somehow they could be friends again. Taking a deep breath, she lifted the latch on the gate and walked up the path. It was impossible to know if anyone was watching her through the thick net curtains screening the windows.

The brass door knocker was polished and shiny. Molly's hand shook as she raised it and then let it drop. No response. She tried again. Still no response.

Her shoulders hunched with defeat, Molly turned round and walked back down the path, blinking away her tears. She felt so bad about what had happened, and about losing Anne's friendship.

She was less than halfway down the avenue

when she heard the sound of someone running up behind her. Turning round, she saw Anne, hatless and coatless, running after her, calling out breathlessly, 'Molly, stop.'

Uncertainly, Molly did so.

'Philip says I'm being mean and that it isn't fair to blame you. He says that he'd have done the same thing in your shoes, and that you were just trying to protect me.'

'Men don't understand. I shouldn't have kept it from you, Anne. I should have told you.'

They each took a step towards the other.

'We've been such good pals, it would be a pity if we were to fall out now,' Anne said huskily.

'I'm really sorry I didn't tell you.'

'Oh, Molly, I'm sorry I was so horrid. It was all such a shock.'

'I'm really sorry.'

'Can you forgive me?'

'Can you forgive *me*?'

Suddenly they were hugging each other, both laughing and crying at the same time as they exchanged apologies.

'We must stay friends for the rest of our lives,' Anne told Molly emotionally, half an hour later, when Molly was sitting perched slightly uncomfortably on the edge of a chair in Anne's parents' immaculate front room. In her hand she balanced the cup of tea Anne had insisted on making her when she had invited Molly in so that they could talk properly. Her parents were out, she explained, and Philip was upstairs resting. 'We've been through so much together.'

Molly agreed, her heart almost too full of emotion for her to be able to speak.

'When this war is over, and me and Philip are properly settled, I want you to come and stay with us. You're the best friend I've ever had, Molly. I wish you had told me about Richard but I can understand now why you didn't.'

'I wish I had done too.'

They exchanged mutually understanding looks.

The war might keep them apart but Molly knew that they would always remain firm friends because of what they had shared.

NINE

'White Rabbits,' said Molly, as she and Johnny met up, one evening the following spring, outside the church hall, where they had been attending a civil defence meeting, Molly with her WVS colleagues, and Johnny with his own rescue group.

'What?'

'It's the first of May,' she reminded him. 'You have to say "White Rabbits" for luck at the beginning of a new month!'

'I wouldn't need no White Rabbits for good luck if you was to agree to be my girl, Molly.'

She gave him a reproving look, and changed the subject. 'Elsie was round at our house last night and she says she reckons she saw Mr Churchill when he were here. Swears it were him she saw. Mind you, if everyone who reckons they saw him did, then half of Liverpool must have seen him,' she laughed.

There had not been any repetition of the night they had shared after the bombing. Molly had made it plain that she wasn't a fast girl and that she did not want to have that kind of relationship, and Johnny, to his credit, had not attempted to press her. They both recognised that their union had been the result of an extraordinary night – a night when they had needed to take comfort from the devastation and destruction all around them. She had allowed Johnny to take her out, though: to the Grafton over Christmas, and just recently she had been going to the cinema with him once a week.

'Courtin' with him, are you?' June had asked her one evening when he had dropped her home.

'He's just a friend,' Molly had told her sister firmly, and that was quite truthfully how she thought of him. It was, after all, only just over a year since she had lost Eddie, and she couldn't imagine any man taking his place in her heart.

She had got up early on the anniversary of Eddie's death and had gone first to church to say a prayer for him, and then to the cemetery where, to her delight, the bulbs she and her father had planted at the back end had been in flower. She had viewed their dancing golden heads through a haze of tears, which had flowed more heavily when she had lifted her head to see how many new graves had extended the perimeter of the cemetery since Eddie's death.

She had felt hesitant and even guilty at first, quietly telling him about her year, and promising him that she had not and would not ever forget him, but then a sense of peace had filled her as though an unseen hand were gently lifting those feelings from her shoulders and freeing her to speak honestly and openly to the young man she had loved, and who now belonged to a place that seemed so very far removed from her.

The news reported in the *Echo* in March, that a baby girl had been found alive under bomb debris in Wallasey after being trapped there for three and a half days, had plunged June back into a mood of dark foreboding and anxiety. Trying to coax her sister into a happier frame of mind had pushed Molly's own most private feelings and concerns to one side. June had been furious when she had been told by the doctor that baby Lillibet was underweight for her age, and to Molly's concern, June's phobias about the safety of air-raid shelters had grown worse rather than better.

'I wish June would go out and stay with Auntie Violet in Nantwich,' Molly had confided to her father. 'She wouldn't have to worry about the shelters out there, and there might be some extra food to spare for Lillibet.'

'Aye, I wish she would go, as well, lass, but June's like me sister and they're as stubborn as mules. Think on, Molly, you can tek a horse to water as often as yer like, but you canna make it drink.'

'Pity it isn't dark,' Johnny whispered in Molly's ear now as she stopped at the kerb to head off across the road and home. 'Not going to ask me why?' he teased her.

Molly dismissed him with a shrug, but he refused to be quelled.

'Then I'll just have ter tell you, won't I?' he whispered. 'If it were dark I could put me arms around you and then I could kiss you . . .'

Molly pursed her lips into a firm line. 'There's going to be none of that going on between us, Johnny,' she told him. 'My Eddie's only bin dead a year and . . .' She stopped speaking when he reached for her hand and held it tightly in his own.

'I'm being as patient as I know how, Molly, but it isn't easy. I want you to be my girl and I want to start courtin' yer proper, like. I made a mistake letting you go once – I'm not doing it again.'

Molly didn't know what to say. She liked Johnny and she enjoyed his company. Her childish sexual fear of his maleness was long gone and she couldn't pretend to herself that she hadn't enjoyed his lovemaking because she had. So why was she holding back? The war had brought the best out in Johnny, changing him as it had done all of them. He relished the danger of the rescue work he did, and was well thought of by the others on the team. So much so that he had now been officially put in charge. Any girl would be proud now to claim Johnny as hers. No one would blame her or look askance at her if they were to start courting, and given what had happened between them she ought to accept. So why did she feel so reluctant to do so? She was a woman now, not a foolish girl any more, and she had seen enough of how the separation caused by war and the different experiences of it could drive couples apart. She and Johnny were sharing their experience of it and she had seen too how that could bond a couple and how, indeed, it could foster a dangerous intimacy between couples who were already committed elsewhere.

'I—'

I need more time, she had been about to say, but before she could do so, Johnny grabbed hold of her and kissed her. Out of the corner of her eye she saw Pearl coming towards them.

'Oh, thank you very much,' Molly reproached Johnny, but he refused to be abashed, simply grinning at her instead, and keeping hold of her hand.

'Nice to see someone is looking happy,' Pearl commented, eyeing them both up with interest.

'Well, if you really want to do that,' Johnny answered, giving her a teasing wink, 'then you want ter find someone who has bought some of them tinned peaches from your hubby that have actually got peaches inside 'em.'

Molly had told Johnny the story about the carrots and he loved nothing better than to tease people.

'It weren't my hubby's fault that there was a bit of a mix-up,' Pearl defended her husband crossly. 'He sold on them tins in good faith.'

515

'You shouldn't have done that,' Molly objected, once Pearl was out of earshot.

'Why not? It wasn't my fault either that them tins—'

'No, not that about the peaches. I mean that you shouldn't have kissed me like that in front of her. She'll have it all over Liverpool by tea time.'

'So what if she does?' Johnny asked her softly. 'I'd be very happy to have folk think of you and me as a couple, Molly.'

'I've just told you, Johnny, it's too soon. And besides, folks round here have long memories. There was all that fuss about that lass and me and you.' Molly could see from his face that she wasn't convincing him.

'Look, I've got to go. Sally's invited our June round tonight to make amends and I've promised I'll make our dad's tea.'

'So them two have finally made up, have they? Last I heard was that your June weren't speaking to Sally Walker.'

'That was just a bit of sommat and nothing, Johnny, and I'll thank you not to go saying anything about it. Sally reckons that her Ronnie and June's Frank should be getting some leave soon. I hope they do. It will do our June a power of good to have Frank home. Do you think we'll see anything tonight?' she asked uncertainly, glancing up towards the cloud-brushed May sky. April had been an unusually quiet month for bombing raids and some people had started to hope that the end of the war was in sight. Molly knew better than that and worried it was the calm before the storm.

'I dunno,' Johnny answered her. 'If Jerry knows that Churchill has had the Western Approaches Command HQ moved from Plymouth to Liverpool we're bound to see some action.'

They exchanged sober looks. The central command for all the shipping approaching England from Canada and North America was now operating from a large secure underground headquarters in Liverpool, and everyone was concerned that it would draw more bombing raids to the city. The occupants of the close had three new residents billeted amongst them, all of them working at the new HQ, and Molly had already exchanged tentative hellos with one of the young women, having seen her on her way to work whilst she was on her own way to the factory.

'Fancy coming for a walk wi' us this next Sunday?' Johnny asked.

'A walk? Where to?' Molly asked cautiously.

'I dunno. Somewhere as I can have you to myself.'

Molly smiled again and shook her head. 'Get away with you!' she laughed, and headed for home.

She reached number 78 just as June was about to leave, Lillibet already strapped into her pram. Molly paused to blow her niece some kisses and watch her rosebud mouth widen into a delighted smile. She itched to take her out of the pram and cuddle her, but she knew how June was likely to react about her interfering with Lillibet's routine if she did. Her duties with the WVS plus her job at Hardings meant that Molly had very little free time, but she still managed to make enough to sing nursery rhymes to Lillibet from the books she and June had shared as children. Molly adored her niece, and couldn't have loved her more if she had been her own.

Over Christmas Molly and Sally, giggly after a glass of Elsie's homemade wine, had whispered together about claiming Dr Truby King's book for the war effort.

'We're allus being told how much we need fuel,' Sally had said virtuously, slightly spoiling the effect by hiccuping loudly.

'I reckon he'd go up in flames right well.'

'You mean our June will when she finds out.'

'I dare you,' Sally had giggled.

Molly looked wistfully at the book, where it lay ready to hand on the sideboard. It had caused so much trouble she'd be pleased to see the wretched thing destroyed.

'Isn't our June back from Sally's yet?'

'No, but it's still light,' Molly pointed out to her father, taking from him the vegetables he had brought back from the allotment.

'Aye but it's gone ten o'clock. What time did she go out?'

'About six.' Molly reached for the kettle and

started to fill it, then broke off as she heard the familiar squeak of the pram's wheels, to tell her father, 'That sounds like June now.

'Dad was just asking where you were,' she told her sister, as she helped to unstrap Lillibet from her pram harness, picking up her niece and giving her a loving cuddle. She was crawling now and giving everyone she knew big loving smiles that showed off her newly cut teeth. Despite June's strict routine, she had a sparkle and spirit that gladdened Molly's heart to see.

'Don't go getting her all excited, Molly,' June protested. 'It's gone ten and she should be asleep.'

'Do you want me to do her a bottle?' Molly offered.

'No, thanks. I gave her one at Sally's and she's not due another now for four hours. She were a bit grizzly earlier on. I hope she's not starting up with cutting another tooth. I still haven't made up me lost sleep from them last two.'

Molly laughed to see the dimples appear in her niece's cheeks as she smiled up at her. Tenderly she stroked the dark tousled curls off Lillibet's face. She was such a pretty baby. Everyone said so, and a loving little thing as well, always holding up her arms to be picked up. Molly knew that June would have something to say if she knew how often Molly did just that, when June's back was turned.

'One of the lads down the allotments was sayin' that he's heard that one of them conchies has moved in on Mabel Street.' Everyone knew about

519

the conscientious objectors, who were exempted from fighting because of their beliefs, but Molly had not actually met one. 'Works up at the hospital, so Ted Hargreaves were saying.'

Dusk had fallen whilst they had been talking, its twilight fading into darkness. June was just reaching out to take Elizabeth Rose from Molly when they heard the warning wail of the air-raid siren. Briefly, all three of them stiffened into silence.

'Quick, let's get down to the shelter,' said Molly, retaining her hold on Elizabeth Rose, and resisting June's attempts to take the baby from her. 'You first, June,' she insisted firmly. 'Dad'll bring the bags.'

Doors were opening up and down the close, as people hurried towards the shelter.

Daisy caught up with Molly, shooing her two sons in front of her. 'Ruddy Jerry. I thought he'd realised over Christmas that he's wasting 'is time trying to bomb Liverpool, because we won't give in to him.' She was having to raise her voice to be heard above the wail of the sirens.

'You not on duty tonight then, Molly?' another neighbour called out as she caught up with them.

Molly shook her head, hurrying into the shelter. As always its sour smell caught at the back of her throat and made her wrinkle her nose.

'Lord, but it stinks in here,' Daisy complained. 'P'rhaps we ought to try leaving the doors open during the day now the weather's warming up a bit,' Elsie suggested. 'Get a bit of fresh air inside.'

'Wot, and have the place stripped out by thieves? Don't be daft, Elsie.'

'Molly, give Elizabeth Rose to me,' June demanded.

'You get yourself settled first, June,' Molly told her calmly, discreetly putting herself between June and the exit. Molly didn't want to risk anything spooking her into trying to leave before the all clear had gone.

They heard the first wave of bombers coming over within minutes of the final arrivals squashing into the shelter and the door being closed.

Everyone started to settle himself or herself down for the night, unrolling sleeping bags and punching them into shape with weary resignation.

'I were 'oping as how we'd seen the last of these ruddy air raids,' one of the men commented grimly.

Molly, who had counted the seconds of the first wave of bombers, wondered if anyone else in the shelter had realised just how many of them there were flying overhead. Far more, surely, than there'd been during the Christmas air raids. The crack and rat-a-tat-tat of the AA batteries exploded like fireworks, followed by the ominous sound of the bombs. Some of the docks were still damaged and unable to be used from the Christmas bombing raids, and by the sound of it they were being targeted again.

A second wave of bombers followed the first, and then a third. The whistling sound of bombs falling, followed by the stomach-gripping silence before they exploded, filled the shelter with a nerve-straining tension. A child started to wail in shocked fear as a bomb exploded somewhere close enough to the shelter to send pieces of debris thudding down on top of it.

'That were close,' one of the men commented uneasily.

June whimpered deep in her throat. She had refused to unroll her sleeping bag, and instead was sitting tensely staring at the door. If June wouldn't try to sleep then she could not do so, Molly acknowledged.

'I don't see why we couldn't have stayed at home,' June told her, panicking. 'There's plenty as does.'

'Yes, and I've seen what happens to them,' said Molly tersely, thinking again of the two children she had pulled out of the wreckage of their own home. The shelter might be cramped and oppressive but it had to be better than staying at home, leaving yourself at the mercy of the German bombers.

'Quick, Molly, this way.'

Johnny had grabbed hold of her hand and was running so fast with her that Molly was afraid she might lose her footing on the slippery cobblestones and fall. Up above them the early May night sky was crisscrossed with the beam of searchlights and the speeding molten silver tracery of the gunfire from the AA batteries. Round after round of ammunition was being fired in an attempt to stem the relentless flood of German bombers blanket-bombing the whole city, determined to destroy Liverpool's docks and the British people's desperately needed lifeline to North America.

Above them, bombers released their cargo of death. Crouching down beside Johnny in the protective shadow of their van, Molly shivered as they watched them explode so close that she could feel the air rushing past her as it was sucked into the explosion and then expelled again. Both she and Johnny were covered with dust.

They were supposed to be on their way down to the docks, but they had become trapped down one of the narrow streets, unable to leave for the bombs going off all around them.

'Looks like the end of the street's had a direct hit. We'll have to turn round and go down Dukerman Street,' Molly told Johnny worriedly.

This was the third night in a row that the city had been blitzed by night-time bombing raids. Yesterday Mr Harding had told Molly not to bother coming into work but to concentrate on her voluntary services duties. He had taken on extra staff to meet the increased demands from the War Office. But with the city being bombed, and families having to be rehomed – many living in the community of tents that had been set up in the fields just outside the city – some girls looked for jobs closer to where they were now living, resulting in a constant turnover of workers.

'I thought the last two nights were bad enough but they were nowt compared to this,' Johnny admitted, checking the sky before urging Molly towards the van.

May wasn't even a week old yet but, for three nights solid, the city had been subjected to a relentless attack from German bombs. As fast as everyone worked during the daytime to deal with the damage of the night before, the bombers returned again at nightfall to begin another round of death and destruction.

'I just hope that our June's all right,' Molly said.

Johnny could hear the anxiety in her voice. 'She'll be fine,' he tried to comfort her. 'Your dad will see to it that she gets into the shelter.'

Molly gave him a wan smile.

'Everyone OK?' Johnny called out as the rest of their small group, who had also taken cover where they could, made their cautious way back to the waiting van.

They had been on their way to Huskisson Dock in response to an emergency call-out, and after Molly had reversed the van back up the narrow street, she drove as quickly as she could towards the fires illuminating the night sky. All around them lay the evidence of the devastating effect the blitz was having on Liverpool and its people. Not that Molly needed to see any evidence. The queues of people forming every night in the buildings where the WVS worked to provide blankets, warm food and what other help and advice they could were proof enough of the growing number of homeless Liverpudlians.

'Hellfire and buckets of blood,' one of the men – a First World War veteran with a bad leg – swore as Molly brought the van to a halt and they all stared at the inferno in front of them.

Opening his door, Johnny called out to a passing ARP warden, 'What's happening, mate?'

'Barrage balloon's bin hit and deflated. It's fell onto a steamer berthed in number two dock,' he told him tersely. 'Steamer's loaded with a thousand tons of shells and bombs, and the ruddy thing's on fire. Port Authority's got every fire crew they can spare trying to put it out. Of course, bloody Jerry's scented blood and he's using the light from the fire to bomb the rest of the dock.' He swore under his breath and ducked as an incendiary bomb exploded, igniting one of the nearby dock sheds, showering everything with burning shards of timber and fiery red sparks. Fresh flames leaped hungrily towards the steamer trapped inside the dock.

Two fire engines came racing past the parked van, followed by a boy on a bicycle, pedalling furiously.

'Hey, you, lad, where do you think you're going?' the ARP man demanded.

'Mill Road Hospital's bin bombed,' the boy told him breathlessly. 'Bomb's fell right into one of the operating theatres. I've bin sent to see if there's any fire engines to spare down here.'

Molly was about to ask Johnny if they were needed more at Mill Road than they were here at the dock, when a port official came hurrying towards them, calling out tersely, 'Out. Out . . . now. We're clearing the dock of everyone apart from the fire fighters. The ruddy ship's loaded to the gunwales with explosives.'

'Let's head for Mill Road and the hospital,' Johnny suggested, following the same line of thought as Molly. He added, 'If it's bin hit then they're going to need as much help as they can get tekkin' patients out.'

'Eh, Molly, it makes me blood run cold just thinking about it, a bomb dropping right onto the operating theatre, and killing everyone excepting for the patient,' Doris Brookes told Molly soberly as they stood together outside her front gate.

'I was on one of the Nightingale wards when we heard about it. We all rushed out to see what we could do to help, and blow me if the ward I'd been in didn't take a direct hit itself.' She spoke with the bemused shell-shocked air that had become so familiar to Molly.

She had been at the hospital herself, after it had been bombed, helping to ferry patients away from the danger. In some cases this had meant taking them on stretchers to church halls to await medical attention because the other hospitals were too full.

The *Malakand*, the steamer in Huskisson number two dock, which Molly and the crew had originally been summoned to help with, had ultimately exploded, showering debris for over two and a half miles, and blowing a hole in the overhead railway. How only five people had been killed, Molly did not know. Lewis's store in Ranelagh Street, the place where June had bought her wedding dress pattern all that time ago, had gone, along with the Customs House and St Luke's Church, down in the city centre. Fires burned everywhere in the wrecked buildings, and with bombs hitting the water mains, it was often impossible to get sufficient water pressure to put them out. Molly didn't think there was a sight more dreadful than a church in flames. Whole streets had been demolished and fire fighters had been coming in from all over the country to do what they could to help. At night Jerry wreaked destruction, and at daybreak, Liverpool's weary citizens dragged themselves back to the heart of their city to start clearing up and doing what they could to keep the trains, buses and trams running. Their spirits were flagging but they wouldn't give in. It made

Molly proud to see her neighbours rallying round each other.

But most important of all were the docks. The man responsible for them, Captain F. J. 'Johnny' Walker, had become a hero to those who knew him and all that he was doing to protect the vessels crossing the Atlantic, bringing into Liverpool the supplies the country so desperately needed.

'How's your June doing?' Doris Brookes asked Molly.

Molly had grown to like Frank's mother over the last few months and admired her fortitude and strength, but her loyalty to her sister made her cautious.

'Elizabeth Rose is cutting some new teeth, so, what with that and the bombs, our June hasn't bin getting much sleep this last week. She's had a letter from Frank to say he'll be coming home on leave soon, though, so she's got that to look forward to.'

'Aye, well, let's hope this time she treats my Frank a sight better than she did last time he were home,' Doris told Molly forcefully.

Molly could only hope so too.

'How much longer is it going to go on for?' June's voice was high-pitched and querulous as she looked almost accusingly at Molly in the dull blue light of the air-raid shelter. It was two o'clock in the morning, and the seventh night of the blitz. Molly had spent the earlier part of the evening helping out at one of the temporary shelters, before hurrying home, dodging falling bombs herself.

To her relief their father had managed to persuade June to take refuge in the shelter, but it was plain to Molly that her sister's nerves were being increasingly badly affected by the constant bombing raids. Molly wondered how long it would be before she broke. She had seen it happen to others; frightened despairing people unable to cope with what was happening to their city and their lives.

A loud explosion close at hand shook the sides of the shelter. June gave Molly a wild-eyed look of terror.

'It's all right, they aren't interested in us,' Molly tried to calm her. 'It's the gridiron they'll be after. Give me Lillibet,' she offered, holding out her arms and smiling at the baby, who had been crying with the pain of her new teeth.

''Ere, June, why don't you try rubbing a bit of me elderberry wine on her gums?' Elsie suggested.

'I'm not risking poisoning my baby, giving her stuff like that,' June refused.

'Suit yourself,' Elsie sniffed, offended. 'But it never did either of mine any harm. Nor you two neither, seeing as yer own mam weren't too proud to use it.'

'Aye, do as she says, June. Then we might all get a bit o' peace. Little 'un's mekkin' more noise than bloody Jerry,' one of the men chipped in, causing June to glare angrily at him, and then swing back to face the door as they all heard the whining dive of one of the small fighter planes that came in with the bombers.

'Ruddy hell, sounds like it's right overhead,' another man commented uneasily, his voice almost drowned out by the sharp staccato sound of the fighter's machine guns.

'I reckon you're right and he'll be after the drivers of one of them ammo trains going through the gridiron. Let's tek a butcher's, Stan, and see what he were after,' Pearl's husband, George, demanded of the man nearest the door, who obligingly started to open it.

'We're going to die! We're all going to die in here!' June suddenly screamed frantically. 'Let me out. I want to get out . . .'

'June, no!' Molly protested, but to her horror June was already on her feet, clutching Elizabeth Rose as she ran to the now open door.

Molly struggled up, crying out desperately, 'Dad, Stan, stop her!' Immediately both men reached for June, trying to hold her back, but somehow she managed to slip through their hands, and run into the street. They could all see the fighter plane banking and turning its machine gun, spewing bullets into the darkness above the bottom of the close and Edge Hill station, and then banking to take another run at its target, so that it was directly over June.

'Shut the ruddy door,' someone called out in panic, 'otherwise he'll get the lot of us.'

They could all hear the fierce staccato noise of the machine-gun fire, and through the still open door Molly watched in horror as June flung herself to the ground in an attempt to protect herself. Oblivious to her own safety, Molly pushed past her father and ran after her sister.

'June!' she screamed.

June lay motionless in the street in front of her. Molly dropped to her sister's side, whilst the fighter sped away.

'June . . .' Molly whispered her sister's name, distantly aware of other people coming to her side and her father's choked voice, as he told her thickly, 'She's gone, lass. She's gone.'

'No!' Molly wasn't going to accept that June could be dead, even though her hands were wet with June's blood; even though she could see where the row of bullet holes punctured her back, as neat as a piece of riveting, her blood glistening black in the moonlight. Molly could hear a thin small cry.

'Ruddy hell, the kiddie's still alive,' George Lawson called out.

Eager hands lifted June and reached beneath her to remove the crying Elizabeth Rose.

'Give her to me.' Molly was still crouching down beside her sister, but she refused to let anyone else take Elizabeth Rose. Miraculously, not a single bullet had touched June's baby but still

Molly clutched her to her breast as if she were in mortal danger.

'I've got her, Junie,' Molly whispered to her sister. 'I've got her and I'll keep her safe wi' me, just like you made me promise.'

TEN

'She was always a good sister to me.'

Frank could hear the defensive tension in Molly's voice.

'And a good wife to me,' he told her quietly.

It was June, the month in which June had been born and for which she had been named. They had come here together to June's grave to lay flowers on it. Frank's leave had not come through in time for him to attend her funeral.

'Me and Dad thought it was best that she should be laid to rest here with our mam.'

'I wouldn't have wanted anything else,' Frank assured her huskily. 'She used to talk a lot about her mam. Missed her badly, she did. She was a lovely girl, so kind and warm. A lot of people couldn't see that – only saw her tough exterior. But I could. I saw it right away. That's what made me fall in love with her.'

It was the most Frank had said since his arrival home earlier that day and Molly kept quiet, letting him unleash all his pent-up emotions. Held tightly in Molly's arms, Lillibet gave a contented gurgle. Molly dreaded having the conversation she knew they must have – about the fate of baby Elizabeth. But she had to tell him sooner rather than later what her sister's wishes had been.

'Frank,' Molly started tremulously, 'a week or so before she . . . before she died, our June started talking about what would happen to the baby if she were gone. It was almost as if she knew, as if she'd had a premonition something was going to happen to her.'

Molly shuddered at the thought. Ever since June's death, she'd thought endlessly of that conversation and wished she'd allowed June to talk about her fears properly rather than hurriedly dismissing them as morbid words.

'She said that she wanted me to take Lillibet and bring her up as my own if anything were to happen to her. She told me so herself.'

Here was the cause of her anxiety and tension: her fear that Frank would insist that Lillibet was to be brought up by his mother. She was, after all, his child.

Molly couldn't bring herself to look at him as she waited for the blow to fall. She could feel his breath against the exposed flesh of her neck as he leaned towards her, his hand a heavy weight on her arm. What was she going to do? How was she going to persuade him that he must leave Lillibet with her? It was only natural that he should want his own mother to raise her but if she let him take Lillibet from her then she would be breaking her promise to June. And besides . . . Molly's eyes blurred with more tears as she looked down into the face of her niece.

'She's all I've got left of June now.'

'I know that, Molly, and I know too that June would want you to be Elizabeth Rose's mother.' Frank's voice was quiet and calm, helping her to take a deep, steadying breath that banished some of her panic. 'She always said you'd be a wonderful mother when you had your own. It's just going to be a bit sooner than you thought,' he smiled sadly.

'But what about you, Frank?' she managed to ask him. 'What do you want? She is your daughter, after all.' It was easier to be magnanimous now that he had acknowledged June's wishes, but Molly feared Frank's emotions were in turmoil and that he might change his mind when he regained control of them.

'I want what's best for Elizabeth Rose, Molly. Me mam is after me to let her mother her.' Molly stiffened and held the baby more tightly. 'And I don't deny that she's got the experience. After all, she brought me up single-handed from a young age, and wi' her nursing on top o' that.'

'I do not want to say anything against your mam, Frank, but she and our June never hit it off and I won't have Lillibet growing up not knowing anything about her mam, or even worse, having it made out to her that she wasn't a good mother.'

Frank made no comment. He knew that June had loved their daughter but he also knew from what his mother and Sally Walker had both told him earlier that morning that Elizabeth Rose was thriving in Molly's care in a way she had not been doing in June's.

'It were that ruddy book that were the trouble, Frank,' Sally had told him in private, not mincing her words. 'You'd have thought it were the bloomin' Bible from the way June carried on about it. But if you ask me, it weren't doing poor little Lillibet any good – all that wakin' her up when she wanted to sleep and then lettin' her cry when she were hungry. I know your mam wants to take on looking after Lillibet, but if you was to ask my opinion I'd say straight off that Molly is doing a grand job. The little 'un knows Molly, Frank. Of course, she knows your mam as well, but – well, if I had bin June then I'd have wanted someone who loved me to be bringing up my baby and not a mother-in-law who didn't.' Sally had flushed bright red as she delivered this statement but she had still looked him in the eye, Frank remembered, and he had understood immediately what she was trying to say to him. His marriage to June might not have worked out as he had hoped – he had felt the last time he had been home as though he were an interloper in her life, whom she simply didn't want to be there rather than a much-loved and missed husband – but he couldn't fault her choice in wanting Molly to bring up little Elizabeth Rose.

It hadn't been easy, though, getting the opportunity to talk to Molly about it. The kitchen at number 78 always seemed to be full of neighbours. Either that, or Johnny was round visiting. The thought of Johnny and his evident desire to court Molly brought a small frown to Frank's face. Johnny had let Molly down once. Frank felt very protective towards Molly. He wasn't going to stand by while Johnny let Molly down a second time, especially if she was going to look after his daughter on a permanent basis.

'I don't have any quarrel with what June wanted for Elizabeth Rose, Molly,' he said to her gently, 'but I'd like to think that you'll remember that me mam is me mam and the little 'un's granny.'

'Of course I will. In fact, I was thinking of asking your mam if she would have Lillibet for me when I'm on duty – if you agree to me looking after her, that is. Mrs Wesley was saying that I could give up me voluntary work now, but I'd like to keep on with it if I can. I like to think I'm doing me bit . . .'

Frank gave Molly's arm a firm squeeze. 'From what I've bin hearing, you've done more than just your bit, Molly. I know for a fact there's two little 'uns have good cause to thank you for saving their lives.'

'Oh, that were nothing,' Molly denied bashfully.

'Can you hold her for a minute?' she asked him, handing his daughter to him before kneeling down to rearrange the flowers on June's grave.

'Me and Dad will come here in the autumn and plant some bulbs like we did for Eddie.' Her voice started to wobble. 'Nearly two thousand killed, there were, during the May blitz, Frank, but when one of them's your own sister . . .' She stood up, her eyes bright with tears. 'If only she hadn't run out into the street like that. We tried to stop her . . . she were allus that scared of being in the shelter. I just wish . . .' Molly's bottom lip started to tremble. Shifting Elizabeth Rose into one arm, Frank reached out with his free hand and drew Molly close to him. He could smell the fresh sun-warmed scent of her hair as she cried against his shirt, her whole body trembling with her grief and loss.

'I still can't believe she's gone,' she wept. 'Every morning I wake up and think she's going to be there, and then I remember. It were bad enough losing Eddie, but losing our June as well . . .'

Frank's own eyes glistened with tears as he held Molly as tightly and protectively as he was holding his own daughter. To anyone watching, they would have looked like a young husband and wife, united in grief but lucky to have each other for support. And, Frank reasoned, so they were.

'I can't believe you mean that, Frank. It's me as should be bringing her up, not young Molly.'

Frank had a tender heart and he hated hurting

anyone, never mind his mother, but his mind was made up and he wasn't going to change it.

'It's what June wanted.' He ignored the grim look his mother was giving him. 'And it's what I want as well.'

'Aye, well, you know my opinion of June.'

'Yes, I do,' he agreed, 'but she were me wife. I'll thank you not to speak ill of her now she's dead, Mam. She thought the world of Elizabeth Rose and I couldn't live wi' meself if I went against her wishes in that regard. Besides,' his face softened, 'you only have to see Molly with the little 'un to know how much she loves her. While there's a war on, I can't be here and I need to know that Lillibet is safe and well. I trust Molly, Mam, and I know you do too.'

'I'll give you that,' Doris agreed unwillingly. 'I've nothing against Molly. She's a good enough girl, and better than most, like I told you before you wed June. Of the two of them I'd rather it had been Molly you'd set your heart on. But have you thought about what would happen if Molly decided to get wed herself and have her own babies?'

Frank frowned and his mother pressed home her advantage.

'Talk is that that Johnny is after courtin' her. And what's going to happen to our Elizabeth Rose if Molly were to marry him? That's what I want to know. Molly might love Elizabeth Rose now like she's her own, but it will be different when she's got kiddies of her own, you mark my words. And besides, you might want to remarry yourself one day.'

His mother's words made him feel uncomfortable. 'That's enough of that, Mam. June's not bin in her grave a month yet,' he reminded her quietly, adding, 'Me mind's made up and I'm not going to change it.'

But the truth was that he was more disturbed than he wanted his mother to see at the thought of Molly marrying Johnny, and not just on Elizabeth Rose's account either.

It was only natural that he should have protective feelings towards Molly, he told himself defensively later. But it still made him feel uncomfortable and guilty to admit just how strong those feelings actually were, and how clearly he could remember how it had felt to hold Molly in his arms, her body soft and warm against his own, in the graveyard. He was a straightforward, honest man, who had remained true to his marriage vows, even when June had denied him her bed and her comfort, but now suddenly and shockingly, to him at least, his body ached with need.

'And I promise I'll write to you and tell you everything that she's doing,' Molly assured Frank as she held Lillibet up to the open window of the train carriage so that he could kiss his daughter goodbye.

540

Frank had told her that she didn't need to put herself out to see him off at the end of his leave, but she had insisted that she wanted to, and he had to fight to stop himself from kissing her more passionately than was seemly when she had lifted her face so innocently towards him.

Whatever had she been thinking of, practically begging Frank to kiss her like that, Molly fretted guiltily, trying to conceal her discomfort by fussing over Lillibet's bonnet, and avoiding looking directly at him.

She wasn't able to relax properly until the train finally started to pull out of the station and her face still felt hot with guilt and confusion when she put Lillibet back in her pram.

Tomorrow morning she would go and visit June's grave and explain to her that she hadn't intended any harm. It had just been a silly mistake, that was all.

'And now we're going to go home and I'm going to tell you a story about your mummy,' she told the smiling baby.

Talking to Lillibet about June was a ritual she had begun within days of June's death. It comforted her and she hoped it would keep June's memory forever fresh in Lillibet's little mind. It was all very well for others, like Frank's mother, to urge her to let the baby forget about her mother, and she knew they meant their advice for the best, but she knew how she had clung to every memory she had had of her own mother and how she had relished those extra memories June had shared with her.

Already she had carefully put away all the mementoes she could think of for Lillibet to have as she grew up and asked for them, even the Dr Truby King book.

She had felt guilty about putting that away instead of using it, Molly admitted, as she pushed the pram out into the warm sunshine. It was wrong of her to blame Dr Truby for the changes they had all seen in June, and to feel that he was partly responsible for her death, she knew. But she still hadn't been able to overcome her own repugnance for the book. Now she comforted herself with the knowledge that she had never kept it a secret from June that her own belief was that the doctor wasn't always right and that June should listen to her own instincts.

It was a lovely sunny day, and once she got home Molly lifted Lillibet out of the pram and put her down on a blanket on the small patch of grass in the back garden, watching her lovingly as she kicked and crowed, and then rolled over onto her back to play with her toes. Making sure she could see her from the window, Molly went inside to turn on the wireless and to gather together some darning that she had been putting off doing. She could sit on the step with it and work whilst she kept an eye on Lillibet. But her mind wasn't really on her darning. Instead, it kept straying to Frank. It had felt so comfortable, somehow, going to the station with him to see him off, just as though they were . . . Molly dropped her darning and sucked her thumb where she had stabbed it with her needle. That was what she got for letting such terrible thoughts into her head, she told herself guiltily. There was poor Frank, grieving over losing June, and she had gone and behaved so terribly.

Tears filled her eyes and she hung her head, whispering helplessly, 'Oh, June . . .'

'I've got sommat to tell you,' Johnny announced excitedly. He had arrived at number 78 only minutes earlier, cutting across Molly's proud urging that he look and see how well Lillibet was crawling.

'What's up?' She gave in but her newly maternal gaze was tracking Lillibet's progress towards the danger of the climbing rose smothering the wall. 'No, sweetheart, don't touch that.' Smiling adoringly, she ran to scoop up her niece, blowing kisses into her tummy and making her giggle.

'Put her down, Molly. I want to talk to you.'

She could hear the impatience in Johnny's voice. 'If I put her in her pram now she'll only make a fuss,' she told him, holding on to the baby. 'What is it you wanted to tell me?'

'I've bin offered the chance to take charge of a new emergency services team that's being set up out Cheshire way. Had me name put forward for it by the top brass here, so I've bin told, on account of what I've bin doing here in Liverpool.'

Molly could hear the impatience give way to pride.

'Of course it will mean moving out of Liverpool,' he continued. 'It'll be worth it. They'll be paying me a fair bit, for one thing, and there's talk of them throwin' in a little house as well.'

Molly didn't know what to say. She was pleased for him, of course, but she also knew that she would miss him.

However, before she could say anything he told her bluntly, 'I want you to come with me, Molly – as me wife. We'll have to get married pretty quick, like, 'cos they want me to start wi' 'em from the beginning of next month. It will mean a fresh start for both of us, Molly.'

'Johnny, I can't leave Liverpool,' she protested shakily. 'It would mean taking Lillibet away from me dad and from her Granny Brookes as well. I know that Frank has said that he's happy for me to bring her up, but I don't know how he'd feel about me moving right away from his mam with Lillibet.'

Johnny shrugged impatiently. 'Then leave her here. I reckon Doris Brookes will be only too pleased to have her to herself. If you ask me it would be a good thing, an' all,' he added darkly. 'You and me deserve to have some time to ourselves, Molly, instead of you having to run yourself ragged looking after someone else's kid. Aye, and what's going to happen if Frank gets tired of supportin' her, or he gets himself a new wife?'

Johnny shook his head firmly. 'No, if you ask me, Molly, it would be best all round if the little 'un was handed over to Doris Brookes to raise, and the sooner the better.'

Molly stared at him in shocked disbelief. 'You can't mean that, Johnny.'

'Why not?' His jaw jutted out pugnaciously. 'You and me – we've got our lives to lead, Molly, and I don't want mine cluttered up wi' someone else's kid.'

There was a huge hard lump in Molly's throat and her heart was thudding heavily into her ribs in shocked misery.

'Lillibet isn't someone else's kid to me, Johnny. She's . . . she's our June's, and she's mine now as well. I promised June that if anything happened to her I'd mother Lillibet for her and, anyway, I don't want to give her up. I love her, Johnny.'

'Aye, and more than you do me, I reckon,' he responded angrily. 'You'll feel differently when we've got kiddies of us own, Molly.' He tried to wheedle her, his tone changing. 'This is our big chance. Think about it. More money, a place of us own . . . you and me together, like we was.' He reached for her hand and she could smell the hot excited male scent of him. Excited but not exciting, she acknowledged tiredly. Not to her any more. Not now, after what he had just said about not wanting Lillibet.

'I'm very pleased for you, Johnny,' she told him tonelessly. 'But I won't be going with you.' When

545

she saw the pain in his eyes she pleaded, 'It's not just Lillibet, Johnny. There's me dad as well. I'm all he's got now, and I'd be worrying meself sick about him. He's not getting any younger, and losing our June on top of losing me mam has knocked him for six. He doesn't say anything, but I've seen him looking at her photograph when he doesn't think I've noticed.' Her voice thickened with tears. She missed June too. 'I can't leave them.'

She dipped her head, unable to look at him, as she said quietly, 'I'm sorry, Johnny, but I can't go with you.'

She winced when she heard the front door being slammed behind him, her tears rolling silently down her face, until Lillibet lifted a little starfish-shaped hand and patted her wet cheek gently.

ELEVEN

'Lord knows when my Ronnie and Frank will be home again, now that the battalion's bin sent to Egypt,' said Sally gloomily. Although officially no one was supposed to know the movements of the troops because of the risk of the information falling into enemy hands, somehow or other word did manage to get through and Sally had come hurrying round to tell Molly that the battalion was now on the move from Sicily. 'Have you heard from Frank? Only it's over a week now since I had a letter from my Ronnie.'

'I did have a letter from Frank last week,' Molly said, 'but I couldn't make much sense of it on account of that much having been censored,' she admitted, heaving a small sigh. 'He did write, though, that he'd got the photographs of Lillibet I'd sent him. She was standing up on her own in them,' she added proudly, turning round to hold out her arms to her niece as she came toddling towards her and then lifting her up onto her lap.

'She's really coming on now, Molly,' Sally approved. 'Walking really well, she is, and she'll be talking next. Have you thought about what you're gonna do about that?' Sally asked her.

'I'm trying to teach her to say "Dada". I keep saying it over and over again to her and—'

'No, that's not what I was meaning. What I was getting at is what is she going to call you?'

'I don't know,' Molly admitted. 'I've got a photograph of our June upstairs and every night when I put Lillibet to bed I show it to her and say, "kiss your mam good night," but she's too young yet to understand.'

'Well, if you ask me you'd be better putting June's photograph away for now, Molly, and letting the little 'un grow up calling you her mam,' Sally told her forthrightly. 'Not that I'm trying to say she shouldn't know anything about your June, but you're doing Lillibet's mothering now, and it will only mek her feel different from t'other kiddies if she has to call you Auntie Molly like she hasn't got a proper mam.'

'I'll have to wait and see what Frank thinks.'

'I wish my Ronnie were coming home.' Sally gave a gusty sigh. 'And I do not know what's to become of us women now, Molly, what with the Government saying that we've all got to register for war work, never mind if we've got kiddies to look after.'

The two women exchanged sombre looks. The Government had also recently lowered the age for male call-up to eighteen and a half, and extended it to fifty, and everyone knew what that meant. There was no point in hoping for a speedy end to the war when the Government was making it plain it needed even more fighting men.

'Wot you doing for Christmas this year, anyway?'

'Dad was talkin' about us going to Nantwich – it won't be the same being here without our June.' Molly's voice revealed her pain. 'But Auntie Violet says that she's got a houseful already so we're going to have to stay here.'

'It's a pity that Johnny took that job, Molly. You must miss him.'

'I did at first,' Molly admitted. She hadn't told Sally the full story about Johnny's ultimatum to her and she wasn't going to do so now. 'But Lillibet comes first.' Her expression softened as she looked down at the little girl snuggled in her lap.

Merry Christmas, mate, and welcome home to Blighty, Frank thought humorously to himself as he hefted his kitbag up onto the overhead luggage rack and looked enviously at the men who had been fortunate enough to secure themselves a seat. The train was packed and still filling up.

The troop ship bringing him back to England had docked in Portsmouth two days ago, on Christmas Eve, and it had taken him this long to travel up to London in order to get a train for Liverpool. He had spent Christmas night sleeping in the underground close to Euston station, joining in with the singsong and gratefully accepting the tea and sandwiches the regulars there had shared with him. Indeed, he considered himself fortunate to have secured a place there, and to have been able to wash and shave before finally boarding this Liverpool-bound train.

His arm ached from the bullet wound that had festered, the cause of his being hospitalised and left behind when the rest of his battalion had left for Egypt. It had been touch and go for a while as to whether or not he would lose his arm, but in the end he had been lucky and the infection had started to clear. The damage it had done, though, had left him with severely weakened muscles in his right arm as well as a deep raw wound where the infection had eaten into his flesh.

Along with the rest of the not-fit-for-active-duty and non-combat forces left on Sicily, he had been shipped back to England.

The man leaning against the wall in the corridor beside him offered him a cigarette, but Frank shook his head in refusal. He had given up the habit whilst he had been in the military hospital and was determined not to take it up again. He intended to put the money he would save on one side for Elizabeth Rose. Just thinking about her made him smile and reach inside his greatcoat to his jacket to remove Molly's last letter and the photographs she had enclosed with it.

'Pretty-looking kiddie. Yours, is she?' the other man asked, peering over his shoulder.

'Yes,' Frank acknowledged, his heart filling with tender pride as he looked at his daughter's picture. Not that he needed a grainy black-and-white photograph to remember how she looked. She had his own dark, almost black, hair, but unlike his, hers curled prettily, just like June and Molly's. Her eyes were like Molly's and he reckoned she had her auntie's smile too. Something twisted sharply inside him and he shifted his weight from one foot to the other. He was itching to unfold Molly's letter and read it yet again. She had kept her promise to write to him regularly, telling him all about Elizabeth Rose, and he had her other letters carefully folded away in his kitbag. June hadn't written very often towards the end, claiming that she was too busy.

June. He had gone into a small church in Portsmouth and said a prayer for her. Molly was right to say that she wanted to keep her sister's memory fresh for Elizabeth Rose, and he wanted to remember the beautiful, excitable young woman he had married, not the woman war had made her.

Once again he felt that painful aching tug on his heart, quickly followed by a fierce feeling of guilty disloyalty. June had not been dead a year, and here he was letting thoughts he had no right to have fill his heart.

*   *   *

Christmas Day and Boxing Day had come and gone, and although Molly had done her best she knew that neither she nor her father had had the heart to celebrate. Christmas Day morning they had gone to the grave, and Molly's father had said heavily that at least June and Rosie were together again now. Afterwards, Molly had left Lillibet with Doris Brookes and gone by herself to Eddie's grave. He seemed so very far away from her now, as though their love for one another had existed in a different life. But she knew she would love him for ever and if things had worked out differently they would have been together when they were old and grey.

Now the grey December afternoon had given way to an even greyer dusk, and Molly's mouth tightened a little to hear Vera Lynn's voice on the radio singing about bluebirds and white cliffs. Her mouth soon softened into a smile, though, when she bent down to help Lillibet build a tower from the wooden bricks she had had from 'Father Christmas'. Doris Brookes had brought them round on Christmas Day afternoon, saying that she'd been having a rummage around in her attic because she'd remembered she still had some of Frank's old toys there.

Right now Lillibet seemed more interested in knocking down the tower Molly had built for her than in building one of her own and, looking down into her happy, innocent face, Molly couldn't stop herself from sweeping her into her arms and kissing her.

'I could eat you up, little Lillibet, do you know that?' she crooned lovingly to her. She frowned when she heard someone knocking on the front door. Her father had gone round to see Uncle Joe, and she wasn't expecting any callers. Putting Lillibet in her playpen, she went to open the door, switching off the hall light as she did so in order not to break the blackout laws.

At first all she could see was a male outline masked by the shadows but then he stepped towards her and the moonlight revealed his face.

'Frank.' She could hear the pleasure in her own voice and feel it in the dizzying beat of her heart, and then he was stepping into the hall and lifting her off her feet, to swing her round, laughing as he kicked the door closed and then suddenly not laughing at all as he held her close and lowered his mouth to her own.

Men – fighting men – said and did all manner of things they wouldn't have said or done in peacetime, Molly knew that, and she knew too it was up to her own sex to make them keep in line, and do what was proper. So why was she wrapping her arms around Frank's neck and kissing him back, for all the world as though she had every right to do so? What he was doing was wrong. Frank was June's, and she had no right to be feeling what she was feeling right now.

Quickly she pulled back from him, putting a safer distance between them, glad of the hall's darkness to hide her burning face and all the other evidence of what his kiss had done to her.

'So the doctor says he's not goin' ter sign yer back up for active duty yet then?' Molly's father asked Frank, whilst Molly sat at the kitchen table, feeding Lillibet, who was sitting next to her in her highchair.

'Here comes a train, choo choo choo . . .' Molly coaxed, holding out a spoonful of mashed potato, making Lillibet clap her hands together excitedly.

'No,' Frank answered him. 'He says me wound's healing up, but he reckons I still won't be able to fire me gun proper.'

'No.' Lillibet refused a second spoonful of the mash, pouting flirtatiously and eyeing her father as she said proudly, 'Dada.'

Molly might have been secretly coaxing Lillibet to say the special word for days, but it still gave her a sharp pang of mingled joy and pain to see the look in Frank's eyes as he got up and walked over to the high chair.

'Yes. I am your dada,' he agreed tenderly.

'I talk to her about our June every night at bedtime,' Molly told him slightly breathlessly, 'but I wasn't sure what you wanted me to do when she starts wanting to say "Mama".' Her colour was high and she couldn't bring herself to look at him. Only yesterday Sally had commented that it would not be long before a good-looking chap like Frank caught some girl's eye.

'Our June's not bin dead a year yet, Sally,' Molly had objected sharply.

'I know that, Molly, but it's different in wartime,' responded Sally. And Molly had not felt able to argue with her.

'I'd better get off to work,' Albert announced, heaving himself up out of his chair. Frank went with him to the door and Molly half expected him to leave as well. Although he was spending virtually all day at number 78 so that he could see as much as possible of Lillibet, he was naturally staying at his mother's. When he didn't leave but returned to the back room, Molly could feel her body stiffening with apprehensive guilt. It had been one thing to acknowledge how she felt about him when she had been a girl, even though he had been June's boyfriend, but it was something else again to acknowledge that she still had those feelings for him, albeit a far more grown-up version of them, when her sister was dead. She felt awkward and angry whenever he was around – awkward with him and angry with herself – and yet at the same time the first thing she thought of when she woke up in the morning was the pleasure of knowing he would be coming round.

'You'd better get off to your mother's,' she told him now, determined not to let him see how she felt.

'There's no rush; she knows where I am.'

Molly had finished feeding Lillibet and she went

to lift her out of the highchair, but Frank stayed her, putting his hand on her arm.

'There's sommat I've bin wanting to say to you, Molly. It's about our Lillibet.' Molly's stomach tightened, her heart lurching sickeningly into her ribs. 'I've bin thinking as how I'd like her to have both a mam and a dad. You and me – we grew up wi' just the one parent so we know what it's like to want to have two.'

He felt as though he were walking barefoot on top of a factory wall cemented with broken glass, Frank admitted. He wished more than anything else he had more time for this, but, as his mother was constantly warning him, ultimately he would be going back to war, and a pretty girl like Molly would have any number of lads chasing after her, even if, from what she'd heard, she'd sent Johnny packing.

It was worse than Molly had thought it was going to be. Much worse. But she had her pride and so she lifted her head and said determinedly, 'If you're trying to tell me that sooner or later you'll be wanting to get married again and when you do, you'll not be needin' me to take care of Lillibet, you don't need to say it. There's plenty enough folk around here told me that already.'

She could see that he was frowning and her heart missed several beats.

'Molly.' He reached for her hands but she pulled them away, folding them onto her lap. 'What's up?' he asked her uncertainly. 'You and me have allus got on well, Molly, and yet since I've bin home this time you've bin like a cat on hot bricks around me – aye, and acting like you can't bear to have me anywhere near you. I thought you and me was pals, Molly.'

Molly's eyes filled with tears that she tried to blink away.

'We are,' she answered him gruffly. 'It's just that I'm that miserable at the thought of you marryin' again, Frank, and tekkin' Lillibet away.'

It was the truth, even if it wasn't the whole of it.

'Eeh, lass. There's only one girl I'd want to be Lillibet's mam, and that's you. That's what I was wanting to talk to you about. To ask if you would think about you and me . . .'

Her heart was pounding so loudly she was surprised the whole street couldn't hear it. If an air-raid warning sounded now, they wouldn't be able to hear it above the racket her heart was making, Molly thought shakily.

Somehow or other he had taken hold of her hands, and he was looking into her eyes, his own filled with earnestness and concern. In another minute he would be kissing her and she *wanted* him to kiss her so badly. But how could she let him when there was June's memory ever present in her mind?

'Molly, will yer—'

She pulled her hands away and jumped up so quickly she nearly overturned her chair.

'No, Frank, no, you mustn't. I won't listen to any more. I can't . . . we mustn't. There's our June to think of.' She shook her head, unable to say any more.

The first thing Molly did just as soon as Frank had gone was pick up Lillibet and go upstairs to her bedroom where she put the baby in her cot and picked up her sister's photograph. She could barely see June's face for her own guilty tears, as she sobbed out her distress and misery to her, before hugging the photograph tightly to her chest.

TWELVE

'Molly lass, what's wrong?'

Molly could hardly bring herself to look at her father. It was four days now since Frank had spoken to her and there hadn't even been one of them when she hadn't woken up longing to be able to tell him that there was nothing she wanted more than to be his wife and Lillibet's mam, and at the same time hating herself for the way she felt.

Today was New Year's Eve and tonight she and Frank and some of the others from the close were all going dancing at the Grafton, whilst her father and Frank's mam looked after Lillibet.

'Come on, lass, you can tell yer old dad, can't yer?' Albert coaxed gently. He hated seeing his little Molly like this. She had allus bin such a happy girl, aye, and a brave 'un as well, and he had begun to hope since Frank had come home that maybe . . .

'It's Frank, Dad,' Molly told him miserably.

'He's said as how he wants me to think about us getting wed so that our Lillibet can have a proper mam and dad, but how can I, Dad, when there's our June?' Tears filled Molly's eyes and spilled down onto her pale cheeks. 'Frank were June's hubby and it meks me feel like I'd be stealing him from her if I were to say yes, but I want to say yes, Dad, and that meks me feel right bad about meself.'

'Eeh, lass . . .' He shook his head sympathetically. Although he'd never upset her by saying so, he knew that as a young girl Molly had been sweet on Frank, and he could see now how distressed she was.

'But if it weren't for our June, would you really want to wed him, lass?'

Molly's flushed face and bent head gave him his answer.

'I don't want to tek what's rightfully June's, Dad. It's different with Lillibet 'cos I'll be telling her all about her mam when she's growing up and she'll know that our June were her mam, and that I love her just as if she were me own for her own sake as well as for our June's, but with Frank . . .'

She went over to her father and put her head on his shoulder. 'Sally Walker were saying only the other day as how Frank is bound to remarry because it's different for men and it's wartime, but you never put anyone else in our mam's place, Dad.'

She felt his chest lift and then fall with his sigh.

'I'll be honest wi' you, Molly. There were times, aye, and lots of them, when I'd have given anything to have met someone who could have been a mother to the two of you and a wife to me, but somehow it never happened. But it's different in wartime, Molly. And do you know what? I reckon if you was able to ask our June she'd say as how she'd rather you was wed to Frank and bring up Lillibet than some stranger. In fact, I reckon if our June is up there looking down right now she'd be telling you that there's nothing she wants more than for her little 'un to grow up with you as her mam. You know how it was with the two of you, Molly. I did me best for both of you, and June mothered you in her own way, but poor June never had anyone to mother her and I reckon I did badly by her by not finding someone who might have done. June missed her mam, Molly, and she wouldn't want her own kiddie growing up wi'out a mam.'

Molly knew there was a good deal of truth in what he was saying.

Her father could see this and he pressed home his advantage. 'June is wi' her mam now, Molly, bless 'em both.' He paused to wipe the tears from his eyes. 'And do you know what? June allus knew as you had a soft spot for her Frank and I reckon if you could ask her now she'd tell you that she wants you to wed him and look after her little 'un. There's no shame in you having feelings for a fine upstanding chap like Frank, Molly, nor any shame in him having them for you. He were a good husband to our June and you were a good sister to her. I reckon folks'll think it only right and natural that you and Frank should wed, especially with you tekkin' on June's little 'un. And I reckon your Eddie would agree with me as well. He wouldn't want to see you all on your own, Molly. He'd want you to be happy, just as you would want that for him if he had bin left here without you. That's what loving someone is all about – wantin' the best for them.'

Frank looked so handsome in his uniform, his thick dark hair neatly combed back off his face and his broad shoulders making him stand out against all the other men, even though the Grafton was packed with people celebrating New Year's Eve. Molly felt so proud to be here with him and yet, at the same time, she felt so shy and apprehensive. Frank hadn't mentioned what he had said to her again, and if it hadn't been for the look she had seen in his eyes earlier in the evening when he had called to collect her, she might almost have thought she had imagined their conversation.

It was almost midnight and her tummy was churning with a mixture of confusing feelings. She wanted desperately to tell him that she did want them to have a future together, but her thoughts of her sister still held her back. The band started to play 'Blues in the Night'. Frank looked at her, and asked, 'Will you dance with me, Molly?'

Her mouth had gone so dry she couldn't speak and had to nod her head instead. Like someone in a dream, she watched as he stood up and then turned to pull out her chair for her. When he led her onto the dance floor, she trembled slightly, and then she trembled even more when he took her in his arms.

She had danced with him before, but never like this, never knowing that he wanted to court her and make her his wife, never knowing that the look she was seeing in his eyes meant that he desired her as a woman.

'Don't look at me like that, Molly,' he commanded her gruffly. 'Not unless you want me to kiss you right here on the dance floor in front of everyone.'

'If we was to be together I'd still want Lillibet to grow up knowing all about our June,' she told him.

Frank missed a step and then looked at her with a mixture of surprise and delight. '*Molly*. Oh, Molly lass!'

'Frank, you mustn't hold me so tight . . .' Molly was breathless and blushing, and oh so deliciously happy.

'Yes, I must,' he told her masterfully. 'And as for Lillibet – of course we'll tell her all about your June, but she'll still call you "Mam", Molly.'

Molly trembled and blushed even more, and now it was her turn to miss a step, so that Frank had to hold her even more tightly and draw her closer to him.

'I'd not want to tek anything that's rightfully our June's,' Molly insisted bravely.

'Me feelings for you belong to you, Molly.'

She looked at him. They had stopped dancing but she hadn't even noticed. She looked up into his kind, loving eyes and then at his familiar smiling mouth and her heart did a somersault.

'When I was a girl I had a right crush on you, Frank.' She could see his smile widening.

'But you're not a girl any more; you're a woman now, Molly, a lovely, strong, beautiful woman. Maybe it's too soon to say this, but I can't help meself. I love you, Molly,' he told her fiercely.

And then he kissed her. Not as a friend, but as a man, and she kissed him back, whilst all around them people broke into cheers to greet the New Year. Somewhere in the distance she could hear Vera Lynn singing about bluebirds and white cliffs, and suddenly it didn't seem as though those days of peace ever after were such an impossibility after all.

I'll take care of him, June, Molly promised mentally. I'll take care of both of them, and your Lillibet will grow up with a proper mam and dad of her own. I promise.

And it seemed to Molly that she felt a small exhaled breath and heard an impatient sigh, and inside her head her sister's voice told her briskly, 'Oh, give over being so soft, our Molly. As if I didn't know that for meself.'

Hettie of Hope Street

Annie Groves

A breathtaking tale of one girl's determination to trace her roots, find true love and succeed in a world where obstacles lurk around every corner.

Hettie is an orphan, taken in by Ellie Pride and her husband to their Preston home and treated as one of the family. But she has never felt she truly belonged.

On the cusp of womanhood, and in love with someone who she is not considered good enough for, she heads for the bright lights of Liverpool to find her fortune.

There, the only way to survive is working in the kitchens of a restaurant. Until, by chance, she is heard singing by the owner...

Whisked to London, Hettie is thrown into a theatrical and colourful world - but one with a dark and seedy side. It is a mad, dizzy, dangerous world and Hettie increasingly feels ill at ease. Thoughts of home and her lost love dominate her mind but she knows she cannot return to the fold.

Then tragedy strikes, and Hettie must decide between her heart and her head, her duty and her desire...

Praise for Annie Groves:

'An engrossing story.'   *My Weekly*

'Heartwrenching and uplifting in equal measure.'
                                                                Take a Break

ISBN-10: 0 00 714959 X

Connie's Courage

Annie Groves

When Connie Pride finds herself alone and pregnant in the rough courts of Liverpool, she despairs. Deserted by her lover, she is too proud to ask her estranged family for help.

Rescued from the gutter, she is offered the chance to train as a nurse. Life becomes a whirl of hard work and long shifts, but also lively evenings at the music hall. Finally Connie has a purpose in life – especially when the wounded of World War One start to arrive in their droves on the hospital wards. If she can stay out of trouble, the future looks brighter. Even love seems possible again...

But then a face from the violent past turns up to shatter all Connie's dreams. All she has built up is threatened. It will take every ounce of courage she possesses to overcome the odds – and a little help from old friends and new...

ISBN-13: 978-0-00-714957-5
ISBN-10: 0-00-714957-3